Nicola

Nicola Cornick

Unmasked

HQN™

ISBN-13: 978-0-373-77303-9
ISBN-10:   0-373-77303-X

UNMASKED

www.HQNBooks.com

Printed in U.S.A.

Dear Reader,

From the Scarlet Pimpernel to Zorro, Robin Hood to William Wallace, the real-life legends and fictional stories of those who fight for freedom and justice have always inspired me. In *Unmasked* I have written an outlaw story of my own! Over the wild heather-clad hills and dales of Yorkshire ride a band of highwaywomen, taking from the rich to give to the poor, protecting the weak and setting right the injustices of society in true Robin Hood style. But the Glory Girls who ride in *Unmasked* are no ordinary outlaws. These are women who defy convention because they cannot bear to sit at home, confined by the traditional role of the Regency wife or widow, who see injustice and feel a burning need to take action.

Nick Falconer, the hero of *Unmasked,* is a man of honor, sworn to uphold the law, and when he is sent to bring the Glory Girls down he is determined to do his duty. But in Mari Osborne, the woman he suspects to be Glory, he finds someone very different from the criminal he is expecting, someone whose principles equal his own…. I loved writing my story of those dashing Regency outlaws the Glory Girls, and I hope you enjoy it, too!

Love from

Nicola

This book is dedicated to Yorkshire, county of my birth, for all the wild and wonderful places that inspired me.

Unmasked

PROLOGUE

Daffodil—Deceit

"THE THINGS I DO for England." Major Nick Falconer stood back and squinted at his reflection in the pier glass in the hall of the Marquis of Kinloss's London mansion. The Marquis was out of Town, which Nick thought was probably all to the good. His great-uncle was notoriously high in the instep and might have cut up extremely rough had he seen his heir's outrageous appearance.

Nick turned to the young man who was leaning against one of the marble pillars and watching him with amusement in his blue eyes.

"What do I look like, Anstruther?"

"You look quite shocking, sir," Dexter Anstruther said politely. "The ribbon is a nice touch, as is the perfume and the patch."

Nick laughed. "And the jacket? Quite dandified, I think."

"Much worse than a dandy," Anstruther said, a smile twitching his lips. "I beg your pardon, sir, but you look like a *molly* with extremely dubious sexual tastes. A rum cove, as my father would have said."

"I do my poor best," Nick said. He picked up his hat, a jaunty wide-brimmed affair with a flirtatious orange feather.

"This place you're going to," Anstruther said, "this club…"

"The Hen and Vulture," Nick supplied.

"Yes." Anstruther looked vaguely uncomfortable. "Is it really the case that one cannot be sure whether… I mean, there are men there, and women…"

"And the men may be dressed as women and the women as men," Nick finished. He grinned. "So I understand. Far too shocking for youngsters like yourself to visit, Anstruther."

"Men dressed as women," Anstruther muttered, rubbing a hand across his forehead. "How could that possibly be attractive?"

"I believe the appeal of such a place lies in the ambiguity," Nick said. "Apparently some of the most beautiful courtesans in London also attend and the skill is in telling them apart from the men in women's clothes."

"Good God," Anstruther said faintly. "It's so…unBritish."

"Just count yourself lucky that you don't have to come with me," Nick said comfortingly. He looked at his companion, sober in his black evening dress. Dexter Anstruther had been assigned to assist him in his current mission by no lesser personage than the Home Secretary himself. The boy had only graduated from Oxford the previous year but he was clever, diplomatic and hardworking, and Nick's current venture, to rein in the wilder excesses of his cousin the Earl of Rashleigh, required assistance from someone with absolute discretion. Dexter Anstruther fitted the bill perfectly.

"How would you dress if you were visiting the Hen and Vulture, Anstruther?" Nick inquired.

"Just as I am—as a repressed English gentleman," Anstruther said ruefully, looking at Nick's somewhat colorful outfit, "rather than the sort of mincing dandy I see before me—with the greatest of respect, sir." He straightened, thrusting his hands into his pockets. "What if Lord Kinloss should hear of this, sir? He'll have a fit. The heir to a Marquisate in a house of ill repute!"

"I'll probably recognize plenty of other peers in there," Nick said, "so no one will be able to point the finger."

Anstruther shook his head in disbelief. "It is difficult to believe, seeing you like that, sir, that you have a certain reputation for ruthlessness."

Nick was adjusting his outrageously lacy collar. "Thank you, Anstruther. Unfortunately I also have the bad luck to be Rashleigh's cousin."

"And the best shot in England and one of Gentleman Jackson's finest," Anstruther said, with an air of hero worship.

Nick smiled. "More to the point, Anstruther, Lord Hawkesbury knows I'll be discreet because no matter how much I hate my cousin, this is a family matter." He tilted his head to one side and patted the patch on his cheek. "Too much, do you think?"

"You look like a whorehouse madam, sir."

"Just the style I was attempting," Nick said.

"Lord Hawkesbury said that this was a delicate business," Anstruther said, shifting from one foot to the other, as though he was not quite comfortable to be in the same room as a man in such dubious attire. "A matter that could cause repercussions through the top ranks of society, he said."

"Yes," Nick said. "It is damnably delicate. You know that my foolish cousin Rashleigh has borrowed heavily from the sprigs of the nobility, Anstruther. He has targeted those youths with generous allowances and lax guardians. And now that his activities are exposed there are peers lining up from Aberdeen to Anglesey threatening to see him in hell. Lord Hawkesbury wants Rashleigh warned off tonight and the money repaid before one of them kills him."

Nick stopped, thinking that in better times Dexter Anstruther himself might have been one of Rashleigh's targets. The boy's father, whilst not titled, had been from a good family and had had a tidy fortune—until he had gambled it all away.

"I had heard that Lord Rashleigh was a scoundrel," Anstruther said gruffly. "I know he's your cousin, sir, but he's still bad *Ton*."

"I couldn't agree more," Nick said affably. "Never could stand Rashleigh myself. He comes from the dissolute branch of the family. My mother's brothers were all worse than scoundrels."

"Dashed nuisance that you have to go to this so-called club," Anstruther observed. "Did you try calling on your cousin at home, sir?"

Nick laughed. "Yes, I tried. He declines to see me. We have not spoken for several years and last time we met he damned me to perdition for refusing to advance him a loan."

"A pity he is a habitué of the Hen and Vulture rather than Whites," Anstruther said. "You could have had a pleasant evening there."

"Whites blackballed him years ago," Nick said.

"You don't surprise me. Unwholesome fellow." Anstruther shifted uncomfortably once more. "I heard Lord Hawkesbury say that he was robbed blind by one of his mistresses a few years back? He said it was the talk of the *Ton* for a while."

Nick's mouth set in a thin line. "Yes, it was. She was a Russian girl. Rashleigh's side of the family had estates there, inherited from his grandmother. He told me once how he had sold his serfs off to the highest bidder." His fist clenched in an instinctive gesture of anger and repudiation. "I think—" his tone hardened "—that that was when I really started to hate him."

He could see that Anstruther was staring at him but he did not elaborate. Nick had spent his adult life in the army, fighting for honor and freedom and principle, to defend the weak and preserve the things that he believed to be right. It was a moral code he believed in, a belief that had only been strengthened by the violent death of his wife some three years earlier. But his cousin, in contrast, treated human life as though it were a commodity to be bought and sold, as though people's very souls were of no account. He sneered at the weak and crushed them under his aristocratic heel. Rashleigh had laughed at the reformers and sworn that those who wanted to abolish slavery were soft in the head. And in Nick's book that made Robert Rashleigh the scum of the earth.

Nick adjusted his hat to a more rakish angle. "That'll do. I'm off."

"Good luck, sir," Anstruther said, holding the door for him. "You are sure you do not need me to accompany you?"

Nick looked him up and down. "A selfless offer, An-

struther, but in that outfit you would stand out like the
proverbial sore thumb." He slapped the younger man on
the back. "I shall see you later, when I am confident you
will be able to report to Lord Hawkesbury on a job well
done."

Out in the street it was a brisk April night with a cold
breeze whipping the ragged clouds across the moon.
Nick settled back in a hackney carriage and winced in
the draught from the ill-fitting door. He had no appetite
for this errand and no time for his cousin, but for the
sake of his family's good name, he knew he had had
to take the Home Secretary's commission. As the
carriage clattered through London's streets he thought,
with no degree of affection at all, about his errant
cousin and the trouble that he had caused from the day
of his birth. There was no doubt, as Anstruther had said,
that the Earl of Rashleigh was worse than a scoundrel.

The hack drew up abruptly and Nick sighed and
jumped down, pushing the plumed hat down farther on
his head as a gust of wind threatened to take it off. His
current garb, he reflected, was about as far from his
army uniform as could be.

From the outside the Hen and Vulture looked much
the same as any low tavern in the Brick Hill area. The
shutters were closed and from within came the flicker
of candlelight, the mingled smell of ale and stale
smoke, and the roar of voices and laughter. Nick
squared his shoulders. He had been called upon to
perform some unusual roles during his career in the
Seventh Dragoon Guards but none had taken him
anywhere quite like this.

He pushed open the door.

Inside it was so dark that for a moment Nick could

not see properly, then his eyes adjusted to the light and he headed for a quiet corner, sliding along the wooden bench behind a rough ale-stained table. The room was almost full. Despite the tavern's reputation, there were only one or two outrageously clad men. One was dressed in an embroidered corset and a trailing golden robe with satin-lined sleeves. He had a well-powdered wig, ear pendants and a beauty patch on one cheekbone that was a match for Nick's.

The inn servant—a slender youth who could actually have been a girl—slopped a beaker of ale down onto the table and gave Nick a flirtatious smile, which he returned in good measure as he slipped the payment into the youth's hand. He looked around the room. As far as he could see, Rashleigh had not yet arrived.

Nick took a mouthful of the ale. It tasted like dirty water and he put the tankard down again quickly. It was threatening to be a long evening if the drink was so poor. He glanced around the room again and caught the eye of a strikingly pretty, masked woman in a tight crimson gown. Like him she was sitting alone in a quiet corner. It looked as though she was waiting for someone. She held Nick's gaze for a long moment and despite their surroundings, despite his outrageous garb sufficient to confuse anyone as to the true nature of his sexual interest, a connection flashed between them that was so intense he felt it like a kick in the stomach.

The girl got up, walked slowly across the room and slid into the seat beside him.

"Hello, darling." Her voice was warm, inviting and very definitely feminine.

Nick thought quickly. In showing more than a fleeting interest in the girl he had no doubt made her think that he was a potential customer. The sort of whores who paraded their wares in places like the Vulture, male or female, did not in general interest him, but he supposed that he would draw less attention if he pretended an attraction to this one, and that would not be very difficult for she was extremely pretty.

He had barely looked at another woman in the three years since his wife had died. Anna had been his childhood sweetheart and their marriage had been an understood thing from the first, an eminently sensible arrangement between two families. They had married when Nick was one and twenty and he had confidently expected to live very happily ever after. It had therefore been both a shock and a disillusionment to find that the reality of their marriage had not lived up to its early promise. Anna was delicate and could not follow the drum and he was young and determined to serve abroad and so they had spent much of their time apart. Nick had told himself that it did not matter, that it was a good enough marriage, better than many, but he knew something was lacking. And so it might have continued for years had not an opportunist robbery in a London street turned violent and he had lost his wife in one vicious moment. He had finally been forced to confront his failure and guilt, and the grief had overwhelmed him, not only for Anna but also for what might have been. His distance from home and the sheer helplessness of his situation only served to compound his remorse, but by the time he had received the news of her death and returned to England, Anna was cold in her grave and his heart was even colder.

He had never felt an interest in another woman since but he looked at this one now and felt an unexpectedly strong pull of attraction. As she leaned toward him he could smell a fresh flower scent on her, light and sweet. He felt her silken warmth wrap about him, a far cry from the stale perfume and sweat he had expected. The sensation went straight to his head—and to his groin. He could not remember the last time he had noticed the scent of a woman but this one filled his senses. It made him feel restless and disturbed in a way he could not quite explain, as though he was dishonoring Anna's memory in some way. He pushed the feeling away and gave the girl a long, slow smile in return. This was, after all, only business.

"Hello, sweetheart," he said. "What can I do for you?"

The girl looked him straight in the eyes. "Several things spring to mind," she murmured.

She was not shy then. She was not even pretending to be shy. Nick did not mind. He disliked artifice in any form. A direct man himself, he preferred bluntness in his dealing with others and whatever she was, she seemed honest.

He allowed himself a moment to study her. She had blond hair that curled about her face, and behind her velvet mask her wide-set, candid eyes were so dark Nick thought they were black until a stray beam of candlelight shone on them and showed up the tiny flecks of green and gold in their depths. She was wearing far too much paint for a young girl but the deep cherry-red of her lips was alluring and drew his gaze. She ran her fingers lightly but deliberately over the lace that edged the low-cut bodice of her gown, back and forth gently across the swell of her breasts, and Nick's eyes followed the movement and he felt the lust slam through his body in response.

He looked up to see her watching him, a knowing look in her eyes.

"What's your name?" he asked. His voice was a little rough.

She gave him a small, secretive smile. "Molly."

Nick laughed. It was a good choice for a place like the Vulture but he doubted it was her real name.

Molly moved a little closer to him. Her slippery satin thigh pressed gently against his leg and once again he felt desire as hard and hot as a punch in the gut. Damnation. He had always considered himself to have iron self-discipline but the only iron thing about him at present was his erection, which was swelling with each provocative slide of Molly's satin skirts against his thigh.

"And who are you?" she whispered in his ear. Her voice was low, slightly husky. Her breath tickled his cheek.

Nick cleared his throat. "My name's John."

She smiled again, that knowing smile. "What are you doing here, John?"

"Looking for company." Nick took a mouthful of the watery beer and appraised her over the rim of his tankard. "What about you?"

She gave a little shrug of her shoulders. The candlelight gilded the pallor of her bare skin, made it look smooth and tempting. There was a scattering of freckles over her shoulders and a tiny, heart-shaped mole above her collarbone that was already driving Nick almost mad with frustration. He found that he wanted to press his lips to it, to taste her skin. He shifted on the bench.

"I'm looking for someone, too," she said.

"Someone in particular, or anyone?"

For a second Nick thought he saw some expression flicker in her eyes, too quick to read. Then she smiled. "Someone special, darling. Someone like you."

Nick leaned toward her. One kiss would do no harm and he wanted it, wanted her, with a hunger that was already hard to control.

She leaned away. "Not so fast," she said. "There's a price."

There always was, with a whore.

Nick raised his brows. "You charge for your kisses?"

"I charge for everything, darling."

The curve of those red lips was very seductive. Nick ran one finger down the bare skin of her inner arm, tracing the curve. He thought that he felt her tremble just a little and admired her skill. The cleverest whores were the ones who seemed innocent.

"And if I want to take something on account?" he murmured.

Her eyes were veiled behind the mask. "It's against the rules." She put her hand on his thigh. "Let me persuade you to open your purse."

Nick caught her chin in his hand, turning her face up to his. "Let me persuade you to break the rules," he murmured.

He felt her go very still beneath his touch, like a wild animal freezing in the face of danger. For a moment Nick thought that he could read abject terror in the depths of those dark eyes and he started to draw back. He wanted no part in coercing an unwilling woman and he understood all too well how some of these girls were obliged to play a role that they hated just to earn enough money to survive.

But then Molly put a hand on his nape and pulled his head down so that his lips touched hers. The surprise held Nick still for a moment as he absorbed the sensation, the touch and the feel of her. Again he sensed a hesitation in her before her lips parted a little and softened beneath his. Her tongue tentatively touched the corner of his mouth, then slid across his lower lip in sweet invitation, and he felt a sudden helpless rush of desire, like the first blindingly hot passion of his youth, so strong it made him ache, so unexpected it shocked him. He had never felt anything so raw for any woman, and certainly not for Anna. Fierce need smashed though him and in that instant he forgot his scruples, forgot his memories, forgot even why he was there, and pulled her to him and kissed her deeply until he was panting and she was, too.

When she tore herself from his grip he was so wrapped up in the taste and feel of her that for a moment he was completely disorientated. Then he saw that she had moved a little way away from him along the bench. Her face was averted and she had a hand pressed to her lips. Nick could see she was shaking slightly. The downward curve of her neck looked so vulnerable that he felt a powerful surge of anger and protectiveness and lust inextricably jumbled into one. Her closeness and her apparent defenselessness unleashed a sudden wave of memories of Anna, terrible, tormenting memories so sharp that they cut him to the core. He had not been there to protect his wife when she needed him. He had failed her in so many ways.

He put his head in his hands for a moment to try to clear his mind. He could not think about this now. He should never have touched the girl and sparked the tangle of memory and desire that had captured him.

With deliberate intent he wiped out the memories and, when he straightened up, he saw that Molly's attention had drifted and she was staring across the room. He followed her gaze toward the door and saw that his cousin, Robert Rashleigh, had come in and was standing preening himself like a displaying peacock. In a white wig, silver cloak, gold breeches and scarlet shoes, he drew all eyes.

The conversation in the tavern fell to a murmur then rose again as men resumed their drink and sport. Nick suddenly became aware that beside him the girl was rigid, upright, vibrating with a strange kind of tension he could not understand. Her attention was riveted on the flaunting figure of the Earl.

"Excuse me," she murmured, and slipped from the seat beside him. She walked straight across to Rashleigh, put a hand on his arm and indicated to the tavern servant to bring him a drink.

Nick's eyes narrowed as he watched the interchange between his cousin and the whore. He felt a fool now for his unrestrained response to her. Evidently he had been without a woman for too long to fall into lust so hard and so fast. Molly, in contrast, had forgotten him already for she was at the door, gesturing to Rashleigh to follow her out into the night, no doubt to a set of rooms nearby. There was no sign of reluctance in her now. The appearance of hesitation earlier must have been only for show—or because she had not really thought Nick worth her time. Her apparent vulnerability and defenselessness had been no more than figments of his imagination. Nick's jaw tightened as he saw her give Rashleigh the same tempting, secretive smile in parting that she had given to him.

He watched as Rashleigh drained his glass of wine in one gulp and ordered a second, which he dispatched the same way, his eyes on the door the whole time. Nick guessed that the girl had asked Rashleigh to give her a few minutes in which to prepare herself before he joined her in her bed. He got to his feet. It was time to spoil his cousin's party. He started to move toward Rashleigh with deliberate intent.

Rashleigh looked up and their eyes met. For a long moment they looked at one another and then Rashleigh turned away abruptly and hurried out without a word. The tavern door crashed on its hinges as it closed behind him. The candles fluttered in the wind and half of them went out. Men cursed as they knocked their drinks over in the dark. Nick blundered across the room and found his way to the door. He was not going to let Rashleigh get away from him now.

The alleyway outside was pitch-black. The tavern sign was swinging in the rising breeze and creaked overhead. Nick stopped, his eyes adjusting to the darkness. He listened intently but could hear no sound of movement. He could not tell which way Rashleigh had gone but he was determined to find him and confront him with Hawkesbury's accusations before Rashleigh gave him the slip and tumbled into bed with that willing little harlot.

Then he saw the glimmer of something in the gutter at the end of the lane, where the narrow passageway joined the high road. His breath caught. Turning, he shoved open the door of the tavern and shouted inside, "Bring a light!"

The landlord hurried to do his bidding, a flaring torch in his hand. Nick could see a fold of the silver cloak, all muddied now from the dirt of the gutter, gleaming bright in the torchlight.

The customers were piling out of the alehouse, scenting trouble. Another lantern flared, showing Rashleigh lying on the ground, his face paint smeared, his wig askew. One of his hands lay outstretched as though clutching after something that had eluded him. Nick could see a knife protruding between his ribs. It was buried to the hilt. Beside him lay a blond wig and a black velvet mask.

Images filled Nick's mind of Anna, lying there in the gutter in his cousin's place, limp, broken, her life drained away. He saw her blue eyes clouding over in death and felt the familiar tide of sickness and guilt wash through him. With an immense effort of will he forced the images from his mind and looked dispassionately down at his cousin's tumbled body. Rashleigh looked undignified in death. His face had fallen and crumpled in on itself. He looked weak and dissolute and pitiful. Nick searched his heart and did not feel a scrap of sorrow. The world was a better place without the Earl of Rashleigh.

The breeze stirred the edge of Rashleigh's silver cloak and stirred, too, the scrap of paper that had been clasped between his fingers. It fluttered free and Nick bent to pick it up. It was a visiting card and on it was printed the flaunting symbol of a peacock in gold. Nick frowned. He had seen that device before. It was similar to the coat of arms of his old school friend Charles, Duke of Cole. He turned it over. On the back was written the words *Peacock Oak,* the estate in Yorkshire where Charles had his country seat.

Nick saw the inn servant at the front of the crowd,

his face thin and terrified in the flickering light. He walked over to him.

"You were standing near to Lord Rashleigh when he was talking to the girl," he said. "Did you hear anything they said?"

"Are you the law?" the servant demanded.

Nick thought of Lord Hawkesbury and wondered what he would make of this mess. "Near enough," he said.

The servant shook his head. There was the sweat of fear on his upper lip and he wiped it away with his sleeve. "He asked if there was a place where they could talk and she said to wait a few minutes and then to follow her across the street. That was all."

Nick held out the card with the golden peacock on it. "Have you ever seen that before?" he demanded.

The inn servant held the card up to the light, peering at it. Then he recoiled, and pushed it back into Nick's hands. He cast one, fearful glance over his shoulder.

"That's Glory's calling card!" He turned an incredulous look on Nick. "Have you not seen it, sir? It's been in all the presses. Glory leaves her card when she robs her victims!"

A hiss went through the crowd, a strange indrawn breath of fear and excitement, for there was only one Glory and she was the most infamous highwaywoman in the country. Everyone knew her name. No one needed an explanation.

Nick straightened up. "Well, I'll be damned," he said softly.

He remembered the touch of the girl's lips on his. She had kissed like an angel. He felt part shocked, part incredulous, to think her a criminal and a murderer. It seemed impossible. He had thought her honest and even now some instinct, deep and stubborn, told him she could not have killed Rashleigh, though the evidence was right in front of him. The wig, the mask, the knife… And his cousin's fallen body that reminded him so sharply, so heartbreakingly, of Anna….

He thought about the strange tension he had sensed in the girl when Rashleigh had entered the room. She had recognized the Earl. Perhaps she had even known him. She had told Nick that she was waiting for someone and that someone must have been Rashleigh himself. All her actions that evening must have been calculated. She had lured Rashleigh outside to kill him in cold blood.

"Shall I call the watch, sir?" The landlord was at his shoulder, his face strained and sweating in the half-light. "Powerful bad for business, this sort of thing." He saw Nick's face and added hastily, "Terrible tragedy, sir. Friend of yours, was he?"

"No," Nick said. "Not my friend. But he was my cousin."

The landlord gave him a curious glance before beckoning the bar servant over with a message for the watch. Nick knew he should go directly to tell Lord Hawkesbury what had happened but he lingered a moment longer, his eyes scanning the dark warren of streets that wound away into the dark. He thought fancifully that the faint, incongruous scent of flowers still seemed to hang in the air. For a second, above the creaking of the inn sign, he thought that he could hear the tap of her heels, see a flying shadow melt into the darkness of the night. He knew he would never find the girl again now.

Word of the murder was rippling through the crowd. People were gathering at the end of the street to peer and point and whisper at the sight of the infamous Earl of Rashleigh dead in the gutter. And beneath the whispers ran the words "It was Glory. Glory was here. She did it, it was her…"

LORD HAWKESBURY was not amused.

When Nick and Dexter Anstruther were ushered into his presence the following morning he was clearly in a very bad mood indeed.

"This is the most godforsaken mess, Falconer," Hawkesbury barked, leaning back in his chair and steepling his fingers. "Murder and sedition on the streets of London, the whole capital stirred up by the deeds of this vagabond criminal! It's in all the morning papers. They are treating her like a heroine for ridding the country of scum like Rashleigh. The whole point of you heading Rashleigh off was to prevent this sort of incident. Instead you spend a jolly half hour with Glory in a tavern and then allow her to wander off and stab your cousin!"

"Quite so, my lord," Nick said, wincing. He reflected that Hawkesbury's mild complexion was a poor guide to his choleric disposition. "But whilst there was, no doubt, a long list of people who wanted to murder my cousin I do not believe we could have predicted that one of them was apparently a notorious highwaywoman."

"You couldn't even recognize a notorious highwaywoman when you saw one," Hawkesbury grumbled, drawing toward him Nick's written statement from the previous night. "Thought she was a harlot, I see." He looked up. "How old are you, Falconer? Two and thirty? You sound as naive as a babe in arms!"

Anstruther shot Nick a sympathetic look. "It's Glory's calling card right enough," he put in, picking up the card that Hawkesbury offered irascibly and turning it over between his fingers. "I read the penny prints. Some of my best sources of information derive from there. And this—" he flicked the card with a finger "—is the sign she always leaves after an attack."

"She has not struck in London before, though, has she?" Nick said. "I understood her to operate only in the north."

The deep frown on Hawkesbury's forehead deepened further. "Thought she was nothing more than a petty felon and rabble-rouser," he muttered, shredding a quill between his fingers. "Now it seems she's involved in treason, as well, and your cousin—" he pointed a stubby finger at Nick "—was part of the conspiracy!"

"Glory is a popular heroine, my lord," Anstruther offered eagerly. "She robs the rich to feed the poor, they say."

Hawkesbury grunted. "You've been reading too many fairy tales, Anstruther! The woman's a criminal, no more and no less." He threw the ruined quill down on his desk and leaned forward, glaring fiercely at Nick. "I have no official authority over you, Falconer, but I'd like to suggest that this is what you do. You've got some army furlough, haven't you? Good!" he added, as Nick nodded grimly. "Then you go to Yorkshire and find this Glory person. You've some acquaintance with the Duke of Cole, have you not?"

"We were at Eton together," Nick confirmed.

"Excellent. He is to host a house party at his York-shire estate from next month, so I understand. You will be one of the guests. There must be some connection between Cole and this felon since the name of his estate was on her calling card!"

Nick nodded. There were worse ways to spend one's leave than as the houseguest of the famously lavish Duke and Duchess of Cole, and Lord Hawkesbury's suggestion was as good as an order.

"Are you suggesting that Charles Cole may be part of a criminal conspiracy, sir?" he inquired.

"Certainly not!" Hawkesbury harrumphed. "Sound man, votes Tory! You can rely on him. No, this female malcontent taunts us, that is all, with peacocks and calling cards and addresses… Pah!" The quill snapped between his fingers. "The sooner you find her the bet-ter, Falconer. Find her and send word to me. I'll make her talk and then I'll hang her."

Nick raised his brows. "Surely she will have to have a fair trial, my lord—"

"Optional!" Hawkesbury barked. "I'd rather shoot her. This is a time of war. The country must be freed from such seditious influences, Falconer." He glared at Anstruther from under his sandy brows. "Popular heroine, indeed. Pah! What a pair you are. It's your mess, Falconer. You sort it out. Anstruther can go with you. He might be useful if he gets over his infatuation with this…this female Robin Hood!"

"So what do we do, sir?" Anstruther said to Nick as, dismissed from Lord Hawkesbury's presence, they made their way out into a chilly London morning.

Nick laughed. "You heard the Home Secretary, Anstruther. We travel up to Yorkshire, find Glory and send word to Lord Hawkesbury. He will make her talk and," Nick said wryly, "then he will hang her."

Anstruther gave him a look. "You met the woman, sir. What did you think of her?"

Nick thought of the girl from the Hen and Vulture. He had been thinking about her for most of the night, remembering the seduction of her kiss and hating the way that despite all the evidence of her perfidy, his body still burned for her.

He set his jaw. "I think she must be the most cunning charlatan in the kingdom, Anstruther," he said, "and she has played me for a fool. So now it is my turn. I shall take great pleasure in hunting Glory down."

CHAPTER ONE

Yorkshire—June 1805

Monkshead—Danger is near

SOMETIMES THE NIGHTMARE would come to her in the depths of the darkness and she would wake cold and shaking, reaching for the comfort of the candle's light. Other times—this time—it caught her unawares, tricked her in that hour before daybreak when the summer light had already started to creep around the edges of the curtain.

She was going to die. She could not breathe. Her wrists were chafed raw from the rope that tied her to the cart and her legs ached intolerably from the long, stumbling miles. She could hear the rumble of the carriage wheels echoing in her head. Her skirt was ripped to shreds and her thighs were criss-crossed with wheals where Rashleigh had leaned from the carriage and plied his whip, laughing as she staggered in the mud. He had sworn to punish her for being seasick all the way from Russia to England. This was his revenge because he had wanted her—wanted to spend the entire voyage in bed with her, no doubt—and instead of pleasuring him her body had thwarted him with her illness. He had told her that she disgusted him.

It was winter and the road was bad. Her feet were bare and blue with cold, her hands numb, her wrists torn. And there was murder in her heart. If Rashleigh gave her but one chance, if there was one single careless moment when his attention was diverted, then she would kill him. It was as simple as that.

But the moment never came. In her dream there was all the anger and the frustration and the pain almost past enduring but never the satisfaction of release. The darkness stretched before her endlessly with no promise of escape. She was a serf, a slave, nothing more than property. She was trapped forever.

Mari struggled awake. The remnants of the nightmare fled. She was lying in her huge bed in her cottage in Peacock Oak. It was light now and downstairs the servants were already awake and at work. She could hear the muted sound of them moving about. Jane would be bringing up the morning tea for her. Soon she would be knocking at the bedroom door, chattering blithely over the beauty of the day as she drew back the drapes and let the sunshine into the room.

There was the rattle of china outside the door, then Jane's knock and the same words that she used each day, "Good morning, madam!"

Mari had always thought that Jane had an amazing capacity for cheerfulness. Even on the gloomiest of winter mornings with the snow piled up on the windowsill and the wind blowing spitefully down the chimney she would remark that it would brighten up later. Jane was their housekeeper and ran Peacock Cottage with the help of one maid of all work and a handyman gardener called Frank, a cousin of hers who was a dour Yorkshire man of as few words as Jane had plenty.

"What a beautiful morning, madam!" Jane had placed the tea tray carefully on the bedside table and gone across to open the curtains. "It will be perfect for her grace's garden party and ball later."

"I hope so," Mari said. She sat up and reached for her wrap. Jane poured the tea from the tiny china pot. It was rich and strong, just as Mari liked it. Strong tea was a proper Yorkshire custom, Jane had said proudly, when Mari had expressed her preference, little knowing that Mari's own tastes had been set years before in Russia, where the black tea had been so strong Mari suspected even Jane would have choked on it.

Beside the cup was a letter and next to that a three-day-old copy of the *Times*. The news reached Peacock Oak a little later than elsewhere but it scarcely mattered. Rural life rolled on its way in this part of Yorkshire with very little change or challenge from day to day and that was exactly how Mari wished it to be.

"I was worrying last night that there might be a summer storm that would flatten all the flowers," Mari said now, "and all our work would be ruined."

"Not a bit of it," Jane said stoutly. "The garden will look beautiful, madam. So many of those lovely flowers you chose for her grace! Mr. Osborne would be so proud of the way you have kept his work alive." Her gaze went to the small portrait hanging on the wall at the side of Mari's bed.

"Ah, yes," Mari said. She smiled, stretched. "Dear Mr. Osborne."

She was very fond of the late Mr. Osborne. An older man, graying, avuncular, he had a gentle face and gave the impression of a manner to match. He had been the perfect husband, rich and kind. Mari felt a rush of affection for him. Sometimes even she almost forgot that Mr. Osborne was imaginary, so real had he become in her mind.

She had never told anyone that she was not a widow. A single woman living in a small village needed a respectable background and hers could not have been more scandalous. The imaginary Mr. Osborne had, in contrast, been a most upright man, the younger son of an obscure clergyman from Cornwall, the owner of a small but profitable business importing and growing exotic plants. Mari had found it remarkably pleasing to create the sort of husband she had required. Mr. Osborne, she was sure, had been shrewd in business but mild in his family life. He had been a temperate drinker, the smoker of the odd cigar on special occasions, but had had no other discernible vices. Certainly he had required nothing from her emotionally and even better, would not have wished for a physical relationship. Which was good because she thought that she never, ever wanted a physical relationship with a man again.

For a moment the nightmare threatened to invade her mind once again, and Mari shuddered. Rashleigh… But she would not think of Rashleigh and the horror of the past. That was dead, gone, buried. Rashleigh himself was dead, after all, murdered in a London rookery two months before.

Marina shivered a little to remember the events of that night. She had never discovered how the Earl had tracked her down to Yorkshire seven years after she had escaped him. Foolishly she had even started to believe that she would be free forever, so when his letter had arrived, threatening blackmail, she had been almost

sick with shock. She had known at once that she had
to confront Rashleigh for the sake of all those he threatened to expose. He knew all her secrets and could have
her hanged for them—he knew that she was a runaway
slave and a thief, and worst of all, somehow he knew
the true identity of Glory and the girls who rode with
her, and he was threatening to tell the authorities and
have them arrested if Mari did not meet with him.

She had had no choice if she wanted to save those
she loved. She had traveled up to London; had arranged
to meet Rashleigh at the Hen and Vulture. She had had
a private room waiting in a tenement across the street,
had told him to wait a few moments before he followed
her, but he never came. And then she had heard the cry
go up that he had been found stabbed to death in the
alley outside.

Mari had not stayed to hear more. She knew that if
people once knew her history as Rashleigh's slave and
his mistress, if they found out that the Earl had threatened her with blackmail, she would not stand a chance.
All the secrets she had tried so hard to hide would
come tumbling out and all the people she cared about
would be ruined. She knew she had the best motive in
the world for murdering Rashleigh and no one would
believe her innocent. So she had run from him for the
second time in her life.

Well, Rashleigh was dead now and no one else
could trace her. She had reinvented herself years ago;
covered her tracks too well to be discovered. She was
not even sure how Rashleigh himself had managed to
find her again, but now that he was dead the secret had
surely gone with him to the grave.

Mr. Osborne had been the opposite of the Earl of

Rashleigh in every way. He was gentle, moderate, kind. She had invented the memory of a paragon, the kind of man who would never hurt her or threaten her or give her cause for grief.

"Indeed," Mari repeated, smiling at the portrait that she had picked up in a pawnshop for two shillings. "Mr. Osborne was a shining example amongst men."

"Lady Hester is taking breakfast in her room this morning, madam," Jane said referring to Mari's companion of the past five years. "She says that she is a little fatigued but will join you for a stroll on the terrace at ten of the clock, before you go to the garden party."

"That would be delightful," Mari said, but mentally she was shaking her head slightly. She knew Hester's ailment and it was not mere tiredness. Lady Hester Berry, the spoiled cousin of the Duke of Cole, was bored, and boredom led her to drinking in alehouses, picking up low company and worse. No doubt this morning she was still half cast away.

Jane was collecting Mari's cup and tidying the tray. She always enjoyed a gossip in the mornings.

"Frank says that there was another attack last night, madam," she said. "That gang, the Glory Girls…"

Mari paused, unfolding the newspaper slowly to give herself time. "What did they do?"

"They stopped Mr. Arkwright's banker on his way back to Harrogate and took Arkwright's money."

Mari raised her brows. "All of it?"

"A tenth of the profits, madam." Jane's eyes were bright with excitement. "A tenth was the money that Arkwright had promised his loom workers and then refused to pay. They say that the Girls gave it back to those who had been cheated of it. Heroines they are, madam!"

"They are criminals," Mari pointed out. "They break the law."

Jane's face fell. She preferred the romance of robbing the rich to give to the poor, rather than the harsh reality of the penal code.

"Yes, madam," she said. "Of course." Her voice warmed with pride. "But begging your pardon, ma'am, I do think that our girls are proper heroines! I know it's not for you to encourage highway robbery but they only hurts those as mistreat the weak and needy."

"Quite," Mari said. "You need not think that I disapprove of the Glory Girls' principles, Jane. I merely remember that highway robbery is a capital crime."

"Yes, ma'am." Jane dropped a respectful curtsy. "Shall I return in a little while to help you dress, ma'am?"

"Thank you, Jane," Mari said. "I shall read the newspaper for twenty minutes or so and then I will be ready."

Jane went out and Mari listened to her footfalls receding along the landing. She did not pick up the paper again. Instead she reached for the letter that had lain untouched on a side table until then. Hester always laughed at the way that Mari left letters unopened for hours when she fell upon hers with excitement the minute that they arrived. But then, Hester fell on life with eagerness whereas Mari had always been rather more careful.

She unfolded the letter. There was a single line of writing, printed in capital letters.

I know all about you. I know what you did.

There was no signature.

Mari did not react to the letter in the manner in

which nine out of ten people would have done. She did not turn pale or cry out. Instead she narrowed her eyes, tapping the letter against the fingers of her other hand.

I know all about you. I know what you did.

The difficulty was that she had done so many things. She had stolen from the Earl of Rashleigh. She had run away from him. She had lied to create an alternative life for herself. She had been present at the scene of Rashleigh's murder. She was party to a conspiracy that robbed the rich to give to the poor…

She had no idea to which of these incidents the letter writer was referring.

She dropped the letter onto the bed, slipped from beneath the covers and went across to the window, drawing back the curtain and standing beside the open sash. A slight breeze caressed her face and flattened her nightdress against her body. The wind was warm and smelled of hay and summer. Jane had been right, it was a beautiful day for a garden party and Mari's friend Laura, Duchess of Cole, certainly knew how to entertain. The event would be the talk of the county for months.

From her window, Mari could see across the lawn to the hothouses where she cultivated her rare and exotic plants. Frank was already hard at work opening the vents in the greenhouse roof and plying his watering can along the row of seedlings. The mellow south wall behind the hothouse separated Mari's land from the deer park of Cole Court. There was a charming white-painted door in the wall through which she often walked when she went to see Laura. Sheep were grazing beneath the spreading oak trees of the park and beyond the grounds the river curled slow and shallow. Nothing else moved in the landscape. A faint heat haze was already rising from the grass.

The view was peaceful but despite the warmth of the day, Mari wrapped her arms around herself as though seeking comfort. She could feel something malevolent in the air. Someone was watching—and waiting.

The letter had disquieted her. Of course it had. That was only natural. Now she thought about it, she realized that the timing of it could not be a coincidence, coming so soon after Rashleigh's death. He must have told someone else her whereabouts. The nightmare was not over after all. She should have known better. She should have known that a runaway slave always had to keep on running.

She knew what would happen next. There would be a demand for money in return for silence and she would have to decide what she was going to do about that. Giving in to bullies and blackmailers had never been her style, though she wondered a little wearily when she would ever be free of the past. She could never forget it, of course, but she could try to live with it, to carry the burden of her history, to keep the secret. If only there were not others so intent on reminding her....

She gave herself a little shake. These blue devils were very unlike her. She was anxious at the prospect of the opening of the new garden and the enforced mingling with the Duchess's guests, of course. She disliked grand social occasions. And then there had been Jane's mention of the Glory Girls' activities. But there was no intimation that the authorities were any closer to identifying the group of female desperadoes who occasionally—very occasionally—terrorized the rich and miserly to redress the balance for the poor and needy.

And the letter… Well, she would just have to wait and see what happened there. Hester would help her. They always helped one another. Hester and Laura were the only ones who knew all her secrets.

With a decisive step, Mari crossed the room to ring the bell for Jane to come and help her dress. It was going to be a beautiful day. The new garden would be a raging success, the Duchess's guests would be suitably appreciative and at the end of it life in Peacock Oak would settle back into the same peaceful routine it had possessed for the last few years. Nevertheless, Mari felt a chill.

Someone was coming. She could sense it. Someone dangerous.

CHAPTER TWO

Wood Sorrel—Secret sweetness

"IT HAS BEEN A HUGE success, I think," Laura Cole said, later that day. She slipped her arm through Mari's and together they walked down the slope from the wooded garden, past the cascade with its secret mossy pools, past the fountain fringed by weeping willow and down to the formal gardens at the back of the house. Cole Court glowed pale in the evening sunshine.

"I am so tired," Laura said. She pulled a face. "And my feet hurt. These gold slippers were such a foolish choice for today! But—" she squeezed Mari's arm "—thank you, dearest Mari, because the whole thing has been *marvelous*."

"I am glad that you have enjoyed it," Mari said. She glanced at her friend. "If it comes to that, you have worked quite hard yourself, Laura, in entertaining your guests. I do not envy you that. Give me plants anytime."

"Oh, some of our guests have been dire," Laura agreed. "So rude! I heard Lady Faye calling you quite the little artisan, Mari. What a poisonous, patronizing toad of a woman she is. And then she was pushing poor Lydia into John Teague's arms all day when all he wished to do was speak with Hester." Laura cast a look around. "Where is Hester? Has she gone home already?"

"You know she takes hours to prepare for a ball," Mari said.

"Dampening her petticoats, I suppose," Laura said. Her rather plain face broke into a mischievous smile. "Oh, what a cat I am! You know that I love Hester dearly, but the gown that she wore for Lady Norris's rout last week was barely decent. Can you not speak to her, Mari?"

"No," Mari said. "I am not her mother." She laughed. "I have tried, Laura, but you know that Hester goes her own way."

"I suppose so," Laura said, sighing. She paused to admire a display of roses growing against the pale red brick of the old walled garden. "Frank tells me that you grew these roses from old cottage garden stock. Are they very ancient?"

"Hundreds of years old," Mari said.

"They look so pretty with the lavender," Laura said. "My own little cottage garden!"

Mari smiled inwardly to see the Duchess of Cole playing at owning a cottage garden when the acres of Cole Court were spread all around them. She had originally met Laura at the Skipton Horticultural Society and Laura had quickly been taken with the idea that she wanted Mari to help redesign the gardens at Cole Court. In vain had Mari protested that the Duchess was quite above her touch and helping to redesign such extensive gardens was a challenge for a more experienced horticulturalist. Laura, with all of a Duchess's disregard for convention, had decided that she wanted both Mari's designs and Mari's friendship, and there was no arguing with her. Laura was so likable and so utterly without the snobbery that often came with high estate that Mari found she could not refuse her. And so Laura had persuaded her and they had worked together on the plans for the best part of two years, and now they were firm friends in spite of Mari's reservations. She knew that letting people close to her was a dangerous business and being the protégée of the Duchess of Cole brought too much attention, attention that she did not crave. She had seen the effect of that today. All society in the county took its cue from the Duchess of Cole and now that Laura Cole had a new garden, everyone else wanted one, too, and they were all clamoring for her designs.

"There is Lady Craven," Laura said, waving. "She tells me that she will be asking you to design a knot garden and a herb terrace for her at Levens Park."

Mari nodded dolefully. "Lord Broughton has already approached me, as has Mrs. Napier and Lady Jane Spring."

"Everyone is talking about you," Laura said. "They think you are most talented."

"They are very generous," Mari said. "I was sure that the Persian Paradise Fountain would not work and that all the fruit trees would be attacked by aphids and die."

"You are too modest, or perhaps too pessimistic," Laura said. She looked at her and sighed. "I am sorry, Mari. I forget sometimes that you have no taste for company and had chosen Peacock Oak to live because it was so quiet."

"Yes," Mari said. She laughed. "That was before you came back to live here! The lawyer made a particular point of telling me that it was a little backwater of a place where nothing ever happened! I thought it sounded perfect—before you arrived!"

They laughed together. "Well—" a shade of bitterness entered Laura's voice now "—I suppose I could have gone back to Buckinghamshire, or to Norfolk or Surrey or another of the Cole seats, but I preferred Yorkshire because it was the farthest I could get away from Charles."

"Oh, Laura!" Mari put a hand on her arm. "Is it truly so bad?"

"Having a hopeless regard for one's own husband and knowing he does not return your feelings?" Laura nodded. "Yes, it is that bad. And now that Charles has joined me here for the summer it is even worse."

"I am sorry," Mari said. "Never having had a husband I cannot understand, but I do sympathize."

"Hush!" Laura looked around. "Someone will hear you and where will the respectable Mrs. Osborne be then?"

"Back in deep trouble, I imagine," Mari said. She glanced across at the clock on the stable block tower. Above it, the weathervane with its iron-carved highwayman was unmoving in the still air. Mari shook her head to see it. Laura's sense of humor took her breath away sometimes.

"I had better let you go and dress," she said. "You will be unconscionably late for your own ball as it is. I will hunt up Hester and make sure that she is ready, too."

"You will come, won't you?" Laura caught her hands. "Just for a little time? Please, Mari—"

Mari had been intending to spend the evening quietly, but now that she saw her friend's pleading face she relented. "Oh, very well. Just for a little. I suppose it cannot do any harm."

"So that is your opinion of the fabled hospitality of the Coles," Laura said, laughing, as she waved a farewell and made her way toward the terrace. "I will see you in a short while."

The gardens were deserted now. The sun was sinking behind the fells and the blue of twilight was settling beneath the trees of the woodland garden. On impulse, Mari slipped off her shoes and stockings and squeezed the blades of grass between her toes, relishing their cool freshness. Like Laura she was exhausted, for she had been tense all day with the strain of meeting the guests, of discussing her garden designs with them, of playing her part and putting on a show. Now that evening had come and the shadows had fallen she wanted the relief of sloughing off that personality, washing it away along with the heat of the day. The trouble with reinventing herself was that every so often she wanted to shake off respectable Mrs. Osborne and be Mari, the girl who had always had a streak of wildness in her.

She stood by the fountain and looked longingly at the refreshing shower of droplets. Her mouth felt dry just thinking about its cool, quenching pleasure. She looked around. There was nobody there. Temptation beckoned. No one would see her. Retreating into the dark shade of pines that bordered the cascade, she started to strip off her clothes.

IT WAS PAST EIGHT o'clock at night when the mail coach from Skipton to Leyburn stopped at the gates of Cole Court and deposited two parcels, seven letters and Nicholas Falconer.

Nick had spent the day in Skipton, speaking with the various forces of law and order that had so far singularly and spectacularly failed to capture the Glory Girls. He had left behind him a disgruntled Captain of the Yeomanry, two angry justices of the peace and a fuming town constable, who were all most put out that the Home Secretary was suddenly taking an interest in their local affairs. Nick had left Dexter Anstruther to smooth them over and Anstruther would be joining him in the morning when all their baggage had arrived from London. For now, Nick was able to look forward to a reunion with Charles Cole, who was one of his oldest friends, and the promise of the legendary Cole Court hospitality.

He threw a word of thanks to the coachman, shouldered his kit bag and started off up the driveway before the lodge-keeper could protest that he had the gig standing by to convey the Duke's guest to the house. The coachman looked at the groom and they both cocked a curious eyebrow at the lodge-keeper. Visitors to Peacock Oak were frequent, for the Duke and Duchess of Cole kept open house, and that very day had unveiled their new pleasure gardens to an audience of invited guests. Most visitors, however, did not travel by mail coach, nor carry their own luggage.

"That's the Quality for you," the lodge-keeper said, shrugging, as he bent to lift the sack of mail. "Do as they please."

"Quality? Him?" The groom stared up the driveway after the fast-disappearing figure. "Shabby as you like and no servant?"

But the coachman knew better. "Old soldier," he said wisely. "Carries his own kit."

"That's Major Falconer," the lodge-keeper boasted.
"Heir to a Marquisate. Scottish title, mind, but even so.
I heard he was at school with his grace."

"Well, stone the crows," the groom said, scratching
his head. "You never can tell."

They sat watching Nick until he passed a turn in the
driveway and was swallowed up between the huge
oaks of the home park. Then an irritable voice from
within the coach asked when they were to resume the
journey. The coachman recollected himself and picked
up the reins and the lodge-keeper waved a cheery hand
and hefted the sack of mail away.

As the sound of the coach died away, silence settled
once again over Cole Court and Nick shifted his bag
from one shoulder to the other to ease the ache. This
was not how he would have chosen to spend his army
furlough, despite the pleasure of renewing acquaintance with his old friend, but then Rashleigh had never
had any consideration for the needs of others and it was
typical that in his death he would cause as much trouble
as in life.

Nick had shied away from all social engagements
since Anna's death, preferring instead the rigors of life
on campaign. Somehow the physical hardship of army
life assuaged the guilty ache in his soul that he had not
been there to help Anna when she needed him. But now
he had been obliged to put aside his own preferences
for a little and rejoin the *Ton* even if it was only as a
cover to hunt down a notorious criminal.

Nick thought about the girl at the tavern frequently,
more often than he wished. The memory of her haunted
him, superimposing itself on the older, more faded
memories of Anna, demanding his attention in a man-

ner that both obsessed him and fed his guilt. He did not seem able to escape her. He had held the girl in his arms and had wanted her. He had desired her more than any woman he had known. He had dreamed about her every night for a week after they had met in the tavern, vivid erotic dreams from which he had woken panting and hard, desperate to assuage the ache in his body. It seemed like a double betrayal of Anna's memory to want to make love with a woman who must be a harlot and a murderer, and the guilt flayed him alive. For hours he had sat with his miniature of Anna clasped in his hand, trying to force his thoughts back on to his dead wife and away from the woman who had bewitched him. He had turned his back on all women since Anna's death, yet suddenly he found himself lusting after a girl who was everything that sweet, delicate Anna was not. He had tried to bury the memory and turn his heart to ice again but he could not forget the girl in the tavern. His emotions, once reawakened, were not so easy to turn off again and he hated himself for it. He had fallen slave to lust and he did not seem able to escape it.

Thinking and hoping that it was just a physical need for a woman—any woman—he had sought out one of the most celebrated courtesans in Town. Their encounter had been torrid and intense and entirely devoid of any real emotion on either side. At the end of the night she had kissed him affectionately and invited him to call on her again whenever he chose, and he had left feeling strangely unsatisfied. His body was sated but his mind felt sharp and unfulfilled. He needed to find the woman from the Hen and Vulture again. He wanted her with an ache that was ever more powerful.

As he walked up the driveway toward the lights of Cole Court, Nick's thoughts turned inevitably once more to the girl in the tavern. Could such a woman really be Glory, the infamous highwaywoman whose band was responsible for the rather quixotic robbing of the rich to give to the poor? Nick was of the opinion that Glory would not have been so notorious were it not for the fact that she *was* a woman. Her deeds had caught the public imagination like a latter-day Robin Hood. Ballads and poems were written in her honor. She was talked of in the taverns and the clubs, her exploits celebrated in toasts and speeches. She was a popular heroine. And now he was here to track her down so that Lord Hawkesbury could hang her. He would likely end up the least popular man in the country if he carried it through. But leaving aside Lord Hawkesbury's commission, he had a personal quest to fulfill. Glory, the girl in the tavern, had played him for a fool and he wanted revenge.

Nick went through the gate that separated the parkland from the formal gardens. Dusk was falling now, painting the sky in shades of peach and blue with the trees standing tall and black against its light. There was the scent of pine and cut grass on the air, and Nick could hear the splash of water. Suddenly he felt intolerably dirty from the long journey. Following the sound, he found himself approaching a flat grassy plateau with a round pool and a small summerhouse. Someone had designed a charming sequence of canals and cascades here. In the half-light the water looked deep and mysterious. A fountain at the center showered down a spray of sparkling drops like grains of corn. Nick lowered his bag to the ground, knelt on the grass beneath the tumbling branches of a willow tree, cupped his hands and tipped the cold water over his head, exulting in the cold shock as the liquid ran down his neck and eased the gritty scratching of his skin. He was tempted to strip off his clothes and leap into the pool, but even as he straightened and his hands went to the buttons of his jacket, he saw that he was not alone. Someone else had had the same idea as he.

From the trees on the far side of the pool came a slender figure so insubstantial in the dusk that she looked more like a figment of his imagination than a real woman.

Or like a figment of those wild erotic dreams that had haunted his nights.

As she crossed the grass she let the white shift slip from her body. The rising moon touched her skin with silver. There was a splash as she stepped into the pool, and Nick heard her involuntary gasp as the cold water from the fountain cascaded over her. She stood still beneath its caress, a creature of fantasy in the moonlight, raising her hands high above her head as the water ran down her body in silver rivulets and scattered jewel bright drops over her cloudy dark hair.

Up at the house the orchestra was striking up for the ball and the music drifted across the quiet gardens and hung on the air, faint and tempting. The goddess ran her hands slowly down her naked length, over her breasts, across the planes of her stomach and the curve of her hips, leaving a trail of shimmering water on her skin. There was a smile on her parted lips, at once sensuous and innocent, that had a direct effect on Nick's groin. He felt his body swelling to what felt like near fatal proportions. His breeches were suddenly intolerably tight, a tourniquet about his most vital parts. It felt like the hottest night of his entire life.

The air seemed full of the scent of honeysuckle. It wound itself around Nick's senses, sweet and seductive. He knew that he was no gentleman to watch, but then she could be no lady. And he would have had to be approaching death to remain unaroused at the sight of the woman in the water. Her head was tilted back as the fountain splashed down on her face, her eyes were closed, the lashes fanning against her cheek, and every line of her body was pure and silver in the moonlight, with the water droplets rolling over her breasts, beading on her nipples and cascading down to the dark juncture of her thighs.

A peacock called its harsh cry from near at hand and Nick jumped, cracking his head on one of the willow tree's low branches. The girl in the pool froze. She turned her head toward him and for a second it seemed that her gaze met his, and then she was gone, running from the pool with the water spangling the grass behind her, scooping her chemise up as she went, before her flying figure was swallowed up in the shadows.

Nick released the breath that he had been holding. His whole body felt hot, hard and aroused. Damnation, he needed that dip in the pool even more now. A shower of cold water was exactly what he required to get his wayward body and feverish imagination under control, or he would be presenting himself for the Duchess's ball in an extremely inappropriate physical condition. The sight of the girl in the fountain had tapped straight into all those dreams he had sought so hard and so unsuccessfully to repress.

He picked up his kit bag. A brisk walk across the garden would have to suffice instead.

By the time that he reached the house, both Nick's breathing and his errant body were under control again. His imagination, however, was proving more difficult to subdue, presenting him with images of naked goddesses with water cascading over their bodies. He blinked when a liveried footman opened the main door of the house and the glare of candlelight spilled out. What he must look like he had no notion, wild-eyed and with the water still dripping from tendrils of his dark hair. The butler was summoned, took one look at the shabby kit bag at Nick's feet and seemed about to send him to the tradesmen's entrance or perhaps dismiss him entirely. Fortunately Charles Cole himself was crossing the hall with one of his guests at the time. He glanced toward the door and his face lit up as he saw his old friend.

"Nick! You're here at last!"

Nick stepped into the hall as the butler, disdain in every line of his body, sniffed and instructed the hall boy to take Major Falconer's bag upstairs, and the haughty aging beauty who had been hanging on Charles's arm looked down her long, aristocratic nose at him.

"*Major* Falconer?" she queried, with just the faintest hint of emphasis on the prefix as though no one below the rank of General could possibly be a welcome guest at Cole Court.

Nick grinned and sketched a bow. "How do you do, madam? Nicholas Falconer, at your service."

"Nick was at school with me, Faye," Charles said. He held out a hand and shook Nick's warmly, his fair, open face alight with good humor. "Nick, this is my cousin's wife, Lady Faye Cole."

"Falconer…" the beauty murmured. Her face cleared. "Oh, the Marquis of Kinloss's heir! I thought for a moment that Charles had taken to inviting the ranks of the *military* to Cole Court!"

"I am a major in the army, ma'am," Nick murmured.

"Well, never mind, never mind." Lady Faye's pale blue eyes bulged. "More importantly you are heir to a Marquisate." Her gaze hardened slightly. "You must meet my daughter, Major Falconer." She smiled, a cold smile that did not reach her eyes. "I was a child bride, of course, and Lydia is but seventeen and only just out."

Nick had no desire to meet the schoolroom daughter of a matchmaking mama, but he bowed politely and Lady Faye drifted off, no doubt to hunt up her daughter and present her like a sacrificial lamb to the new arrival.

"I'm sorry about Faye," Charles Cole murmured, taking Nick's arm as his cousin's wife drifted away on a cloud of nose-numbing perfume. "My cousin Henry always was an abject fool when it came to women. You remember Henry? Then you'll know what I mean. But she could at least have waited until you were through the door before lining you up as a prospective son-in-law."

"Someone should warn her that I am not good son-in-law material," Nick said, a little bitterly. His parents-in-law had never reproached him for his treatment of Anna but his remorse was sharper because he knew he was culpable.

Charles sighed. "If you are solvent and have all your own teeth, then you are eligible, old chap."

Nick gave a groan. "Tell them I'm penniless, for pity's sake, Charles."

"I could do that, but then I would be lying. And what about the Marquisate?"

"Put it about that my uncle has disinherited me, or something." Nick laughed. "I'm sure he would do if he could. He finds me very unsatisfactory—doesn't approve of his heir working for a living. Speaking of which, I *am* here to work, Charles, not to be distracted by debutantes."

"So I understand." Charles threw a rather theatrical look over his shoulder and Nick realized that he was probably going to make a poor conspirator. "Hawkesbury sent a letter before you. Might have known that Rashleigh would continue to cause trouble from beyond the grave."

"Naturally. He never had any consideration."

"Where is Anstruther?" Charles asked, looking around. "Is he not with you? Now he really is ineligible, poor lad. Faye won't be throwing Lydia in Anstruther's way, not now that his father has disgraced the family name."

"Dexter arrives tomorrow," Nick said. "I left him in Skipton, smoothing over matters with the constable."

"Of course, of course." Charles looked furtively excited. "I must say this business has certainly enlivened my summer. Usually I find the country a dead bore. Now Hawkesbury says…" Charles drew closer and whispered loudly, "You are to fill me in on the details and I am to offer you all aid I can in catching the Glory Girls."

"Right," Nick said, trying not to laugh.

"But tonight—" Charles turned as the ballroom door opened and several couples spilled out into the cool of the checkered hall "—tonight you are to meet my guests and mingle. Who knows, you may discover something useful."

Nick nodded. "Of course. I—" He stopped abruptly.

The front door had opened and two late guests, both female, were being ushered into the hall by a deferential footman. One was a beauty of maybe seven or eight and twenty. She could command a room. As imperious in her own way as Faye Cole, the arrogant tilt of her blond head demanded that everyone should look at her and Nick thought that most men would be only too willing to comply. She was dressed in a shockingly low-cut ball gown of scarlet that barely covered her nipples and looked as though it had been dampened for good measure. Very bold, Nick thought, with all the goods in the shop window. He heard Charles sigh.

"That's another of my cousins, I'm afraid, Lady Hester Berry. The perils of a large family…"

But Nick was not listening. He was looking at the other woman. She was hanging back behind Lady Hester and he could see from the way in which her gloved fingers gripped her evening bag that she was nervous. She looked younger than Lady Hester, a little pale, small but voluptuous, her hair covered by a fashionable turban, her body swathed in an expensively modest gown that nevertheless clung lovingly to every one of her curves.

Nick stared. He had seen those curves recently covered in no more than droplets of water.

She turned her head and met his gaze. He had thought that her eyes were black until the lamplight struck across them and he saw the flecks of green and gold in their depths. The recognition hit him then so hard and so fast that he almost lost his breath. It could not be a coincidence. Surely, *surely* this was the girl from the Hen and Vulture? She had been wearing a blond wig then, and a mask, but the one thing that she could not disguise was the unusual color of her eyes. He stared at her, admiring the curve of her cheek, the sensuous fullness of her lips—not stained a harlot's cherry-red tonight but a tempting pale pink—and the vulnerable line of her neck. He was almost certain— as sure as he could be without kissing her—that it was the same woman.

Her gaze widened slightly as it met his and he knew in that moment that she had recognized him, too, though whether as the man she had kissed in the tavern or as the man by the pool—or both—he could not be sure. He watched her and waited coolly for her reaction.

It was not long in coming. She raised her chin and gave him the most perfectly calculated cut-direct that he had ever experienced. She looked through him as though he simply did not exist.

Nick's lips twisted with appreciation. She was a very cool customer indeed.

But could this oh-so-proper lady truly be the notorious Glory, the harlot from the tavern? She was certainly the naked nymph from the fountain.

And he had the advantage. His sudden appearance must inevitably have shocked her, no matter how well she concealed it. So now was the time to make a move before she had the chance to rally her defenses.

"Who is that?" he murmured, and heard Charles sigh again.

"I told you, old fellow, that is my cousin Hester—"

"No," Nick said. "The other lady."

"Oh." Charles sounded taken aback, as though no one should be able to see another female in the room when Hester was there to dazzle. "That is Mrs. Marina Osborne. She is a neighbor of ours."

Mrs. Osborne. Nick's eyes narrowed. She sounded extraordinarily respectable.

"She's married?" he asked.

"No." Charles sounded wearily amused, as though Nick was not the first person to ask. "She is a widow— a rich and most devoted widow. They say she buried her heart with her late husband."

Nick smiled. A rich widow. What a perfect cover for the questionable Mrs. Osborne. She had a husband to lend his name and respectability but, conveniently, not his presence.

"They always say that about apparently virtuous widows," he said.

"Sometimes it's true," Charles said. "You are a cynic, my friend. And you have absolutely no chance whatsoever if you are planning to fix your interest there. She is reputedly as cold as ice."

Nick thought once again of the tempting beauty of Marina Osborne as the drops of water caressed her naked body.

"We'll see," he said. He straightened his shoulders. "Introduce me."

CHAPTER THREE

Indian Jasmine – Attraction

"THE MOST GORGEOUS MAN in the room is staring at you, Mari," Lady Hester Berry whispered. "I do believe he intends to make your acquaintance."

Mari knew. The second she had entered the hall she had been aware of the man standing to Charles Cole's right. She had been conscious of every gesture he made, every glance in her direction. She had seen him look at Hester, then look at her, and then—extraordinarily—continue to hold her gaze as though no one else in the room existed.

Such a thing had never happened to Mari before. One of the many reasons she loved having Hester as a companion was that Hester was the most perfect camouflage. Mari was accustomed to being looked through, over and around by men who were searching the room for Hester. She welcomed it. That was not to say she had no suitors of her own. There were plenty who admired her fortune if not her person. But she was mainly accustomed to men trying to charm her solely so that she would speak well of them to her friend.

This dark stranger broke every rule. He had looked at Hester and then he had looked at her and he had not looked away again. In that moment Mari had known, instinctively, since she had not seen him clearly, that he had been the man beneath the willow tree in the garden and that he had recognized her as the naked nymph swimming in the fountain.

A second later, as he stepped into the light, she had also known—with a certainty that made her heart drop to her satin slippers—that he had also been the man in the tavern in London the night that Rashleigh had been killed. He was the man that she had picked up whilst she had waited for Rashleigh to come, the man she had *kissed.*

He looked different, of course. That night he had been dressed somewhat ambiguously. Yet she had sensed as soon as she had seen him that it was a disguise rather than his true persona, for there was something hard, intense and entirely masculine about him that he had *not* been able to disguise. It was something that, to her shock, had called to all that was feminine in her.

She shivered beneath the folds of her silver shawl and drew it a little closer around her. The kiss had been a mistake. An aberration. Normally she hated kissing. It disgusted her. She seldom even touched another person. Such closeness made her fearful. Which made it even more extraordinary that she had forgotten all her own rules when she had kissed this particular man.

She had spent the months since meeting him trying, unsuccessfully, to forget the kiss, to forget him. When Rashleigh had appointed the Hen and Vulture as their meeting place she had known she could not sweep in wearing her widow's weeds if she wished to remain inconspicuous. So she had chosen Molly's fetching disguise but as soon as she had arrived at the club she had realized her peril when a drunken dandy had tried to pick her up. She had looked around the club for another man whom she might use as decoy, as protector, and her gaze had fallen on him. But as their conversation had progressed she had realized she had a tiger by the tail.

There had been something about him that had intrigued her, attracted her. She had never felt like that before in her whole life and it had been heady, like a draught of the strongest wine, tempting her, calling to her wild side. A part of her had been incredulous and disbelieving that after the way Rashleigh had treated her she could *ever* feel like this, and it lured her into further indiscretion. When he had leaned in to kiss her she had panicked for a moment, afraid that she would feel all the revulsion that she had felt for Rashleigh, her skin crawling, the fear threatening to close her throat. But it had passed in an instant and instead of disgust she had felt a sensation that was sweet and strong, sweeping her past hesitation. She had brought his lips down to hers, led by instinct, wanting to explore the taste and texture of him. The quick rush of desire that had flooded her had taken her by surprise and, when she withdrew from him, she had seen the echo of that passion and that surprise in his eyes, too, and her world had reeled.

He was a dangerous man, a man who could almost make her forget the past. She had thought that she would never see him again, that she could forget what had happened between them. She had been wrong.

And now it seemed he was dangerous for another reason. He had been at the Hen and Vulture the night

Rashleigh was murdered and he was here now, and that could be no coincidence.

Mari raised her chin and very deliberately broke the eye contact between them.

"He is not so handsome," she said now to Hester. "His nose has been broken in the past and has not set straight. And I prefer fair hair to brown." Even so, there was little to fault in his appearance, and she knew it. He had very straight, dark brows above equally dark watchful eyes, cheekbones and a jawline that looked as hard as rock and a very firm mouth. Mari remembered that mouth with a little shiver of recollection.

"Nonsense," Hester was saying. "You are too particular. He looks—"

"Tough," Mari said, with another shiver.

"Yes," Hester allowed. "Very direct." She smiled. "He is not for me, I think. But I do believe that he is the most handsome man I have seen in Peacock Oak these two years past."

"Peacock Oak being well-known as a center of excellence for masculine beauty," Mari said.

Hester gave her a flashing smile. "I will allow you to be an expert in matters botanical, Mari, but not in matters pertaining to the opposite sex. There, I think, you must bow to my superior knowledge."

"Your extensive knowledge," Mari agreed.

Hester gave her a tiny kick with her slippered foot. "Here they come," she said. "He must have asked Charles for an introduction."

"Then he cannot take a hint," Mari said. Her heart had started to beat a little faster now despite her outward calm. "I just cut him dead."

"Must you do things like that?" Hester asked. "I wish to meet him even if you do not."

"I fear I have to cut him," Mari murmured. "He was the one I told you about earlier. The one who was watching me in the fountain."

Hester clapped a hand to her mouth. "Oh! No wonder he was staring!"

"And," Mari continued, "I am almost certain that he is also the man I met in London."

Hester looked at her blankly and she spelled out, "The one at the Hen and Vulture, Hes, the night that Rashleigh was killed."

All the color fled Hester's face, leaving her pale beneath her paint. "Damnation," she breathed. "Can it be a coincidence?"

"I don't believe in coincidences," Mari said bleakly.

Hester bit her lip. "Is it too late to run away, do you think?"

"I fear so," Mari said. She looked thoughtfully at the purposeful figure advancing toward her. "I suspect that if I did," she said, "he is the sort of man who would run after me. And catch me."

"Then what are we to do?" Hester whispered. She still looked very pale. "I am hopeless at dissembling—"

"Then don't try. Leave it to me."

Charles Cole was bowing before them. Mari dropped a demure curtsy. She had always kept her distance from the Duke who was more, she was sure, than simply the easygoing country squire he pretended to be. Having her own secrets to keep made her more sensitive to the deceptions of others, though she was not sure exactly what Charles Cole's secret was.

Hester offered her cousin a cheek to kiss. "Good

evening, Charles," she said. Mari could tell that despite her nervousness, she was making strenuous efforts to behave normally and she felt a rush of affection for her friend. Hester had insisted on accompanying her to London on the dreadful journey to confront Rashleigh. She had waited for her at Grillons Hotel. Mari had told her everything that had happened that night, for they always shared all their secrets. But now, for the first time, she was wishing that there were some things she had kept from Hester, too, so that her friend should not feel this terrible pressure to protect her. Mari had looked after herself before when there had been no one else to care for her. She could do it again if she had to. She did not want Hester to suffer for her past.

"Good evening, Hester," Charles said, making sterling efforts not to look down the front of Hester's dress where her bosom rather flaunted itself. He bowed more formally to Mari. "Mrs. Osborne."

"Your grace." Mari tried not to look at Charles's companion and failed singularly. She could feel the weight of his glance on her like a physical touch, and when she raised her eyes, there was a look in his that made her heart jolt and delicious shivers run along her skin. His glance on her was hard, appraising. She felt a heat start to burn deep in her stomach and was shocked. She had thought that Rashleigh had taught her all about men, all about their baser instincts and how far they would go to indulge them. When she had run from him, she had run from the desire ever to have an intimate relationship with a man again. She had thought never to want to. Yet this man had overturned those certainties before with just one kiss and now he was doing the same with one look.

She reminded herself sternly that he must be here with a purpose and that she could not afford to drop her guard for a moment. Her attraction to him could only weaken her. It made her vulnerable to him and that she could not permit.

"May I introduce Major Nicholas Falconer," Charles Cole was saying smoothly. "He is an old friend of mine come to spend the summer in the country. Nick, my cousin Lady Hester Berry and a friend of ours, Mrs. Osborne."

Nicholas Falconer. He sounded safe enough and he bowed to Mari with scrupulous courtesy. But when he took her hand in his, his touch felt dangerous. It also felt shockingly familiar on the basis of just one kiss.

"How do you do, Major Falconer?" Mari made her voice as colorless as possible.

"I am very well, thank you, Mrs. Osborne," Nick Falconer said. He took her arm and drew her a little away from Charles and Hester. He did it with supreme confidence and an absolute determination to separate her from their companions. It had happened before Mari had even realized what he was about.

"I beg your pardon, Mrs. Osborne," Nick Falconer said, "but have we met before?"

Mari met his gaze. It was dark and direct. Suddenly she felt quite cut off from everyone but Nick himself, for his broad shoulders blocked out Hester and Charles and all the other guests. He had drawn a little closer to her as a group of people passed by, chattering and laughing, on their way to the refreshment room. One of his hands was holding her elbow, lightly, but with a touch that made her entire body tingle with awareness. She could smell the scent of him, a combination of summer nights, sandalwood cologne and something more personal and intimate. His clothes were creased and dusty from his journey but that did not detract one whit from his air of authority. Here was a man accustomed to taking what he wanted. She could tell. She doubted that many women would refuse him.

The awareness shivered between them, intense, compulsive. It felt as though he was conscious of every inch of her beneath the gray silk of her evening dress. Mari broke the contact only with difficulty.

"I am sure that we have never met," she said.

He gave her the same slow smile that she remembered from that night at the tavern. "Would you have remembered me?"

Definitely. I could not forget you....

"I have a good memory," Mari said coolly, "but you do not feature in it."

He raised an eyebrow, completely unmoved at her set down. "Strange. You seem very familiar to me."

Mari gave him a cold smile. "On the contrary, Major Falconer, you are the one who is overfamiliar—and not very original in your approach, either."

He smiled again. It was devastating. "And yet for all your denials I am certain that I recognize you," he said, "although you do look very different with your clothes on."

Mari could feel herself clutching her reticule so tightly that the catch bit into her fingers. So he was going to be *that* direct. Not many men would be so blunt but she might have known that he would waste no time on courtesies. She knew he was deliberately provoking her, testing her to see what her reaction would be. No respectable woman, after all, would admit to swimming in the nude in a garden fountain. So if she *did* admit it, it would be tantamount to confessing that she was of easy virtue and then, well, judging by the look in his eyes, it would not be her planting schemes he would be interested in discussing…

Damn it all to hell and back. She admitted to herself that he had her trapped. What was to be done? It could be the ruin of her reputation if he spoke out about what he had seen. On the other hand, her indiscretion in the garden was not as damaging as those other, life-threatening secrets that she absolutely had to keep. She could admit to being the woman in the fountain but never, ever to being the harlot at the Hen and Vulture.

"I know it was you in the fountain," he said softly, whilst her trapped mind ran back and forth over the possibilities. "You may protest if you wish but I believe I would recognize you anywhere."

A shiver ran along Mari's nerves and she drew the silver shawl more tightly around her shoulders. Oh, yes, he recognized her from the gardens but did he know her from the tavern, as well? It felt as though they were already deeply involved in a game of hunter and hunted and any admission she made could be so very dangerous.

Challenge him. See how far he will go, what he will give away….

She had always been a gambler. She had had to be in order to survive. Sometimes to throw down the gauntlet was the only way.

She gave a little shrug. "Very well. I concede that I was the woman you saw in the fountain. I thought I was unobserved. It was…careless of me."

He flashed her another smile, a disturbingly attractive one. Her toes curled instinctively within her slippers and her heart did another giddy little skip as though she was a schoolroom miss developing a *tendre* rather than a mature woman of five and twenty.

"I like it that you do not pretend," he said. His voice was intimately low. "Ninety-nine women out of one hundred would have claimed not to understand me."

If only he knew. Sometimes she forgot where the pretence began—and where it ended.

She gave him a very straight look. "Of course they would, and who could blame them? A reputation dies all too easily, as you must know, Major Falconer."

"So why are you different? Why did you admit it?"

Mari met his quizzical dark gaze and felt a little breathless. "I am not different. I do not wish you to be the ruin of my reputation, Major Falconer. But equally, I know that you saw me, so what can I say?" She spread her hands in a gesture of surrender. "I was bathing. You saw me. It would avail me little to pretend otherwise. So I must rely on your behavior as a gentleman and hope you will not speak out."

It was not the whole story, of course. It would be impossible to tell him the truth, that sometimes the role of the respectable widow grated on her and she felt an impossible desire to be free. She could not tell him that it was this impulse that had led her to strip off her clothes and revel in the fresh coldness of the fountain. That was too intimate a thing to confide to a virtual stranger, a dangerous stranger who already saw far more than she wished.

When he remained silent, watching her face, she raised her brows. "Was that all you wished to say to me, Major Falconer?"

She saw his lips twitch into a smile at her attempted dismissal of him.

"No, it was not all." He reached forward. His fingers brushed against her neck very lightly and lingered, warm against her skin. "You had better hide that curl if you do not wish anyone else to guess your secret. Your hair is still wet. You must have rushed home and dressed in a great hurry."

Mari's hand flew to her neck where the wayward curl of hair nestled against her throat. It felt feathery, soft and damp, drying from the warmth of her body. She pushed it beneath the edge of her turban, her fingers suddenly clumsy. She could feel the color suffuse her face as Nick continued to watch her.

"Hair as black as midnight," he said. "I remember."

There was a heat in the pit of Mari's stomach as she thought of what else he might remember about her. Her whole body felt as though it was on fire. But then the memory of Rashleigh—his violence, his touch—slithered into her mind and turned her blood to shards of ice and this time she could not erase it.

Not all men were cruel like the Earl of Rashleigh had been. She knew that. She knew that some were all that was chivalrous and honorable. But she had no desire to find out for herself which were good and which were not. She could never trust a man; never let him close to her, and this man least of all when he could bring them all down. So she had to put an end to this disturbing attraction now. She had to finish matters before they really began.

"I have to ask you to forget everything that you saw, sir," she said coldly, "and never speak of this again." Indignation swept through her and she could not quite stifle it. "Indeed," she said, "if you had any claim to the title of gentleman, you would not have been watching anyway."

She saw the laughter lines around his eyes deepen and felt a strange tug of feeling inside. "My dear Mrs. Osborne," he sounded amused, "you ask too much. I am a man first and a gentleman second."

"A very long way second!"

He inclined his head as though conceding the point. He took her hand again, drawing her close. His breath tickled her ear. The icy feeling that was wedged beneath Mari's heart threatened to melt in the heat of his touch.

"You are a widow, Mrs. Osborne," he said softly, "and as such, I assume, you are familiar with the way a man thinks on such matters as—" his voice dropped further "—physical desire?"

Mari repressed a shiver. Oh, yes, she knew all about the way a man thought about lust. Rashleigh had taught her more degrading things than she ever wanted to remember. She looked down her nose at him.

"The thought processes of a man on such subjects are scarcely complex," she said coldly.

Nick laughed. "Quite so. Then you may imagine how *I* felt on seeing you naked and soaking wet with the water cascading over your body and the droplets catching the last of the light—"

Her whole body suffused with blistering heat, Mari wrenched her hand from his. "Major Falconer!"

"Call me Nicholas. Or Nick, if you prefer, since we already know one another so well and are likely to know each other even better."

"Major Falconer," Mari repeated, "you are re-

markably—indeed, distressingly—obtuse. I have no interest in encouraging your attentions to me. I am a respectable widow."

"All appearances to the contrary, Mrs. Osborne," Nick interrupted smoothly.

Mari stared at him. He was right, of course. No woman who displayed herself so wantonly in public could possibly claim the right to modesty. It was the richest irony that she had allowed herself to swim only because she was certain she was alone and now it turned out that the one man in the entire kingdom whom she would wish never to meet again had been the one man standing watching her.

"If you are looking for a lover—" Nick began.

Mari's temper snapped. "Major Falconer, I am not! I must ask you to desist from speaking of such matters! As for what you saw in the gardens, you will desist from even *thinking* about it—" She broke off as Nick shook his head.

"Oh, no, Mrs. Osborne. I give you my word that I will tell no one of what I saw, but you cannot ask me to forget." He smiled. "You cannot erase my memories."

Mari had an all too vivid picture of what those memories might look like. She took a deep, steadying breath.

"Very well. If I have your promise of silence then I suppose I must be content."

He bowed mockingly. "Of course. No gentleman could promise less."

Mari bit her lip. She was not sure if she trusted him to keep silent. It should have felt like a partial victory and yet the spark in those dark eyes suggested that it was anything but.

"Thank you," she said warily.

He shrugged easily. "Once again, a pleasure. And if you tell me that we have never met before, then I shall, of course, believe you. But…" He hesitated, and Mari's overtaxed nerves tightened a further notch, "I wonder… Do you ever visit London, Mrs. Osborne?"

It took every last ounce of self-control for Mari not to jump. She met his gaze and saw nothing there but polite inquiry. He had the most perfect face for games of chance, she thought. He was able to hide every emotion behind a wall of impassivity. And yet she thought she knew where this conversation was heading now. Despite her disguise, he must have recognized her from the Hen and Vulture. He must know she had been the one there that night, waiting for Rashleigh.

Why had he come to Peacock Oak? Did he know her true identity? Had he come to accuse her of Rashleigh's murder?

Mari thought of the consequences of unmasking and the fear took her breath away. She closed her eyes for a second to steady herself, reminding herself that she knew none of this for certain. Even if he suspected her, he could prove nothing.

"I go to London very seldom, Major Falconer." The evenness of her voice surprised her. "I have no need of the diversions of Town when I am so sincerely attached to the country."

Nick inclined his head. "Odd. I thought perhaps that we might have met there a few months ago?"

Mari smiled and shook her head. "I have already said not, if you recall, Major Falconer. And I advise you not to push your luck—or your familiarities—too far."

Their eyes met and held with the clash and challenge

of a sword thrust. Then, with inexpressible relief Mari saw the figure of Laura Cole approaching. There was a faintly worried expression on her face, as though she had realized that Mari was in trouble and was coming to the rescue. Mari was so relieved she wanted to hug her.

"I do believe your hostess is coming to welcome you," she said. "I wish you a pleasant stay at Cole Court, Major Falconer."

Nick detained her with a hand on her arm. She felt the warmth of his touch through her sleeve as though her skin was bare. "I will see you again, Mrs. Osborne?"

"I doubt it, Major Falconer," Mari said, and saw his teeth flash white as he smiled.

"You misunderstand me, Mrs. Osborne," he said. "It was not a question. I *will* see you again. In fact, I would stake on it."

"I do not play games," Mari said. She released herself very deliberately from his touch. "Goodbye, Major Falconer."

CHAPTER FOUR

Rosemary—Remembrance

NICK LEANED HIS BROAD shoulders against the ballroom doorway and watched Marina Osborne dancing the cotillion. Laura, Duchess of Cole, had welcomed him in the vague, sweet manner that he remembered and then she had drifted off to speak to some of her other guests and Nick thought that he would retire for the night rather than join the festivities. He felt tired and dirty from the journey. He was not dressed for a ball, as Lady Faye Cole had not hesitated to point out when she had passed him in the doorway and had practically sniffed to imply that he smelled rather insalubrious from his travels.

Mari was dancing with Faye's husband, Charles's cousin Henry Cole. Nick watched the elegant sway of her gown as she moved through the steps of the dance. When she and Henry came together, he grabbed at her with the overexcited playfulness of a puppy and she withdrew, an ice maiden in silver satin. Nick did not know Henry well for, although he belonged to the junior branch of the Cole family, he was older than Charles by several years and so Nick had never spent much time in his company. Henry had always struck him as a typical country squire, his life a round of hunting and shooting and fishing, gorging himself at table, drinking hard and suffering the gout in consequence. His color was certainly high as he danced with Mari but that, Nick thought, was probably due to a different kind of excitement from that engendered in the field. As he watched, he saw Henry surreptitiously squeeze Mari's bottom as she passed him, a clumsy but lascivious gesture that made Nick clench his fists in disgust. For a moment Henry bent close to her ear and made some remark that had the color searing Mari's face. No one else had seen his actions—Nick realized that Henry had made very sure of that. His opinion of Charles's cousin fell several notches from an already low starting point.

Nick found that he had already taken a couple of steps forward, with every intention of intervening, when he saw Mari dig the spokes of her fan into Henry's ribs with a force that had him almost doubling up in pain. Henry reeled out of the dance, coughing and spluttering and Mari raised her brows, a look of most perfect concern on her face. Nick relaxed a little and smothered a grin. Henry Cole had got what he deserved and clearly Mari Osborne could take care of herself. Of course she could. She did not need *his* protection. For a moment he had almost forgotten that she might be a criminal and even a murderer, blinded as always by the complicated mixture of raw desire and deeper need that she seemed to evoke in him.

As a soldier, Nick had honed a fine instinct for danger, when to attack, when to withdraw and bide his time, to trust his gut feeling, to listen to that intuition which other men sometimes derided. It had led him to make judgments and decisions that on more than one occasion seemed to fly in the face of practicality and sense and yet they had proved correct in the long run. His instinct had kept him and his men alive. And now his instinct was telling him that Mari Osborne was Glory, the harlot from the tavern, and he wanted her. Lusting after Mari Osborne, the clever, devious, disreputable widow ran counter to everything that he had always believed in about himself and what he had thought he wanted from a woman. She could not have been more different from Anna. And yet his hunger for her was intense, burning him up.

He shifted, uncomfortable with both his thoughts and the physical effect that they had on him. He had found crossing swords with Mari intensely stimulating. He had admired the coolness with which she had countered his attack and the manner in which she had weighed the odds and decided which matters to concede and where to fight him. She was a clever strategist and he relished the game between them. And since they possessed such a powerful mutual awareness, he would use that attraction to bring her down. He would get close to her. He would seduce the truth from her. And he would not forget for a moment that this was all in the line of duty. In playing the game he would be able to slake his desire for her and then the white-hot passion that seared him would burn itself out.

"She turned you down then," Charles Cole said in his ear, with a certain satisfaction.

Nick straightened up. "She did. In no uncertain terms."

Charles laughed. "I did warn you," he said. "She's as cold as the driven snow. Always has been."

Nick raised his brows. "Does she have many disappointed suitors then?"

"Plenty of men are interested in her fortune," Charles said, "even if she is a little gray mouse of a woman."

Nick looked at him. Charles was a man, albeit an apparently happily married one. Could he not *see* how alluring Marina Osborne was if one looked beneath the dowdiness of her attire? But perhaps he could not. Charles skated across the surface of life, seldom seeking deep meaning. He had been like that for as long as Nick had known him. Perhaps he could not see the rich curves and tempting lines of Mari Osborne's body and perhaps it was a good thing, too, for Nick had a powerful feeling that he would want to take any man who looked covetously on Marina Osborne and pull his neck cloth so tight it choked him.

With a palpable effort he forced himself to relax. His feelings were becoming too involved and it was clouding his judgment. This was precisely what had happened to him at the Hen and Vulture when Mari's warmth, the touch and the taste of her, had invaded his senses and played havoc with his judgment. She had played him for a fool then. It would not happen again. Now they would play on his terms, not hers.

He watched as Mari made her way off the dance floor and disappeared through the doors that opened on to the terrace. Her gray dress blended in with the pale shadows and she was gone from his sight. With a slight jolt Nick realized that Mari's deliberately drab appearance was as much a disguise in its way as the blond wig and mask had been at the Hen and Vulture. She was trying to efface herself, perhaps to escape the fortune hunters, perhaps for another reason. Could she be deliberately creating a persona as far from that of Glory, the female hellion, as possible?

"I think," Charles said suddenly, surprisingly, "that Mrs. Osborne might be shy. She is not at ease in social situations. I have often observed that she would prefer to avoid gatherings such as this."

Nick reflected cynically that Charles might have made an interesting point—that Mari Osborne avoided company—but attributed it to the wrong reasons. No woman who dressed as a courtesan and picked men up in a tavern like the Hen and Vulture could possibly be shy, but again she might be deliberately playing a role that was the opposite of the highwaywoman heroine, Glory.

"Well, if she is shy, then she is most unlike your cousin," he said, nodding toward Lady Hester Berry, the vivid center of a group of male admirers further down the room.

"Chalk and cheese," Charles agreed. "Poor John Teague—" He indicated an older man standing slightly apart from the group and watching with an air of weary amusement. "He never gets a chance. He's been in love with Hester for years but I think she barely sees him."

Teague glanced toward them and Charles beckoned him over. "Come on," he said to Nick. "There's better refreshment in my study than you'll find for Laura's guests. And Teague has lived in this area awhile. You may find he can throw light on your case."

They repaired to Charles's study, a room off the hall where Charles had stashed a very fine bottle of brandy against the need to fortify himself to deal with his cousins.

"For," he said wryly, "Henry and Faye may be family but I fear that I have little in common with them and Faye will try to foist her daughter on any or all of my male guests, like a fishwife pushing her wares."

"A shame," John Teague said lazily, accepting a glass of brandy and folding his long length into an armchair, "for Miss Cole is a fetching little chit—" He broke off to see Charles's quizzical eye upon him. "No, I do not have an interest there myself!" he said hastily. "You know me better than that, Charles."

Nick had been watching Teague and weighing up how far to take him into his confidence. Charles had introduced the older man as a friend and indicated that he was reliable, but Nick liked to make his own mind up on such things. Certainly Teague, with his shrewd expression and open manner, seemed pleasant enough. But even at Eton, Charles had been quick to trust, and whilst it was an admirable trait to look for the good in everyone, it could be damnably awkward if you found that the man you had thought honorable turned out to be less than sound. So Nick said nothing of Rashleigh's murder, merely indicating that he had been sent by Lord Hawkesbury to investigate the civil disturbance caused by the Glory Girls. Teague raised his brows and said he was surprised that Hawkesbury should concern himself with such a small domestic matter.

"They are a bunch of petty criminals, highwaymen, no more," Teague said. "Gossip has it that they are females, but I doubt it very much."

"Gossip has it that they are gently bred females," Charles interposed, "and I think there may be some truth in it."

"Do they ride sidesaddle?" Nick asked.

Charles laughed. "Not they! They ride astride like a pack of huntsmen!"

Teague shot him a look from beneath lowered brows. "There was nothing gently bred or remotely feminine about the felons who held up my coach two weeks ago, old chap," he said. "The ringleader had the gruffest voice this side of the alehouse and sat his horse like a trooper."

"What did they stop you for?" Nick asked mildly.

Teague turned his shrewd gray eyes back to him. Nick remembered what Charles had said about Teague being one of Hester Berry's suitors and remembered that he had almost pitied him to hear it, but now, seeing the keen intelligence behind those eyes, he started to wonder if Hester knew John Teague very well at all. He did not seem the kind to tolerate her flirting with a great deal of equanimity.

"What do you mean, old fellow?" Teague asked.

Playing for time, Nick thought, and wondered why.

"I understand that the Glory Girls always have a reason for what they do," he explained. "The redistribution of wealth to the poor, for example, if a mill owner is cheating his workers. Or the liberation of the oppressed if farm laborers are forced to work long hours."

Teague gave a crack of laughter. "If you say so, Falconer. All they wished to liberate in my case was my money."

Nick pulled a face. "Are you sure it was the Glory Girls?"

Teague shifted and took a mouthful of brandy. "Certain. They boasted of it."

Nick shrugged and let it pass. It was odd that in Teague's case there appeared to have been no ulterior motive for the attack when all the other cases he had read about had been prompted by some injustice. But perhaps the gang that had attacked Teague were impostors trading on the Glory Girls' name and reputation. That happened often enough when one set of thieves wanted to borrow some of the luster of another.

"My favorite," Charles said, with a reminiscent grin, "was the time they kidnapped Annabel Morehead on the way to her wedding. Her father's face, when he realized that all his scheming to marry her off for money had been in vain!"

"That was richly deserved," Teague agreed. "And Miss Morehead was extremely grateful." He looked thoughtfully at Nick. "You will find plenty who do not look kindly upon your plan to capture the Glories, Falconer. Some people see them as popular heroes—or heroines—hereabouts."

"I doubt that Arkwright's banker is one of those," Nick said. "I must go to Skipton in the week and speak with him about the attack a few nights ago."

"I doubt he will still be Arkwright's banker after that fiasco," Charles said. "Edward Arkwright does not condone incompetence in his employees and losing a tenth of his profits would be a heinous sin in his books."

"Perhaps he should look to his own business practices, then," Nick said. "He was the one who cheated his workers out of their money, so I understand."

Teague cocked an inquiring brow. "You sound surprisingly sympathetic to these felons, Falconer," he said. "Surely Lord Hawkesbury expects you to fulfill his commission with the full weight of the law?"

"I imagine so," Nick said. "Don't mistake me,

Teague. I do not condone highway robbery or extortion and I do intend to find these criminals." He drained his brandy glass. "Charles, have you ever been held up on the road?"

"No," his host said, sounding, Nick thought, slightly disappointed to admit it. "But I keep a pistol in my carriages so I can wing them if they try and attack!"

Nick laughed. "I see. So, gentlemen, is there anything else that we know about the Glories?"

"No," Teague said.

"They are reputed to meet at one of the hostelries on the Skipton road," Charles said, after a moment.

"I recall," Teague said. "The King's Head, is it not?"

"Either the King's or Half Moon House," Charles agreed.

"I will call there," Nick said, "and see what I may discover. And if we entertain for a moment the idea that the Glories *are* a band of gently bred females—"

Teague shifted, clearly uncomfortable. Once again, Nick noted it. And wondered.

"Seems preposterous," Charles muttered. "Can't see Laura or Faye or Reverend Butler's wife leading a band of mounted desperadoes."

"No," Nick said. "On the other hand there must be others. Does Mrs. Osborne ride?"

Charles and John Teague exchanged a look. "Occasionally," Charles said after a moment, "but she is a poor horsewoman."

"Hester rides like a jockey," Teague said, "but surely you are not suggesting that Cole's cousin is a highwaywoman, Falconer? That's outrageous!"

"I am not suggesting anything at the moment," Nick said, unruffled. "I am merely asking."

There was an awkward silence. "I've sometimes wondered about Mrs. Osborne," Charles said suddenly.

"Oh, come now, Charles!" Teague had gone a little red in the face. "Just because she made her money in trade!"

"It isn't that," Charles said. He, too, had gone a little red. "I know Laura has taken her up and Hester likes her, but…" He stopped, looking uncomfortable.

"It is true that she is a little reserved," Teague said gruffly, "but when one gets to know her…" He took a deep breath. "She has been the truest friend to Hester that one could ever ask for, and to Laura, too, if you would only admit it. Laura is lonely here in the country with you up in Town so often—" Teague stopped and cleared his throat as Charles shot him a less than friendly look. "They have a genuine mutual interest in the horticultural society," he finished, a little lamely.

"I'm glad to hear it," Charles snapped.

Nick said nothing. There were interesting undercurrents here, he thought. He had not realized that Charles left his wife in the country when he went up to London to take his seat in the Lords. He wondered why they spent so much time apart. And then there was Teague, who evidently was in love with Hester Berry. His defense of Mari Osborne might well spring from his loyalty to Hester. But what of his discomfort when the Glory Girls were mentioned? It could be that Nick was getting too close in his questions and that Teague knew it. Mari Osborne's apparent lack of skill as a rider, for example, could be as much an elaborate ruse as her dowdy appearance. Whatever the case, it was clear where Teague's sympathies lay and that made him a man worth watching, as well.

Nick stood up and stretched. "Thank you for your time, gentlemen, and for the brandy, Charles. If you will excuse me, I will seek my bed. It has been a long day."

As he went out, Charles was offering John Teague another glass but in Nick's view Teague's thoughts did not appear to be on the excellence of his host's cellar. He was gazing into the distance and the expression in his gray eyes was very bleak indeed.

MARI HAD FOUND a dark corner of the terrace where the honeysuckle twined around a pretty little arbor of her own design. She curled up on the cushioned seat, wrapping her arms around her knees, careless of crushing the silk of her gown. It was a warm night with a gentle breeze from the moors that carried with it the smell of gorse and bracken and, rather more agriculturally, sheep.

When she had walked away from Nick Falconer, her first instinct had been to run and hide until she had the chance to gather her thoughts. She knew, however, that for the sake of her charade, she had to appear utterly unconcerned by their encounter. Accordingly she had gone into the ballroom and had accepted the first offer to dance made to her, which had, unfortunately, been from Lord Henry Cole.

Mari detested Lord Henry. A big, bluff hunting man, he hid a vicious nature under an outward show of bonhomie. He reminded her of Rashleigh in too many ways. For some time now Henry had been pressing her to show him what he referred to as "kindnesses" and what Mari knew to be sexual favors, implying that her bed had been cold too long and he was just the man to fill it. When he had squeezed her in such a disgustingly familiar manner during the dance, she had felt horribly sick, his big, sweaty lustful hands reminding her of Rashleigh's importunities. She knew that his liberties would only get worse. He seemed inordinately excited by her resistance, the kind of man who saw refusal as a challenge that simply has to be overcome by force.

Mari shuddered. To make matters worse, she knew that Nick Falconer had been watching her every move with that dark, implacable gaze of his. She thought that he had probably been the only one to see Lord Henry touch her, for he had started toward them as though he were about to intervene. He had looked positively thunderous. The realization that he had been coming to her aid made Mari feel very strange. She had felt a compound of relief and security and *trust* that she had never experienced in her life before. She wanted to throw herself into Nick's arms and simply soak up the strength and protectiveness of him. It was an instantaneous and inexplicable reaction but more importantly, it was extremely dangerous because of *course* she could not trust Nicholas Falconer. He was the last man on earth she should allow close to her. He could expose the truth about her. She had the horrible thought that perhaps *he* was the author of the anonymous letter, the fate that was about to catch up with her.

"I know all about you. I know what you did…"

The panic threatened to overwhelm her, tight bands around her chest, the fluttery wings of a thousand butterflies in her stomach beating frantically to break out. She had been troubled by such attacks on and off since she had run away from Rashleigh. They happened whenever the past loomed too close, whenever it seemed that she could not escape. Because sometimes it seemed that she could never get away, never be free.

She dug her nails into the palms of her hands and tried desperately to calm her shaking. Breathe deeply. Distract yourself.

She thought about what she might do now that Nick Falconer was here. She could run away. She could start all over again. She had done it before. But if she did that, Rashleigh would have won again and she would not let that happen. She was too strong to let that happen.

The feeling of panic was passing now, the tightness in her chest easing, her breath coming more easily. She pressed her forehead against her knees and felt the cool silk of her skirts against her hot cheek. Suddenly she felt bone-weary. It had been a very long day.

There was a step on the terrace beside her and a swish of silk and Mari straightened up hastily, pushing her tumbled hair back from her face. Her turban—she hated it anyway, the ridiculous thing—lay discarded on the terrace beside her. She made a grab for it but then realized that the newcomer was only Hester so she relaxed again.

Hester sat on the balustrade beside her and passed her a glass of cold champagne. It felt smooth against Mari's rough throat.

"Are you all right, Mari?" Hester's voice was troubled. "What happened? I saw you leave the ballroom."

"I am very well." Mari gulped some more champagne. "Lord Henry annoyed me. I hate his importunities."

"He molested you again." Hester sounded disgusted. "I am so sorry, Mari. He is a blackguard to do so, especially when he knows you are an unprotected female. What can we do? Shall I get John Teague to call him out, or…I know—*Glory* can call him out!"

"No," Mari said, feeling a little better. Hester's suggestion had almost made her laugh. "I know John would do that for your sake, Hes, and I am sure it could only add to the luster of Glory's reputation for her to fight a duel, but there is no need. It only upset me because it reminded me of Rashleigh. Most of the time I can shut out such thoughts but sometimes…" She shook her head. "Anyway, I stabbed Lord Henry with my fan and I think I bruised him."

"Good," Hester said, with satisfaction. "A pity you did not crack his ribs." She swung her legs beneath her silken skirts but within a moment the movement had stilled. Her voice changed, became serious. "I have been asking some questions, Mari. About Major Falconer, I mean. He is a widower, heir to a Scottish Marquisate."

"Lady Faye will be delighted," Mari said dryly.

"I imagine so. But the rest is not so delightful," Hester said. "He is Rashleigh's cousin on his mother's side, Mari, and when Rashleigh died without issue, he inherited everything that was not entailed."

Mari almost dropped her champagne glass. Nick Falconer was Rashleigh's *cousin?* Suddenly it felt illicit to have been attracted to him, shameful and wrong. Even if he were not cut from the same cloth as Rashleigh, they were related, tied by blood. And if he had inherited all of Rashleigh's property then he might well have inherited *her* along with Rashleigh's other possessions. She had run away but she had never been freed. She had been Rashleigh's chattel, body and soul. She felt sick.

"Oh," she whispered. She cleared her throat. "I did not know." She put her glass down very carefully. "I *knew* it could be no coincidence that he was here! That must be why he was in the Hen and Vulture that night, Hes. He had gone to meet Rashleigh. Perhaps—" Her anxiety was rising again and she fought hard to control it. "Perhaps Rashleigh told his cousin about me," she said. She looked at Hester and rubbed a hand across her brow, her head aching intolerably. Suddenly the past pressed frighteningly close. "Do you think that is why he has come here? Does he know I am his property? Does he intend to take up the blackmail where Rashleigh left off?"

Hester slid off the balustrade and came to sit beside her, passing a warm arm comfortingly around her shoulders. "Do not even think it, Mari!" she said sternly. "I am sure it is nothing of the sort. Rashleigh may have threatened to expose your past and reveal your links to the Glory Girls but I am sure he told no one else of his evil plans. That sort of scoundrel always keeps his secrets."

"I hope that you are right," Mari said, with a shudder. "It is true that whilst I was with him I never met any other member of his family and he never spoke of them so I imagine he cannot have been close to his cousin. But Major Falconer must know that the Earls of Rashleigh once owned serfs in Russia."

Hester's arm tightened. "What if he does know it? That is all in the past."

"No, it is not," Mari said, shivering. "You know that legally I was never given my freedom. I am still a serf."

For one long, terrifying moment the memories crowded in and she was back in the study of the house in St. Petersburg, where she had lived for the first seventeen years of her life. Rashleigh's father had taken her from her parents when she was a child and had educated her on a whim, instructing her in all the arts that an English lady would learn. He was an eccentric, an academic and a collector, and Mari had come to realize that in an odd sort of way she was part of his collection. He had wanted to see if he could take the child of Russian serfs and transform her into something approaching a lady.

But when his son had inherited her, he had had other ideas of the role of his father's seventeen-year-old protégée. In her mind's eye Mari could still see Robert Rashleigh strutting into the house and plundering it whilst his father's body was not yet cold upstairs. He had lolled back in his father's chair, appraising her with his insolent gaze.

How piquant of my father to try out such a foolish notion as to educate you and give you ideas above your station, girl! But never mind, all serfs are bred to be no more than bed warmers and soon you can take up your duties on your back.

He had leaned forward and pinned her with his icy-blue gaze.

You see, I have a proposition for you, my dear. An offer you cannot refuse. You and your family are serfs. You belong to me body and soul. So I am offering you a proposal—a rather piquant one, I think you'll agree. If you give me your body to do with as I wish I will give your family their freedom, their souls, if you like…

She had accepted his proposition.

Of course she had, for how could she have refused, knowing that her family's very freedom was at stake?

She had had no real choice. She was trapped. So she had traded herself, her virginity, her innocence, her very life, for their freedom from slavery. She had become the Earl of Rashleigh's mistress.

The only remarkable thing about it was that Rashleigh had kept his word, giving money for her sisters' education, buying her father a small plot of land near Svartorsk and giving him grain and animals enough for him to forge a living from the soil. But then Mari had come to realize that it pleased Robert Rashleigh to be magnanimous sometimes, so that amidst the cruelty and avarice, he occasionally displayed a careless generosity that would surprise her. At first she had taken it as a sign of hope—that there was good in him after all. Later she came to realize that he did it precisely for that reason—to make people think there was hope in order to take a perverse pleasure in proving them utterly wrong. He had freed her family on whim because he wanted to prove he had the power to do so, the power of life and death, the power over freedom or slavery. And then he had set out to exact thorough and devastating payment from her, subjugating her body to his will.

With a shudder she pushed the memory back into the furthest recesses of her mind.

"Don't think like that, Mari," Hester said now, recalling her to the present. "You are not a possession. You belong to nobody but yourself. Legally—" she waved a hand around vaguely, with the kind of aristocratic disregard for convention that always made Mari laugh "—there may be some boring argument that someone could make against you, I suppose, but that will never happen." She paused. "I think it is most likely that if Major Falconer does have a purpose in coming to Peacock Oak, it must be to solve his cousin's murder."

There was silence whilst they both thought about it.

"But how did he know to come *here?*" Mari spread her hands wide. "Unless Rashleigh told him where to find me…"

Hester was shaking her head. "I don't know, Mari. But I think that until we find out, you must be very, very careful."

Mari nodded. She felt frighteningly uncertain. From the questions he had asked her that evening she thought that Nick Falconer surely suspected her of Rashleigh's murder. It could be no coincidence that he had come to Peacock Oak. She already knew he was strong and ruthless in his pursuit of what he wanted, and if his aim were justice, he would hunt her down. She refused to think of the other, even more frightening possibility that Rashleigh had told his cousin everything about her and that Nick was there to take up the blackmail where Rashleigh had left off. She tried not to think that he might have come there to claim *her*.

Hester was right. She had to be very careful indeed. Say nothing, admit nothing, show no fear….

"He cannot prove a thing," Hester said now, "least of all that you killed Rashleigh, since you did not."

"No," Mari agreed.

"And even if you had," Hester said, her voice as hard as iron now, "no one could condemn you, Mari. Not if they knew the truth. The man deserved to die horribly a thousand times over for what he did to you."

There was a silence between them. At the beginning of their friendship, when Hester had suggested that they

should share a home, Mari had decided to tell her all
about her background. Hester and Laura Cole were the
only people she had ever told, the only ones who knew
that Mari had reinvented herself as Marina Osborne, respectable widow. Even then she had omitted the worst
details of Robert Rashleigh's vice, not wanting to either
relive it or to inflict on her friends the horror of what she
had experienced. Mari thought that she would never forget Hester's appalled reaction and the look of utter shock
on her face when she heard the tale. Hester, who had
believed herself so outrageous, so worldly wise and
cynical, had been shaken to the core by Mari's disclo-
sures.

She had heard Mari's tale in silence and then she had
squared her shoulders and told her that Robert Rashleigh was a despicable man who deserved to die for
what he had done and that Mari must never, *ever* feel
sad or ashamed or lonely ever again. Mari had appre-
ciated her kindness and her generosity of spirit more
than Hester could ever know, but even so there were
things that she could never tell her friend, things she
could never explain about the shackles that were on her
mind if not her body. She had been a serf all her life.
One of her earliest memories was trying to grasp after
what it truly meant to be free. She had asked the old
Earl to explain about serfdom but he had just laughed
at her for what he called her philosophical interests.
And when she was twelve and he had asked her what
gift she would like for her birthday, she had asked for
her freedom and he had given her instead a mouse
made of spun sugar.

The old Earl of Rashleigh had treated her as a toy
but it was his son who had made her his plaything, had

taken away her self-respect and her innocence and sometimes she despaired that she could ever forget.

She finished the champagne and smiled wryly to think of the little serf from Russia sitting on a Duke's terrace and drinking his champagne. How far she had climbed. How far she had to fall, if Nick Falconer should suspect her, if he had uncovered that she was his cousin's runaway mistress, a slave, a thief and a criminal.

"He is a difficult man to deceive," she said, thinking of Nick.

Hester looked at her sharply. "What do you mean?"

Mari swung her champagne glass thoughtfully between her fingers. "Only that he is clever, Hester, and ruthless and strong. I am so afraid that he will catch me out sooner or later."

Now Hester looked horrified. "But, Mari, you cannot let him! You must lie to him and keep your nerve. Think of the consequences if you do not! You could bring us all down—"

"I know," Mari said. She felt immensely weary. This, she thought, was hardly the moment to tell Hester how much Nick Falconer attracted her nor that she had a mad desire to trust him.

"Do not worry, Hester," she said. "You have always cared for me. I will not let you all down."

"All you have to do is to carry on as though nothing has happened," Hester said, calming a little. "Besides, it could all be a hum. Major Falconer was at school with Charles. It might just be a coincidence that brings him here to Peacock Oak and nothing to do with Rashleigh at all."

"As I said before, I don't believe in coincidences,"

Mari said bleakly. She put the empty glass down gently on the balustrade. "I think I shall retire. Laura will understand that I am tired after the day's festivities."

"I will come with you," Hester said at once. She stood up and brushed down her skirts. "This ball bores me. It is the same old faces. I shall drop you at home and then travel on to Half Moon House."

Mari's shoulders slumped. "Oh, Hester!"

The light spilling from the ballroom windows was bright enough to illuminate Hester's rueful expression.

"I know. You think me wanton."

"It is not that," Mari said. She struggled with her feelings for a moment. On the nights when Hester did not come back, she lay in her bed and fretted the night away as though she were Hester's mother. "I worry about you, out on your own, in bad company. And then there is Lord Teague. If he knew…" She stopped.

Hester snapped her fingers. "John is my friend, nothing more."

"But he wants to be more," Mari argued. "He cares about you. He loves you, Hester!"

Hester slipped her hand through Mari's arm. "Let us not quarrel," she pleaded. "You are tired and anxious, and I am bored. You know how these events stifle me. So you will go to your bed and I will go—"

"To someone else's," Mari said dryly. She sighed as she spoke for there was no changing Hester. She and her husband, Jack Berry, had been as wild as each other, forever encouraging one another to new feats of madness. From things that Hester had said, Mari had understood that she and Jack had quarreled like cat and dog, and yet something had bound them together. In Jack's case the madness had ended in an early death on the hunting field. In Hester's, Mari was not sure where it would end.

They went back inside and Hester sent a footman to fetch their cloaks. As they crossed the hall to leave they saw Nick Falconer emerging from Charles Cole's study. For one infinitely long, loaded moment his eyes met Mari's and she stared, unable to look away. She thought of her own words and Hester's response.

He is a difficult man to deceive....

You must lie to him! You could bring us all down....

It was true. If Nick Falconer knew her history, knew everything his cousin Rashleigh had known, then conceivably it might ruin all those whom she cared about the most. For herself, she sometimes felt so tired of the struggle to be free that she did not care. But she could never bring danger to Hester or Laura. They had shown her nothing but kindness and friendship. Even so, looking into Nick Falconer's dark eyes and wondering what he wanted from her, Mari had a conviction that she could not escape their encounter unscathed.

CHAPTER FIVE

Witch Hazel—A spell is upon me

NICK AWOKE EARLY the morning after the ball and made his way downstairs. Streaks of silver dawn light were fading from the sky. The musicians, their faces drawn with tiredness, were packing up their cases. The servants were starting to scrub, polish and dust the house back into a state of tidiness. Nick knew it would be some time before his fellow guests rose from their beds, so he partook of an early breakfast and set off to walk a path that led up through the beech woods to the fells above.

One of the first rules of army tradecraft that he had been taught was to understand and prepare the ground. Accordingly he wanted to see the lie of the land at Peacock Oak and understand the area over which the Glory Girls rode.

Charles had told him the night before that Hester Berry and Marina Osborne lived at Peacock Cottage, a house that had once belonged to his land agent and which Mari had bought from the estate some five years before. Nick could see it below him as he climbed higher up the hill. The word *cottage,* he thought, was picturesque rather than accurate, for it was a substantial dwelling with a beautiful walled garden and greenhouses built against the south-facing wall. He remembered hearing that Mari had advised Laura Cole on the redesign of the gardens at Cole Court. The botanical interests were obviously hers. It was an intriguing thought—the highwaywoman with a passion for horticulture. Nick shook his head at the image. Mari Osborne was becoming more of an enigma with each thing he learned about her.

Beyond Cole Court and Peacock Cottage, the grounds fell away down to the water meadows of the River Wharfe, where the sheep were grazing placidly in the early morning heat haze. Over the stone bridge was Peacock Oak village and the Skipton road, cutting its way through the high fells on its journey south. It was good ambush country, Nick thought. The road was narrow and twisting and there were plenty of places to hide. He wondered about the horses. Charles and John Teague had said that the Glories met at one of the hostelries along the road, the King's Head or Half Moon House. Perhaps they stabled their horses there, as well. He would have to go there and have a few pints of ale with the local villagers. The difficulty, as he already knew, would be in getting anyone to talk. If the Glories were part of the local population then the villagers would probably guard their secrets well. The Girls were heroines to them, for their work amongst the poor and oppressed. He knew that if he asked questions, in all probability, he would get no answers. Men's gazes would slide away and they would answer evasively and he would know that they would never tell him the truth. Some loyalties went very deep.

There was the echo of hooves on the cobbled track

farther down the hill and Nick looked down through the beech trees to see Marina Osborne on a chestnut mare. Surprisingly she had no groom leading her, but was alone. This morning she had forsaken the drab gray of her ball gown for a smart riding habit in dark green. Her black hair was drawn back into a tight knot, but a frankly frivolous little hat ruined the severity of the outfit. The horse was picking its way gingerly along the path and Mari was sitting equally gingerly in the sidesaddle.

Nick watched her thoughtfully for a while. He had wondered if Mari's apparent lack of facility in riding might be a deliberate ploy, for how could she be Glory if she could not sit a horse with confidence? Yet now he could see that her lack of skill was no pretence. It would be impossible to feign such incompetence. She sat on the sidesaddle as though she were perched on a chair and about to fall at any moment. She held the horse's reins but exerted no control with them. The simple fact was that she seemed a very poor horsewoman indeed.

He watched her make a complete hash of leaning down to open a gate, losing her footing in the slipper stirrup in the process and, he was almost certain, cursing under her breath.

A moment later he was scrambling down the hillside as a small creature ran across the path, the mare shied, and Mari, with no control over the horse at all, tumbled from the saddle to lie still on the track.

By the time he reached her, the horse had calmed and was cropping the grass beside the path. It looked at him from the corner of a bad-tempered eye. Mari's saucy little hat had come off and was stuck upside down on a nettle.

"Mrs. Osborne!"

She was lying still, her hair falling out of its severe knot to cascade around her shoulders, her eyelashes dark against the pale curve of her cheek. Then she rolled over and Nick could see that, far from being knocked unconscious by the fall, as he had assumed, she had been winded and was literally fighting for breath. He grabbed her arms and forced them wide, then drove her wrists hard into her stomach. It was a primitive and painful treatment—he knew that from personal experience— but it was effective because it drove what remaining wind there was out of her body and allowed her to start breathing afresh. He let her go and she sat up, panting.

"There is no need to maltreat me, sir!"

Although she still sounded breathless her eyes were snapping with anger. Nick laughed. It seemed there was not much wrong with her.

"I did you no hurt and I saved you from choking for breath," he said. "You should be thanking me, not berating me."

She did not reply, but gave him another furious look from those gold-flecked eyes. He judged her to be recovering well enough and went across to pick up the horse's reins. It came with him docilely and allowed him to tie it to the gate.

Nick went back and offered Mari a hand to help her rise. She ignored it and scrambled to her feet. Her face was flushed now and there was a long streak of dirt down her cheek. Her hair was awry and her riding habit sadly crumpled. Nick thought she looked utterly tempting, ruffled and disheveled. Unbidden, the image of her in the fountain the previous night rose in his mind, her skin pale in the moonlight, cool, sweet, oh, so desirable.

Hot and hard on the heels of the memory came the impulse to kiss her. The strength of the urge shocked him. He could imagine how warm and sweet she would taste. Her mouth was full and very, very sensual, made for kissing. He wanted to strip her crumpled riding habit from her and explore the delicious, voluptuous body beneath. One step closer and she would be in his arms....

No. His mind intervened, slamming down on his desire, imposing the image of Anna's delicate innocence between him and the woman before him. What the hell was the matter with him? He had sworn to seduce the truth from her but that would be a cynical ploy on rational terms, not at the whim of his wayward body. He was here to expose her as a criminal, not to forget everything he believed in whilst he threw her down in the leaves and made love to her. Even if she was no highwaywoman, and her ineptitude in the saddle suggested that she surely could not be, he was still certain that she had been the woman he had met in London, a woman who had been masquerading as a whore and could well be a murderer or a murderer's accomplice. If he was going to get close to her and expose the truth, he would need to be as devious as she surely was.

"You should not ride out alone when you are not very good at it," he said. "You could get into difficulties."

She shot him another look under which the anger smoldered. "I can manage, I thank you."

"No, you cannot. If I had not been here—"

"Then I would not have been pummeled and battered like a prize fighter!"

Nick shook his head. "Next time I will leave you to fend for yourself, madam."

"Please do so. I have no need of your assistance if it comes in that form." Mari straightened up and he saw her wince slightly.

"Have you twisted an ankle?" he inquired.

"No!" The flush in her cheek deepened. "My head hurts a little, that is all."

"A touch of concussion, perhaps. Let me help you." He came across to her and put out a hand but she stepped back, very firmly out of reach. There was wariness in her eyes now, as well as a startled physical awareness that she could not quite hide. For all his determination to be cool and in control, the emotions crackled between them like burning sticks.

"Thank you." Her tone was formal, quenching the fire. "I shall be very well. I will walk the horse home—"

Nick fell into step beside her. He had no intention of allowing her to go so easily.

"No, you won't," he said. "Not alone."

She looked at him. "This is absurd, Major Falconer. I have no need of your further *assistance*—" she invested the word with some sarcasm "—having suffered enough of it already."

Nick leaned casually against the gate and fed the horse a handful of grass. "You seem very eager to be free of my company, Mrs. Osborne," he said. "Most women are not so quick to dismiss me."

Another scornful flash of those glorious eyes was his reward for this. "Well," she said sweetly, "I am not amongst their number. I do not beg for you to stay. I told you last night that I had no desire for your company."

Once again the air between them crackled suddenly with something potent, something heavy and intense.

Once again Nick was wrenched by a primitive, masculine urge simply to drag her off to the nearest byre and make love to her on the bed of hay within. He saw her expression change, saw the echo of his raw desire in her eyes and started to move purposefully toward her.

The horse nudged him once, hard, in the stomach and he almost doubled over with the pain. When he straightened up, Mari Osborne had moved prudently out of his reach.

"I fear that Star is as evil-tempered as I am, Major Falconer," she said. "Pray forgive us both, and do not be offended by my lack of enthusiasm for your company." Her head was bent, her expression hidden from him. "My only concern was for you. I assumed that you must have been on your way somewhere when you stopped to help me. I would not wish to delay you further."

Nick allowed himself a smile at this blatant piece of falsehood. "How thoughtful of you, ma'am. But I was going nowhere in particular, merely enjoying a morning walk."

She looked at him sideways from under those deliciously long lashes. "You are up early for the morning after a ball."

"So are you."

She unhooked the horse's reins from the gate and looped them over her arm. Her back was turned to him. She did not reply. Nick was impressed. In his experience, very few people let silences hang. Mostly they rushed to fill them. It took nerves of steel to resist that urge, particularly if one were hiding something.

"Perhaps," he continued, "you do not sleep well?"

She flashed him a look that would have withered a cactus. "Perhaps you should keep your impertinent observations to yourself, Major Falconer."

He grinned. "I see. You will not give me an insight into your sleeping habits?"

"Certainly not!"

"But you have no guilty conscience to keep you awake?"

Her eyes narrowed. "I get up early because I enjoy the summer morning, that is all."

She gestured to a small purse that was attached to her waist. "This is the best time to collect the plants I use for my herbal remedies."

Nick raised his brows. "I see you are the modern equivalent of the village witch, Mrs. Osborne. Who would have thought it?"

"It is medicine, not witchcraft," she said. Her face was flushed now, her brows arched in genuine disdain. "You do not strike me as a superstitious man, Major Falconer. To consider herbal remedies magic not science is willful ignorance."

She opened the purse to check that the contents were not damaged and the sweet scent of mint hung for a moment on the air. Apparently satisfied, she clipped the purse more firmly to her waist and then guided the horse back through the gate. When she turned to close it behind her, Nick caught it in one hand and held it open to pass through. Mari's brows immediately snapped down in an intimidating frown.

"Why are you accompanying me, Major Falconer?" she demanded. "There is absolutely no need and I have already expressed a disinclination for your company."

"I do believe that my road back is the same as

yours," Nick said pleasantly. "It will reassure me to accompany you so that I can ensure you take no further hurt."

There was no doubt that she was irritated by his insistence, but the only sign she gave was to bite her rather luscious lower lip very firmly between her teeth as though repressing some sharp retort. Nick retrieved her saucy little hat from the grass and handed it to her.

"This is yours, I believe." He turned it over in his hands. "A curious choice, if I may say so, Mrs. Osborne, for a woman who presents herself as an irreproachably respectable widow."

Mari frowned as she took it from him. "Whatever can you mean, Major Falconer? There is nothing remotely disreputable about this hat!"

Nick gave her a wicked smile. "It is very provocative, Mrs. Osborne. Just like you. You are what you wear." His smile grew. "Or what you do not wear."

Mari took the hat and crammed it down fiercely on her head, squashing it slightly in the process.

"You are scandalous, Major Falconer," she said, with arctic cold.

"Not I," Nick said. "You are the one whose behavior is outrageous, Mrs. Osborne, and it surprises me that no one in Peacock Oak has yet realized it."

She gave him a look of searing scorn. "Whereas you, Major Falconer, have been here all of a day and think yourself *so* perceptive that you know me already. I assure you that you know nothing!"

"What I do not know," Nick said, "I intend to find out."

She looked at him and the challenge flashed between them, along with a sensation so hot and primitive that Nick felt it rip through his body. He held himself still through sheer willpower and held her gaze, and Mari was the first to lower her eyes.

"That sounds most tedious, Major Falconer." Her voice was only a little uneven. He saw her take a deep breath, as though to steady herself. "I am no interesting subject for your study."

"On the contrary," Nick said, "you fascinate me, Mrs. Osborne."

The glance she flicked him was contemptuous. "You sound like a man with too much time on his hands, Major Falconer. I am surprised that the army can spare you for the whole summer." Her dark, mocking gaze traveled over him. "How will they manage?"

"I am sure they will scrape through somehow," Nick said.

She inclined her head, a slight smile still on her lips, but once again she did not reply.

They had reached the path that led down to Peacock Cottage and Nick put a hand over hers where it held the reins. It would do no harm to ruffle her feathers a little more, he thought. He had every intention of deliberately provoking her each time they met until the truth was revealed between them. This blistering awareness that heated his blood and found an echo in her response to him could be used against her, to make her susceptible to him. He had seldom faced a more enticing prospect than that of seducing the truth from Mari Osborne.

"If you already know that I am an army man, then it seems you have been asking questions about me," he said. "Admit that you have a curiosity about me, too, Mrs. Osborne."

He expected her to withdraw from his touch and she did remove her hand from his, but gently. Her lips were curved into a smile that was faintly scornful.

"Acquit me of any personal interest in you, Major Falconer. The clue to the fact that you are an army man is, after all, in your title. I have heard gossip of your profession, nothing more. At the ball last night, Lady Faye was full of your dashing exploits."

Nick smiled straight into her eyes. "Then you disappoint me, Mrs. Osborne. I was hoping for much more than that."

Mari's hand tightened on the reins momentarily. "You will be waiting a long time if you hope for more from me, Major Falconer. I have no interest in idle flirtation. Now, if you will excuse me—" She turned away.

"Wait!" Nick said. "You have dropped something."

He passed her the card that Rashleigh had had clenched in his hand on the night he died, Glory's visiting card with the flaunting golden peacock on it. And he watched her face for every little reaction.

She took it in her gloved hand. There was a slight frown of puzzlement between her brows but nothing more, no recognition, no fear. It appeared that she had never seen anything like it before. She turned it over and her brows rose slightly to see the words *Peacock Oak* on the back.

"This is not mine," she said.

"But if you recognize the handwriting," Nick said, "perhaps I could return it to the right person."

Mari looked at it again briefly, but shook her head. "I have no notion whose crest this is, nor whose handwriting." She handed it back to him. "I am sorry I cannot help you. Good day, Major Falconer."

Nick watched her walk away down the path to the house. The chestnut mare was taking advantage of her, sidestepping, pausing to snatch a mouthful of food from the hedge. Nick grimaced to see such indiscipline. Either Mari Osborne was a better actress than he gave her credit, or she could not control a horse to save her life. And if she was not pretending, she most certainly could not lead a gang of female desperadoes intent on redressing the injustices of the rich toward the poor, the strong toward the weak. She could not be the notorious Glory.

And then there was the visiting card. Nick sighed, running his fingers over its smooth edges as it lay in his pocket. He was an observant man, accustomed to spotting even the tiniest nuances that would give away a man or woman in a lie. They would look away, blush, say too much or too little. But Mari Osborne had reacted in none of those ways. She had seemed entirely honest.

On the other hand he was still certain, on instinct alone, that Mari was the woman he had met that night in the Hen and Vulture. And that put her at the center of his investigation. She had to be involved. There had to be a link. He would find it somehow.

He watched her go through the archway into the stable yard and disappear from sight. His blood still beat with the intensity of their encounter. He had come so close to kissing her. Only the thought of dishonoring Anna's memory had prevented him. Yet now when he thought of Mari he remembered the naked abandon with which she had splashed in the fountain, the intimate slide of her tongue against his when she had kissed him, the erotic entwining of her body around his in all his most heated dreams. He felt his body harden in response to the mere thought and almost groaned aloud. He remembered that night in the Hen and Vulture when he had believed that he had iron self-control and Mari had been able to undermine that self-discipline with just one kiss. It could not be allowed to happen again. He would use Mari's awareness of him as another weapon in the armory, to undermine her resolve and break down her resistance. He would have the truth from her eventually and he would not allow himself to become distracted from his purpose. He was in control now.

LADY HESTER BERRY woke with a headache. She lay for a moment with her eyes closed, listening. It must be late. The alehouse was already astir; there was the sound of barrels being rolled deep in the cellar and the chatter of voices and the crash of pots from the kitchen.

Hester groaned. The drink and the sex had made her oversleep, careless of time. And now she would have to ride home in full daylight, wearing last night's ball gown, looking just what she was, a harlot who had been tumbled in a cheap tavern.

Beneath her nose the bedsheets smelled none too clean, of sweat and stale straw. But then, she thought, if she chose to couple with the groom, she could not really complain if he smelled of the stables.

She opened her eyes. He was lying beside her, on his back, snoring. He was a big, muscular lad she had seen working in Josie's stables when they had taken the horses there after the last venture with the Glory Girls. She could not even remember his name—if she had ever known it. Last night she had seduced him easily, sweeping into Half Moon House in her ball gown, pointing at him and beckoning him to follow her upstairs. He had wiped the ale from his mouth with the back of his dirty sleeve and followed her amidst the catcalls and cheers of his fellows. She had been aware of Josie's disapproving eye upon her and had not cared, in the same way that she had not cared earlier in the evening when Mari had told her she was concerned about her. Hester knew that her friends worried but it did not stop her. Sometimes she thought that nothing could stop her. She and her latest conquest had made love with a brutal frenzy that had, for a time, satisfied her wildness and need. Hester stretched and felt herself ache; she knew there were bruises and scratches on her body.

Last night she had wanted him. Now she wanted him gone. She shoved him hard and he snorted awake.

"Get your clothes and leave," she said.

He stared at her for a moment and she could smell his stale breath on her face and see the saliva crusted at the corner of his mouth. He slid from the bed, grumbling under his breath, and struggled into his breeches. Hester lay and watched. For all his glowering looks and muttered imprecations, he did not refuse to go. None of them ever did.

After he had gone out, and the door had crashed closed behind him, Hester lay still, staring up at the cracks in the plaster ceiling. Out of the corner of her eye she could see her ball gown lying discarded on the floor. It looked tawdry and crumpled in the daylight. Hester turned her head to look at it and noticed a tear in the bodice. Her cloak had disappeared entirely and her evening slippers were tumbled in the corner of the room.

The door banged open and Josie Simmons marched in without a knock. The landlady of Half Moon House was a big woman in every way, physically large with a big personality and a very loud voice. She brandished a feather duster threateningly at Hester.

"Get up, milady, and get you gone home. I need to clean the chamber!"

Hester put her hands over her ears to block out the bellowing. "Any chance of breakfast, Josie?"

"None," Josie said rudely. "Now get your backside out of that bed." She had never stood on ceremony with Hester. They had first met years before when Hester had gone to Half Moon House to take her drunken husband home after one of his many bouts of carousing. A firm if unlikely friendship had developed between the two of them over the years. These days Josie hid the Glory Girls' horses and rode out with them when they could find a cob large enough to bear her weight. She was a formidable woman whose own husband had run off with the potboy years before and had never been heard from since, and against all the odds Josie had turned the tavern around to make a healthy profit.

Now she stood, hands on hips, looking down at Hester. "What are you at, madam? You've run through all my grooms and serving men and in the villages they're talking about you like the trollop you are—"

Hester winced. Josie never spared anyone's feelings.

"And sooner or later your cousin the Duke will get to hear of it, or that nice Lord Teague…"

Hester put the pillow over her face then wished she had not because it smelled of her perfume from the previous night and, like everything else, seemed stale.

"That is all I ever hear," she complained. "What about that nice Lord Teague, why not *marry* that nice Lord Teague. I am sick of hearing how nice John Teague is!"

"You could do worse," Josie pointed out.

Hester pushed the pillow aside. "But he could not."

Josie did not contradict her and after a moment Hester turned the subject. She did not want to talk about herself. She had been running away from herself ever since her husband, Jack, had died.

"You have had no trouble since the Girls were out a three nights ago?" she questioned.

"No." Josie sniffed. "No questions, no one looking around. But if you carry on like this, you'll bring trouble on us all."

Hester remembered saying the same thing to Mari only the previous night. All their fates and futures were wrapped up in Mari and her identity. If she gave in, crumpled under the pressure, then Hester knew they might all be doomed. She shuddered. She knew Mari was strong but she had been through so much—far more than anyone could be expected to bear without running mad. Hester could still remember all too vividly Mari's despair when Rashleigh had tracked her down, and her anguish when she had decided she must meet him again, to try to buy his silence.

It was Mari who had inadvertently created the Glory Girls. One day she had gone to take fresh vegetables from her kitchen gardens to the villagers in nearby Starbotton and had returned almost incoherent with rage, telling Hester of the appalling working conditions in the local lead mine, the property of a hard-nosed businessman called Sampson.

"It is well nigh slave labor!" she had stormed to Hester. "It's iniquitous! Mrs. Dell's son broke a leg because he was so tired he fell down the mine shaft, having been made to work for twenty-five hours without rest! And then when Mrs. Dell went to Sampson to ask for aid because her son was the only breadwinner and could not work whilst his leg mended, Sampson laughed in her face!"

It had been in that moment that the Glory Girls had been born. Hester knew that for Mari it was a point of principle to make some redress, to ensure in some way that people did not have to suffer the sort of injustice that had beset her own life. Mari always burned with the need to right perceived wrongs. She had built the school in Peacock Oak, she provided food and medicines for the poorer villagers and she gave a fortune to local charities, and all without drawing attention to her benevolence. It was as though she was driven to do whatever she could to help others. Whereas Hester freely admitted that on her part, riding out with the Glory Girls—leading the Girls—was just another aspect of her quest for excitement. She was not moved by principle, only the need to satisfy her lust for adventure.

Mari never rode with them. She did not have the ability. Hers was the cool head behind the planning, Hester the one who carried the plans through. Josie rode with her, and Josie's lover, Lenny. Lenny was actually a man but he was allowed to be an honorary girl for the purposes of highway robbery. But most shocking, most scandalous of all was the fact that Laura Cole was part of the group. Hester smiled to think of what Charles, that stuffed shirt of a man, would say to see his wife of ten years riding hell for leather across the county. But then, if only Charles did not neglect Laura so and leave her alone to go to Town for months on end, she would not be so unhappy and looking for other diversion.

They involved no one else, trusted no one else. And if one of them should be unmasked, then they were all in deep trouble.

Josie picked up the tattered ball gown and threw it to her. "Come along. Some of us have work to do."

Hester slipped from the bed and dressed as best she could in the remnants of her gown. Josie left her to it, thundering back down the stairs to harangue the kitchen maids. Peering into the spotted mirror, Hester winced at her frowsy reflection. But this was a part of her ritual. The night before was wicked and wild, the morning after humiliating.

She went down into the bar. In the bright morning light it looked drab and smelled of old beer. A maid was scrubbing the flagstone floor. She looked up when Hester passed, staring at her. Hester swept by with her head in the air. She always ignored those stares. But then she opened the door and was assailed by the fresh summer morning. The sun was already climbing high in a blue, blue sky, the air was sweet and the warmth of the day enfolded her like a mother's embrace.

And to her horror, Hester felt the tears start in her eyes and run down her cheeks unchecked and she did not even know why she was crying but she thought that her heart might break.

CHAPTER SIX

Tiger Lily—I dare you to love me

MARI WAS IN the greenhouses when Hester arrived back from Half Moon House later that morning. She had taken a tisane of wild mint to ease her headache but when Jane had suggested she should rest, Mari had declined and had taken herself off down to the gardens. It was one of the few places where she felt any peace. But this morning not even the earthy smell of the soil and the hot bloom of the roses could soothe her.

Nick Falconer troubled her. He troubled her a great deal. The sweet stirring of her blood that his presence caused was enough to disturb her. The raw desire she could see in his eyes and feel in his touch both seduced and scared her. It made her want to take a risk, to try to put the past behind her, to test the theory that not all men were evil and cruel in their lust. Worse, she felt a terrible, insidious, instinctive desire to trust him and tell him the truth.

But Nick was not a man she could trust. She could trust no one.

She was no closer to discovering whether he suspected her of his cousin Rashleigh's murder for he kept his secrets very well whilst seeking to unmask hers. Only that morning he had thrown down the gauntlet to her when he had promised to learn the truth about her.

"What I do not know I intend to find out."

She was terrified that one of the things he might find—one of the things he might already *know*—was that she was his property.

Mari sighed, and straightened her shoulders. She had to keep him out. Out of her life, out of her head. Already she was afraid that his disconcertingly perceptive dark gaze saw too much. Sometimes he seemed to see directly into her soul.

With a muttered curse Mari tried to block Nick Falconer from her mind, to block out both the promise and the danger he represented. She concentrated, rather fiercely, on her rose cuttings. Tiny green shoots of new growth showed on their woody stems. She bedded them down gently in their little pots.

She had always had an interest in botany. The old Earl of Rashleigh, thinking it a subject suitable for the English lady he wanted to turn her into, had had her educated in the science of plants alongside the other feminine accomplishments of reading, drawing, painting, sewing and music. At the house in St. Petersburg she had pestered the gardeners to tell her everything they knew, practical knowledge, not the book learning she had gained in the Earl's library. She was never permitted to go out beyond the garden walls but for years that did not matter to her. The gardens and the hothouses were a paradise of scent and color, an escape into another world.

When she had first come to Yorkshire, the fortune she had stolen from Rashleigh had enabled her to buy

Peacock Cottage. It had been the natural beauty of the
fells and the turning of the seasons that had helped to
heal her. She had spent hours and hours planting her
garden, watching the seedlings grow, seeing her plans
mature in front of her eyes. She had felt peace and ful-
fillment and a growing sense of freedom. Slowly, carefully, she had explored that unfamiliar liberty like a
butterfly stretching its wings in the warmth of the sun.
She had felt safe for the first time since she had met
Robert Rashleigh….

It had been an illusion. She did not feel safe anymore. The past was closing in on her. Nick Falconer
was closing in. She had had five years of peace and
freedom, and now it was about to be shattered.

There was a thunder of hooves from the courtyard
and Mari looked up to see Hester clattering in and
jumping down from the saddle. She shouted for her
groom. Mari saw that she was wearing her torn evening
gown and was vaguely surprised that Josie had not lent
her an old skirt and a shirt as she normally did. But perhaps this was Josie's way of expressing her disapproval
for Hester's behavior; behavior Mari sensed would
come to an explosive climax all too soon.

As Hester ran down the garden toward her, Mari
could see the stain of tears on her cheeks. Even now,
Hester was wiping them away furtively with the back
of her hand, like a little child.

Mari rubbed the soil from her hands and went out
to meet her.

"Hester? What has happened?" Hester was always
looking for trouble. If someone had hurt her, abused
her… Mari felt her heart lurch and the memories swirl
in to claim her. "Are you ill?" she whispered.

She saw Hester's expression change as her friend realized what she was thinking and then Hester gave her a hard hug.

"No! Of course not. I'm so sorry, Mari." She threw her hat down on the grass and herself down after it. "Josie was foul to me—she practically threw me out—and then on the way home I met John Teague."

Mari winced. "Oh, no!"

"He asked me where I had been and, since I was in my ball gown, I could scarce pretend that I had not been out all night." She chewed her lip. "It was most unfortunate."

Mari thought it was probably worse than unfortunate. John Teague was not stupid and might already have an inkling of Hester's nighttime activities.

"What did you tell him?" she asked.

"Oh, merely that I had spent the night with a friend," Hester said, with an airiness that was almost entirely unconvincing. "He did not even trouble to answer me, but rode off without a word and with a face like thunder. He is so rude!"

"You push him too far," Mari pointed out.

"I know." Hester shrugged pettishly. "But it is his own fault that he allows me to treat him so!"

Mari simply looked at her and after a moment Hester picked a blade of grass and started to chew it. She looked at Mari out of the corner of her eye.

"What are you thinking?"

"I am thinking," Mari said, "that I wish you would leave my lawn alone to grow properly, rather than pluck it to shreds."

Hester cast the blade of grass away. "I'm sorry. I am very bad, am I not, Mari?"

"No," Mari said shortly. "You are like a spoiled little girl, and you know it. A shame your papa was so indulgent to you, and that your cousin Charles is so soft that if he knew of your exploits—which he may well do—he would not lift a finger to stop you, either!"

Hester laughed and jumped to her feet. "Oh, Mari, you sound so severe! What a harsh parent you will be one day!"

"I doubt it," Mari said. She turned away, the sun pricking her eyelids. She had seldom allowed herself to think of having a husband and a family. The idea seemed unfamiliar, strange. Surely it was not, could not, be for her. And yet the longing took her sometimes when she woke in the night feeling so lonely. She had made a new life for herself but she could not people it with the family she sometimes wanted for fear that her true past would be exposed. She could let no one close. And now, if the past did come to claim her, even her new life would be under threat.

"I met Major Falconer in the woods when I was out collecting my herbs," she said.

"Oh, so did I!" Hester said, eyes sparkling suddenly. "Now *he* stopped to say good morning to me most civilly. There was a young man with him, too—a *most* handsome young man—called Dexter Anstruther. Apparently he arrived only an hour or so ago to join Charles's house party."

"Did he?" Mari said, brows raised. "And did both he and Major Falconer see you like that, Hester?" she added. "Dressed in your ball gown and riding astride?"

"They did," Hester said. She stooped to retrieve her bonnet from the lawn. "They looked most impressed at my prowess on horseback."

"I am sure they did," Mari said, "given that I had fallen off at Major Falconer's feet earlier this morning."

Hester sighed. "Oh, Mari, not again! Remember what I taught you—"

"I do remember. But I have no proficiency." Mari sighed, too. "Forgive me, Hes. I am no credit to your teaching."

Hester smiled and squeezed her arm. "And Major Falconer? Did he pick you up and dust you down?"

"Very roughly," Mari confirmed, wincing at the memory. "And then he proceeded to interrogate me all of the way home." She paused. "He showed me a card, Hes. He pretended I had dropped it. It was like a visiting card, with a golden peacock on it—" She stopped dead as she saw Hester color up ever so slightly. Hester blushing was so unusual that Mari knew at once she was as guilty as sin.

"Do you know about this?" she demanded.

"I?" Hester opened her eyes very wide with perfect, false innocence. "Why would I?"

"So you *do* know!" Mari said wrathfully. "Hester—"

"It sounds like Glory's calling card." Hester capitulated. "When Glory robs her victims, she leaves a calling card. Have you not read about it in the press?"

Mari put up a hand to her head. "I believe I must have missed that little detail," she said sarcastically. She shook her head incredulously. "So you leave a *calling card?* Hester, do you remember *any* of the things I told you about how to behave when you ride out as Glory?"

"You said not to be reckless and not to draw attention to ourselves," Hester said, a little sulkily.

"Correct." Mari took a couple of short strides away across the grass. Her head was aching again, the sort of ache that could not be soothed with an infusion of mint. "And do you not think that a flaunting, ostentatious, golden peacock on a calling card is perhaps a little on the obvious side?"

"No more," Hester said, with spirit, "than dressing up as Haymarket ware and picking a man up in a tavern, or swimming naked in a fountain, only to discover that you have a very interested audience!"

There was a pregnant pause.

"Very well," Mari said, after a moment. She could not quite bite back her smile. "I have to concede that you are right there. I am equally as bad as you."

"Yes, you are," Hester said triumphantly. "You try to be respectable but you always fail. You are wild like me."

"Not quite like you," Mari said. "At least I have *some* common sense." Her smile faded. "But the point is that Major Falconer appears not only to be taking an interest in me but also an interest in Glory. And I have been thinking. Do you remember the newspaper reports after Rashleigh had died? They blamed the murder on Glory! We were struck by it at the time but we thought that some enterprising felon had stolen our identity for his own ends. But now I wonder if there is more to it than that."

Hester chewed on her lip. "Hmm. Where did Major Falconer get the card from?"

Mari sighed. "I thought I was asking you that," she said sarcastically, "since you are the one who apparently hands them out."

Hester shook her head. "But I do not know."

"If it was with Rashleigh's body," Mari said thoughtfully, "then that might be the reason Major Falconer came to Peacock Oak."

Hester gave a little, heartfelt groan. "In which case how did *Rashleigh* get the card?"

"I think someone gave it to him," Mari said. "The same person who told him where to find me and what my connection was to the Glory Girls." The light summer breeze breathed gooseflesh along her skin. "I think Rashleigh had the card and Major Falconer found it. He believes that I am Glory and that I killed his cousin. He's come here to find proof." She sat down on the grass and gestured to Hester to join her. She rested her chin in her hand and stared up at the impossibly blue summer sky. "We are in deep trouble, Hes."

"But you are not Glory," Hester argued, "so he cannot pin that on you."

"I am as much Glory as you are, or Laura or Josie," Mari argued. "The execution of the raids may be yours but the idea was mine. And anyway, that is not the real problem. The real problem is anticipating what Major Falconer intends to do now he has found us."

"I see now that handing out a calling card was a mistake," Hester said. She bit her lip. "Hmm, I suppose I should have thought that the peacock is a little *too* like Charles's coat of arms."

Mari gave an exaggerated sigh. "You might as well have given him directions," she said. "Though, as it happens it is not entirely your fault." She turned her head to look at her friend. "Someone had written the words *Peacock Oak* on the back, though I did not recognize the hand."

"It must have been the person who told Rashleigh who you were and where to find you," Hester said. She rolled over and propped herself up on one elbow. "But who could that be?"

Mari shook her head. "I don't know. I wish I did. It is hateful to think that there is somebody out there who knows all our secrets and could bring us down." She sighed. "I did not tell you before, Hes, but I received an anonymous letter yesterday. It said that the sender knew who I was—and what I had done."

"So it arrived on the very day that Major Falconer comes to Peacock Oak," Hester said thoughtfully. "Can that be coincidence?"

"I don't know," Mari said. Once again she shivered to imagine what it could mean if Nick Falconer knew her history, knew her secrets and could ruin them all. It might not be Nick, but there was somebody out there who could…

"Someone is playing games with us," Hester said with a little shiver. "What can we do?"

Mari sat up abruptly. "All we can do is what we have already resolved to do," she said. "Tell Major Falconer nothing. Show no weakness. Whatever he believes, he will have to prove it. And until he shows his hand we are playing a waiting game." She sighed. "I do not like this. It feels as though he holds all the cards and we have none."

"And if your anonymous correspondent is someone else?"

"Then we have two problems on our hands rather than one," Mari said dryly. "And we have to wait for them to reveal themselves also."

"Glory could warn Major Falconer off," Hester said eagerly. "Frighten him, make him give up the case—" She stopped to see Mari's pitying eye on her.

"No, I suppose that would not serve."

"Certainly not. Major Falconer is scarcely a man to be frightened off by anything," Mari said. "And Hes," she added, fixing her friend with a severe frown, "no riding out with the Glory Girls. Take no risks."

Hester rolled over on to her stomach on the grass, propping her chin in her hand. "Life is going to be unconscionably boring if I have to behave well all the time."

"Life is going to be unconscionably short if you do not," Mari said. "Now, I suggest that you go and change into something more respectable and I will go and take something for my headache and later, when we have had time to think, we may talk about what else we are going to do."

"I could fetch you some mint tea," Hester said generously, "given that I am the cause of your headache."

"It would take vats of it," Mari said. "I was thinking more in terms of laudanum and then I need worry about nothing at all. I am in jest," she added, at Hester's look of alarm.

Arm in arm they made their way up to the terrace and in through the garden door. Hester went off to the scullery to fetch some hot water to wash and Mari made her way into the hall. From behind the closed kitchen door she could hear Jane's voice raised in alarm over the state of Hester's clothes, and Hester spinning her some tale about falling from her horse and ripping her gown. Mari shook her head slightly over Hester's glib lies.

There was a vase of lilies on the hall table, scenting

the cool air with a hint of the exotic. Beside the flowers, on a silver tray, were two letters. Absentmindedly Mari picked the first one up.

I know who you are. I know what you did. You will pay me for my silence.

Icy slivers of fear slid down Mari's spine. She could still hear Jane's and Hester's voices but they seemed to have faded to a murmur at the back of her mind. She could feel the warmth draining from her. Nick Falconer's face rose before her eyes, the straight, dark brows, the uncompromising line of his jaw, his mouth. Surely he could not be the one who threatened her like this? Mari's instinct told her that he would never do such a thing. He was too direct, too plain spoken. He was an army officer. He was supposed to be on the side of the angels.

But she could not trust her instinct. She could trust nothing and no one. Worse still, if it were not Nick who threatened her, then someone else was out there who knew her history and wanted to use it—and her—for their own ends. Once again, as on the previous night, she felt a terrible, insidious desire to go to Nick Falconer and tell him the truth about herself, to draw on his strength and ask for his protection. Her heart screamed at her to do it and her head told her she was nothing but a fool and it was the surest way to the gallows.

She crumpled the note fiercely in her hand. If there had been a candle alight, she would have burned the note there and then. And she knew that she would permit no one, neither some stranger in the shadows nor Nick Falconer himself, with his deep, dark perceptive gaze, his sinfully tempting mouth and his incendiary touch, to take everything she had gained away from her. Whatever happened, she would not succumb to him.

LAURA MATILDA ANNE Elizabeth, twelfth Duchess of Cole, sat before the mirror in her dressing room, her chin resting on her hand, and stared despondently at her reflection. She was wearing an evening dress and had dismissed her maid, as she was about to go downstairs for dinner and the evening's entertainment. But now she hesitated for one long moment, staring at herself, wondering if what was inside showed on the outside.

She hated house parties. She hated the fact that she spent half of the year rattling around Cole Court on her own and the other half with the place full of strangers she had no wish to get to know better.

All she wanted was to spend time with Charles and most fervently of all she hated the fact that he showed no desire to spend time with her.

Tonight there was to be a card party, another entertainment for her guests, another opportunity for Lord Henry Cole to bray about his exploits on the hunting field, for Lady Faye to push poor Lydia into the lap of some local landowner in the hope of an advantageous marriage, another chance for Nick Falconer to watch them all with that disconcertingly observant dark gaze of his, as though they were all exhibits in a freak show. Laura liked Nick—she sensed that he was a very straight and honorable man—but he frightened her, too. He saw too much. She knew it would not take him long to realize that she was desperately in love with Charles and that, shamefully, her husband, Nick's oldest friend, had no time for her at all.

Laura had been in love with Charles Cole since she was eleven years old. She was the elder daughter of the Earl of Burlington, whose land marched with the Cole Yorkshire estates, and she had known from her earliest years that she was intended for a dynastic match. It was her destiny and she had accepted it without question. She was bred for it. Marriages of convenience were what the daughters of Earls *did*. What they did *not* do was fall in love with their future husbands in an unbridled, passionate and entirely uncontrollable manner. She had transgressed the rules of aristocratic liaisons and had humiliated herself in the process.

Often, when Charles was in London and she was in Yorkshire, she would sit in the library and wonder what he was doing at that very minute. Was he attending the House of Lords? Was he at his club? Was he—unbearable thought—making love to an opera dancer or in a Covent Garden whorehouse? She sat and tormented herself thinking about Charles but she doubted that he ever wasted a moment thinking about her. When they had first been married—ten years before—she had suggested eagerly that she should accompany him when he went up to Town and had been crushed when he had refused. He had not done it unkindly, for there was nothing cruel about Charles, but his indifference hurt her more than any malice would have done. It was the very absence of feeling at the heart of their relationship that pained her.

When she had confided her misery in Hester and Mari, they had both agreed that she should travel to Town unexpectedly one day to surprise Charles. Laura had thought about the idea. She had got as far as packing a portmanteau and summoning the carriage, but then her courage had failed her. What if Charles was in bed with his mistress when she rolled up on the doorstep? She had no idea if he had one but she thought it entirely likely that he would. Most men had certain needs, so she had heard, and he seldom satisfied them in her bed. How could he? Their beds were over two hundred miles apart. Even worse than contemplating surprising him with another woman was the thought that he would greet her arrival with a complete lack of interest, throw her a word across the breakfast table and return to his newspaper. She knew that Hester, so much more tempestuous than she, would *demand* Charles's attention but Laura was not like her cousin-by-marriage. Laura was restrained, elegant, the perfect Duchess.

Laura stared into her own hazel eyes. She felt more akin to Mari, with her mysterious past and her icy outward shell, than she did to vibrant Hester. Laura knew all Mari's history and understood that the one thing that they had in common was that they both wore a disguise, Mari as a respectable widow and Laura herself as the perfect Duchess. They were both impostors.

Laura sighed, stood up and tried to smooth the creases from her gown. It fell straight to the ground. She had no bust and no waist to speak of. She felt as angular and sexless as a washboard. It was no wonder that Charles shunned her bed.

Her guests were already assembled when she walked into the blue drawing room. She knew that she should have been there earlier to greet them and she could tell from Charles's expression that he was a little surprised by this departure from her usually faultless behavior. She saw the ring of faces watching her. It was the same people, night after night, the same conversation and the same entertainments. Sometimes her life felt like a whirling top that never stopped spinning through the same scenes.

Mari was absent tonight. She had sent a note to apologize for an indisposition brought on by falling from her horse—again. Laura had smiled ruefully to hear of it because Mari was utterly hopeless at riding but insisted on trying all the same. Hester was there of course, although Laura wondered why, since she knew that these predictable social events bored her to tears. And there was John Teague, still gazing forlornly at Hester, and Henry Cole with his rheumy eyes from too much drink, and Faye, her mouth turning down at the corners with discontent. There was Nick Falconer chatting with Charles and looking inordinately attractive in evening dress, and next to him Dexter Anstruther who was, as all the maids had noticed, an extremely handsome young man. Laura's gaze moved on to Charles himself and immediately he eclipsed everyone else in the room. She felt a hopeless, desperate wave of love submerge her, just as it always did. Their eyes met and he gave her a slightly quizzical look as though checking she was quite well and that she would not let him down in front of their guests. Laura gave him a faint reassuring smile in return and wondered, suddenly hysterical, what they would all say if she burst out, "Good evening, everyone! I have something to tell you all. I am one of the notorious criminal gang who ride out as the Glory Girls and take from the rich to give to the poor. I am telling you this because secretly I am hoping to be found out—and finally shock my husband out of his *intolerable* indifference toward me!"

She imagined Charles's face if she did it, imagined wiping that uninterested expression from his features and replacing it with astonishment, disbelief, anger. At least she would have made him feel something for her. Anything would be better than nothing. In that moment her love for him teetered on the edge of hatred.

She took a deep breath.

"Good evening, everyone," she said. "I do apologize for keeping you all waiting. Shall we go in for dinner?"

HESTER DID NOT COME home that night. Mari lay awake listening for the sound of the carriage and her friend's step on the stair but it never came. She heard the clock strike two and eventually she fell into a light sleep troubled by dreams that had her tossing and turning for the rest of the night. Jane's face was disapproving when she brought the morning tea and, when Mari got up, she saw that there was one cup untouched again on the tray and her heart sank.

It was to raise her spirits that she went out early again, immediately after breakfast, taking the path that led down to the river this time. She walked slowly, listening to the crunch of last year's beech leaves underfoot and making very sure that no one was following her. She valued the freedom of being out in the open air. It was also a pleasure to be walking, not riding. Really, she was not sure why she persisted in trying to succeed at something she was clearly not very good at. Native stubbornness, she supposed. Her mother had always maintained that she was too obstinate for her own good.

For a second the clear, tumbling water of the river shimmered before her eyes and she blinked back the tears. The most difficult thing to bear of her entire experience had been the discovery that her family had perished the same winter that Rashleigh had brought her to England. As soon as she had escaped him she had made discreet inquiries. She had had some wild dream that she might pay for them to join her, somewhere safe, somewhere they could all be together. The news that they had died in a fever epidemic that had swept the country had been the final blow. It had almost destroyed her.

With a sigh she placed her little straw basket down on the grassy bank at the side of the river and sat down beneath a wide-spreading oak to remove her shoes and stockings. She had deliberately chosen one of her oldest gowns this morning, a demure dress of striped pink and white that she had joked to Hester made her look ridiculously like a debutante. Hester… For a moment a frown marred her brow. Much more of this behavior from her friend and she would go to Half Moon House herself and drag Hester out of the bed of whichever farmhand was her current fancy. Hester's dangerous and self-destructive behavior simply had to stop.

She rolled her stockings up neatly and placed them in her shoes, then picked up the little basket and walked across the soft grass to the water's edge. A kingfisher, startled from its perch on an overhanging branch, winged away along the river with a soft cry.

The river was low because it had not rained in a long time and the water only came up to her knees. The mossy stones slid beneath her bare feet and the soft, smooth sensation was delightful. She loved feeling so close to the earth, loved watching the way the bright green fronds of the ferns uncurled themselves amongst the damp stones and the way that the purple saxifrage peeped from between the roots of the trees. On the other side of the river, though, she had found a veritable treasure trove, a secret that she shared with no one. She settled the basket a little more firmly on her arm, tucked up her skirts and picked her way carefully over the slippery stones and through the fast-flowing water.

In a patch of chalky soil on the far bank was the plant she sought, its tiny scarlet fruits glistening ripe in the sun. She had learned from her reading that wild strawberries liked the limestone ground hereabouts, and when she had found her own crop of them, she had been delighted. They were exactly like the ones she grew in her hothouses, only smaller and sweeter, and the fact that they were hidden away here by the river and no one knew of them made their flavor all the more delicious to her.

She had nearly reached the bank and was about to scramble out when the stone beneath her feet shifted without warning and she almost fell. Grabbing for a branch to steady herself she felt the stones shift again, slipped, felt her balance go, and knew she was about to fall headlong into the river. The inevitability of it flashed through her mind and then an arm came hard around her waist and someone scooped her up into his arms and she was held hard and fast.

For a moment she froze in shock and fear.

"Dear me, Mrs. Osborne," an amused male voice said in her ear, "you do seem to have an affinity with water."

Nick Falconer. Strangely, as soon as she knew his identity, Mari's fear melted. It was replaced by indignant mortification and she wriggled hard to be free. Immediately his arms tightened around her until she could barely breathe.

"Hold still," he said, "or you will have us both in the water."

He strode to the bank and took the slope with what seemed to Mari to be insulting ease. His grip was firm and she could feel the strength in him. It was supremely disconcerting. No one had ever held her like this before. She felt her body heat up as though it was burning from the inside out, molten, excited, expectant.

"Put me down!" she said breathlessly, overwhelmed with sensations she could not begin to understand.

In response Nick went down on one knee and tumbled her into the middle of the strawberry patch, following her down into the soft, sweetly scented grass.

"As you wish," he said, smiling.

Mari lay still for a moment, winded and bemused. The smell of hot, dry hay was all around her, mingling with the fresh, sharp scent of the strawberries and the faint lemon tang of cologne on Nick's skin. Mari's head spun at the assault on her senses. She felt dazed, as though she could scarcely breathe.

Nick propped himself on one elbow beside her.

"You don't seem very grateful to me, Mrs. Osborne," he said. His lips were only inches away from hers. His voice fell. "Twice I go to the trouble of rescuing you and get no thanks for it." His eyes on her, he plucked a strawberry and bit into it hard. Mari felt a hot jolt through her entire body.

"Were you looking for these?" he continued. "They are delicious. Have I stumbled on one of your secrets, Mrs. Osborne?"

Mari found that she could not speak, could not move. The ground was warm beneath her and above Nick's head she could see the bright clear blue of the sky and feel the heat of the morning sun beating down on her body. The rush of the water was in her ears and the scent of the strawberries was all around her. Suddenly she felt sultry and wicked and wild in a way that she had never experienced before, a feeling compounded of the rampant lushness all around her and the aching spiral of desire that was inside her. It was madness but it held her in thrall.

Nick brought a strawberry to her lips and she bit into it, relishing the taste of it on her tongue, feeling the juice run. She heard Nick groan and then his mouth covered hers and his tongue licked the juice up and swept inside, tasting her, kissing her as though he wanted to take all of her.

Mari gasped. The feelings in her were so potent, so unfamiliar. After the horrors of her past and all the barren years since, she was utterly dazzled. Her whole body ached for him. She felt hot, shaky and hungry. Her body felt ripe, as though it was ready to open to him.

His tongue thrust against hers again, teasing, taking. Of her own volition, Mari's hands tangled in his hair. It was silky soft beneath her fingers, a contrast to the rough line of his jaw. He tasted of strawberries and heated desire. She opened her mouth beneath his and drank in the heady sensation of his kiss. She felt intoxicated, drunk with passion.

His mouth left hers and he began to kiss and lick his way down her throat. Mari's heart raced as the heat within her spread and pooled low in belly. Nick pressed his lips to the place where the pulse beat in the hollow of her neck, just above the fastening of her gown.

"I want you." His voice was ragged. "I want to strip this prim little gown from you and take you here in the grass by the river—"

Mari's breath caught on a moan and his mouth returned to hers, roughly now, demanding, possessing, sending shards of pure need through her body. His hand came up to cup her breast through the cotton dress, and she felt the nipple harden against his fingers and squirmed with frustration at the layers of cloth that separated them. Then he moved above her, so that his weight pinned her down, and for the first time something cold and fearful touched Mari's mind, cutting through the pleasure that filled her senses. She felt restrained, trapped. His hands had moved to undo the fastenings of her gown. She could feel his erection hard against her thigh and tried to move away, but he was kneeling on her skirts and she could not shift an inch. Panic started to rise in her and the sweet need drained from her body like water slipping away through her fingers, impossible to recapture.

And then she heard voices, loud voices close by on the packhorse bridge, and the rumble of wheels on the road, and her mind cleared of the last shreds of desire and she froze as she realized that they were in full view of anyone who passed by.

Nick had realized it, too. She felt him shift and then sit up and she opened her eyes to see him looking down at her, the hard, heated desire still in his eyes but fading now as reality intruded on them. She scrambled to sit up, part in panic and part in embarrassment, but Nick caught her arm in a warning grip and she kept still until the cart had passed and the danger of being observed had gone. Then she sat up and smoothed her skirts around her bare ankles with hands that shook, and avoided looking at him as she tried desperately to think what to say, what to do. She could not believe what had almost happened to her. There had been no fear in her, no bitter memory, until the moment that she had felt constrained and the realization of Nick's physical dominance had filled her mind, pushing aside all pleasure.

"Next time I'll choose somewhere more private." Unlike her, Nick did not sound as though he had lost an ounce of self-assurance.

Next time…

Mari's mind reeled at the thought, half yearning, half afraid. Nick had not realized, of course. How could he understand when he knew nothing of her experience and she could not tell him? He had thought only that she, like him, had been pulled from that sensual spell by the passing of the cart and the realization that they might be overlooked.

"There won't be a next time, Major Falconer." Her voice came out like a croak and she cleared her throat. "I made a mistake," she said. "It won't happen again."

Nick took her chin in his hand and turned her face up so that she was forced to meet his gaze, and she saw the demand and the determination in his eyes and caught her breath, because his need called such a deep response from her. One that she could neither under-stand nor deny.

"You do mistake," he said. "We shall be lovers, Mari, you and I. It is inevitable."

A shiver chased down Mari's spine. He sounded so certain and she felt so unsure, so *tempted*. Yet in the end she also felt afraid and it was that emotion that she knew would win, because of her history, because of what it had done to her.

Nick dropped a brief, hard kiss on her lips and for a moment she felt the echo of their passion through her whole body and then he was walking away and Mari felt the past fall around her like a shroud.

We shall be lovers, Nick had said, but Mari knew that could never be. She had caught a glimpse of what passion might have been like in another place, another time, but now she had to accept that it would not, could not, be.

CHAPTER SEVEN

Tansy—Resistance

"So, ANSTRUTHER," Nick said the following morning as he and Dexter Anstruther rode down to Peacock Oak village on their way to the Skipton road, "you have now had two days in which to assess our fellow guests. What do you think of them? Are there any that strike you as potential highwaywomen?"

"Only Lady Hester Berry, sir," Anstruther said, laughing. "I believe she would be capable of anything. She is very wild. Riding astride, staying out all night…"

"The sort of woman your mother warned you against, eh?" Nick said. "I saw her flirting with you at the card party the night before last."

"I think that Lord Teague would probably call me out if I responded to any of Lady Hester's overtures," Anstruther said, turning a little pink about the ears. "But I cannot envisage any of the other ladies as part of the Glory Girls. It seems an absurd idea."

"I agree with you," Nick murmured, "but we must be open to all possibilities. The Duchess of Cole, for example. I hear she rides exceptionally well. A lot of these country women do."

"Not her grace!" Anstruther looked horrified, thereby confirming Nick's suspicion that he was developing a somewhat surprising, youthful *tendre* for Laura Cole. He recovered himself quickly. "I cannot imagine it, sir. She is the perfect, elegant hostess, not a highwaywoman."

They crossed the River Wharfe by the humpbacked bridge and the road wound upward into the village. As they breasted the rise Nick could see Marina Osborne crossing the green, a basket over one arm. She was wearing a cream-colored spencer over a dark blue gown and had on a straw bonnet with matching blue ribbon. She looked fresh and pretty, and Nick caught Dexter Anstruther looking at her with something much more than a casual regard, and felt a possessive fury grip him. It was coming to something, he thought, when he was starting to feel jealous of Anstruther, and all because he looked at a pretty woman with admiration. But he could not help himself. His unsatisfied lust for Mari Osborne rode him hard and gave him no peace. He had dreamed about her again the previous night, a tangled dream of passion and wanting in which Anna's ghost reproached him for his lack of fidelity and he woke drenched in sweat and torn between desire and guilt.

He had not seen Mari since he had kissed her in the water meadows the previous morning. She had not attended the picnic that Laura Cole had arranged in the gardens that afternoon, nor the musicale in the evening. Nick had found himself looking for her, wanting to see her, aching to see her, if he were honest. He had told himself that he had driven the encounter with Mari by the river exactly as he had intended, that he had been in control, had set out coldly and calculatedly to seduce her. But the raw need he felt for her contradicted his claim. He knew that as the seducer he was in equal danger of being seduced.

He had kissed her in the Hen and Vulture and again beside the river, and he knew for certain now that it was the same woman. She had tasted sweet and shockingly familiar. It felt as though his body already knew her intimately.

"I say, sir," Anstruther was saying eagerly now, "who is that lady crossing the green?"

Nick laughed. "That," he said, "is our prime suspect, Anstruther. You are about to meet Mrs. Marina Osborne."

"That lady in the navy blue, sir?" Anstruther said, wrinkling up his eyes. "Surely she cannot be the woman we seek. She looks far too reputable."

"Anstruther, Anstruther." Nick sighed. "When will you learn? Glory does not habitually gallop around on horseback wearing a black cloak and demanding people's valuables. Part of her skill lies in her ability to appear respectable. Not," he added quietly, "that I necessarily think Mrs. Osborne *is* Glory now that I have seen her lamentable riding ability. But that she is the woman I met at the Hen and Vulture, dressed and behaving like a whore, I am certain."

He grinned at Anstruther's shocked, scarlet face and swung himself down from the saddle and into Mari's path. After their kiss Nick was curious to see just how she would react to him. She had been willing and eager in his arms the previous day even though she had retreated from him when they had been in danger of being interrupted. But she could not hide the passion in her nature. He was sure she would take him to her bed soon.

"Mrs. Osborne!" he called. "How do you do, ma'am? We were just speaking of you. May I introduce my friend Dexter Anstruther?"

"Your…your servant, ma'am," Anstruther spluttered, sending Nick another speaking look. "A pleasure to meet you."

Nick watched Anstruther's blush deepen as Marina Osborne smiled very prettily at him. There was a pink color in her cheeks that morning and the straw bonnet framed her face most flatteringly. As usual, despite the warmth of the morning, she was buttoned up to the neck. Nick felt a wayward and powerful urge to unbutton her there and then.

"How do you do, Mr. Anstruther?" she said. "I have heard much about you from Lady Hester."

Anstruther blushed again to the tips of his ears and as he seemed utterly unable to frame a suitable reply, Nick stepped forward and took Mari's gloved hand in his. She was avoiding his gaze and looked a little shy. It made him cynically amused that she had her act to perfection.

"You seem very well recovered from your near fall in the river yesterday, ma'am," he murmured. "I am so glad that I was able to be of service to you."

Mari's gaze flicked to his face before her lashes came down to veil her expression. "I am very well, I thank you," she said, removing her hand from his grip. "Pray do not let me keep you from your business."

Nick laughed. "You do not seem particularly pleased to see me again, ma'am."

"I have no feelings on the matter," Mari said, very sweetly.

"You claim to be indifferent to me?"

"I make no claim to anything at all," Mari said. She smiled impartially at him and at Dexter Anstruther. "I beg that you will excuse me, gentlemen. I have parcels to distribute."

Nick looked into the basket. There were piles of oranges and lemons nestling within. The previous evening he had heard Lady Faye comment waspishly on Mari Osborne's charitable activities, another way, Lady Faye had implied, in which she pushed herself forward inappropriately.

"Expensive commodities," he commented. "Do you hand them out to the poor and needy, ma'am?"

Mari looked a little flustered. "I suppose you could say that, Major Falconer."

"You are generous."

"I do what has to be done."

Nick smiled at her. "And do you rob from the rich, as well as give to the poor in order to do what has to be done?"

Mari's gaze came up to meet his very sharply. For a moment their eyes clashed and Nick held hers very deliberately. He felt the same sensation he always experienced on looking at her—an impact as though someone had punched him in the gut. Her eyes were so candid. How was it possible for her to be a counterfeit when she could look like an innocent schoolroom miss? She truly was a mistress of deceit.

Then, to his surprise, she smiled at him. "What a vivid imagination you have, Major Falconer," she said. "I assure you that I am no Robin Hood. Good day to you." She turned and nodded a polite farewell to Dexter Anstruther and put her hand firmly on the gate of one of the cottages that bordered the village green. A moment later she was knocking at the door and showing the contents of her basket to those inside. She stepped over the threshold and was lost from view.

"She has the nerve of the devil," Nick said, under his breath, as he swung himself back up into the saddle. "Well, well." He turned to Anstruther. "I wonder about Mrs. Osborne's other charitable activities, Anstruther. Pray make inquiries."

"Yes, sir," Anstruther said. "She seems a very charming lady," he added. "I am sorry, sir, but I cannot believe…" His voice trailed off and he looked unhappy.

"Believe it, Anstruther," Nick said grimly. "Mrs. Osborne is no lady. She is an impostor. And I will expose her as a fraud if it is the last thing I do."

Anstruther rubbed his forehead. "But without proof, how is such a thing to be achieved, sir?"

"I will seduce the truth from her, Anstruther," Nick said. He saw the younger man's uncomprehending expression and added, "Get her to reveal the truth—and a great deal more—by bedding her."

The tips of Anstruther's ears glowed liked beacons. "I say, sir," he protested. "That's simply not cricket!"

"I know," Nick said. He laughed. "Sometimes we all have to do things that are less than chivalrous, Anstruther. The end justifies the means."

"If you say so, sir," Anstruther said doubtfully.

Nick encouraged the horse to a trot. The contact he had had with Marina Osborne, brief as it had been, had made him burn with wanting her. It was always the same; that impact, that blow to the heart that deprived him of breath. He wanted rid of it before it distracted him, betrayed him altogether. He had to seduce her, bed her, get the truth from her before he was utterly be-witched. With a muffled curse he kicked the horse to a gallop, leaving Anstruther in his wake.

As Mari emerged from Mrs. Bean's cottage she saw Laura Cole driving slowly up the hill in the Cole Court gig. Laura waved energetically when she saw her and Mari crossed the road to join her.

"I am so glad I saw you," Laura said, leaning down to give her a hand up onto the gig seat beside her. "I need to speak with you. Can I drive you back?"

"Thank you," Mari said, smiling. She waited whilst Laura put the gig in motion with her usual no-nonsense capability.

"I was sorry that you did not join us last night," Laura said. "I wondered if you were perhaps deliber-ately avoiding someone. Major Falconer, perhaps?" She smiled at Mari's vivid blush. "I noticed that from the start he appeared to admire you exceedingly."

"He may do so," Mari said. "Or he may be pretend-ing to admire me. I am not sure." She looked down at her gloved hands, locked so tightly together in her lap, then up into Laura's face. "Oh, Laura," she burst out, "how am I to tell? For all my history I have so little real experience. He kissed me yesterday and I felt—" She wriggled on the seat. "I felt all hot and excited and truly *wicked* in the best possible way!" She stopped; bit her lip. "I never thought that it would happen," she said quietly. "Not after Rashleigh. It seemed impossible."

"And now you find that it is possible," Laura said.

"Yes. Maybe. But then something happened…" Mari hesitated, looking at her friend. Although she and Laura were close, she was not at all sure that she could speak to the Duchess of Cole about such intimate matters as a man's arousal. Talking to Hester would, of course, be a different matter entirely. Hester would have no qualms on such a topic, indeed she would probably be indelicate enough to mention comparative size and length and go into details that would make Mari blush with mortification. Laura, though… Well, one simply did not mention erections to a Duchess.

"I suppose you felt his erection," Laura said helpfully. "I imagine that could make you quite nervous."

"Laura!" Mari squeaked.

"What?" Laura shot her a look of amusement. "Are you thinking that I can know nothing of such matters? Well, it's true I know very little about sex, but we were talking of your problems, not mine."

"Yes, well, you are correct," Mari said, recovering herself. "It made me fearful." She shivered. "He seemed so strong, so forceful."

"But he is not Rashleigh," Laura said gently.

"No." Mari shivered. "And maybe you are right. Maybe, one day, with a man who is gentle and patient—" She stopped. "At any rate," she said, "that man cannot be Major Falconer. Hester has told you that it seems he has come to Peacock Oak to trap the Glories? He thinks I am his cousin's murderer. His attentions to me can only be a means to an end—a way of discovering the truth about Rashleigh's death."

Laura shook her head. "That would be the behavior of a blackguard. I cannot believe it of him."

"Believe it," Mari said sadly, "for I am sure it is true." She sighed. "I am attracted to Major Falconer. I am even afraid that I might be falling in love with him because he seems strong and protective and honorable.

So a part of me wants to believe that he is a good man and that I may trust him with the truth about myself and about Rashleigh's death. But we both know that is madness for *of course* I cannot trust him. I am a runaway slave and, if I confess, I will hang."

"He might not see it that way," Laura said slowly. "You are not culpable, Mari—"

"Yes, I am in the eyes of the law," Mari argued. "You know it is true, Laura! Besides, whatever I say will lead inevitably to the Glory Girls and I cannot expose you and Hester and Josie and Lenny to that danger. So—" she shrugged "—I cannot do it. I cannot take that risk. I cannot trust Major Falconer."

Laura was silent for a long time. "I understand what you are saying," she said slowly, "and I fear you are correct. You cannot confide in him."

Mari shook her head. Some of the brightness seemed to have gone out of the day. She knew that Laura was right. She had come to the same decision herself. And yet the need to trust Nick Falconer made her ache. It was instinctive. It was also destructive and dangerous. So next time she met him she must push him back to arm's length and resist both her attraction to him and the deeper, more insidious desire to tell him the truth.

"It is a pity that the Glories cannot ride out at present," Laura said, turning the gig onto a narrow track that led alongside the river, "for I was at Starbotton just now and I see that Sampson is enclosing all the common pasture at Starbotton Raikes. John Teague tells me that Sampson has told all the villagers to find grazing elsewhere or he would take their livestock, too. He is an odious man."

Mari felt a familiar rush of fury through her blood as unstoppable as an incoming tide. It was always the same. When she heard a tale of injustice or greed on the part of the local landowners or employers, she wanted to run straight down there to confront them. The activities of the Glory Girls gave her enormous satisfaction in righting a few of the inequalities that beset rural life. It was not enough—it was never enough—but it helped. Her charitable work, the education, the food, the firewood in winter, felt like a tiny drop in an ocean of disparity, where the weak suffered and died if they had not enough to clothe, feed and warm them, and the powerful sat before the roaring fire and stuffed themselves with meat.

"That is…unfortunate," she said quietly.

"John has already challenged Sampson about it," Laura said, "but Sampson has the law on his side. He has bought the land. He simply laughed in John's face and told him he was a fool not to take advantage himself."

"And you and Hester want to ride out and teach Sampson a lesson?"

"Yes." Laura drew the gig to a halt on the grassy bank by the side of the river. "Has Hester not spoken to you of it?"

"I have not seen her this morning," Mari admitted.

A little frown puckered Laura's brows. She lowered her voice until it was barely audible above the sound of the water.

"Was she out all night again?"

"Yes."

"This has to stop, Mari, or something terrible will happen."

"I know," Mari said unhappily, "but what can I do? She will not listen to me. I know she is unhappy but I am powerless to help."

Laura shook her head. "She was always like this, unable to settle, searching for something. For a while Jack's madness masked hers—actually I think they made one another worse—but when he died and she lost all her money and Starbotton Hall to boot, it started again."

"Perhaps Charles could help—" Mari started to say, but fell silent as Laura shook her head.

"Charles would be no help," his wife said bitterly. "He would be scandalized if he knew of his cousin's behavior. He is beyond conventional, Mari. Truly I think he is the most boring man I know. I have spent years wishing desperately for his regard only to discover that he has nothing by way of feelings to give me and I am locked into the most tedious life imaginable."

"Laura!" Mari was genuinely shocked now. She had realized that Laura and Charles were not close—how could they be when he spent so much time apart from her?—but until that day in the gardens Laura had been supremely loyal, never uttering a word of criticism of her spouse. "I am sorry," she said a little awkwardly. "I had no idea that matters were as bad as that."

"We are a fine pair, Hester and I!" Laura said, urging the horse to set off again. "The one too wild and the other too staid."

"There is nothing very staid about riding out with the Glories," Mari said.

"No." Laura's porcelain fair face flushed a little. "It is my escape, I suppose. Not a very noble reason to ride out, but the only one I have." She took one hand from the reins and squeezed one of Mari's clasped ones. "Do not pity me, Mari. After all, I am a Duchess and that has some compensations."

"I suppose it must," Mari said, but for the first time she was wondering what they were. Having money and influence was all very fine but when there was an empty chasm beneath, no love, no warmth and a huge mansion to rattle around in alone, all the money in the world could not compensate. And Laura was so generous, so loving as a person. Mari's heart ached for her, that she had no object on which to expend that love.

"We are not so different, you and I," she said. "It amazes me that our backgrounds are so far apart and yet we are so similar in so many ways."

Laura smiled. "So you understand, then. What do you say? Shall the Glories ride against Sampson?"

Mari laughed aloud. "Yes. Yes, they shall. It is reckless and very probably mad, but I cannot see such injustice and stand aside." She thought about Nick Falconer and it felt as though a shadow had tiptoed across her grave. "Just be careful, Laura," she besought. "I have lost so much. I could not bear it if anything were to happen to you or to Hester."

Laura smiled. "It will not."

"If you do ride out," Mari said thoughtfully, "make it after the Midsummer dance on Friday night. Everyone will be cast away and their drunken recollections will greatly enhance Glory's reputation later."

"Gracious," Laura said. "What a splendid idea! It is fortunate Glory has your resourcefulness, Mari." She turned the horse in at the gate of Peacock Cottage. "It will be Glory's last ride. I promise."

"It had better be," Mari said, and once again she was thinking of Nick Falconer, and his determination to bring the Glory Girls down.

THE PIANOFORTE, Nick thought, was one of the most refined torture implements invented by man. Already that evening he had been obliged to sit through the noisy playing of Miss Lydia Cole, which privately he had considered quite shockingly bad. Lady Faye had talked all the way through her daughter's performance in order to comment on what a talented girl she was and how she would make someone a lovely, biddable wife. Her sharp glances and pointed remarks were not lost on Nick, who knew that he was being lined up as first choice of son-in-law and could scarce bear the thought. Miss Cole herself seemed, as John Teague had said, a gentle girl, but her mother was a harridan.

Miss Cole had given her place at the instrument to Lady Hester Berry, who was now playing Bach with a great deal more melodrama than that composer had surely ever intended. Tonight she was wearing a plunging gown in emerald-green, which revealed a vast expanse of bare skin. There were bruises visible on her arms and what looked like a scratch on her collarbone, but Hester was wearing them like trophies and making no attempt to hide them. Nick had seen John Teague take her on one side and ask her about them, and Hester had brushed his questions away with a laugh and Teague had flushed, apparently with anger.

Nick sympathized with Teague's frustrations. He had had an exasperating day himself. He and Dexter Anstruther had traveled to Skipton to meet with Edward Arkwright's banker to discuss the robbery perpetrated by the Glory Girls the previous week. Desmond, the banker, had been angry and vicious in his condemnation of the highwaywomen, but Nick suspected that because his pride and his employer's pocket had been hurt he was exaggerating the case. The man was full of what an immense, rough, uncouth woman Glory had been and how her cohorts were a bunch of ruffians.

"Give to the poor?" he had snorted. "The only ones benefiting from that robbery were Glory and her gang!"

Nick had judged his witness statement as good as useless. The highwaywomen were all six feet tall, rode like men, had deep gruff voices and carried pistols. It had been dark, so Desmond had seen nothing else. They had taken a tenth of Arkwright's profits from the coach and had left Desmond and the coachman tied up in a field, with a calling card tucked impertinently in their pockets.

"Next time," Nick said, "why not travel by daylight?"

Lady Hester's dashing performance hit a jarring note and Lady Faye Cole, who was seated at Nick's side, leaned closer to whisper in his ear.

"Dear Hester is somewhat *theatrical* in style, is she not?" Lady Faye flicked her fan. "I think it must be the plebeian influence of Mrs. Osborne. Her husband worked for a living, you know."

"So do I," Nick said.

Lady Faye's eyes bulged. "My dear Major Falconer, that is quite different! You are an officer in His Majesty's army!"

"I still get paid," Nick said. He stretched. Over Lady

Faye's shoulder he could see Lord Henry Cole snoring on the sofa with his mouth open, and beyond him, Marina Osborne talking with the Duchess of Cole.

Tonight Mari was wearing a gown of rich purple, as demure and high-necked as Hester's was low cut and daring. Her hair was uncovered and it was drawn back tightly in the same severe style she had worn whilst out riding. She should have looked dowdy but her hair was so deep black in color that it gleamed rich and fine in the candlelight. Nick itched to touch it, to release it from its tight confines, to see it spill across her bare shoulders and feel it run through his fingers. The contrast of the jet-black hair and the creamy pale skin of her shoulders would be unbearably seductive. Nick knew that instinctively and the thought tormented him. In his fevered imagination he had already undressed Mari and made love to her there on the sofa that was, in fact, occupied by Lady Faye Cole.

Nick remembered the tantalizing dusting of freckles that Molly from the Hen and Vulture had scattered across her shoulders and the little heart-shaped mole. If only Mari Osborne did not favor such concealing gowns he would be able to see if she, too, had freckles there and so confirm another piece in the puzzle. Had they not been interrupted, the previous day by the river, he would certainly have unbuttoned her bodice and bared the tender skin of her shoulders to his gaze. And he would not have stopped there. He thought of peeling the purple gown from Mari's body, very slowly, of exposing the curves of her breasts and their pert pink tips. He wanted to taste her….

He shifted slightly, trying to concentrate on what Lady Faye was saying rather than on his growing arousal. Never had he had such trouble keeping his mind on a commission. The bewitching Mrs. Osborne, counterfeit or not, would drive him to distraction before he solved this case.

"To think that we should see the widow of a *cit* in the blue drawing room at Cole Court," Lady Faye was saying. "It is Laura's fault, of course. She is far too *democratic* in her tastes. It is most inappropriate for a Duchess."

Nick thought that Laura Cole and Marina Osborne did seem very easy in one another's company. The previous couple of nights, when Mari was absent, Laura had seemed strained and tense and Nick had wondered if she was ill. Now Laura was smiling at something Mari was saying, but her fine hazel eyes strayed constantly to Charles, who was talking to John Teague. He seemed unaware of his wife's scrutiny and after a moment Nick saw Laura sigh and turn away.

"Her grace met Mrs. Osborne at the Skipton Horticultural Society, I understand," he said.

"Indeed!" Lady Faye's discontented mouth turned down farther at the corners. "That is what I mean, Mr. Falconer. Horticultural Society, indeed! As though the Duchess of Cole should be mingling with such people. So common! What does one employ gardeners for if one is going to tinker in such matters oneself?"

"It sounds most entertaining," Nick said lazily. Privately he thought that Lady Faye considered that she herself would have made a much better Duchess than Laura. It was a tragedy from Faye's perspective that Henry was from the junior branch of the Cole family.

"Hester attends the meetings, too," Faye sniffed, "and she knows nothing about plants and cares even less. Yet when I invited them to join me for some card playing with the other ladies of the parish, they declined!"

"Incomprehensible," Nick agreed smoothly. He saw Faye gesturing surreptitiously to her daughter Lydia to join them, and got to his feet. "Excuse me, Lady Faye."

He had been seated away from Mari at dinner and had been obliged to escort Lydia Cole, and apart from a brief exchange of pleasantries he had not spoken to Mari at all. The urge to be close to her was now strong, so strong that he could resist no longer. And he thought that although Laura Cole's drawing room was not necessarily the most ideal spot for a seduction, a conversation with Mari might offer him the opportunity to progress their affair.

He took his teacup and walked across to where Laura was presiding over the pot. She looked up and smiled at him. "Another cup, Major Falconer?"

Nick was very aware of Mari sitting beside the Duchess. She was deliberately not looking at him. Her head was bent, her dark lashes casting a shadow against the curve of her cheek. She was studying her clasped hands rather intently. Nick put his cup down on the table.

"Thank you, your grace, but I must decline. I came across because Lady Faye has been singing Mrs. Osborne's praises and I wished to ask her advice on my planting schemes."

Laura's rather beautiful mouth curled into a smile. "Did you so, Major Falconer? Planting schemes—what a novel approach. But I will gladly give my place to you."

She squeezed Mari's hand and stood up. "There was

a matter upon which I wished to ask Hester's advice, dear Mari. We can continue our conversation later?"

"Of course," Mari said, and for a moment Nick saw her face relax into warmth. "Thank you, Laura."

Nick took the Duchess's vacated seat and watched with interest as Mari placed her cup precisely on the table and folded her hands again. There was something very deliberate in her movements as though she was arming herself for a confrontation. When she finally lifted her eyes to his, he once again felt the jolt of the contact like a kick in the stomach. He wanted this woman so badly. He wanted to hold her against him and plunder that tempting mouth with his own. His mind was telling him she was a charlatan, his body that she was the most desirable creature he had ever seen. He knew which he wanted to listen to.

"Good evening, Major Falconer." Her voice was low and unhurried and reflected none of the heat that Nick felt within. "I am not sure which of your statements just then was more untruthful—that Lady Faye has been singing my praises or that you have a need of botanical advice."

Nick smiled. "If you think my excuses unconvincing, Mrs. Osborne, what do you think could be my real reason for approaching you?"

Mari shrugged carelessly. "As to that, I can have no notion, Major Falconer."

"No? Not even after our encounter by the river?"

Her gaze touched his face, and then she looked away. "As to that, I have already told you that it was a mistake on my part and on yours—" she hesitated "—I suspect it was merely part of a plan you have for me."

Nick was fascinated. Had she divined his true purpose in planning to seduce her? Was she being even more daring, and intimating that she knew his true purpose here in Peacock Oak—and that he would never catch her?

"Do you think so?" he murmured.

"Yes." Her dark eyes mocked him. "I am a rich widow, you see, and you—" she smiled "—you may well be a fortune hunter."

Nick's lips twitched. "You have met many such, Mrs. Osborne?"

"Oh, many and a many," Mari said.

"They profess to admire you?"

"Always. But they admire my fortune more."

"Whereas I," Nick said gently, leaning toward her, "am heir to a fortune, and thus do not need yours. And I admire you sincerely."

The smile that curved Mari's lips was cynical. "You cannot admire me sincerely, Major Falconer. You have met me on only a few occasions. Any sincere emotion takes time and experience to grow."

Nick made a slight gesture. "I am misled, then, by the feeling that I have met you more *frequently* than you claim. At least half a dozen times, by my reckoning."

The color crept under her skin. "How odd."

"And disturbing," Nick said, "to feel that one knows a person more intimately than they pretend."

Mari's luscious mouth was tight with scorn. "There is nothing intimate in our acquaintance, sir."

"I beg to differ." Nick lowered his voice. "I saw almost every intimate inch of you in that fountain, Mrs. Osborne, and having done so can only burn to touch every place that my eyes have uncovered." He shifted.

"I would have done so yesterday—would have made love to you—had we not been interrupted."

He saw Mari bite her lower lip, her incredibly full and sensuous lower lip and felt his body jolt in response. The world of Laura's drawing room, the other guests, the buzz of conversation about them, even his memories of Anna, had all retreated to the edges of his mind. He could focus on Mari alone and the dazzling need to possess her.

Mari was fidgeting with her teaspoon. "I think you refine too much upon one kiss, sir," she said. "It was no great matter."

"How crushing for my self-esteem," Nick said. "I shall have to try to do better in future."

"Pray do not put yourself to so Herculean a task on my behalf, sir," Mari said. She raised her eyes to his. "As I said, I made an error and I tend to learn quickly so I will not make the same mistake again."

Nick reached out and lightly touched the back of her hand, and she let the spoon fall into the saucer with a slight tinkle.

"I would like to believe you," he said softly, "just as I think you would like to believe yourself, Mrs. Osborne, but the truth is that you want me, too. You kissed me back. Admit it."

He could see that she was disturbed by his words. The color in her face was the flush of arousal now although her refusal to meet his gaze showed that she was fighting it. She fidgeted with the seam of her dress, pleating it between her fingers.

"Major Falconer—"

"Yes?"

"It is true—I did kiss you back." She spoke very

softly, so quietly that he had to strain to catch her words. She sounded very candid. He would have believed her had he not known her better, known her for a counterfeit. "I did not intend to," she said. "It took me by surprise and so I…I responded." Her voice strengthened. "But Major Falconer, I would ask that you disabuse yourself of the belief that I share any of your feelings. I do not wish for a love affair."

Nick smiled. "You depress my pretensions."

"I hope so. I have no use for your admiration."

Nick leaned closer until his breath stirred the tendrils of hair that escaped the confines of the knot. So far she had been the epitome of the respectable widow, word perfect, irreproachably virtuous, but for the unwilling arousal he had seen in her eyes. Now he felt the tiniest tremor of awareness go through her at his proximity. She was not indifferent to him, very far from it. And he was prepared to go as far as he had to in order to test that virtuous facade and uncover the tavern harlot beneath.

He leaned forward and allowed the back of his fingers to brush the skin of her neck, very gently, as though by accident. She felt warm, soft and so smooth he wanted to run his hands over her whole body to see if it was equally as perfect. Her skin heated beneath his touch and blushed a pale rose. He felt a sudden wrench of pain for Anna, then, for her delicacy and her honesty and the fact that he had not deserved her. This relationship with Mari was based on little but deceit. And yet there was some truth in it, for there was no pretence in his desire for her.

"You say you have no wish for an affair but you know you lie," he whispered. "Take me as your lover."

He felt her whole body stiffen. She drew back from him slightly. Her lips were parted, her breathing shallow. There was shock in her face and something else that quickened his pulse. He waited, his mouth dry, for her response. In that moment he wanted nothing more than to take her to his bed. He had all but forgotten the Glory Girls. As for Rashleigh, he could hardly have cared less about his murderer. The man had been a blackguard and it was good riddance. He wanted nothing other than Mari, her naked body entwined around his, her mouth open and willing beneath his own.

"You move too fast." Her words came out as a whisper.

"I know when I want something."

"You are outrageous."

"I know it. But so are you. You match me in every way although you pretend otherwise. You are far from proper, Mrs. Osborne, and we both know it. I have seen you in your true guise."

Her chin came up. "Now you go too far, sir."

"I go nowhere near far enough," Nick said, "but I shall go much further." He saw Mari give a quick glance over her shoulder at the Duchess's guests, chatting and laughing and totally oblivious of the spell that held them both in thrall. "Not now, perhaps," he said, "but at a time of my choosing."

He saw a flicker of expression in Mari's eyes and then she gave a little sigh and sat up straighter.

"The answer is no, Major Falconer."

Nick was not a strategist for nothing. He knew when to retreat. "Very well," he said. He sat back and smiled at her. "Forgive my importunity. But I wonder whether you would care to ride with me tomorrow? You could explain matters so much more clearly to me if we were alone and we could…pledge ourselves to reach a better understanding."

He saw with amusement that she was about to give him a crushing set down, but before she could do so, Lord Henry Cole gave a loud snort and lurched awake, turning toward them. "Riding? Did someone mention a ride?" He spun around unsteadily on Charles. "When is the hunt going out, dear boy? Can't wait to see the fillies mounted, eh?" He gave Mari a lascivious wink.

"You must hold me excused, my lord," Mari said. Suddenly she was as pale as chalk. "You know that I do not ride well enough to join the hunt."

Nick watched curiously as she smoothed her skirts with fingers that shook slightly. There was something here that was more than Mari's dislike of Lord Henry, he thought. He had seen the way she had dealt with the persistent peer at the ball; she was not afraid of him. Yet now she was breathing in short, shaky breaths and looked almost white enough to faint. He caught her fingers in his, his desire for her suddenly overlaid by concern.

"Mrs. Osborne? Are you quite well?"

"I… Yes…" For a moment her dark eyes were unfocused as though she were gazing inward on something terrifying. "I beg your pardon." She straightened and removed her hand from his. "Yes, I am quite well, I thank you, sir. But I am afraid that I must decline your invitation to ride. You have seen for yourself that I am not proficient."

Nick knew this was true but he thought it could not account for such acute anxiety. He frowned slightly. Had she had a hunting accident in the past that might have made her so nervous?

"Have you ever been out with the hunt, Mrs. Osborne?" he asked slowly.

"No." She had locked her shaking hands together now in a vain attempt to quell their trembling. "I dislike the hunt. It is barbaric."

"It is but sport."

She looked him directly in the eyes. And now there was no pretence, no desire, no deceit, nothing but pure, blazing anger.

"Sport?" she said. "Tell that to the hunted, Major Falconer. You have no idea what you are talking about. Excuse me."

And with a soft swish of satin skirts she rose to her feet and walked away.

SOMEHOW MARI MANAGED to quell her panic whilst she crossed the huge expanse of marbled hall and waited for the footman to call her carriage. Somehow she must have provided a coherent reply to Laura's anxious questions as her friend came hurrying out of the drawing room to check that Mari had not been taken ill as a result of the lobster patties they had had for dinner. And somehow she had kept her expression studiously blank as Nick Falconer followed Laura from the room and paused for a moment, watching her thoughtfully as she stood in an agony of impatience, desperate to be alone.

Eventually the carriage pulled up at the door, Mari climbed inside and the blessed darkness enclosed her. She leaned back and closed her eyes. The familiar panic was like a tide racing through her, sweeping aside all thought and reason, claiming her, fiercely, as its own. The feral baying of the hounds echoed through her head. She could feel the chill of the water numbing her feet as she crouched in the stream and waited for them to pass by. She could hear the thud of the beaters' sticks in the grass, the horn calling to the dogs as Rashleigh's men hunted her across the winter fields. A wave of heat swept through her body, setting her shaking, and then the panic started to recede a little and her mind began to clear and she could hear the rumble of the carriage wheels on the road and knew she was safe.

Safe.

Free.

People spoke of liberty and freedom so lightly and many had no idea what it truly meant. Her grip on both safety and freedom felt so tenuous. For all her childhood and the first part of her adult life she had lived at the whim of others. She had been a possession, property. She had bought her physical freedom at such a high price and had known that because she was still technically a serf, because her owner had never set her free, she could be captured and taken back and forced back into slavery.

Nick Falconer was Rashleigh's heir. He might even be her master. She thought of the anonymous letters. At the very least he might discover the truth about her and then she would lose all she had fought so hard to gain.

Never trust a man, never let him close, never let him hurt you, never give him that power….

The attraction she felt for Nick Falconer was ruthless but she had learned hard lessons in a hard school. She would not give in. She had retreated tonight into the shell she had created for herself, her reinvention, Mrs. Marina Osborne, virtuous widow. It was not who she really was. She was not even sure it was the person she wanted to be. Occasionally she would catch a memory of little Marina, the child who had lived for her first seventeen years in St. Petersburg and had tumbled in the snow with the other children of Lord Rashleigh's serfs. That child had been fierce, strong, forever chasing after new ideas and desperately grasping after liberty but never actually free.

The person Mari wanted to be had been lost seven years before, taken from her home and family, swept away from all that was familiar by Rashleigh's selfish cruelty, her innocence stolen. But now, looking back, she could see that she had never really been sure of whom she was. Rashleigh's father had taken a child and turned her into an approximation of an English lady for his own pleasure; she had been some sort of experiment to him, not a real person. He had taken her from her parents when she had been no more than a baby and had named her Marina. Her parents had not even had the power to name her. They had no will, no right, to resist. Thus was the lot of a serf.

When she had created Marina Osborne she had tried to make the life for herself that she thought she had wanted. She had her cottage and her garden and her plants. She had good friends who loved her. She had taken the money she had stolen from Rashleigh and had tried to use it for good. And she had dismissed the impossible dreams of a husband and family because Rashleigh's legacy to her had been fear and mistrust. Along with her virginity, he had stolen her hopes for the future.

Under other circumstances Nick Falconer might have been a man that she could have trusted, a man with whom she could have rebuilt that future. But although she wanted him, she knew his seduction had a deliberate purpose. He wanted to trick her into trusting him, into telling him the truth. And she had to keep silent for her own sake and the sake of all those she loved and protected.

She shivered a little as she remembered his whispered words.

I have seen almost every intimate inch of you... Take me for your lover....

She had wanted to, had wanted *him* with a desire all the stronger and more poignant because she had thought she would never feel like that. But she had chosen the wrong man. Even if he was not cynically trying to exploit her attraction for his own ends, he could still be her downfall. It could never be. She had to ignore both her awareness of him and the insane urge that prompted her to trust him, to run to him, to draw on his strength. Mrs. Marina Osborne might be a counterfeit but it was all she had to hide behind. She had to hold firm and hope—and pray—that she would never be found out.

"ANSTRUTHER," Nick said a little grimly, on returning to the drawing room, "I need a drink. You had better join me at Half Moon House. I wish to make some inquiries about the Glory Girls."

Dexter Anstruther looked less than delighted at this enticing prospect when the alternative was to sit gazing surreptitiously at Laura Cole, but he went helpfully enough to fetch the horses and within a few minutes they had excused themselves from the house-party guests and were riding out on the Skipton road. Nick had no qualms about riding at night. They had pistols and the moon was waxing full so they could see the way clearly. He reflected that it was, in fact, the perfect night for a raid by the Glory Girls, but nothing moved in the still landscape and there was no sound other than the hoot of an owl in the beech wood and the bleat of the sheep down by the river.

Anstruther seemed disinclined toward conversation, which suited Nick perfectly since he was preoccupied in thinking about his discussion with Marina Osborne. And this time his thoughts were not on seduction, or his relentless desire to possess her, nor on the habitual guilt that those feelings aroused in him because of Anna's memory, but on the very last thing that Mari had said to him.

Sport? Tell that to the hunted, Major Falconer.

He had wondered at the time if that comment had been directed at him, for certainly he was pursuing her, unyielding in his determination to unmask her and drive her to tell him the truth. And yet he thought it was another memory that had haunted her thoughts at that moment, and one so powerful that it had made her almost physically ill. He felt a wayward pang of sympathy as he remembered her pallor and the way she had drawn on some inner strength to compose herself. Then he stifled his feelings. This was no time to weaken. He should take her vulnerability and exploit it ruthlessly to gain what he wanted.

The lights of the tavern pricked the darkness and they left the horses with the ostler and settled into a corner of the taproom. The noise and the fug of smoke and the smell of ale reminded Nick of the Hen and Vulture. Anstruther had engaged one of the inn servants

in conversation in the hope of gaining some information on the Glory Girls but from the man's blank expression and the way that he was shaking his head, it
seemed that little of use was forthcoming. A short
while later the landlady, a fearsome-looking woman
built like a brick outhouse, came into the bar and stared
hard at them, hands on hips, as though sizing up
whether to pick them both up in one hand and throw
them out onto the street.

"They don't like strangers at the Half Moon," Anstruther said ruefully, burying his face in his tankard of
ale.

Several hours later, and having drunk considerably
more than he had intended, Nick was in a bad temper.
They had heard no mention of the Glory Girls all evening and none of their bland inquiries had elicited any
useful response. Taken together with the lack of information he and Anstruther had gained that day from
Arkwright's banker in Skipton, it meant that the sum
total of Nick's inquiries so far was precisely nothing.

As they clattered out onto the road toward Cole
Court, Anstruther brought his horse close alongside.

"Did you have a chance to visit the stables, sir?" he
asked, in a low voice.

Nick had, in fact, made a point of dropping in to the
stables on his way back from the jakes, on the pretext
of checking on his own mount. The ostler, a surly looking man, had seemed unimpressed by Nick's care for
his horseflesh and had answered his questions in mono-
syllables, but it had at least given Nick the opportunity
to size up the other horses that were stabled there.

"Yes," he said. "I thought there were a couple of
mounts that might suit a dashing highwaywoman."

Anstruther grinned. "Aye, sir. A very nice bay mare with a flash, just like Arkwright's banker mentioned." He lowered his voice still further. "She was shoed backward, sir."

Nick turned his head and gave him a sharp look. "You are sure?"

"Yes, sir. A highwayman's trick, sir."

Nick whistled soundlessly. Shoeing a horse backward was an old ploy to throw any pursuers off the trail.

"Well, well," he said slowly. "And Lady Hester Berry was riding back this way when we met her in the woods that morning a week ago. Perhaps she has acquaintance at Half Moon House."

They strode into the hall of Cole Court just as John Teague and Charles Cole were emerging from the study, laughing and joking together and looking almost as badly foxed as Nick was starting to feel.

"You look as though you've had a hard night, old chap," Teague said, sobering slightly. "Any luck with your inquiries at Half Moon House?" He cocked a brow. "I assume that was where you went?"

"Quiet, man!" Charles hushed him in a comically loud whisper. "We don't want everyone to know Falconer's business!"

"I should think they all know it already," Teague said easily, "news traveling as quickly as it does around here."

"Well, there's damn all news tonight," Nick said abruptly, and noticed that Teague smiled with just the slightest edge of relief. "I am for bed," he added, refusing Charles's eager offer of a nightcap, "but before I go I wondered if either of you recollected the first name of Mrs. Osborne's husband?"

Teague looked startled and it was Charles who replied. "I believe it was Phineas," he said. "Or possibly Phileas. Something of that sort." He rubbed a hand over his forehead. "She seldom speaks of him, and always as Mr. Osborne rather than by name."

"And where did he come from?" Nick pursued.

"Wasn't it Dorsetshire?" Teague suggested, his tone just a shade too casual.

"Cornwall," Charles said. "The Truro area. His father was a clergyman."

"That should make the family easy enough to trace," Nick said pleasantly, and saw Teague frown slightly.

The emergence of Lady Faye and the Duchess of Cole from the blue drawing room put an end to further conversation between them. Lady Faye gave a little, repressed scream to see so many gentlemen in their cups and recoiled in horror. Laura Cole's hazel gaze slid over them, lingered for a moment on Charles's flushed, foxed face, and then touched Nick and Dexter Anstruther with equal indifference. Nick saw Anstruther blush and start to stammer an apology but it was too late. Laura had gone.

"Anstruther," Nick said quietly, as, somewhat sobered, they climbed the stairs to their chambers, "have you noticed how John Teague tried to misdirect our inquiries? On my first night here he did a similar thing when he pretended to know very little about the Glory Girls."

"Protecting Mrs. Osborne, perhaps, sir?" Anstruther suggested.

"Perhaps. Or Lady Hester Berry." Nick frowned. "I require you to do something for me, Anstruther. I fear it will demand a spirit of self-sacrifice."

Anstruther smoothed a hand over his tousled locks. "Of course, sir."

"I need you to go back to London," Nick said. "I am sorry to tear you away from the charms of the Duchess of Cole after only a week, but there is some work that requires your specific talents and besides, I don't think that Laura Cole is in the market for a lover."

Anstruther's face blushed an even deeper red. "No, sir," he said. "I mean, yes, I am sure you are quite correct. I never really imagined that she would be, sir. I will go to London in the morning. What is it that you require me to do?"

Nick drew him to one side as a housemaid passed them with a hasty curtsy. "You heard the Duke of Cole. I need you to find out about Phileas or Phineas Osborne, who was apparently the son of a clergyman from Truro, and specialized in the importing and selling of exotic plants. I would also like details of his death approximately five years ago and any information you can find out about his widow."

"What exactly are you expecting me to find, sir?"

"I do not know," Nick said grimly, "but I am beginning to wonder if you will find much at all." He looked at Anstruther's puzzled face and articulated the suspicion that had been forming in his mind for some time. "Specifically, Anstruther, I am beginning to wonder if the sainted Mr. Osborne ever existed."

CHAPTER EIGHT

Bilberry—Treachery

"NEVER MIND about your fancy men for now," Josie hissed, when Hester stepped through the door of Half Moon House a couple of nights later. "Lenny's here. Some flash cove has been asking questions about Glory. He's been here *and* to the King's Head. Come downstairs. No one can hear us there." She bundled Hester out of the crowded taproom and down the steps into the cellar where Lenny was sitting on the edge of a beer barrel, a pint of ale clasped in his hand. Hester thought that he looked even more lugubrious than usual in the dim light. Even his moustache drooped.

"Tell her, Lenny!" Josie said.

Lenny looked glum. "It's true. Flash London cove, looked like an army man, staying with your cousin at the Court."

"Tall, dark—" Hester began.

"Handsome," Josie said, nodding. "That's the one."

"Major Falconer," Hester said. She sighed. "Damnation! We were hoping that if he found nothing, he would cease his questions, both about Mari and the Glories." She stopped, sighed again. "He is damnably persistent."

"Why's he interested in little Mrs. O?" Josie inquired. "She done something wrong?"

"No more so than you or I," Hester said ruefully.

"Then we'll all hang together," Josie said with a cackle.

"At least Mrs. O ain't out half the night riding about the county," Lenny pointed out. "Can't pin Glory's activities on her if we all keep our mouths shut."

"No." Hester sat down heavily on the barrel next to Lenny. "But he is trying to pin other things on her and once he starts digging around, we'll all go down if we're not careful. Damnation!" she said again. "Was he in earnest in his inquiries?"

"Asking questions," Lenny said. "Offering money. That's in earnest." He was a man of few words.

"Offering money?" Hester raised her brows. She was starting to feel very nervous now, knowing how desperate some of the local families were to find the next farthing. Would their loyalty to the Glories hold steady?

"No one took it," Josie hurried in to say. "No one told him anything. But you know how it is, milady— there's those as would sell their own grannies if the price was right."

"Came sniffing around the stables, as well," Lenny said, "looking at the horses. At that time of night! Next time we go out we need to switch the nags. If we're going out." He cocked a brow. "What about Midsummer night tomorrow? Do we ride against Sampson's enclosures?"

Hester nodded. "We ride. And damn Major Falconer. In fact, I think we should teach him a lesson."

She smiled to herself as she climbed the steps to the

taproom. Riding out with the Glories always raised her spirits. She knew that Mari had said she would be a fool to ride against Nick Falconer, but perhaps Mari was wrong. Still thinking and planning, she strode straight past the hopeful grooms and farmhands without even noticing them and rode off into the night.

"A VILLAGE DANCE?" Lady Faye Cole said in the sort of tone that implied that Laura had suggested an orgy. "My dear Laura, I really do not think so."

It was breakfast on Midsummer's day, and Laura had just outlined to her guests the plans for that evening's entertainment.

"Sounds rather amusing," Lord Henry Cole said loudly, gaining a dark glare from his spouse. "Will that little filly Marina Osborne be there, Laura? Rather fancy seeing her flashing her hocks in the jig, what!"

"I imagine that she will attend, cousin Henry," Laura said coldly. She hated Henry's lascivious comments, hated his hunting language in general, ever since he had looked at her critically on her wedding day and told Charles to cover her and get her in whelp as soon as possible.

"It is Mari who sponsors the dance, after all," she said. "We merely lend the villagers a barn for the occasion."

"Mrs. Osborne sponsors the event!" Lady Faye looked down her nose. "Oh, no, no, no, no, no, Laura! How very inappropriate. Henry, you certainly must not attend."

Henry ignored her. "You'll be joining us, eh, Charles?" he called across the table. "Come and tread a measure with your lady wife, eh?"

Charles rustled his morning paper irritably. The fact that he was reading at breakfast and largely ignoring his guests, leaving her to bear the brunt of the conversation, seemed to Laura inexcusable. But then, Charles had appeared somewhat preoccupied of late and his duties as host did not always seem to be foremost in his mind.

"Dancing?" he said. "Not I, Henry, I thank you!"

"Quite right," Faye said, her chins quivering approval. "It is not at all suitable for a *Duke* to dance with his tenants."

Laura felt all her happy anticipation in the event start to drain from her. She had been looking forward to the dance as a change of scene, a break from the suffocating evenings in the drawing room listening to poor piano playing, Faye's malice and Henry's innuendo. Now, looking at Charles buried once more in his newspaper, she felt a sort of exasperation with him that was entirely new. Had anyone, ever, been so utterly wrapped up in their own concerns and so indifferent to the needs of others?

"Charles, dear," she said carefully, "I do think that, as the landlord, it would be most obliging of you to attend—"

The paper rustled again. Charles did not even look up. "I said no, Laura."

Laura felt crushed. She could feel the tears sting her eyelids and clenched her hands beneath the tablecloth.

I am a Duchess. I will not cry at my own breakfast table.

She looked up to see Nick Falconer watching her with his disconcertingly shrewd dark gaze. For a moment Laura, vulnerable and distressed, felt absolute terror as she thought that Nick could expose the Glory

Girls and send them all to the scaffold. Now that she was looking at him and measuring the cool ruthlessness she could see in his eyes, Laura thought that Hester's plan for the Glories to ride out that very night was probably very ill conceived.

Then she straightened her spine.

I am a Duchess. I will not slouch in despair.

What Nick Falconer did not know, he could not prove, and if they could help Mari with their plan then so much the better.

"Major Falconer," she said brightly. "Can I prevail upon you to make up the party with myself and Lord Henry? I am persuaded that Lady Hester and Lord Teague will certainly be there, as well."

Nick inclined his head slightly and smiled at her, a warm smile that made Laura realize with a slight jolt what a very attractive man he was. He had charm to burn, she thought, and for some reason the picture of Dexter Anstruther popped into Laura's mind at that precise moment and brought an entirely inappropriate blush to her cheeks. She found herself wishing he had stayed for the dance—and then wondered why on earth it should matter to her.

"I should be delighted to attend, your grace," Nick said, and Laura heard Lady Faye give a disapproving sniff.

"That's splendid then," Laura said, smiling radiantly. "The carriages leave at eight." And she tried not to worry that the Glory Girls had most certainly bitten off more than they could chew this time.

MARI HAD NOT SEEN Nick Falconer for a whole week but he had scarcely been out of her mind for a minute of that time. He obsessed her thoughts during the day and stalked her dreams every night, nights when she would toss and turn, and awaken flushed and aroused, as though her deceitful body was intent of betraying her even when she tried to rule it with her mind.

She had tried to throw herself into planning her planting schemes for autumn and had also accepted some of the commissions offered to her by Laura's friends. She could not help but think that the *Ton* would not be so quick to praise her designs when she was carted off to Newgate to hang, although given the fickle nature of fashion it might well be the case that were her past exposed and she were accused of Rashleigh's murder, her work might become even more of a novelty. During the day she drew up different designs and discussed ideas with Frank, tended her hothouses and weeded her borders and wished for once that the gardens at Peacock Cottage were not quite so perfect and might afford her something more to do, physical work so hard it exhausted her and tired out mind and body before the night came. But each night was the same, filled with hot, disturbing dreams and each morning she would waken before Jane brought the tea and would lie there feeling as tired as though she had barely slept at all.

The day of the Midsummer dance was another glorious summer's day and the air was heavy with the scent of roses and the light was just starting to fade from the western sky as Mari and Hester walked the short distance from Peacock Cottage to the barn where the dance was being held. Knowing what a crush the event could turn into, both of them had dressed in old cotton summer gowns, Hester in blue and Mari in pink.

Mari had fastened her hair into one thick, black plait that reached halfway down her back. It was not elegant but it was practical and this was no *Ton* ball.

True enough, the barn was already packed when they arrived. The high, haunting melody of the fiddle was clear over the sound of the wind in the beech trees, and when they reached the barn, there was a huge fire blazing in front of it and torchlight spilling out from the interior.

"You have done the village proud again, Mari," Hester said approvingly, looking at the piles of food on the trestle tables. "Cider from our own orchards! I wondered for what occasion you had been hoarding it. My, we shall all be three sheets to the wind before midnight!"

They made their way through the throng and into the barn's interior. The sheep that normally inhabited the place had been banished and all trace of them fortunately swept away. The air was sweet with the scent of the roses that Mari had grown especially to entwine around the rafters. They mingled with strands of ivy and their petals floated down gently to be crushed beneath the dancing feet and release more scent into the air.

"Laura's guests are already here," Hester whispered in Mari's ear. "I might have known Faye would decline and refuse to allow Lydia to come, too, but only look— I do believe that Charles has cried off, as well. How stuffy he can be!"

John Teague came upon them then and grabbed Hester's hand, pulling her into the dance without so much as a word. Mari laughed at Hester's blank look of astonishment as Teague whirled her into a jig. One of these days, she thought, Hester would see John Teague for what he really was; not the stalwart friend who was safe and reliable, nor the slightly dull peer who was a pillar of neighborhood society, but as a man who, she suspected, hid rather a lot of passion for Hester beneath his very proper exterior.

A moment later she forgot about Hester's *amours* as she felt a prickle between her shoulder blades and the goose bumps rose on the sensitive skin of the back of her neck. She turned slowly. Nick Falconer was standing in the shadow of the doorway, his eyes fixed on her with disconcerting concentration. He started to move toward her through the crowd, apparently oblivious of the people blocking his path and the greetings thrown to him by Teague and Hester. He moved purposefully, with the same deliberate intention as he had done on the night he had arrived in Peacock Oak, and when he reached Mari's side, she found she could neither speak nor move, so captured was she by the look in his eyes.

"Your hair…" he said. He raised one hand to touch the strands that had escaped her plait and curled around her face. His voice was gruff. "You look about eighteen."

Mari's awareness of him was intense. She smoothed the wayward wisps of hair back with a hand that trembled slightly and in doing so her fingers brushed his. The cool shivers of desire sparked in her blood instantly. The week of his absence had done nothing so much as increase the intensity of her feelings. This was like nothing she had ever experienced before. His slightest touch was incendiary.

"Good evening, Major Falconer," she said. Her

voice came out as a thread of a whisper. She saw the sudden flash in his eyes as he recollected who she was and where they were. His hand fell to his side and he took a step back.

"I beg your pardon, Mrs. Osborne," he said. "Just for a moment I forgot myself." He smiled, a slow, rueful smile, and her traitorous heart missed a beat. "It seems to be a surprisingly frequent experience when I am near you," he added. "Would you care to dance?"

Mari had not been intending to dance that night, least of all with Nick Falconer, but now she found that he had taken her hand and pulled her into the fray before a refusal could pass her lips. Generally, dancing made her feel uncomfortable. The proximity it gave to a man, the license it granted him to touch her, were things that she disliked and tried to avoid. Yet tonight, with Nick, the wild, magical mood of the music swept her up and she found her heart lifting with excitement.

They danced a jig and a country-dance where the rules were nothing like the decorous conventions of the ballroom. Farmers' lads were taking advantage to steal a kiss from their sweethearts, Hester was held very firmly in John Teague's arms and whenever Nick and Mari came together she was acutely conscious of his hands on her waist or her back, warm, intimate, holding her close. They stirred an insidious throb deep inside her body, an ache that was building and burning. She whirled and spun in the dance, giving herself up to the music and the spirit of the evening and following no more than her instincts in entrusting herself to Nick's hands. It felt dangerous, tantalizing, irresistible.

The wild beat of the fiddle softened and became

dreamy, and Nick pulled her closer, his arms going around her. She looked up into his face. At such close quarters she could see the lines around his eyes, laughter lines that deepened when he smiled, and the stubble that darkened his cheek and jaw. She resisted an insane urge to run her fingers over the hard planes of his face. She wanted to see them soften. Wanted him to soften for her. She felt warm and melting inside.

Nick bent his head and his lips grazed her neck. She drew back a little in surprise, trying to mask the sharp delight that had swept through her at his touch. Their bodies swayed and his thigh brushed the material of her gown, momentarily hard against her softness.

"I hear this dance is the fashion in the country," he said, and she saw the corner of his mouth lift in a smile.

"It is like no dance I've ever known before," Mari commented dryly.

He pressed his cheek fleetingly against her hair. "I know. I do not think there is a man here who is complaining, though."

The music rippled and swelled around them and the dancers linked hands and spun and swayed together, and once again the music caught Mari up and swept her away. She was conscious of nothing but Nick. He filled her whole awareness.

When the music finally stopped, there was a burst of appreciative applause from the dancers and Mari blinked as though released from a dream. Nick let her go gently and with reluctance. They were standing in a shadowy corner of the barn and he was smiling down at her. Something shifted inside her, a tug of feeling deep within. She felt shaken by the force of it. She knew that her smile had faltered and as he saw it, his own expression changed and focused, his eyes darkening, their expression masculine and primal.

"Mari—" he said, and her pulse raced to hear him say her name.

He cupped her face in his hands, his thumb brushing the fullness of her lower lip. "I believe I had something to prove," he said softly.

Mari shivered. "You should not have taken it as a challenge," she whispered.

"Maybe not. But I did."

His lips were about an inch from hers. He leaned closer.

"My turn, I think, eh, Falconer?" Lord Henry Cole's jovial tones broke the moment and they moved apart so hastily that Mari almost tripped. Lord Henry put a hand on her arm and she tensed, still shaken from that moment with Nick. She had almost kissed him again. She had almost let her defenses down. How could she have been so foolish, so careless, after resolving to keep him at arm's length?

"Thank you, my lord," she said, turning to Lord Henry, "but I think I will sit out the rest of the dance."

Lord Henry turned a nasty shade of red. "No need to spoilsport, m'dear. One little jig won't hurt."

"No, truly, I—"

Lord Henry's grip tightened on her. "Come along, m'dear. Tally ho!"

Mari's skin pricked, the icy shards of revulsion chilling her blood at the latent violence she felt in him. She broke away from him. "My lord, I do believe you are not listening to me," she said. "I have no desire to dance with you. I ask that you leave me alone."

"You heard Mrs. Osborne, Cole," Nick said. His

tone was pleasant on the surface but there was something ugly beneath. He had taken a step forward and she could feel him standing at her shoulder. "Don't make me reinforce her wishes," he added gently.

Mari watched as Lord Henry backed away, stammering his apologies. For a moment there had been an expression of the most primitive possession in Nick's eyes and it had shocked her to the core, but when he turned back to her he had banked it down and sketched a bow with careless courtesy. "If I can be of further service, Mrs. Osborne—"

"Much as I appreciate your support, Major Falconer," Mari said, her temper flaring, "I can take care of myself."

"That has been apparent all along, Mrs. Osborne," Nick said. He was smiling slightly. "A pity you did not have your fan in order to deliver another sharp stab in the ribs, as you did at the ball."

Mari could feel herself blushing. "You saw that? I thought you had."

"I did. And applauded the neatness of your maneuver." His dark eyes swept her face. "Fortunate for Lord Henry, perhaps, that you did not have a knife to hand."

The words dropped into frozen silence. Mari felt stricken. For the duration of the dance she had forgotten that Nick suspected her of Rashleigh's death. She had given herself up to the pure pleasure of the music and the night and his company. She had been swept by a raw, demanding passion for him and now she felt a fool to have been so misled, for clearly he had not forgotten for one moment. It was as she had suspected—his pursuit of her was no more than a means to an end, a means to seduce her into revealing the truth.

"If you think me so ruthless, Major Falconer, it surprises me that you risk dancing with me yourself," she said coldly. "But then, I suspect you are a man who likes to gamble with danger."

His fingers closed around her wrist and he held her still. "You are correct," he said, his voice so low only she could hear. "I do. Or rather, I like to gamble with you, Mrs. Osborne. It is very…stimulating."

She looked up into his eyes. The expression there was hot and hard and shockingly arousing. Mari's breath caught.

"And I will win," Nick added, his fingers tightening. "Make no mistake."

For a long moment they stared at one another and then Mari shook him off. "You can gamble all you wish," she said, "but you cannot beat me, Major Falconer." She dropped him the slightest of curtsies and walked away. And though she was shaking, she did not falter and she did not look back once.

NICK WAS FURIOUS with himself. Not once, but twice in one evening, he had forgotten his purpose and allowed Mari Osborne to get beneath his guard. When he had seen her he had been poleaxed by her demure appearance, just as he had that day by the river. She had looked almost like a young girl rather than a widow, worldly or otherwise. And later, when Henry Cole had blundered upon them in his callow way he had been taken by a possessive fury so potent that he would happily have hit the other man across the barn. That was not the calculated action of a man who was in control of his feelings.

He reached for a flagon of cider and drank deep,

tasting the bite of the apple and the rougher flavor of
the alcohol behind. It was inexcusable in him to neglect
his duty and even more disloyal to forget Anna—for
he *had* forgotten her for the entire time that he had been
dancing with Mari—and lose himself in the moment.
He felt confused and ashamed, as Anna's memory
seemed to slip from his mind even as he grasped after
it. He had never felt remotely possessive of her in the
way that he wanted Mari.

He watched Mari as she sat chatting with Laura
Cole, the two of them perched on a bale of hay now
like country girls at a fair. Lord Henry had found a bux-
om lass from the village to dance with who was a great
deal more forthcoming than Mari had been, and the two
of them were kissing one another with great abandon
in a dark corner of the barn. Hester and John Teague
were still locked in each other's arms, dancing in a
dreamy fashion that bore no relation to the music at all.

As the dance wore on Nick drank more of the cider
and noted that it had a kick like a mule. Hester and John
Teague had finally torn themselves from each other and
Teague had asked Mari to dance, which she did grace-
fully and with none of the abandon that Hester had
shown. Hester was, indeed, drinking almost as much
cider as the village stalwarts and her hair had come
loose from its ribbon and her face was flushed red. She
looked completely cast away.

No doubt Laura had seen the same signs that he had
for a moment later she had signaled that she was ready
to leave. Teague supported Hester out to the carriages
and Laura caught Mari's arm and beckoned to Nick to
come across. It seemed to him that Mari was anxious
to avoid his company, which was, he supposed, no

great surprise after the exchange between them earlier. She was tapping her foot impatiently on the ground and looked as though she would have walked away rather than be civil to him had Laura not been there.

"I am persuaded that you will not mind traveling back with Major Falconer, Mari," Laura said, smiling ingratiatingly at them both. "Hester and Lord Teague have taken the first carriage and I must speak with Mrs. Butler about the arrangements for the harvest festival, so I am sure that they will convey me home whilst we talk. Which leaves—"

"The two of us," Nick said, favoring Mari with a mocking bow. "Delighted, Mrs. Osborne."

He saw Mari flash him a less-than-friendly look that warned him to decline Laura's offer. He chose to ignore it. It was too bad if she did not want him in her carriage. Laura had offered him an unexpected opportunity and he was going to take it.

"There is Lord Henry Cole, as well," Laura said. "He could take you up, Mari, but he seems to have disappeared. He brought his curricle—so foolish at night! I think he must have been trying to impress someone but anyway, there is only room for one to drive with him."

"Well, how perfect," Mari said. She turned to Nick. "You may drive back with Lord Henry, Major Falconer."

"I think Lord Henry is too occupied to wish to tear himself away," Nick said. "Besides, that would leave you alone and unprotected in the carriage, Mrs. Osborne, and I could not be so lacking in chivalry as to do that."

"Pray do not concern yourself," Mari said sweetly. "As we discussed earlier, I am well able to take care of myself."

"I am sure you are," Nick conceded. "Nevertheless, I would like to drive with you, Mrs. Osborne."

"It is but a step," Laura said, looking from Mari's stormy face to Nick's sardonically smiling one. "You will be home in a moment, Mari."

"Then as it only a step," Mari said, "perhaps Major Falconer would care to walk. Or, even better, *I* will walk back."

"Alone?" Nick raised his brows with theatrical surprise. "Is that not rather unconventional, Mrs. Osborne, and you so *respectable* a lady?"

He thought Mari looked as though she would like to stab him there and then.

"It is not precisely respectable to be alone in a closed carriage with a gentleman," she pointed out, through her teeth. "Walking is the lesser of two evils, Major Falconer."

At that moment, Lord Henry Cole staggered toward them, waving his whip. "Tally ho, my little filly! Are you driving back with me?"

"Now I am definitely the lesser of two evils," Nick said, under his breath. "You do not want Lord Henry pursuing you all the way back to Peacock Cottage, Mrs. Osborne."

Laura waved a hand in relief. "Quite right, Major Falconer. That is settled then. Excuse me, please. Mrs. Butler will be waiting."

She hurried off and Nick offered Mari his arm. "Shall we?"

Mari placed her hand upon it with obvious reluctance and he smiled. "As the Duchess said, it is but a short journey home. Your purgatory will soon be over."

He led her out to the lane, handed her up into the

carriage and settled in the opposite corner. The coach set off with a slight jerk and he thought he heard Mari sigh, though whether with relief or tension he could not be sure. He watched the skipping moonlight cast her face in its pure white light. She looked young and innocent and he felt some emotion shift within him and deliberately pushed it away.

"Tell me," he said casually, "have you or the Duchess or Lady Hester ever been stopped on the road by the Glory Girls, Mrs. Osborne?"

He heard Mari catch her breath in the silence.

"The Glory Girls?" she said. She shifted slightly; cleared her throat. "Why do you ask, Major Falconer?"

"I understood," Nick said gently, "that they are very active in this area."

"I suppose so," Mari said, after a moment. He could detect nothing more than a casual indifference in her voice now, after that initial, betraying catch. "Do you have a particular interest in female miscreants, sir?"

Nick smiled. "Only some, Mrs. Osborne."

There was a slight pause. Again, as when he had questioned her that time in the beech woods, Mari let the silence hang. Again, Nick admired her nerve.

"Well," she said, after a moment, "the Glory Girls have never stopped any of us, Major Falconer, and I would not really expect it. Laura is very well regarded, as you have probably seen tonight, and Hester—" she paused, then laughed "—well, everyone loves Hester. It is hard not to."

"And they admire you for your charitable activities, I imagine," Nick said. "Before this week I had no idea that you were such a benefactor, Mrs. Osborne. Foodstuffs and medicines for the villagers, a feast for the Midsummer dance, almshouses for the homeless…"

In the moonlight he saw a faint smile light Mari's features. She was relaxing a little with the apparent innocuousness of his conversation, which was exactly what Nick wanted. What could not be gained by outright seduction could, perhaps, be achieved by a more subtle approach. The end result would be the same—the exposure of the truth between himself and Mari Osborne. He was almost certain that she had expected him to pounce on her in the carriage and he took great pleasure in confounding her expectations. For now…

"You should not forget, of course, that I am also responsible for appointing the schoolmistress of whom the Duke so heartily disapproves," she said.

"Yes," Nick said. He had heard that Charles did not support the village school. "I wonder why?"

"His grace does not agree with the education of women." There was a shade of scorn in Mari's voice now.

Nick felt surprised. He had not known that about Charles, but when he thought about it he supposed that it fitted his friend's rather conventional stance. "And you do?" he asked.

"Of course." Mari smoothed her skirts. "Girls have every right to the same standard of education that is given to boys, Major Falconer."

"You speak with feeling," Nick said. "Perhaps," he added, "you have experience of geometry and astronomy and mathematics? Would you wish that tedium on the fellow members of your sex?"

Mari laughed unexpectedly, a low, throaty chuckle that caught at his senses. "I believe that females should

have an equal right to be bored to death by such subjects as males do."

"Did you experience that masculine education yourself?"

He felt the chill in the carriage at once, an arctic cold
that seemed to sweep right through her and leave her
rigid and frozen. Whether it was because he had
touched on something painful to her or simply because
he was prying into her past, he was not sure, but he
sensed immediately that she had no wish to pursue the
conversation further.

"I did not," her voice was low now, forbidding further discussion. "I had a very conventional upbring-
ing."

Still he persisted. "All the feminine arts?"

"Naturally."

"But no riding lessons."

He thought that she was almost betrayed into a smile
at that. "No riding lessons," she agreed. "I have never
had any talent for it at all."

"I could teach you," Nick said. "I like a challenge."

"So I have observed." She fidgeted a little. "Major
Falconer, you know I would be foolish in the extreme
to accept your offer."

"How so?" Nick raised his brows. "I ride well and
I am a good teacher."

Mari turned her head so that only her profile, clear-
cut in the moonlight, was visible to him. "You are being
deliberately slow, Major Falconer," she said. "I am not
minded to accept any of the offers that you make to me."

Nick laughed. "A pity," he said. "I should apologize,
I think, Mrs. Osborne. It is simply that you…tempt me
beyond control."

It was close to the truth, close enough to make him uncomfortable, and he could see that it troubled her, too, because he was sure that she felt the same. He acted then, quite deliberately and ruthlessly, to take advantage of her confusion and prove to himself that he was still in command of his desires.

"Mari—" He moved until he was beside her on the seat and touched her cheek, feeling the silken smoothness of her skin beneath his fingers. Once again he heard her catch her breath. She did not draw away.

"This is…" Her words were barely more than a whisper. "I do not understand why I feel like this… It is all wrong…"

Nick hesitated, wanting to ask her why but sensing it was too soon. If he pressed her too hard, too quickly, she would withdraw from him and he would learn nothing. This time he had to go very slowly if he was to trap her into confiding in him.

He rubbed his thumb experimentally along the line of her jaw and felt the instinctive way in which she turned her head into his touch, pressing closer. He slipped his hand around to her nape, beneath the heavy plait, and applied the tiniest amount of pressure to bring her lips closer to his. He could hear the quickness of her breathing and feel the sweet, scented warmth of her. His senses started to reel and he clamped down mercilessly on his own needs and concentrated on Mari, bringing his mouth gently down on hers.

Her lips softened beneath his and she gave a little sigh, opening her mouth to the subtle but relentless demand of his. For a moment Nick's mind was clear, calculating, and then he sank inexorably, inescapably, into a sensual excitement so intense that it destroyed coherent thought. He kissed her with a fierce passion, plundering her mouth until it was swollen and tender from the pressure of his. He rained little kisses over her cheeks and throat and exulted in the soft sounds of surrender that they drew from her.

His mouth returned to hers, hot and insistent, and his hand slid up to cup her breast. He felt her melt in his arms, sweet and urgent, and then suddenly the carriage slewed across the road and pulled to an abrupt halt, and they almost tumbled straight off the seat and onto the floor.

"We are the Glory Girls! Stand and deliver!"

The command came out of the darkness and Nick heard Mari give a gasp, this time, he thought, of shock and fear. There was an ominous thud and then the door swung open abruptly. In the aperture stood four horsemen, all masked and cloaked.

Nick looked at Mari and was surprised to see on her face an expression of almost comical amazement, which was followed swiftly by anger and then puzzlement, before she wiped her face clear of any emotion at all. He had no time to think about her reaction, though, because the leader of the gang brought her horse around in an ostentatious but beautifully controlled circle in front of them. It was a pitch-black stallion that was snorting and trying to rear. It was not, Nick noted, the bay with the white flash that he and Anstruther had seen at Half Moon House a few nights back. The Glory Girls had evidently changed their horses.

Nick sent up a quick prayer that Hester Berry—and he was certain that it had to be Hester, for who else could ride as well as she and have the sheer nerve to carry off the role of the notorious Glory—had not consumed such vast quantities of cider at the dance that she lost control of the stallion. She had only one hand on the reins because the other held a wicked-looking silver pistol that gleamed in the moonlight. He did not even dare wonder what might happen if she was half cut and could not fire straight.

The leader reined in before the open door of the carriage and addressed them.

"We are the Glory Girls! We are here to demand recompense for the poor! You—" the pistol moved toward Mari "—I'll take that pretty little gold chain you have around your neck, madam, in payment for *your* misdeeds."

The voice was very unlike Hester's husky drawl. The woman put out a gloved hand and pulled the chain from Mari's throat, breaking it. Nick heard Mari catch her breath and saw a thin line of blood trickle down her neck where the links of the chain had snapped and cut her skin. For the first time he felt a flicker of doubt that this was a pretence, least of all one that Mari had conspired with.

"And you—" The woman's voice hardened as she turned to Nick and he had the sudden, unnerving feeling that she genuinely wished to shoot him where he sat. "Hand over your money."

"I have none with me," Nick said. "We have been to the village dance. We carry no valuables."

Glory looked down at him. "The convention," she said, and he had the impression that she was smiling, "is your money or your life. Which do you wish to offer?"

"It'll have to be my life, then," Nick said, "as I have no money."

Glory wheeled the horse around again. "Very well," she said indifferently. "Get out of the coach, both of you." She looked at Nick. "You first. No tricks."

Nick had thought that had she made Mari descend first, he might have tried something, tried to unseat one of the other riders, perhaps, who sat in a silent, watchful circle around the coach. Now he did not have that option. He was becoming less certain by the minute that this was a charade presented with Mari's complicity. The tension he could feel in her, the way that Glory had taken the necklace from her throat, the whole tone of the encounter, seemed wrong. There was something else here other than a performance played out simply for his benefit.

Glory's pistol menaced him and he jumped down onto the road and waited as one of the girls came forward and tied his hands roughly—very roughly indeed, they certainly seemed to bear a grudge—behind his back. The rope cut into his wrists and Nick winced. She was strong, whoever she was, and a disconcerting instinct told him that for all her slightness of figure, this "girl" was actually a man. Certainly she did not smell like a woman and when she dropped the rope at one point and bent down to pick it up, he heard her swear in language that would not have shamed an army trooper.

"Kneel down," his captor barked.

It was undignified but the man was holding a pistol and Nick had always been a pragmatist. He knew he would have to wait his chance to fight back, so he obeyed. For now. Glory rode up to him, put one booted foot against his chest and forced him farther down on his knees. He noted that she had very big feet.

"I'll speed you on your way to your maker in a moment," she said, "and take pleasure in it." She turned back to the carriage. "You," she said to Mari. "Get out! I want you to watch."

Nick waited. He could not move because the man who had tied him up had his pistol cocked by his ear. All his senses were on alert, waiting and watching for the moment that he could strike back and disarm them.

He saw Mari gather her skirts in one hand and jump down from the coach to stand on the road in the moonlight. Nick was watching very carefully now. What he had thought at first was a fine theatrical performance was turning into something far darker.

"Tie her up," Glory said, and Nick felt the shock slam through him. He had not expected that. The suspicious part of him, the cynical part, had still thought it might all be a charade. Now he knew it could not be. Mari could not be complicit with this. His mind started to race. How to effect an escape, how to end this, how to help Mari… He moved and immediately his captor jabbed the muzzle of the pistol into his neck with a growled, "Keep still!"

"Stop!" Mari said, and Nick's attention snapped back to her. "If you want to tie me up, you'll have to shoot me first." She had taken a step backward so that her back was against the panels of the carriage and she was looking up at Glory defiantly in the moonlight. "I don't like being told what to do," she said, very quietly.

Nick felt the pistol that was next to his ear jerk as the man who held it moved in surprise. So they had not expected resistance. He waited, tensed. Glory turned the horse again and brought it close in to Mari's body.

"Just do what we say, darling," she said softly.

"No," Mari said. "I won't." She took a deep breath. "Go now," she said. "You've taken my necklace. That's enough. Don't try and tie me up. I don't want to have to kill you."

Glory threw back her head and gave a peal of laughter. "*You* shoot *me?* You'd shoot Glory?"

"Yes," Mari said. There was a pistol in her hand now and Nick suddenly remembered Charles Cole saying that he kept firearms in all his carriages against the danger of attack by footpads or highwaymen. She must have taken it before she jumped down and hidden it in her skirts. He wondered if she knew how to use it.

"I'd shoot without hesitation," Mari was saying. "And I think you would find that rather difficult to explain."

Nick didn't wait to see whether she would make good her claim. Taking his captor by surprise he twisted around and felled the man with a well-aimed kick to the back of the legs. He crumpled at his feet with another most unladylike curse. Hampered as he was by his bound hands, Nick hurled himself toward the nearest horsewoman in an attempt to unseat her. The horse reared as she tightened her grip on the reins and he threw himself away from the flailing hooves. A shot sounded close by. The coach horses, terrified, set off down the road in a mad cacophony of noise with the coachman shouting as he tried to regain control. Nick heard Glory calling to the others and the man he felled scrambled up and into his saddle and then they were gone in a wild clatter of hooves, the moonlight shining brightly and briefly on their flying cloaks before the beech wood swallowed them up and the sound of the horses died away to quiet.

Mari hurried across to him. He could feel her quick breath against his cheek, the warmth of her body where it pressed against his and the tremor in her hands as she struggled with the knots that bound him.

"You're not hurt?" he said urgently.

"No." Her voice was almost steady but her trembling betrayed her reaction. "I fired into the ground. I was afraid I would hit someone if I aimed at them."

"That," Nick said dryly, "is rather the point of carrying a firearm."

"I know." The catch in her voice was halfway between laughter and tears. "But I have never shot anyone before and I did not want to start tonight."

Nick thought of the messy way in which Rashleigh had been stabbed and left dying in the street. Would Mari Osborne have been any better at stabbing a man to death than shooting one? After this evening's encounter he rather thought not. It was too immediate and for all her defiance, she did not appear to have the cold-blooded experience to carry it off. Something shifted inside him, something that felt oddly like tenderness for her.

"You were very brave," he said.

She made no reply. She was still grappling with his bonds and did not appear to be making much progress. "I cannot undo these knots," she said. There was distress in her voice now, something close to tears. "They have tied you so tightly!"

"I don't think they liked me very much," Nick said wryly.

The rope caught, vibrated with tension and dug more sharply into his wrists, and he smothered a gasp of pain.

"I am sorry." Mari sounded really shaken now. "I am doing my best—"

"You are doing fine." Nick kept his voice steady. He could hear the raggedness in hers, the catch in her breathing. Something was distressing her greatly, something more than the mere fact that he had been tied brutally tightly. The memory of her reaction to the mention of the hunt came into his mind and the transparent whiteness of her face as she had looked inward, as though on something truly terrifying. She was reacting in the same way now, as though it was not what was happening in the present that disturbed her but something that she could remember, something unbearable.

"Just keep calm," he said. "You are doing very well."

The shaking in her hands eased a little and the rope came loose at last. Nick stretched the cramped muscles of his shoulders with relief. "Ah, that's better." He rubbed firmly at his wrists to restore the circulation to his arms. The wheals left by the rope stung him and showed raw and dark in the moonlight.

Mari had not moved. She was holding the rope loose in her hand but she was staring at the marks on his wrists, a blank look on her face, as though she were in shock. He took her hands in his gently and felt the tiny tremors that still racked her body. He was startled to discover that though the night was warm, her fingers were as cold as though it were winter.

"Everything is fine," he repeated.

"No, it isn't!" Suddenly she came alive beneath his

hands, vibrant with anger. "It is *not* fine! They tied you up. They hurt you!"

He was shaken by the strength of her distress and her anger. "I have come to no harm."

She shook her head and for a moment he thought he saw the glimmer of tears in her eyes in the moonlight. She wrapped her arms around herself as though for comfort. He could see the way she shook.

"I can't bear it. I can't bear what they did." Her voice broke on the words.

He took a step forward and caught her gently by the upper arms.

"Mari," he said, "tell me what is wrong."

Her head was turned aside as though she was ashamed for him to see her distress. He stroked her arms very gently, drawing her a little closer to him. Her body was tense and she stood rigid before him, braced like a bow, resisting his attempts at comfort, shutting him out.

"You don't understand," she said, and there was despair in her voice. She sounded broken.

"Then explain to me," Nick said. "Tell me so I can help you."

He saw hope flare in her eyes for a moment and felt the excitement quicken his blood. She was going to talk to him. She was actually going to confide at last. He was so close to hearing the truth....

Then she shook her head. He could feel her withdrawing from him.

"I cannot," she said. She sounded wretched. "I am sorry... I truly wish..." She shook her head. "No, I cannot."

The frustration slammed through Nick to have been

so close and yet still denied. He took a step toward her but then there was a shout from farther down the road and a moment later the coachman was puffing up the hill toward them, a light in his hand. John Teague was at his shoulder.

"Falconer! Mrs. Osborne!" Teague's face was drawn and the strain showed in his eyes. "What has happened? I am but this moment returned from taking Lady Hester back to Peacock Cottage—" He broke off as he saw the marks on Nick's wrists. "What the devil? Are you injured, Falconer?"

"Nothing but a scratch," Nick said. He spoke to Teague but looked directly at Mari. "It was the Glory Girls, Teague."

"The Glories?" Teague looked thoroughly confused. Nick saw him glance at Mari, who had been standing silently, head bent. "But surely… I mean… The Glories? Tonight?"

"Indeed," Nick said grimly. "They robbed us."

"Robbery?" Teague repeated. There was an odd tone in his voice. "The Glory Girls are avenging angels, Falconer, not highwaymen."

"I thought," Nick said, "that you said they relieved you of your purse only a few weeks before I came to Yorkshire?"

He felt rather than saw Mari turn slightly to look at John Teague, but when he glanced back at her, her face was quite expressionless. It was enough, though. He knew that Teague had in all probability lied about the robbery for the same reason that he had tried to misdirect his inquiries all along, to protect Hester Berry. And by the same token he knew that both Teague and Mari knew that the gang that had held them up that night must indeed be the Glory Girls and they were both covering up for them. He remembered the look on Mari's face when the coach had been stopped; the surprise, puzzlement and fear in her eyes. She had not been complicit in the attack but as soon as it had happened she had realized what the Glory Girls were doing. She might not ride with them but as he had suspected, she was deeply embroiled in their activities.

The only thing that he could not understand was the violence of Mari's reaction when she had freed him from his bonds. It had not been feigned and it argued deep distress. Even now her fingers were straying to the cut on her neck where the blood had dried in a thin smear and he could see that she trembled slightly.

"We must get Mrs. Osborne home, Teague," he said abruptly. "She has taken some hurt. And I think any questions must wait until the morrow."

Mari's head came up and she met his eyes and he knew she had read the unspoken threat in his words. Tomorrow, he thought, he would challenge her about all the secrets that lay between them. It was time to bring the deception to an end.

"Hester!" Mari was so angry that she marched straight into Hester's bedroom with barely a knock. She stopped at the sight of her friend reclining lazily in her bed, eating the remains of a plate of bonbons. "I want to talk to you!" she added wrathfully. "What the devil do you think you were doing? You were supposed to be over at Starbotton, knocking down Sampson's enclosures, not playing at highwaymen with me and Major Falconer!"

"I know," Hester said, with her mouth full. "We

thought it would be so much more effective to stop you and Major Falconer on the road, because you would not know about it and would therefore seem completely innocent—"

"Innocent! Effective!" Mari was so furious she could barely speak. "First you trick me and then you point a pistol at me! I almost shot you for that!"

"Not me," Hester said. "Laura."

That stopped Mari in her tracks. "*Laura?* You mean, that it was Laura who was acting the part of Glory? Dear God, I almost shot the Duchess of Cole!"

"You were magnificent," Hester said admiringly. "We never imagined that you would play your part so well. And if you did not recognize Laura as Glory then it is certain that no one else will do."

"Well," Mari said furiously, when she had got her breath back, "I am glad that *you* are so pleased with your evening's work!"

Hester darted a quick look over her shoulder. "Keep your voice down, Mari! Jane will hear you. And besides I have the headache."

"Jane is in the kitchen drawing me a bath and making me some supper," Mari said, "and you should not have drunk so much tonight. As it is I am surprised that you did not fall off your horse under the influence. Oh, Hes—" her tone changed "—of all the crack-brained, idiotic, addle-pated, downright foolish ideas!"

"But did it work?" Hester inquired, scooping up the last sprinkling of crumbs from her plate. "I was sure that if the Glories held up the two of you together, Major Falconer would see once and for all that you simply could *not* have any connection to Glory yourself and he might leave you alone. That was why Laura arranged it so that you would be in the carriage with him."

"Astound me," Mari said crossly. "I had worked that one out for myself."

"Of course," Hester said, eyeing her with slight trepidation. "Of course you had. And we thought that if we warned Major Falconer off, as well, he might go back to London and give up the hunt for the Glory Girls."

"A spectacularly bad idea," Mari said, "since your so-called warning will have made him all the more determined to track them—you!—down! Aargh!" She sat down on the bed regardless of the mud and sheep droppings clinging to her skirts. "What did I tell you? Do not draw attention to yourself, do not do anything reckless, do *not* attempt to warn Major Falconer away…."

"I know," Hester said. "You are the only sensible one amongst us."

"I begin to think so," Mari said. "I thought that Laura at least had some sense but it appears she has an appetite for self-destruction equal only to your own."

"She is angry with Charles," Hester said apologetically.

"So this is the way that she punishes him? By trying to get caught?"

"Well, it would be one way of getting him to notice her," Hester said.

Mari made an aggravated noise and jumped to her feet. "He will notice her well enough when she is swinging on a gibbet!" She ran a hand over her hair. "Oh, Hester, you play at this with no idea what you are doing!" The anger went out of her to be replaced by a terrible weariness. "I was terrified this evening," she said, trying to make Hester understand. "*You* terrified me. All of you. And as for Major Falconer…" She stopped. "Lenny tied him too tightly, Hes. He really hurt him."

"He doesn't like him," Hester said. "He feels protective of you, Mari, of all of us." She bit her lip. "I am sorry about your necklace. Laura did not mean to hurt you. She was very upset. But we had to make it convincing, you see. I will buy you another, I swear—"

Mari shook her head. "Don't. Don't say that, as though it will put all to rights. You have no idea." She put a hand to her head. "What have I done, Hes? I should never have started this. I've created a monster and it has to be stopped."

Hester pushed the empty plate aside and scrambled down the bed. "I don't understand! The Glory Girls work for good! We never hurt anyone except in their pride or their pocket." She glanced at Mari's face. "Oh, I know tonight was different but we never meant to hurt you! How can you even think it?"

"Of course I do not believe you would deliberately have hurt me," Mari said. Her mind was full of Nick Falconer, of the marks on his wrists and the searing, terrible memories they had conjured in her mind, memories that played out in her nightmares. The violence with which she had reacted to seeing Nick's injuries had frightened her. Even now she felt sick to think of it, sick to think of Nick being hurt. Her reaction disturbed her and she could not even begin to start explaining it to Hester.

"What we do is wrong, Hes," she said slowly. "I am as much to blame as those of you who ride. I see that

now. We treated it lightly, but tonight I was so frightened." She walked wearily to the door. "I am too tired
to talk about this now. I need to sleep. No…" She saw
that Hester was going to say something placating.
"Pray do not speak to me until I have calmed down or
I might be inclined to turn you in myself. Especially
as the reward has gone up to fifty pounds!"

She paused with her hand on the doorjamb. "When
he came to find us, John Teague said that he had only
just left you here, Hes. Was that a lie?"

Hester's eyes were very bright. "John? Did he say
that? Bless him for covering up for us!"

"It means," Mari said patiently, "that he knows what
we are about. And apparently he also told Major Falconer
that the Glory Girls had robbed him a few weeks back."

Hester raised her brows. "Did he so? He is very
loyal. He will not give us away."

"I sometimes wonder," Mari said crushingly,
"whether you deserve his loyalty, Hes. Good night."

She went out and made her way along the landing
to her own room. Jane had filled a tub with water
scented with rose petals. With a little sigh, Mari slipped
off the pink gown and her underclothes, and slid into
the warm water. It was blissfully sweet smelling and
relaxing. Slowly her tight muscles started to ease and
the painful ache of fear and grief in her stomach was
soothed away. The cut on her neck throbbed a little and
she rubbed it absentmindedly.

She had not told Hester a quarter of her feelings. She
had not told her that when they had threatened to tie
her up the thought of being constrained had reminded
her too vividly of the way that Rashleigh had shackled
her to his coach, and brought back every horrible, ter-

rifying detail of her nightmares. She had not told Hester that when she had seen the wheals on Nick Falconer's wrists, she had felt physically sick, trapped in the memory of a past that she could not escape. All her defenses had been stripped away to the point that she had nearly, so very nearly, told Nick everything. And if John Teague had not arrived when he had, she was fairly certain that Nick would have demanded the truth from her anyway and she would not have been able to resist. She thought of the quiet calmness of Nick's voice as he had soothed her panic, the gentleness in his hands as he had held her, and she shivered. She had felt doubly a fraud as she had worked to release him, guilty for her complicity in the Glory Girls activities even though she had not known of this particular attack, and so distressed at what they had done to him that she could barely keep calm enough to free him. When he had praised her for her courage, her knowledge of her own cowardice in knowing the truth and not telling him had cut her deeply.

She slid deeper under the water, scrubbing at her body as though to rid it of the stains on her mind. It only seemed to make matters worse that before the attack she had been in Nick's arms, responding so openly and so urgently to his desire. They were locked so tight in a tangle of her own making now that she was not sure she could ever unravel it.

She heard Hester go down the stairs and knew she must be heading for Half Moon House, but she did not move to stop her.

She scoured herself until she was almost raw and the water was cold, and only then did she get out of the bath and curl up in her bed and try to sleep.

CHAPTER NINE

Pink—Ardent love

HESTER WAS UPSET. She felt that she had failed her friends. She knew that the Glory Girls had upset Mari by their attack in ways that she could hardly understand. She had talked about it with Laura in advance and the two of them had thought that Mari would probably be angry, but Hester had not anticipated this reaction, this distress. And she knew that Mari had not fully confided her feelings in her although she was hurting. There was a wedge between them now.

Then there was John Teague, so loyal, so devoted. He had covered up for her because he cared about her, despite the casual carelessness with which she treated him. He was too good for her, too honorable, too gentlemanly. She did not deserve Mari's friendship and she knew she certainly did not deserve John Teague's love. She felt miserable at her own behavior and there was only one thing to do to banish her loneliness and the blue devils. Still half drunk, she strode into the taproom at Half Moon House and saw all the grooms and farmhands that had been at the dance. They were watching her and she felt a frisson of excitement and lust run through her. She could use one of these eager men to help her forget her misery. It was all she was good for.

"You," she said carelessly, pointing at a young laborer whom she had seen at the inn the week before. He looked about nineteen, well built and muscular with callused hands. Hester's body shivered in anticipation of those hands touching her. "Come with me," she said.

There was a ragged cheer from around the taproom and someone slapped the lad on the back. He downed his pint in one gulp and grinned as the ale dripped down his chin and stained his tunic. Hester did not care. The rougher the better, as far as she was concerned.

She was already halfway up the stairs as he started to follow her. Hester never waited for her lovers, never looked back in case she thought about what she was doing and hesitated. She went into the bedchamber and stood by the window, her back turned, tapping her fingers on the wall.

He seemed to be a long time following her. There was a crash downstairs, followed by a swell of noise, then, finally, his footfalls on the stairs. He sounded eager now, taking the steps two at a time. Hester heard the door close, the key turn in the lock and the creak of the bedsprings beneath his weight.

"You took your time," she said, without bothering to turn around.

"Good evening, Hester," John Teague said. "As you did not care for my style of wooing, I thought we would do this your way."

"TALK TO ME," Teague said. He was propped on one elbow beside Hester on the bed and was trailing a finger down her spine in a most distracting way. Hester made a little, soft noise of surrender and sheer exhaustion and rolled over to look at him from beneath half-lowered lids. Her body felt full and heavy, utterly sated and yet deliciously alive.

"You didn't want to talk before," she said teasingly.

Teague leaned over and kissed her, and his hand came up to cup her breast, his touch sending endless quivers of feeling along her nerves.

"No," he murmured against her mouth, "and truth to tell I do not want to talk now but I do want to get you away from this place."

He got up and gathered his clothes together whilst Hester lay still and watched him. The pleasure was draining from her now and she had a horrible feeling that everything was about to go back to as it had been before, and all the exciting, intimate and thoroughly indecent things they had just done to one another would be stifled under layers of civilization and propriety.

"I don't want—" she started to say, but he turned toward her and interrupted her for the first time in their entire acquaintance.

"This time it is more a question of what I want than what you want, Hester," he said.

Hester was so taken aback that she did not say anything else and a second later Teague had picked up her cloak, stripped the bedclothes from her, wrapped her up and scooped her up in his arms. She tried to struggle but as soon as she did the cloak fell open, revealing her nakedness.

"Put me down!" She was outraged at his high-handedness. "How *dare* you?"

"I dare many things," Teague said calmly, "as you are about to discover. I have had enough of your willfulness." He freed a hand briefly to unlock the chamber door then pinioned her tightly, her arms around her sides, as he carried her downstairs.

"Lie still," he said in her ear, "or the entire taproom will see you nude and despite your dalliances with half the men here, I do not think that would please you."

Hester burned with mortification. He knew all about the men, all about her lovers. He knew everything.

There was absolute quiet as he carried her through the bar. A pin dropping would have sounded loud in the silence. Looking around, Hester saw the avid faces of the farmhands and grooms, and the black eye sported by her original choice of lover that evening. Her gaze moved on to take in Josie's appalled expression and she closed her eyes and almost groaned aloud at the embarrassment of it all. Previously she had pretended that she did not care. Now she could pretend no longer.

Teague said not one word, but kicked the outer door open and then Hester felt the cool night air against her skin as she was tumbled unceremoniously into his carriage and he gave the coachman the order for home.

The short journey was accomplished in absolute silence and, when they reached Starbotton Hall, Teague simply picked her up again, carried her up the stairs and threw her down on his bed, where she rolled out of the cloak and lay sprawled in naked abandonment, staring up at him. By now, Hester was absolutely furious with him for humiliating her in the tavern and in front of his servants. She struggled to her feet, shrugging off the cloak, gloriously unconcerned about her nudity. She turned on Teague, trying to kick him and scratch his face.

"How dare you treat me like this? How dare you?"

"You're becoming repetitive, my love," Teague said, an undertone of amusement in his voice. "It was about time that someone did dare. You are spoiled and your behavior is a disgrace."

He put out a negligent hand and caught Hester by the wrist, pulling hard so that she tumbled down onto the bed with him and across his knee. A second later she felt his free hand come down across her bare buttocks.

Her skin stinging and her pride, too, Hester tried to wriggle to be free of that tormenting hand, which was now smoothing in a circular motion over her bottom and bringing with it such a sweet, scalding heat. She struggled against him and against the insidious pleasure she was feeling, but Teague held her down with one hand in the small of her back and spanked her again, a second, third and fourth blow. Hester's flesh started to grow pink and warm and the tormenting need she felt in the pit of her stomach made her want to groan aloud. When he slid his fingers between her legs and felt the moist core of her, Hester could not hold back a moan of mingled anger and need.

"You bastard!"

Her head spun as the spanking started again, peppering her tender flesh with burning heat. She struggled against his restraint, all the time growing more and more inflamed with lust, and at last succeeded in rising to her knees on the bed. All she could think of, all she wanted, was to assuage the ache of her body with his. She was furiously angry and unbearably aroused. She thought she would probably die if she could not have him. She grabbed the waistband of his breeches and ripped it open, her fingers seeking and finding his iron-hard erection and drawing an answering groan from him at last. She straddled him and ground down on him, swift and hard, her moan of ecstasy smothered by his kiss, matching his movements, driving them both on, until they both exploded in mutual climax.

They lay breathing fast and entangled together in the bedclothes until Hester turned on one side to face him.

"For an old man," she said, a provocative smile curving her lips, "you do quite well."

This time when he took her, her screams of pleasure echoed from the quiet walls of her old home.

NICK FALCONER was not asleep. He lay on his bed, hands behind his head, staring into the darkness.

When he had arrived back at Cole Court there had been a letter from Dexter Anstruther awaiting him. Nick had taken it up to the privacy of his room, where he had crossed to the desk, sat down and opened it at once. Strangely he had felt a pang of anxiety as he had unfolded it, as though a part of him did not want to know the information it contained. His reaction, he knew, was in some way tied up with the complicated feelings Mari Osborne had aroused in him that night. Not the lust and the desire, but the admiration he had had for her courage, the protectiveness her vulnerability had produced in him. He had respected her bravery and had been moved by her distress, and now his feelings were utterly confused for he *knew* she must have some connection to the Glory Girls and yet her fear and her pain had not been feigned.

With a sigh he had turned his attention to the letter. After the initial pleasantries, Anstruther got straight down to business:

I can find no one of the name of either Phileas or
Phineas Osborne in the Truro region between the
dates you have given, nor can I find any record
of Mr. Osborne's parentage or marriage. My first
guess would be that either the information we
have relating to Mr. Osborne is inaccurate and I
am searching for him in the wrong place, or al-
ternatively, that he did not exist at all. There is no
record of a Mrs. Marina Osborne in either Cornwall or elsewhere before 1800, when she purchased the property in Peacock Oak, Yorkshire.
She seems to have appeared from nowhere. In
cases similar to this that I have investigated, the
subject has usually adopted a false name and
persona under which they are now living and it
is impossible to trace their history prior to that
point unless you know their previous identity.
The reason for the adoption of a new identity is
usually either a criminal one or, in some cases,
occurs where a woman has had a child out of
wedlock, or wishes to conceal her identity as a
man's former mistress....

Nick had sat back in the chair, the letter clasped
loosely in his hand. He was not shocked. He was not even
very surprised. He had realized that he had already known
what Anstruther had told him, or at the least suspected it,
but now he wished that it were not true. Marina Osborne
was a liar, a charlatan and very probably a criminal.

He had turned back to the letter to blot out his feelings. There was little more of import, apart from a
brief paragraph at the end.

Lord Hawkesbury asks me to tell you that he has released into your possession all the papers belonging to your late cousin Rashleigh. He has read through them all for the purposes of the current investigation but can find no information that is germane to our inquiries and so has arranged for them to be sent to the house in Eaton Square.

Nick had winced to think of his great-uncle's displeasure when his London house became cluttered with Robert Rashleigh's collection of French pornography. He supposed that at some point he should sort through his inheritance from Rashleigh and set matters in order. The prospect was not an enticing one but it had to be done.

Now, several hours later, Nick was lying awake and thinking of Mari Osborne. Tomorrow, he resolved, he would confront her with her false identity. He would tell her that he had proof she was an impostor. He would break her and make her tell him the truth about Rashleigh's murder and the Glory Girls.

On impulse he went across to the desk and took from the drawer the little portrait of Anna in the silver locket that he carried with him everywhere. The shape of it was so familiar in his hand and the silver engraving worn by his touch. He snapped it open and looked down on her face, as he had done so many times before. Usually it comforted him. Tonight it did not. Never had Anna felt so distant from him, so lost.

He reminded himself that this was what he had wanted from the first. He had resolved to get close to Mari, to seduce her into trusting him or at the very least telling him what he wished to know. Tonight he had almost succeeded in that aim. Tomorrow would be the culmination of his plans. He had been every bit as calculated and ruthless as he had intended, and if a part of him was ashamed at that behavior he had only to remind himself that he was doing this in the interests of justice. Now at last, with the truth revealed between them, his troubling desire for Mari Osborne might be laid to rest when she was revealed as a criminal and very possibly a murderer.

He should feel glad, because this was exactly what he had wanted.

Even so, it was a long time before he slept.

LAURA WAS NOT SURE what had woken her that night. For a moment she lay still, her mind drowsy and confused by sleep. Then the sound came again, a soft scraping noise from her dressing room next door and, surely, a muffled curse. Laura slid from the bed and tiptoed across to the door, opening it a crack and peering out.

The moonlight filtered through a gap in the curtains but warmer and stronger was the light from the candle on the side table. It illuminated the walls with their ancestral portraits and it also illuminated her husband, who appeared to be rifling through the contents of the chest that contained her petticoats and drawers. For a moment Laura thought she had discovered the cause of Charles's indifference to her—his hands were full of feminine underwear, after all—but then she realized that the focus of his search was not her clothing but her jewel box, which was at the bottom of the chest. Not realizing that she was there, he had pounced on the box with an exclamation of satisfaction and was now busy rummaging through the contents. The candlelight glinted on the fine diamond necklace that had been one of her father's wedding presents to her.

Laura found her voice. "What on earth are you doing, Charles?"

Charles jumped as though he had been bitten and in that moment Laura realized it was the first time in their marriage that she had ever questioned him about anything. He looked confused, taken aback and then rather alarmed at her tone.

"Hello, old girl. I was simply looking…" His voice trailed away as he looked down at the jewelry in his hands.

Charles, Laura thought, with some pity, was not a man who could think of good excuses quickly.

"Perhaps," she suggested, "you wanted to check if I kept my jewelry safely locked away?"

"Yes!" Charles grasped at this excuse desperately. "Should be in the bank, of course. That would be much better."

"Of course," Laura said politely. "But then you could not take the pieces that you needed, Charles. I had wondered where my silver locket had gone, and my pearl earrings. I would have accused my maid, but I know her to be entirely trustworthy."

Charles drooped. "Oh, Lord. I thought you wouldn't notice, old girl. Thought you wouldn't mind."

"You thought I would not mind that you were pilfering my grandmother's heirlooms?" Laura said, raising her brows. The anger was licking along her veins now and it felt surprisingly good. "Why on earth would you think that, Charles? Because I never made a fuss before?"

Charles shifted from one foot to another. He looked utterly discomfited, and Laura felt a sudden rush of sympathy for him. He had married an aristocrat he had thought was his equal in cold blue blood and after ten years she was turning into an unpredictable woman whose feelings and emotions were dangerously close to the surface. He was watching her out of the corner of his eye, as he would a horse of uncertain temperament.

"Steady on, Laura," he said, replacing the necklace in the box and closing the chest rather gingerly. "No harm done."

"How much do you owe, Charles?" Laura asked. Certain matters were clicking into place in her mind now; her husband's frequent absences in Town, his refusal to allow her to join him, the faded patch on the wall where a rather fine portrait by Hogarth had hung… He could scarce gamble away his inheritance in Skipton without someone noticing, but in London there were so many more opportunities.

"How much," she repeated, and he looked away shiftily.

"Forty," he muttered.

"Forty *thousand?*" Mentally Laura doubled it. That meant that he had gambled away his inheritance and her dowry into the bargain. The flicker of anger within her grew, expanded, started to blaze. Not that he needed anything to leave to his heirs since he had not begotten any, but how long would it be before word got around about his financial troubles? Perhaps, Laura thought, word was already out in London and that was another reason why he did not want her there.

"You had better take my grandmother's rubies," she

said. "Those are worth about forty thousand. They should stave your creditors off for a little while."

Charles blinked at her. "Take the rubies? I can't do that, old girl!"

Laura knew that he would have taken them anyway in the end, even if he deluded himself that he would not. The pictures would have gone from the walls, the jewels from her case; even the furniture might have started to disappear. And, she thought, the extraordinary thing was that neither of them would have said anything. For ten years she had been unhappy in her marriage and had said not a word, and she would have carried on forever in silence because that was what she had been taught Duchesses did. Her husband would have denied her the pleasure of going up to Town, the pleasures of company and she would not have challenged him because she had promised to obey him when she took her wedding vows. He could have ransacked their home, taken everything of value, and she would not have broached the subject because she never complained, never asked for difficult explanations. In the privacy of her chamber she might have stared into her mirror and felt despair, but she would never have told Charles how she felt and he would never have thought to talk to her about it.

She thought of the time that she had caught Hester sneaking out to lead the Glory Girls and how Hester had looked terrified because she had thought Laura would inevitably be so outraged and appalled that she would give the game away. Hester had never realized how much Laura envied her for her unconventionality and her outspokenness. Laura had always felt like the caged canary to Hester's free-flying hawk.

But not any longer.

Laura looked at her husband, with his weak chin and his trapped, darting gaze, and something shifted deep within her. Something finally broke that could never be repaired.

"When we next go up to London, I will come with you to the solicitor's offices and we shall discuss the full extent of your debt and work out a plan to retrench," Laura said. She saw his face twitch at her use of the word *we,* but carried on regardless. "It will be delightful to be up in Town again. I cannot think why I have not made the journey before." She swished across the room toward him and he actually retreated a few steps. "Perhaps Papa might advance us a loan to help clear some of the more urgent bills," she said thoughtfully. "I will ask him."

"D-don't!" Charles stuttered. "Don't tell your papa about this!"

Laura ignored him. "After all, Papa would be most concerned to hear that you were obliged to hawk my jewelry about the place in order to pay your gambling debts."

"Laura." There was a note of desperation in Charles's voice now. "I pray you not to involve Lord Burlington. There is no need!"

"Well, perhaps not." Laura smiled. "I shall think about it. Now, I suggest that you go back to bed, Charles. All this worry cannot be good for you and we have a house full of guests to entertain on the morrow."

"Yes," Charles said, with relief. "Yes, of course. Good night, old girl."

Laura watched him scurry away to the door and listened to the sound of his footfalls fading along the corridor.

Remembering the hopeless passion she had felt for him so recently, she could scarce believe it. Now, she thought, she almost hated him. Her loathing and her anger were so hot inside her that she thought for a moment that she might burst; she might explode like a firework. There was only one way to get rid of such restless fury. Taking her candle, Laura made for her closet and reached for her riding clothes.

A LITTLE LATER, as the first streaks of dawn were beginning to lighten the eastern sky above the fells, the landlady of Half Moon House was roused from her bed by a persistent knocking at the inn door. Grumbling, she made her way down the stairs and drew the bolts, holding her candle high in one hand and her pistol in the other as she confronted the cloaked and masked stranger on the doorstep.

"Mercy," she said after a moment, lowering the pistol. "It's you, madam! I thought the Glories did not ride out again this night?"

Laura laughed. "I am going out alone, Josie, to do what we originally promised and burn Sampson's ricks to the ground. I have come for a horse." She looked thoughtfully at the candle flame. "And a flaming torch, as well, I think. Yes, that will be a nice touch. The tale of Glory's torchlight dawn gallop through the villages will soon be the talk of every inn and club in the country."

"Take care, madam," Josie said. Her face was troubled. "Sometimes I think that the devil is in you even more than in Lady Hester."

Laura laughed. "Very probably, Josie." She adjusted her gloves. "Could you lend me the white gelding to-night, please? He will look the best in the torchlight. I intend to make sure that everyone remembers Glory's last ride."

"MERCY ON US, MA'AM," Jane said the next morning as she brought Mari's cup of tea, "Glory was out alone last night and burned Mr. Sampson's ricks and set fire to his fences! There is such a to-do in the village this morning, ma'am! They had to bring buckets of water from the river, and by the time they had put the fire out there was none of his hay left!"

"Glory?" Mari said. She rubbed the sleep from her eyes. "I thought—" She stopped.

Jane bustled around the bed to draw back the drapes. "Frank said that Glory rode through Starbotton like an avenging angel with a torch in her hand." There was a misty look in her eyes. "He said the horse was pure white and there were sparks flying from its hooves and a circle of fire about Glory's head. Fair puts the fear of God in you, doesn't it, ma'am?"

"It does indeed," Mari said. "Please could you lay the green cambric gown out for me this morning, Jane? I shall be attending to my hothouse and so do not re-quire anything smart to wear."

"Yes, ma'am," the maid said, recognizing this change of topic for what it was. "No tea for Lady Hester this morning, ma'am," she added, her mouth pursing with disapproval. "She is not here again!"

"I expect she has gone out for an early morning ride with Lord Teague," Mari said easily.

"Aye, ma'am." Jane's tone suggested that if Mari believed that, she would believe anything. "Is that all, ma'am?"

"Thank you, Jane," Mari said.

When the maid had gone out, she took her teacup, slipped from the bed and walked over to the window, in much the same way as she had on the morning Nick Falconer had first come to Peacock Oak. Across the valley she could see wisps of smoke rising in the still air. Shaking her head slightly she curled up on the window seat with her cup.

"This has to stop," she said, under her breath. A rueful smile twisted her lips. "Even so, I would have liked to have seen it. Circle of fire, indeed! And I'll wager she took that showy white gelding on purpose."

IN THE BREAKFAST PARLOR of Cole Court, the Duke was buttering his eggs with bad-tempered vigor. Neither Lord Henry, nor Lady Faye, nor their daughter had yet risen to face the demands of the day and so Charles and Laura were obliged to eat alone together, a fact which Laura observed seemed to make her spouse uncomfortable after the events of the previous night.

"Blackett tells me that the Glory woman has been out again," Charles said, "burning Sampson's barns." He rustled his newspaper irritably. "It's a damned disgrace! I'm a justice of the peace and I'll see her hang! Do you hear me, Laura? This just won't do!"

For a moment Laura wondered how much he knew, but when she met his eyes, he looked away and made a business of picking up the paper again. At any rate, she thought, he will never tell me what to do again. Not after last night.

She reached for the honeypot and spread the golden substance lavishly over her toast. She smiled sunnily at her husband. "Just so, my love," she murmured. "I am sure you will."

CHAPTER TEN

Fig–I keep my secrets

"I AM SO HAPPY!" Hester burst into the hall just as Mari was coming down the stairs for breakfast. "I have been with John all night—don't scold, Mari, we are to be wed—and I am so happy I could burst!" She grabbed Mari by the hand and dragged her into the parlor where the maid was setting out the fresh bread and butter and honey. "Will you be my matron of honor, Mari? The banns are to be read next Sunday for the first time of asking. Charles is being very stuffy because he heard I was with John and he insists we wed as quickly as possible." She gave Mari an impulsive hug. "Who would have thought it?"

"I would, for one," Mari said, smiling. "The only wonder is what took you so long."

"Yes." Hester blushed. "I was very foolish and I have treated John very badly. I see that now. But I was lonely and sad—" Her face fell and she squeezed Mari's hand all the tighter. "I am sorry, Mari," she said quietly.

A lump rose in Mari's throat. "Do not be," she said. "I am glad for you, even if I am to be an old widow woman living on my own!" She felt the loneliness grip her heart. She understood what Hester was trying to say. Her friend knew that her newfound happiness would only increase Mari's isolation.

"We will still be friends," Hester said, looking anxious, "and Starbotton is no great distance."

"Of course not," Mari said. "And perhaps this is the opportunity for me to appoint some staid matron as my companion to make up for my own scandalous character!"

"Well, I wouldn't do that," Hester said, sliding into her seat and reaching for the coffeepot. "That would not suit you at all." She stopped and put the pot down with a thud. "Oh, Mari, I do so want you to be happy. I want you to be as happy as I am!"

Mari looked at her; Hester, her friend, flushed with love, her eyes dreamy, and in that moment she felt so pleased for her and so wrenched with sadness.

"I cannot wait to live at Starbotton again," Hester was saying. "Really I do not know why I did not accept John sooner so that I could go home!"

"Perhaps," Mari said calmly, "because you did not realize quite how good in bed John would turn out to be. A pity, because if you *had* realized sooner, we would have been spared all your roistering at Half Moon House."

"Mari!" Hester turned a gratifying scarlet.

Mari shrugged. "Is it not so?"

"I suppose so," Hester said. She bit her lip. "I have behaved very badly—"

"Never mind. You can turn into a pattern card of respectability now," Mari said. "You will be Lady Hester Teague of Starbotton Hall, and Laura will be untouchable as the Duchess of Cole and Glory can slide into legend where she belongs."

"But what about you?" Hester looked anxious again. "What about you, Mari?"

"I shall do very well," Mari said, ignoring the painful knot inside her. "I shall devote myself to good causes."

"Perhaps you are correct about the Glories," Hester said, on a sigh. "John says that Major Falconer has been sent by the Home Secretary himself to bring us to justice. I realize that we cannot ride again."

"John knows that?" The cold fear struck Mari's heart. Nick Falconer had been sent by the government to find the Glories? It was even worse than she had thought.

"He had it from Major Falconer himself," Hester confirmed.

The maid came back and Mari turned the conversation to the wedding and the trousseau, and Hester's face lit up and she chattered on about going to Skipton for gowns and not having enough time for all the preparations, and she barely stopped talking to eat.

It was only later, when Hester had rushed back to Starbotton Hall with unseemly haste, that Mari sat alone drinking a second cup of coffee and feeling melancholy. She was happy to see Hester so radiant but it seemed a cruel contrast to her own situation.

Just for a moment the image of Nick Falconer rose in Mari's mind, the hard, clear planes of his face, the uncompromising line of his mouth, the dark perceptive gaze of his eyes. Just for a moment she permitted herself to wonder what it would be like to spend her life with a man like that; to share the good times and the difficult times, to bear his children, to have someone to trust in and to love and to cherish. She knew Nick could not be that man, at least not for her. In another time, perhaps, another existence…

With a sigh, she put down her cup. She knew Nick would seek her out today. After the events of the previous night, it was inevitable. She could run, of course, or she could hide away and refuse to see him, but in the end that would make no difference and anyway, she was weary now of running and hiding, of believing herself safe and discovering that she was not.

She knew Nick would want answers; that today would be the time he chose to demand from her the explanations he wanted in his subtle and merciless determination to reveal the truth.

She could not give them to him. No matter her desire to trust him, that troubling impulse that always prompted her to tell him the truth. One glance at Hester's radiant face had been enough to convince her that she had to protect the Glory Girls against any accusation. In revealing her own history to Nick she would allow him to get close to Hester and Laura and the others. So she had to think of a way to keep their secrets.

She got to her feet. It was another beautiful day, perfect for spending time in the gardens. It was the place that gave her the most peace, so she would work there today.

And when Nick Falconer came, she would be ready.

"MRS. OSBORNE?"

It was late that afternoon, the shadows were starting to lengthen and Mari was in her hothouse by the south wall, repotting some seedlings of sweet marjoram. She jumped when she heard Nick's voice and spun around, spilling some compost onto the wooden floor. Suddenly the enclosed space of the greenhouse felt tiny and very, very hot. She wished that she had opened some of the air vents in the roof. She was aware of the soil staining her fingers and the sweat beading her brow. She raised the back of her hand to wipe it away and then remembered, too late, that she would have made her face streaky with dirt. Her hair was scraped back beneath an old scarf and she was wearing an ancient gown of pale green cotton and she was sure she looked rumpled and shiny and grubby.

She had actually started to believe that he was not going to come to see her that day, had started to hope that he might be going to leave her alone, that she would not need her carefully assembled half-truths and protestations. But she might have known that he would not give up so easily. After all, he had been commissioned by the Home Secretary himself to discover the circumstances of Rashleigh's death and the link to the Glory Girls.

You must lie to him, Hester had said at the very beginning, and daily, hourly, her ability to do so seemed fatally undermined by both her attraction to him and the disturbing desire to confide in him. That was his skill, and her danger. He could make her forget the past. And even when she was aware that he was using her feelings with the most skillful manipulation, still it seemed that she was not immune to him. The previous night, at the dance, she had felt the strength of that attraction. She had allowed herself to think of that sweet seduction and to remember the way that he had held her, kissed her, down by the river. Her body had ached for him and for the satisfaction of slaking her loneliness with his touch, so that when he had taken her in his arms in the carriage, she had been all too ready to succumb.

But later, when the Glory Girls had sprung their attack and she had been shaken to the core to see marks of violence on Nick's body, she had realized how damaged she was and that she could never ever reveal that vulnerability to any man. The depth of her feelings had confused her, suggesting that her attraction to Nick as not simply physical but was far deeper and more dangerous than that.

And now she was trapped in the greenhouse and Nick Falconer was leaning against the door frame, arms folded, looking disturbingly masculine and utterly implacable. He was blocking the only escape and looking at her with such a disconcertingly thorough appraisal that it made her feel as though the ground beneath her feet was shifting slightly.

"Major Falconer." Mari cleared her throat. "I did not realize you had called."

"I did not call at the house," Nick said. "I wanted to see you alone. I hope that you have recovered from the experience of last night?"

"Yes, I thank you." Her voice sounded rusty and awkward, like a green girl tongue-tied in the presence of a gentleman. She raised a hand again to rub her brow and felt the old green gown slip a little from one shoulder. Embarrassed, she quickly pulled it up again, but not before Nick's glance had gone to her bare shoulder and the flash of heat in his eyes sent an answering burn through her whole body.

Nick took a step toward her and Mari's stomach clenched with a mixture of nervousness and sheer sensual attraction.

"I have waited a long time," he said, "to see my suspicions confirmed."

He took a step closer. The back of Mari's thighs came up hard against the greenhouse shelf and she braced her hands against its edge.

"What do you mean?" Her words were a whisper.

Slowly, almost negligently, Nick put out a hand and slid the edge of the old green gown down over her shoulder. It felt intimate. It felt as though he was undressing her. Her exposed skin prickled for his touch.

"So," he said, "Mrs. Osborne of Peacock Oak is everything that is proper and respectable." He tilted his head, watching her intently. "But what about Molly, the ravishing little whore from the Hen and Vulture? She had a scattering of freckles just there…" His fingers drifted across her shoulder and Mari felt the gooseflesh breathe along her skin.

She made a sharp movement and caught the edge of one of the little pots of marjoram. It fell to the floor, spilling soil as it went, and smashing to pieces.

"Damnation!" Mari said, staring at the shards. For one terrifying moment her mind was completely blank. She did not know either how to refute his words or how to escape. And it was far too late now anyway. Through her reaction she had betrayed herself more thoroughly than she could have done with mere words.

"Now that," Nick said with a smile, "sounds more like Molly than Marina Osborne."

Mari could feel the panic building in her chest, threatening to choke her. "Major Falconer—"

"Let me spare you the trouble of denials, Mrs. Osborne," Nick said, suddenly cold and deadly, "for both you and I know that you *were* the woman in the club that night." He took another step toward her. "Ever since I came to Peacock Oak I have been working to prove it."

Mari's knees suddenly threatened to give way. The heat in the greenhouse seemed overpowering. She could not breathe. She shook her head. Even though she had suspected this all along, to have it confirmed by him so starkly, finally to see her absolute danger, terrified her.

"I do not know what you are talking about."

He laughed. "Of course you do. What does it take for me to prove it—should I kiss you until you admit it? You kiss just like the girl in the Hen and Vulture, and I should know."

Mari swallowed hard. "You would not do that."

"I would if that was what it took to make you admit the truth. There is some honesty in kisses."

He was so close to her now that she could smell the scent of fresh air on his skin and hear his breathing. It sounded calm and steady, nothing like the tumultuous rush of her pulse. Quickly, desperately, Mari reviewed her options.

She could persist in her denials. He would give that short shrift.

She could admit the truth. That would only be the start of her troubles, troubles that might well end on the scaffold.

She could challenge him, dare him to kiss her and prove his point.

He had called her a gambler and now she had to risk all.

Tilting her chin up, she looked him in the eyes. "Very well, then," she said. "Prove it."

She saw his eyes widen as though she had surprised

him, then darken with a raw desire that sent an answering spear of need through her, and then he took her chin in his hand, just as he had done that first night in the club, and turned her face up to his. When his lips were a mere inch away from hers, Mari closed her eyes.

She had thought that she could do this. She had willed herself to clear her mind, to remain unresponsive and to block the sensation of the kiss out until it was over. But it was not so simple.

His mouth covered hers and her heart raced as sweet, forbidden pleasure swamped her body. She forgot that she did not enjoy kissing. It was different with Nick. It always had been.

Her hand came up to brace against his chest but the impulse to hold him at arm's length was lost as soon as it formed and instead she found her fingers curling into his shirt. She knew she was making a mistake, losing control, but the seduction of his kiss blew away all reason. The scent of his body mingled with the heavy, earthy smells of the greenhouse and filled her senses. She remembered the kiss in the tavern and the kiss by the river, remembered the sharp hunger she had felt for him then and was swept by an undeniable longing and a dizzy desire. Instead of pushing him away, she drew him closer still.

His fingers slid down her throat, lingering on the erratic pulse at the base.

"You always taste the same as I remember," he said, against her parted lips. "Very sweet."

"No—"

"Yes."

He nipped at her bottom lip and Mari gave a little gasp and he slid his tongue into her mouth again, delving deep, tasting her, savoring her, drawing a fierce response from her that she could not hide. His hand fell to her shoulder again, sliding aside the green cotton dress so that he could press his lips to her bare skin where the freckles dusted it. His tongue flicked over the curve of her shoulder and his hand fell to cup her breast, his thumb circling her tight, hard nipple. Mari's knees weakened and she groaned as the sensation ripped through her body.

"So," he said, raising his head, "you lose."

"No." Mari dragged in a deep, painful breath. "You have proved nothing."

"I have proved that you kiss me as though you mean it." His thumb slid over her nipple again and she shuddered. He bit down on the tender lobe of her ear.

"Admit it, Mari," he whispered. "Tell me the truth."

Oh, she was so tempted. Bewitched, bewildered, seduced by his touch, she wanted to trust him. Never had the walk to the hangman's noose seemed so easy.

"There is nothing to tell." She held on—barely—to the shreds of her sanity. "I admit that I respond to you, that is all. And that can be no real surprise to you when you have tormented me with the fact these three weeks past."

He laughed, a low laugh of masculine triumph, and his mouth returned to hers, insistent, demanding, deep.

"I wondered when you would forget to wear a high-necked gown," he murmured against her lips. "You have such a sweet scattering of freckles on your shoulders. I have ached to see them again. Had we not been interrupted that day by the river, or last night in the carriage, I would have stripped your gown away to expose them."

Mari drew back a little. Her lips felt swollen, stung by his kisses. Her heart felt bruised at the proof of his calculated seduction. She had suspected that that was what he intended, of course, but to hear it confirmed made her feel wretched.

"I think you mistake me for another woman," she said.

"I do not. That is what I have been telling you." His hands were hard against her back, holding her close to him. She could feel his arousal and her stomach knotted with a mixture of fear and longing.

"We can play this game for as long as you wish," he said. "I'll allow it is most pleasurable—but you will never convince me."

"And you will never make me confess to something I did not do."

"You already did." He held her a little way away from him and his dark eyes scanned her face thoughtfully. "Your reaction when I accused you was not that of an innocent woman."

Mari looked down at the cracked pieces of the plant pot and the telltale scattering of earth on the hothouse floor.

"You startled me, that is all."

"Of course. And then I challenged you. And although you said that you did not understand what I was talking about, you were not even remotely convincing." He smiled. "For a criminal, you are a poor dissembler, Mrs. Osborne."

Mari was afraid that it was true.

"You can prove nothing," she said again. "When you can, pray come back. Until then, good day, Major Falconer."

He laughed. "You are sending me away?"

"Of course. What does your case amount to?" Mari held his gaze as coolly as she could. "A scattering of freckles and the response to a kiss? It is scarce sufficient."

He smoothed some of the spilled soil between his fingers. "I know you are an impostor," he said slowly. "I know Mr. Osborne did not exist."

Mari's heart gave an erratic thump. The panic caught at her throat. He had made inquiries. Of course he had. He might know far more than he was disclosing. Rashleigh might have told him everything… But until he revealed the extent of his knowledge, she was not going to give anything away. She could not. Five lives depended upon her silence. She took a deep breath and fought down the fear, locking it out for as long as she could.

"I still do not know what you are talking about."

"Yes, you do. You are not Mrs. Osborne, virtuous widow. But I think we both already know the extent of your virtue—or lack of it—do we not?"

Mari held his gaze, desperately trying to decipher how much he knew. His expression was dark, closed, as he watched her.

"You base your assumptions on no more than a vivid imagination and wishful thinking, Major Falconer," she said, as steadily as she could. "As I said, unless you can make good your claims, I suggest that you leave and do not trouble me until you have something you can prove."

The silence that followed her words was as taut and tense as a lightning storm. Mari held her breath. She could feel the churning sickness of the panic pressing closer, but still, she held it at bay. Then he nodded.

"Very well." He laughed curtly. "You have the devil's own nerve, I grant you that." He gave her a mocking bow. "I shall be back. The next time you hear from me there will be nothing you can do to refuse me. Good day, Mrs....Osborne."

Only when she was sure that he had gone did Mari permit herself to crumple slowly to her knees, picking up the shards of pot with shaking fingers.

She had not believed that he would go.

But he would be back. He would respond to every challenge that she set him. She might be determined, but he was ruthless and she would never win. She knew she was running out of time.

MARI THOUGHT about Nick Falconer for the rest of the afternoon, throughout dinner, which she ate alone, Hester not having returned, and again whilst she sat in the drawing room after the meal, drinking tea. She thought about the alternatives and came to the conclusion that she had to leave Peacock Oak, quickly and silently, and go somewhere that Nick Falconer could not find her. She had reinvented herself before and she could start all over once again. All it took was courage. And at least she would have her freedom and Hester and the others would be safe.

"Excuse me, ma'am." She realized that the maid had come in and was waiting for her attention. "I found this under the door—" The girl was holding out a letter. "I am not sure how long it had been there."

Mari took it automatically. "Thank you, Betty."

"Ma'am." The girl curtsied and went out quietly and Mari unfolded the letter and started to read.

She had not taken in more than a few words when

she realized, with a cold blow to the heart, that it was another anonymous letter, the third.

You belong to me now that Rashleigh is dead, and I want you. Meet me at the Star House at midnight or the others will suffer. I know all about you. I know about the Glory Girls, too. Such highborn ladies… Such a terrible scandal… Only you can buy their safety if you give yourself to me.

Mari felt numb. Her thoughts tumbled back over her conversation with Nick earlier that day. She had sent him away with instructions not to trouble her unless he had something new to say. She had challenged him and now, surely, he had responded.

"You belong to me now that Rashleigh is dead, and I want you."

The letter had to be from Nick. Who else could have sent it? He was Rashleigh's heir. She did belong to him. She was his property. The first letter had arrived on the same day that he had. He had been biding his time, playing games with her, awaiting his moment. Now that moment had arrived.

Once before, she thought numbly, a man had offered her a bargain—her family's future for her own enslavement. It had been no true choice. She had had no alternative. She had bought freedom for them with her own body.

Now someone was threatening her with almost the same words and she knew, with a deepening sense of disillusionment, that it must be Nick. She knew what he wanted. He had made no secret of it from the start.

He wanted her, and now he was demanding her submission.

She thought about their last encounter, that very afternoon, in the hothouses. He had given her the chance then to tell him the truth and she had refused. Now he had finally shown his full hand. Rashleigh had told him about her, just as she had feared. Their game was over and he was demanding what was his.

She remembered Hester saying that John Teague had told her Nick had been sent by the Home Secretary himself and her feeling of painful disappointment deepened to think that not only would Nick use her as callously as his cousin had done but he would also be corrupt enough to betray the man who had sent him. He was an officer in the army. He was supposed to be on the side of right. But he had proved himself as venal as Rashleigh. Her instinct to trust him had been utterly wrong.

He knew about the Glory Girls. He knew about Hester and Laura and Josie and Lenny. It was precisely what she had feared all along; the one thing that she had hoped would not be true. Mari felt faint to think of the power of life and death that was in Nick's hands now. She felt sick to think of what he could do to rip apart their lives: Hester, who had just found her true happiness with John Teague; Laura, who hid behind her facade as the perfect Duchess and ached with loneliness beneath it; Josie, who had struggled her entire life. They had taken her in and shown her love when she had had no one. And now she was the only one who could stand between them and ruin.

It sickened her that she had thought Nick Falconer had come to Peacock Oak for justice, that he was sup-

posed to be a man of honor, and yet he would compromise his principles with such evil blackmail.

She thought of the pistol in her desk drawer but
knew almost at once that such a course would not
serve. She could shoot her blackmailer, she might even
get away with it, but there were no guarantees that
someone else would not know the secret. Rashleigh's
death had proved that. She had thought that it would
set her free, but he had already told Nick of her existence. Maybe Nick himself had shared the secret. There
would always be someone else. A runaway slave could
run all her life but there would always be another master waiting.

She stood up, smoothing her skirts with little
anxious movements that she was not even aware she
was making. She felt cold inside, as though once again
she had locked away all the emotions and feelings that
had unfurled within her over the last five years of
freedom. She had done this before when Rashleigh had
made his bargain with her. She could do it again. She
could give herself to Nick as his mistress in order to
save those she loved.

She glanced at the clock. It was five minutes to nine
on a beautiful summer evening. She had three hours
ahead of her in which she would do nothing other than
concentrate on how important it was to save Hester and
Laura and the others. She would think of nothing else,
feel nothing else. Enslavement was nothing to her
when she could lock away her true self within and no
one could touch it.

You belong to me now.

Like Rashleigh, he could possess her body and try
to take her soul but he would never break her spirit.

Except… She shivered in the breeze from the open window. Except that she was very afraid that she could not shut Nick out as she had done his cousin. From the first he had threatened all the defenses that she had so carefully erected. From the first she had wanted to trust him and lean on his strength and be with him.

He was not like his cousin.

Mari closed her eyes briefly. That was an illusion, of course. He was exactly like his cousin. He had proved it by sending the letter. He had told her from the first that he wanted her and now he had moved to make that desire a reality. And she had to ensure that she did not, for a moment, weaken and give him more than her body, for if she fell in love with him, as she had feared she was doing, her enslavement would be complete, a matter of emotion and not simply a physical relationship. She had to make sure that never, ever happened. It was the very last thing that she could withhold from him.

Very slowly she went upstairs to prepare for their meeting.

CHAPTER ELEVEN

Dittany—Passion

IT SEEMED TO NICK that no one was very eager to linger after dinner that night. John Teague made some spurious excuse about needing to return to Starbotton to consult his estate manager, Lord Henry Cole complained of gout and said he intended to go to bed early and Charles did not offer Nick his customary nightcap but retired to his study alone. Since it was a clear, starry and warm night, Nick thought that he would take a walk in the gardens before he, too, retired to bed.

It was as he was passing the stables that he thought he saw Lord Henry Cole, miraculously cured of his gout, slipping away across the deer park and glancing furtively over his shoulder to make sure he was not spotted. A little later, pausing by the cascade to watch the silver water tumbling in the moonlight, Nick also thought he saw the shadow of a man lurking behind the bushes. He stopped and listened but there was no sound and dismissing the idea as fanciful, he walked on to the Star House. This small, star-shaped gazebo had been placed on a low mound facing the fountain where he had seen Mari Osborne bathing on the first night he had come to Peacock Oak. And now, in a re-creation of that moment, his heart leaped as he saw Mari leaning on the wooden balustrade and gazing at the fountain. She was dressed in a filmy gown that looked gossamer pale in the moonlight and her arms and shoulders were bare.

Nick had been thinking about her for almost every moment since their encounter that afternoon. Mingled with those thoughts had been the memories he had of the previous night, of Mari's courage as she had faced down their attackers, her distress as she had struggled to unfasten the bonds that had held him. The more he thought about her the less able he was to disentangle his instincts from his suspicions and the lies. He knew her to be an impostor yet he sensed she was in some sort of terrible trouble. She had sent him packing that afternoon with a coolness that belied the desperation he had seen beneath the surface.

Perhaps he was deluded. Perhaps he was a fool, misled by the part of his anatomy that was certainly not thinking but very definitely feeling. Perhaps he only wanted to exonerate her because he had held her in his arms and wanted her more than any woman he had ever known. Perhaps lust was clouding his judgment. All those things might be true. Yet his stubborn instinct could not be shifted. And so he had decided to take an enormous risk. He was determined to tell her every-thing, why he had come to Peacock Oak, what he thought he knew of her, to place it all before her, to urge her to trust him and tell him the truth.

And now seemed as good a time as any.

He went up the steps to the terrace.

MARI HAD ARRIVED at the Star House at eleven, so anxious that she knew she was ridiculously early. There was no one there. The light of the full moon poured in, illuminating the little room that she had designed as a retreat for Laura and Charles. The charm of the idea mocked her now, for she knew that Laura and Charles would never share the intimacy of a night here gazing at the stars and instead it was to be the scene of her own seduction, but not in the way that she wished. Never in the way that she wished it.

She moved through the quiet room and went out onto the little terrace, with its white balustrade. The fountain was in front of her, the splash of the water loud in the night. Away in the woods, an owl called. Mari shivered as the night breeze breathed along her skin. Mindful of the part she had to play, she had chosen to wear a pale yellow dress, which was cut low and left her arms bare. She knew it was not the cold that made her tremble, for the night was hot. She knew it was nervousness and expectation.

There was a step on the wooden stair, the shadows shifted, and a man crossed the terrace toward her.

It was Nick Falconer.

Mari's heart did a little skip of pure anticipation, and at the same time she felt, conversely, desperately sad that in being there he had confirmed he was her blackmailer, the man who owned her.

The moonlight fell on his face. His expression was watchful, unreadable.

"I thought it would be you," Mari said, "but I hoped—" She stopped. What point was there now in telling him that she had hoped she was mistaken, that she had hoped he would prove to be a better man than his cousin had been? It did not matter what she thought. She was trapped. She was his property.

She shivered. The memories of the past clung like wisps of smoke no matter how she tried to shut them out.

He took a step closer. "Why did you think it would be me?"

"Because you are Rashleigh's cousin." Mari thought that if she could keep this very practical, very calm, she would survive. She could shut out all emotion and keep the past locked away. She had done it before. Whenever Rashleigh had touched her, she had absented herself from her body so that whilst he might have thought he possessed her, he had never conquered her. She looked at Nick's dark face and felt the panic close her throat. She was not sure if she could do that with this man. Right from the start his touch had undermined her defenses. He had invaded her very thoughts. She was not sure if she could shut him out, but she had to try. She had to use every trick she had ever learned to keep him from knowing how vulnerable she felt, how vulnerable *he* could make her feel. She might belong to him, he might legally be permitted to do whatever he wished with her, but she would show him no emotion. She was a slave but he would not be permitted to possess her soul, as well as her body.

"You are his heir," she said again. "When I received your letter, I knew he had told you about me—who I was and where to find me."

She stopped. He had made a slight movement, quickly stilled, but he did not speak.

Mari thought back to the note. The most urgent thing, the most important thing, was to make him swear to keep his word.

"You promise that you will honor the arrangement

you offered in the note?" she said. "If I give you what you wish, you will keep your word?"

His face was still shadowed. "Of course. I will keep my word."

She did not trust him now—of course she did not—but she had no choice. Rashleigh had made an unholy bargain with her seven years before; now his cousin was enforcing a similar one. The only thing that mattered to her was that Hester and Laura and the others would be safe. The only people she truly cared for, the ones who had loved and stood by her, had to be protected. She could save them.

"If you break your promise—" She stopped, for a moment too choked with emotion to say more. "If you do not keep to the agreement, then I will make you pay."

Nick moved into the moonlight. "How? Will you kill me, as you killed Rashleigh?"

"I did not kill him," Mari said. She knew that in saying it she was admitting she had been the girl at the Hen and Vulture but it hardly seemed to matter now. Nothing mattered anymore.

Nick shifted a little. "Tell me. Tell me what happened at the club the night Rashleigh died."

Mari walked across to the balustrade and leaned both hands on it. Why not? Why not tell him the truth? She was already in his power. And she was tired of carrying the burden of it all alone.

She could sense that he had moved to stand behind her but she did not turn.

"I did not kill him," she said again. "It was not my doing."

"Then who did?"

"I do not know. Rashleigh had told me to meet him there. I had taken rooms across the street where we could talk privately. I told him to follow me and went out first."

"Your wig and mask were by his body."

"I discarded them in the alleyway. I had no further use for them. Rashleigh knew who I was."

"Because you had been his mistress?"

"Of course. I was only in disguise because I did not wish anyone else to see me."

There was a second's pause. "So why did you pick me up that evening?" Nick asked. "Why risk exposure?"

Mari shrugged. "I only did it because I felt conspicuous, sitting in the tavern on my own. If I had known who you were—"

"Yes?"

"I would not have chosen you."

It was not the whole truth. Mari knew that something had drawn her to Nick that evening but she would not tell him that. She knew this was the first of many lies she would have to tell to keep him from invading her innermost thoughts, to prevent him from understanding how she felt. She could tell him the facts, dispassionately, but she did not want him to know *her*. That was too intimate and it would cause her too much pain. It would permit him too close. Just as she had previously had such a strong instinct to trust him, now all she wanted was to keep him at bay.

She heard him sigh.

"I did not realize at the time that Rashleigh had told you about me," she said. "It was only when you came to Peacock Oak and your anonymous letters started to arrive that I realized someone else knew who I was, and where I was." She turned her head slightly. "That was why you were at the tavern that night, wasn't it?"

"I was there to meet him," Nick said.

Mari felt a little sick. She knew Rashleigh so well, knew all the sordid games he must have had planned for that night. He would have invited his cousin along for some sport with his blackmailed former mistress. She could almost hear Rashleigh's mocking tones ordering her to pleasure him whilst his cousin watched, blackmailing her to depravities that were the stuff of her nightmares. She nearly put her hands over her ears to shut out the ghost of his voice. Intolerable memories… She shuddered.

Nick put a hand on her arm and she jumped as though burned.

"So you claim that he was following you out when someone stabbed him in the street."

Mari moved away, unconsciously smoothing down her arm where Nick had touched her.

"I told him to wait a few moments before he followed me. I went to the room and waited for him, but he did not come. Then I heard the hue and cry in the street. I realized what had happened, so…"

"So you ran away." There was no expression in Nick's voice, but still, Mari felt defensive.

"Yes." She schooled her voice to calm. "I was afraid. It looked bad for me—"

"Of course. A lovers' quarrel."

"We had been lovers." It sickened her to refer to what had been between herself and Rashleigh in such a way when there had been no love in it. "It was a long time since we had met."

"How long?"

"Seven years."

"How did it end?" Nick asked. "Why did you leave him?"

Danger threatened. Mari knew she could not tell him the truth. She knew that if she said that she had run away, Nick would want to know why. Then there was the money she had stolen. Robbery was a capital offense and stealing from Rashleigh would see her hanged. But even more importantly, if once she started to unlock the secrets of that dreadful night, she would no longer be able to hide her feelings and keep the past from invading her mind. All the hateful, frightening, horrific images would come tumbling out in a riptide, flooding through her body and sweeping everything away. She had kept them hidden for seven years, locked away in a dark place where no one could reach them, but now those locks and bolts seemed so flimsy, so insecure. Nick was getting too close. His quiet persistence was dangerous. It felt as though everything she had worked so hard to forget was in danger of spilling out. Everything that she had tried to rebuild was under terrible threat. Her life, her very self, was going to disintegrate before her eyes. She looked into the void and felt terrified. She could not let this happen to her. So she had to lie.

"Did he not tell you how we parted?" She held her breath, hoped that Rashleigh had been too vain to tell his cousin the truth of how his mistress had stolen from him and run away.

"No," Nick said. "He told me very little about you."

"Oh." She felt a huge relief that he did not know already and that she could keep the horrific memories buried in the dark where they belonged. "Well, he pensioned me off, Major Falconer. He was very generous."

There was a silence. "He paid you off?" For a second she heard stark disbelief in Nick's voice and felt anxious that he might challenge her. Then his tone changed, flattened. "I...see," he said. "I had no idea Rashleigh was so generous to his discarded mistresses."

"We had exhausted our interest in one another," Mari said expressionlessly. "I am sure you understand such matters, Major Falconer. So he paid me off on the basis that I should live quietly in the country. Which I have done."

The silence hung heavy between them. Mari was not sure if she had convinced him. But it seemed that it had been as she had hoped—Rashleigh had been too proud to tell anyone of the way in which she had cheated him. There might have been rumors, but nothing was certain. In Rashleigh's vanity and silence lay her sanity, for it meant that Nick would ask no questions about the past that would open up all the horrible, painful, unbearable memories she had buried so deep.

"So it was a mutually convenient agreement?" Nick's voice was quiet, his words echoing her thoughts.

"Of course."

Mari's hands tightened into fists, her nails digging into her palms. Her hatred of Rashleigh was like bile in her throat. "Major Falconer, to escape drudgery, to be a rich man's mistress was a dream for many people I knew."

That was true, but it had not been a dream for her. Her mind screamed, *Why did he choose me?* And once again she could see Rashleigh strutting through the house in St. Petersburg, eyeing his father's priceless artifacts with a merchant's eye. The serfs had all been lined up for his inspection and he had stopped in front of her.

"This is the one my father had clothed and educated, is it not..."

She had only been seventeen but she had seen then that her fate was sealed. There had been a cruelty in Rashleigh that had delighted in taking the little girl, the toy his father had created and indulged, and breaking it. She pressed her knuckles to her mouth to prevent herself from screaming.

Nick's footsteps crunched on the wooden panels of the pagoda as he walked a little way away from her.

"So he pensioned you off, but then, seven years later, he sent for you?"

"Yes."

"Why?"

Mari forced a smile and hoped it looked convincing. "I imagine he had planned some sort of...reunion. Something mutually enjoyable and financially beneficial."

She closed her eyes momentarily and felt the hot tears sting behind her lids. She could guess what Rashleigh had really wanted. He had been searching for her ever since she had run away from him. He wanted revenge. He had written that he had tracked her down and that if she did not agree to meet with him, he would expose her for who she was, and see her hang for the theft of his jewelry all those years before. And he had made it plain that he also knew about her involvement with the notorious gang, the Glory Girls. And so she had gone to Rashleigh to try to strike an agreement just as she had come to Nick now, to prevent the truth coming out, to stop her friends from being ruined and to bargain with whatever power she had to save them.

Nick did not reply and his silence stretched her over-taxed nerves close to breaking.

He had come to stand directly behind her and suddenly her physical awareness of him overwhelmed her. When he put both hands on her upper arms, she shivered, but it was no longer with revulsion. Nick could draw a response from her that Rashleigh had never been able to command. She did not understand it and she could not control it, but it frightened her, as well as holding her unwillingly fascinated.

"So now you come to strike a new agreement with Rashleigh's successor." He bent his head and his lips touched the curve of her neck. "You received the letters and you are willing to give yourself to me."

Her mind cried out against it even as her traitorous body trembled. The tragedy was that she knew she could have admired this man, loved him even, if he had had the honor and integrity she had once imagined. But now he had shown himself to be as venal and callous and immoral as Rashleigh himself, a man prepared to stoop to blackmail to ensure he could take what he wanted, a man prepared to hide his true nature behind a facade of honor. She felt a sense of betrayal and a desperate disappointment that she had once thought him a principled man.

But she was his slave. She did belong to him.

"I am." She fought the emotion rising within her.

He turned her to face him. His hands were warm on her bare arms, sending little quivers of sensation along her nerves.

"You will do whatever I ask of you?"

"I will."

His mouth took hers in a sudden fierce kiss that had her catching her breath. Her mind reeled.

"I want all of you." He sounded harsh. "Body and soul, Marina."

Mari stepped back. She spread her arms wide. "You have my body. Why ask for more?"

"Because I want everything." He was standing before her, tall, straight, commanding. "I demand it."

He stepped in close, so close she could feel the heat of his body. "Did you give Rashleigh everything?" he asked roughly.

"He did not ask it of me." Rashleigh had not been the man to ask for her mind when he could have her body. He had not cared.

"Well, I am not like my cousin." He put a hand on her waist, drew her to him so that they were touching. She could feel his arousal, already hot and hard against her. "I wanted you from the start. All of you."

Mari tilted up her chin. "I offer you exactly what I offered Rashleigh," she said. "It is a business arrangement only. If that is not enough…" She let the words die away.

The tension spun out between them and then he gave a groan and pulled her to him.

"It will have to be enough."

His mouth came down on hers, the kiss hard and demanding. For a moment Mari stood still beneath the onslaught. She had not intended to resist, merely to endure whatever he chose to do to her. But now the heat of his embrace, the relentless seduction of his mouth on hers, drew a response from her. Her mind turned cloudy with passion, her need for him swamped all other thoughts. She parted her lips and her tongue tangled with his and he made a noise of satisfaction deep in his throat to have wrung a response from her. The flames licked her, burned her, surprising her with sensations she had never imagined. For a moment she fought against the assault on her feelings, but then she let go and felt her mind spin away into darkness.

His mouth had gentled on hers now and was exploring her intimately. One of his hands slid upward, cupping her breast and teasing the nipple with the tips of his fingers. Mari gave a gasp and he took advantage to deepen the kiss still further. Then he wrenched himself away from her and stood back, and Mari felt so shocked and bereft that she almost fell.

"Unpin your hair." His voice was low and rough.

Her hands shook as she pulled out the pins that held up the Grecian knot. A couple of them fell from her fingers. She heard them hit the wooden floor of the pergola and spin away. Behind her the fountain splashed, silver in the moonlight.

She felt her hair loosen and then it started to fall, black and straight, around her shoulders and down her back.

"That's better." She heard his sigh of satisfaction. "I have wanted to see you like that."

He came to her, sliding one hand into her hair and bringing her mouth back up to his with determined force. His palm was against her cheek and it felt warm and a little rough. She yielded with only the slightest murmur now, her mouth bee-stung from his kisses, her whole body quiescent. Yet when he raised a hand and started to unbutton her dress, she drew back.

"Here?"

"Why not?" She could not read his expression in the moonlight. The movement of his fingers did not still. Another button gave. "I want to see you naked in the fountain again."

Mari shook. "But anyone might see—"

"You did not care about that last time."

Another button gave. Then a fourth.

"Turn around."

She did as he bade her, mutely. Her heart was slamming so hard beneath her bodice that she thought the material must be trembling with the force of it. She felt the slow, inexorable slide of his hand down her back as the material of her gown fell apart with each button that was unfastened. When the dress fell to her waist, she stepped out of it without him asking. She was lost, held in the sensual spell he had cast. She refused to think.

He stood back once more. His face was dark.

"Unfasten your chemise. Take your clothes off."

Mari shuddered. The sensual spell was pierced and she felt cold. Rashleigh had said those words to her. She fumbled with the laces of her petticoat and felt the bodice hang open. The cool night air caressed her breasts, hardening the peaks still further. She closed her eyes and slipped the petticoat from her shoulders.

Nick did not touch her. Her skin burned as she waited in an agony of impatience and fear. The night breathed chill along her nerves. She wanted to cover herself. She felt so exposed but she forced herself to stay still.

When she opened her eyes, it was to see him watching her. His look made her burn all the more. He took one step forward and slid a hand along the curve of her waist. When his body covered hers, it was warm and the contact made her gasp. His mouth took hers with a violence that made her shake with relief that the waiting was over.

Nick picked her up in his arms and carried her, not out to the fountain but deeper into the pergola, where a cushioned bench was positioned against one wall. It was dark here and the noise of the fountain was muted. The moonlight lay in bars across the floor. He laid her down amidst the cushions and left her briefly to strip off his clothes. Her mind floated free now. She could absent herself. Soon this would be over. She had wanted him so much but she had never wanted it to be like this, like it had been with Rashleigh.

Nevertheless when he joined her on the couch, his body hot and hard against her own, she felt the flames of desire burn all the deeper. His hand came up to stroke her breast, the other to slide over the curve of her hip, bringing her into sudden, shocking contact with his arousal.

Her mind was split. A part of her could still taste the sweet, drugging seduction of his kisses but it was over-laid now with a terror that made her shrink from him. She had thought she could keep him out of her mind and her emotions, that she would be able to build a wall against him that would protect her, but now his de-mands on her and her own needs had made that impos-sible. Her defenses shivered, faltered. The past pressed agonizingly close.

He touched her, brought his lips down to her breast, and the wall smashed and she started to think and feel with terrifying intensity. She had always wanted him but she could not bear for it to be like this, like her loveless transactions with Rashleigh. That was intolerable. All the shame and the misery and the longing for what might have been fused within her and she caught her breath on a sob. She tried to stifle it and felt as though the sobs would rack her whole body and tear her apart. Her mind was full of Rashleigh and screamed for escape. Her skin crawled with sudden revulsion.

He felt it. His hands, so demanding upon her body a moment before, stilled completely. He raised a hand and very gently turned her head so that the moonlight fell across her face. He brushed her tangled hair back and his fingers lingered on her cheek.

"Mari?"

Unbelievably there was tenderness in his voice.

It shattered the last of her defenses. She had been so careful to distance herself, to remind herself that even if he could draw a response from her body, he could not invade her mind. And then he had done just that.

Rashleigh had never shown her any tenderness. He had not cared. Nick did, and his gentleness, his compassion, was enough to break through the last of the protective facade. Suddenly she could feel again, not only with her body but deep in her heart. And it hurt. It hurt so much that Nick cared when everything else was wrong between them. She thought she could not bear it.

"No!" Mari tore herself away from him and struggled to sit up, disoriented by the darkness and what had happened.

Her mind felt sluggish, confused. All she was aware of was the most excruciating pain. She swung her feet to the floor and made a grab for the pile of clothes that she saw at the foot of the couch. She wanted something, anything, to cover herself. As she scrabbled the garment over her head, she realized that it was Nick's shirt. It smelled of him. It was still faintly warm from his body.

No matter. Anything would do now. She started to move toward the door.

"Wait!" Nick was beside her, his hand on her arm.

"No!" Mari tried to pull away from him as the panic started to pound in her chest. "Let me go!"

His hand fell to his side. It was all she needed.

She ran.

Instinct alone guided her along the path to the deer park and she flew like an arrow to its target until she reached the door in the wall that led to the gardens of Peacock Cottage. She slammed through the quiet house regardless of waking anyone and did not stop until she was in her bedchamber.

The candles were still lit, burning down to their sockets.

Mari stopped, panting for breath, then ripped off the shirt and kicked it violently away from her across the floor. Naked, she stood before the mirror and stared at her reflection in the glass. Outwardly her body looked so innocent, so how could it be so knowing? How could it hold so many hateful secrets that made her want to scream with the shame of it? How could she be so damaged inside and for it not to show on the outside? How could she ever have thought that she could leave her past behind and feel differently with another man? She felt so angry and ashamed and confused that she never, ever wanted anyone, least of all Nick, to know the truth about her.

There was a sound downstairs and she swung around, frozen to think that Nick might have followed her. But it was only the grandfather clock winding itself up to strike the hour of twelve.

The candle guttered and went out. All the fight seemed to leave Mari's body and leach away, and she burrowed beneath the blankets of the bed and scrunched herself up into a tight ball, closed her eyes and willed the darkness to come and take her away.

NICK FALCONER SAT silent and alone in the pergola for a very long time.

He had dressed slowly, minus one shirt. He could smell Mari's perfume on his skin and still feel the imprint of her touch on him. The desire that had raced through his blood so uncontrollably was cooling now but, when he found her gown, he held it to his face and inhaled her scent on an impulse, and felt an echo of that ache inside him again.

He did not understand why she had run from him. Even though he had been utterly consumed by his need for her he had sensed some kind of sudden withdrawal in her and had stopped to make sure that she was all right. Her face in the moonlight had looked quite blank of expression and then she had run away as though all hell were at her heels. If he had not known her history, known she was experienced, he would have sworn she had been afraid. But that made no sense. Rashleigh's mistress must surely have been as debauched and degraded as he. She could be no shrinking virgin.

Nick had been startled to find Mari at the pergola in the middle of the night but had quickly realized that she had mistaken him for someone else, someone who had apparently arranged to meet her, secretly and anonymously, someone who knew her true identity.

Mari, he thought, had given a great deal away without realizing that she was talking to the wrong man.

He knew now that she had been Rashleigh's mistress and that she had benefited from such an arrangement.

To escape from drudgery to be a rich man's mistress was a dream...

If he had not heard the words from her own lips, he would not have believed them for it seemed so contradictory to the Mari Osborne he had thought he was beginning to know, the one he was going to beg to trust him and tell him the truth. But that was all over now. He had been misled by his instincts, misled by his desire. He had at last seen her for what she really was.

He thought about her words. Maybe she had been born a maid-servant and had seen Rashleigh as a means to escape from servitude. It seemed that she and his cousin had used each other for mutual pleasure and benefit.

He smashed one fist into the palm of the other hand. She had chosen her path and it was not her fault but his if he had secretly started to hope that she was so much better, so much finer, purer and sweeter, than she had turned out to be. In truth, she was a whore with a whore's mind, as well as a harlot's body. Everything had a price. Had she not shown that the very first time they had met, in the Hen and Vulture? He was no more than a fool to have been misled by a consummate actress.

He had never intended to allow matters to go so far with Mari. He had played along with the masquerade at first for information—he had wanted to know the truth of how Rashleigh had died—but then he had become so jealous and angry that he had forgotten his good intentions, forgotten his principles, forgotten everything in the heat of Mari's seduction. When she had spoken of being Rashleigh's mistress, he had felt a searing rage that made him demand everything that had once been his cousin's. Every privilege, every favor, every kiss, every caress... His jealousy had been uncontrollable. He had never felt for Anna an ounce of the white-hot possessive rage he had felt then for Mari, and somehow that simply made matters worse. Even now, thinking of the taste of her and the silken warmth of her body beneath his hands, he could have groaned aloud.

He put his head in his hands, then straightened up and went down the steps to the pool, where he doused his face in the cool water from the fountain. His mind cleared a little and the simmering anger within him eased and at last he found he was able to think dispassionately. He picked up Mari's discarded clothes from the terrace, scrunching them up in his hand in a mixture of frustration and puzzlement, and walked slowly down the gardens toward the house.

He thought about Mari's words when they had first met that night.

When I received your letter, I knew he had told you about me—who I was and where to find me.

Except that Rashleigh had not told him. He must have told someone else, someone who had been sending her anonymous letters.

If you do not keep to the agreement, then I will make you pay.

She had sounded fierce, furious, threatening to kill him if he broke his word. And now Nick wondered about this agreement. Could the mysterious letter writer be blackmailing her? It would explain the author's anonymity and Mari's anger. Nick thought that he would give a great deal to know about that agreement.

Pondering on it, Nick crossed the parterre and went into the house.

The hall was empty. Carrington, the butler, greeted him politely, as though his grace's guests frequently returned from midnight strolls in the grounds wearing fewer clothes than they had gone out in.

Nick went upstairs, thinking about the information in Anstruther's letter and how it had matched with what Mari had said about Rashleigh paying her off and her agreeing to live quietly in the country. Evidently she had invented a history and identity for herself. Living in a quiet place like Peacock Oak, it would be important to have a background that was irreproachably respectable, hence the husband who had been a clergyman's son. But such lies could make her very vulnerable to blackmail.

He lay down on the bed and put his hands behind his head. Did he believe what she had told him about Rashleigh's death? She was a liar and an impostor and yet he was inclined to think she had told him the truth. Perhaps she was capable of honesty after all.

He kept very still, concentrating, his mind running over everything that had happened and all that she had told him.

Something in the story did not fit.

He frowned. Something was not right. He could sense it.

He rolled over on the bed and lay facing the window where the curtains were not drawn and the moon poured in its bright white light. On the chair lay Mari's golden gown, shimmering in the moonlight. It seemed to taunt him with all the things that he did not know or understand.

Now that he had seen Mari Osborne in her true colors he knew he would do well to forget the disturbing impulse that prompted him to dig deeper. He would do well to forget Mari altogether; forget the taste and the touch of her, forget her sweetness in his arms and the aching need he had for her. He should go back to London, tell Hawkesbury that she was not the woman he sought for murder and highway robbery and give himself time and space to think clearly about who that murderer could be. Perhaps then he could untangle his emotions from this case and lay his feelings for Mari to rest.

Once again, as he had the previous night, he took Anna's locket from the drawer and opened it to look at the picture inside. Her image smiled back at him, calm and untroubled. He felt the familiar wash of guilt sweep through him. He had not been there to help Anna when she needed him. He had failed her.

Was he about to fail Mari, too?

With an oath he snapped the locket shut and lay down and attempted to sleep but the doubts and questions in his mind disturbed him and gave him no rest.

Mari had run from him. She had been afraid.

She had been Rashleigh's mistress. *She had been afraid...*

He lay awake all night.

CHAPTER TWELVE

Coltsfoot—Justice shall be done

"I AM WORRIED about you, Mari," Hester said over a late breakfast a couple of days later. "You are too pale and you haven't been to your greenhouses for three days so I know there must be something wrong. Are you sick?"

Mari tried to smile. She felt tired and listless. It was the same weariness that had possessed her when she had first known her secrets were to be exposed and all she had struggled to gain was under threat. She felt too tired to move, too tired even to think. She felt as though she was in a dream that nothing could penetrate. Since the night at the Star House with Nick she had hidden away, nursing the terrible scars on her mind that their encounter had forced so cruelly into the light, and she had not cared about anything else at all.

"I am very well," she said. "I felt a little unwell for a couple of days but it is quite past now."

"Jane said that Major Falconer has called twice but that you have refused to see him," Hester said, reaching for the jam pot. "She said she was afraid he would ignore her excuses and demand an interview with you. What is going on, Mari?"

"Nothing," Mari said. She made an effort. "I find this heat very enervating. I wish that it would thunder and clear the air."

"Well, it won't happen today," Hester said. "Frank says that the weather will not break until tonight. Laura has arranged an archery tournament for Miss Cole and her friends today, but I fear it may be too hot for it." She stood up. "I promised I would spend a dull hour at the Court cheering them on. I suppose you will not come with me? No? Well, before I forget, here is a letter that arrived for you yesterday. I do not know who brought it. I found it in the hall."

After Hester had gone out, Mari put out a hand and reached slowly for the letter, unfolding it with a singular lack of interest.

It was printed in capitals on a single sheet of parchment.

I was waiting for you at midnight at the Star House. You cannot play these games with me if you wish to ensure the safety of those you care for. Meet me tomorrow, or the truth will be exposed. I want what is mine, bought and paid for.

Mari stared at the note. At first she did not understand. Then she felt nothing but shock as the words slowly impinged.

She had made a terrible mistake. It had not been Nick who had sent her the anonymous letters. Her mysterious blackmailer was still unidentified.

Her trancelike state shattered. She felt angry, and the anger swelled and grew until it blocked out all other feelings. Nick had tricked her. He had allowed her to believe that he was her blackmailer. She had told him so much—too much. She had given such a lot away. She had almost given herself.

She shredded the letter between her fingers. So Nick Falconer had not been the venal, callous man she had thought him, the man who, like his cousin, had been prepared to blackmail a woman to get what he wanted. He had not sold his principles. But he was almost as bad because he had deceived her thoroughly to find out the information he had wanted. He had led her on deliberately so that she confided in him. And he had nearly—so very nearly—seduced her. He would have done so had she not run away.

She would deal with the true blackmailer later. Now she would deal with Nicholas Falconer.

There was a red haze of fury before her eyes now. Suddenly all her emotions switched back into life, as though someone had set a flame to tinder. She was burning up with anger and it felt good, strong and powerful. She got to her feet. She took Nick's shirt, which Jane had laundered so beautifully and left, somewhat pointedly, on the silver tray on the hall table, and she marched out of the house, across the garden and through the gate into the deer park, all without pausing for breath.

Laura's guests were already assembled, sitting beneath a big white marquee on the south lawn. It was midmorning and tea was being served. Mari could hear the civilized chink of china as the servants handed around the cups. Miss Lydia Cole and some of her debutante friends were performing at the archery butts and Lady Faye and the other matrons were watching and applauding enthusiastically. Mari could see Nick standing at the edge of the group, chatting to John Teague. She looked at them all and thought of the years she had spent portraying herself as the irreproachably respectable widow and how she was about to smash the whole illusion now and that she no longer cared.

She walked up to the archery butts and draped Nick's shirt over it. Then she strolled over to Miss Cole, who was watching her with lively interest, and asked to borrow her bow. By now Laura's guests were starting to watch her. She could hear the lowered voices, the curious whispers.

She raised the bow, took aim carefully and shot the arrow into the center of the target, piercing Nick's shirt somewhere in the region of the heart. Impaled on the arrow, it flapped like a flag of surrender in the summer breeze. There was dead silence from the pavilion now. Mari handed the bow back to Lydia with a polite word of thanks and walked directly up to Nick. She ignored John Teague, ignored Hester and Laura, ignored everyone else as though they simply did not exist. She was conscious of nothing and no one but Nick himself.

"Major Falconer," she said, "if you ever trick me again, I will shoot you."

And without waiting for any response, she turned on her heel and walked away.

HE CAUGHT UP WITH HER before she had taken more than twenty steps away, catching her arm and drawing her beneath the spreading branches of one of the home park oak trees, in order to hide them from the prying eyes of Laura's guests. Mari did not care. She was so angry that she would have said whatever she had to say in front of an invited audience.

"Mrs. Osborne—" he began.

"Don't pretend to misunderstand me, Major Falconer," Mari cut in.

"I won't," Nick said.

That stopped Mari momentarily in her tracks. It was not what she had been expecting, but then he had always been a very direct man.

She could see one of the servants taking his shirt down off the butts now and Lydia and her friends resuming their display.

"You are angry with me," Nick said.

"Correct." Her gaze came back and focused fiercely on his face. The anger burned so hard and so bright inside her she thought she might be consumed. She looked at him and the intensity of her feelings shook her. Whatever there had been between them had always been powerful, passionate, extreme. Now it was unstoppable.

"You are angry because I led you to believe that I was the man who had written you the anonymous letters," Nick said.

"You are *so* perceptive, Major Falconer." Mari wanted to hurt him, to lash out. She barely held herself under control. "I can see why Lord Hawkesbury thought to send you to unmask me. You must be a real asset to him."

Nick took a step closer to her and she fell silent, suddenly powerfully aware of his physical presence. Even now, after all that had happened, she was not, could not be, indifferent to him.

"I did not lie to you even once that night," he said slowly.

"No," Mari said bitterly, "you merely allowed me to make assumptions."

"Exactly."

"Why?"

There was no tone of apology in his voice as he answered. "Because, as you have no doubt guessed, I needed to know what had happened to my cousin." His gaze examined her face and Mari felt herself burn beneath it. "I needed to know," he said quietly, "that you were not a murderer."

"I see." Mari's fury was almost choking her. "You needed to know that I was not a murderer so you tricked and very nearly seduced me. And that is supposed to make all right. Well, Major Falconer, the purity of your motives does *not* excuse your actions. You are a deceitful, dishonest, cunning, conniving traitor!"

He smiled at her. It was devastating. "I accept your reproof. You have every right to be angry with me. Forgive me, but I had to be sure."

"You pretended to be attracted to me from the start," Mari continued, trying to ignore the perfidious impulse that was prompting her to excuse him.

"That," Nick said, "was no pretence."

"And you set out to seduce me with deliberate intent."

"Again, that is true, but my desire for you was not feigned."

Mari took a deep breath. "You would have made love to me had I not run away from you."

"Yes." Nick shifted a little but his dark gaze remained fixed on her. "I would have made love to you," he said. "I wanted you to the exclusion of all else. I freely confess it."

They looked at one another whilst the anger and

something far stronger smoldered between them, then Nick straightened. "And I do believe," he said quietly, "that I have as much right as you to be angry. You told me a pack of lies that night."

Mari caught her breath. Suddenly his tone frightened her far more than his words. It was very gentle, terrifyingly so. "Everything that you told me hung together as a story," he continued. "It might even have been true. But it was not." He rested a hand against the trunk of the oak. "I thought about it all night." His eyes met hers and Mari felt the slam of her heart through her entire body. She was surprised she was not shaking visibly with it. "I thought about *you* all night, and about why you might lie to me."

Nick reached out and touched her cheek, and she closed her eyes in despair. "I think," he said softly, "that you lied because you are alone and in danger and you are afraid."

His insight stole her breath. It seemed impossible that he had not believed the story she had spun for him. Impossible, and very, very dangerous, because now he was within a whisker of piecing together the truth and she had to stop him.

"You are imagining things," Mari said. She wanted to sound abrupt. Instead she knew she sounded scared.

"I am not," Nick said, with an absolute certainty that shook her. "I could help you," he said, "if you were to trust me—"

"Trust you!" Mari said. Once, she had longed to do precisely that. Even now, after all that had happened between them, she felt an insidious urge to confide in him, this man who had set out deliberately to seduce the truth from her and had almost succeeded. She wondered bitterly how many more times she needed to remind herself to trust no one.

"You ask me to trust you now, after all that you have done?" she said. "You can take your trust and your help, Major Falconer, and…and you know what you can do with them!"

"When you ran from me that night, you were afraid," Nick said, and his quietness cut straight through her anger and pinned her with a helpless despair that she would never be able to deceive him, that in her heart she did not want to and that she needed him now as much as she had ever done.

"What did Rashleigh do to you, Mari?" he said. "I know what sort of a man he was. What happened between you? What are you afraid of?"

"Nothing," Mari whispered. Her lips felt stiff, bloodless. The heat of the day faded, the grass of the deer park shifted beneath her feet. She fought to keep the memories in the dark place where they belonged. She could not bear the thought of telling him all the hateful, painful details of her history. "I was his mistress," she said. "It was as I told you."

"It was not." Nick's tone was implacable.

There was silence for a moment and then Mari sighed.

"Let it go," she said. "Please. I swear, that I told you the truth when I said I had not murdered your cousin, Major Falconer." She took a deep breath. "And so that there cannot be any further misunderstandings between us, I will also say that I cannot help you in the matter of the Glory Girls. As for the rest—" her voice broke "—as for those things that you have asked me about myself and the Earl of Rashleigh… Those are matters that cannot be set to rights."

Nick caught her hand in his. "It is never too late—"

"Yes, it is," Mari said. She thought of her history as Rashleigh's mistress and the scars it had left on her, and the secrets she had to keep.

"It is too late for me," she said. She slipped her hand from his. "You should go back to London, Major Falconer, and not return to Peacock Oak."

Nick took a step back and she thought her heart would break. She knew that she was right, that there were too many secrets and lies between them, too many reasons why they could never be together, and yet for a moment her heart ached fiercely for what might have been.

"I will go back to London," Nick said, and Mari felt her spirits sink even as she knew he was doing the right thing.

"Thank you," she said. She smiled a little. "And thank you for believing me, Major Falconer, when I have given you every reason not to do so."

"I will go," Nick said, "since you ask it of me. But I will come back, Mari. There will come a point when you are ready to speak to me, and then I will come back and we shall see what can be undone and what cannot."

Mari pressed her hands to her cheeks. Her battered heart could not bear for him to prove now that he was as good and honorable as she had always hoped he would be. "Nicholas, please," she said beseechingly.

"No," Nick said. He smiled faintly. "I will respect your wishes for now, Mari, but you must know that there is no point in trying to dissuade me. I will be waiting for you for as long as it takes. There is nothing so bad that it cannot be put right."

She watched him go. He walked past the pavilion without pausing to speak to anyone, and disappeared in the direction of the house. Mari saw Hester glance anxiously across at her, but she shook her head. For a moment the tears blinded her eyes. She had sent Nicholas Falconer away and she hoped to be able to forget his strength and his honesty and his integrity, qualities she ached for, because with her past she could not match them nor give him anything in return.

Later that day, Hester had come back to Peacock Cottage and told her that Nick was indeed returning to London, and Mari had known that he had accepted her word and felt both glad and desperately sad. Hester was quiet, and Mari could see that she wanted to ask what had happened between the two of them but did not want to pry. Mari sent her back to John Teague at Starbotton Hall, which was where she knew Hester really wanted to be, and then she took the shreds of the final anonymous letter and sat re-reading it at her bureau whilst she thought about what to do. She knew that she had to deal with it, to wipe the slate clean. She would tell her blackmailer to expose the truth and be damned. She had to dare to believe that he had no proof that could hurt Laura or Hester or Josie or Lenny. She could not keep running, could not keep living in fear. She could see that now, now that she felt awake and alive again. To see him, to deal with him, was the only way that she could be free.

Accordingly she waited until the long case clock had struck eleven that night, donned a dark cloak and took her pistol from the drawer in the desk. Hester had not returned and Mari was glad. If she had told Hester what she was doing, her friend would have insisted on accompanying her and she wanted no witnesses to this very private meeting.

The moon was bright as she went through the gate into the deer park and picked her way between the trees until she reached the driveway and beyond that, the formal gardens. It reminded her of the night when she had run toward Nick Falconer in a panic of fear and desire. Now, though, her mind was icy clear. The fear had lifted.

The gardens were still and quiet in the hot night. Mari found a spot beneath the weeping willow by the fountain and waited. She wanted to see her blackmailer arrive. She wanted to know his identity before he saw her. In the massing banks of storm clouds to the west, she could see the flicker of lightning. The full moon was peering from behind the scurrying clouds now and the whole night seemed full of menace.

On the terrace of the Star House a shadow stirred. Someone was mounting the steps and heading for the door.

Mari kept very still, craning her neck to see if she could recognize him, but the night was too dark now. She saw the figure slip the latch. He crossed the threshold into the darkness inside, leaving the door ajar. A moment later Mari saw the flare of a lantern within.

Moving very quietly, she slid from the cover of the bushes and skirted the fountain. The pool reflected the faint light of the moon. The canal stood silent and still whilst in the rock garden the water from the fells tumbled down the hillside toward the river. The roar it made masked all other sounds.

Because of the noise she did not hear the second figure until it was almost too late and it was nearly upon her. At the last moment she saw it approaching and stepped behind the trunk of the tall silver birch, and the woman walked straight past her and up the steps of the Star House, disappearing through the half-open door. As she slipped through the door Mari saw the lamplight fall on her face. It was Laura Cole.

Mari's heart raced. Laura here? Had she made an assignation? It seemed impossible in the extreme. Mari waited a moment and then resumed her cautious progress toward the Star House, ghosting silently up the steps to stand by the door, her back against the wooden panels of the wall, straining so that she might hear the conversation within.

It was Laura who was speaking. Her voice was low-pitched and perfectly calm, almost conversational.

"Were you expecting someone else, my dear? You seem strangely put out to see me. I saw you creeping out of the house and thought it might be interesting to follow you. So here I am—and most curious about your reason for being here in the middle of the night."

Mari heard her companion grunt a reply, and after a moment, Laura resumed.

"It seems ironic, does it not, Charles, that it was Mari who designed this house as a place where the two of us could retire from our public lives to enjoy a little intimacy? Ironic, I mean, in the sense that you chose it as the place for your seduction of Mari rather than of me?"

The shock hit Mari squarely in the stomach. She felt icy trickles of horror and disbelief creep down her spine. It was *Charles* who had written the notes, Charles who had threatened to expose her and bring the Glory Girls to justice, Charles who had claimed to have bought her from Rashleigh and to own her body and soul. And Laura *knew*. Laura, whom she loved, Laura who had been one of her most loyal and dearest friends. She felt the cold sweat prickle her skin.

Charles was blustering. "Don't know what you mean, old girl. What has Mrs. Osborne to do with this?"

"Oh, Charles." Mari thought that Laura sounded as exasperated as a governess with a slow pupil. "You always underestimate me, my dear. Do you not realize that I know all about your sordid attempts to blackmail Mari into becoming your mistress? I guessed it was you as soon as I heard about the letters. I know how you sent her those desperate little notes threatening to expose the truth about her and about the Glory Girls! I thought it unworthy of you, my dear, but then I suppose that snake Rashleigh was the one who told you of Mari's past? You always were far too deep in his company and so easily led. I could forgive the gambling and your stealing my jewelry," Laura finished gently, "but not your blackmailing of Mari, and not your *disgusting* attitude toward slavery. I will never forgive that."

There was a heavy silence. Mari could feel the sweat running down between her shoulder blades now. Her muscles were cramped tight with the effort of keeping still. The moon had vanished behind the suffocating darkness of the storm cloud and the only light came from the golden pool cast by the lantern.

"Now, just a moment, old girl…" Charles's voice cracked a little with telltale tension. "I swear, I have no notion what you are getting so exercised about. Came up here to…to have a bit of peace and quiet, don't you know. I wanted to…to think. All those guests… The house party… A fellow never gets a moment to himself."

"I see." Mari could hear Laura's footfalls echo off the wooden floor. Her shadow crossed the pool of light cast by the lantern. "You wanted to have time to think. I do believe that is the poorest excuse that you have come up with since your lies to me about your theft of my jewelry." The contempt dripped from her voice. "Well, I have had enough, Charles. I have had enough of your lies and your deceit and your blustering and your pathetic excuses. Rashleigh *sold* Mari to you like the sickening scoundrel he was. Do you think I do not know that? Do you think I have not worked out everything? But you were a coward. You did not dare come out and claim her openly. How could you? Slavery is disgusting and you pretend to oppose it. But instead you sent her anonymous letters, you blackmailed her in the most repellent manner that I have ever seen."

There was a silence, broken by Charles's mumbles of self-justification. "Didn't realize that she would tell you…"

"You didn't realize that she would tell me? She told Hester and Hester told me. Mari is my friend, Charles, and I have more respect for her than I will ever have for you again!"

"It wasn't like that," Charles muttered. "I admit I made a fool of myself over her. I wanted her as my mistress but it is no great matter." His voice changed into a pathetic attempt at confidence. "You understand how it is in society, old girl. It is the way of the world—"

The sharp slap of Laura's hand against Charles's cheek snapped the silence and Mari jumped.

"It may be the way of the world, it may be *your* way, but it is not *my* way," she said. "I suppose there have been other women, all those times you were in London without me?"

The silence was painful, assenting. A moment later Laura resumed, "You will leave Cole Court tomorrow morning, Charles. I understand that Major Falconer returns to London on the morning coach. Well, you may travel with him."

"Travel by stage?" It seemed to Mari that Charles was more appalled at the thought of that than anything else that Laura had said that night. "I say, I can't do that, old girl. Think of my position! I'd be a laughing-stock if I didn't take the carriage. Don't make me."

"You will travel by stage," Laura said relentlessly, "and if I hear one word more—one word, Charles— from you about threatening to expose the Glory Girls, then Glory herself will personally hunt you down and shoot you. Do you understand me?"

Mari could hear naked fear in Charles's voice now. "Never meant it, my love. I would never have spoken out, I swear."

Once again Mari could hear the sharp clip of Laura's heels against the wooden floor. "Before you go," she said, "there is something else I need to know."

"Anything!" The eagerness in Charles's voice was pitiful. "Ask me anything, old girl, and I swear, I will tell you the truth."

"How did Rashleigh know that Mari was here in Peacock Oak?" Laura said. "Did *you* tell him where to find her, Charles?"

"I didn't know who she was," Charles protested. "We were having a drink one day and I started to tell him about your unsuitable friendship with a merchant's widow. He seemed very interested—"

"I am sure he was," Laura said dryly, "when he realized whom she was." She sighed. "Poor Mari! Of all the unconscionably bad luck, to choose Peacock Oak without knowing that you were hand in glove with Rashleigh!"

"The *Ton* is a small world," Charles muttered.

"Indeed. And it was Mari's lawyer who recommended Peacock Oak as a quiet place to buy a property, and he is of course, our family lawyer, too."

"Most inappropriate," Charles said. "I cannot think why he takes on the middle classes as clientele when he has our business."

Mari heard Laura give a snort of amusement. "You are a more tragic snob even than Faye, my dear. And was it Rashleigh who told you about the Glory Girls, too? How did he find out about us?"

"It wasn't Rashleigh." Charles's words fell over themselves in his haste to get them out. "It was the other way around. I told him. It was a mistake! I was drunk! I never meant to tell anyone. I had seen you ride out one night last summer and could not believe it. I set a servant to watch you and he told me about the others, about Hester and that woman who owns the inn on the Skipton road. I meant to keep it a secret, I swear, but I had one of Glory's cards that Hester let slip and Rashleigh saw it—"

"So you knew all along," Laura said. Mari could hear the ring of bitter amusement in her voice. "And to think that from the first I wanted to be found out, I wanted for you to know, Charles, so that you might notice me, so that you might realize I was more than just a cipher wife, more than just the bloodless aristocrat that you had married." Her voice rose. "I wanted your regard, Charles! I wanted your love! And now I cannot understand why I *ever* wanted it."

Mari slipped away. Whatever happened between them now was no concern of hers. The shock of knowing that it had been Charles who had bought her from Rashleigh was subsiding now although she could not quite believe his hypocrisy. On more than one occasion in the past, Laura had told her with pride that Charles backed the abolitionists and had spoken out against slavery in the House of Lords. It seemed now that his words had been a sham. Her skin crawled to think of him as a man who had wanted her as his mistress. Not by one word or one deed had he betrayed to her his interest in her. Had it been Lord Henry, as she had secretly suspected, she would not have been surprised. But Charles, Duke of Cole, the perfect, conventional country gentleman… She had wondered once what his secret was and now she knew. She felt desperately sad for Laura who had loved him and wanted his love in return, Laura who was so generous that she had not uttered one word against her, so giving that she had not blamed Mari for her husband's betrayal.

The thunderstorm was creeping closer now and the rain had started to fall in huge fat drops that splattered on the ground, raising the hot smell of the dust. Mari was soaked by the time she found her way back to Peacock Cottage. She stripped off her wet clothes and hung them up in the drying room, then jumped into bed and curled up beneath the blankets, listening as the rising wind threw the rain against the window. She wondered if Laura would ever mention her encounter with Charles to her, and thought that she probably would not. Laura was as secretive as Hester was open. There would be no explanation offered as to why the Duke of Cole had abandoned his house-party guests in the middle of summer, nor any comment made on the decision of the Duke and Duchess to live separate lives. The threat from the blackmailer would simply disappear and for that Mari could only be grateful.

The morning coach from Skipton would also carry Nick Falconer back to London and Mari knew that she should also be grateful that he would be gone from her life. Hester would be married in ten days' time and a new chapter in the life of Peacock Oak would unfurl.

Mari stretched out, feeling the cool brush of the bedclothes like a lover's caress. She knew she should try to rest. She could sleep now knowing the threat from the blackmailer was gone. But the threat from the past? That was not so easily dismissed. If Nick chose to ask questions on his return to London, he might find out about Rashleigh and the manner in which she had run away from him.

When you are ready to speak to me, I will come back and then we shall see what can be undone and what cannot….

She turned her head against the pillow. Nick Falconer, as she already knew, was a man of his word and she had a feeling that the fate that tied her to him had not finished with her yet.

LONDON IN JULY was hot and dusty and empty of company. Nick's first task had been to give Lord Hawkesbury a report of his work in Yorkshire and it was not a meeting that went particularly well.

"So," Hawkesbury said, steepling his fingers and leaning his elbows on his desk, when Nick had ended his report, "you have identified the woman from the Hen and Vulture but discovered that she was neither Rashleigh's murderer nor the criminal Glory. You have not found the real Glory or apprehended her gang, and you have no notion who killed your cousin." His brows snapped down. "In short, you have completely failed in all aspects of your inquiry."

"Yes," Nick said. "That sums it up, my lord."

Hawkesbury sighed loudly. "This woman—your cousin's whore—you are certain of her innocence?"

"I am," Nick said. He felt his temper rise with animosity at Hawkesbury's disparaging description of Mari and tried to clamp down on his anger. He hated to hear her spoken of with such a lack of respect.

"Apparently he pensioned her off on the basis that she should live quietly in the country," he said. "She had nothing to gain from his death."

"*Humph.*" Hawkesbury sighed again. He toyed with a quill, snapping it in half.

"This is most unsatisfactory."

"Yes, my lord." Nick allowed himself to relax infinitesimally. He was protecting Mari quite deliberately. From the moment he had seen the fear and vulnerability in her, he had resolved that he had to return to London to make sure that Hawkesbury's inquiries did not harm her. In the fullness of time he hoped she would trust him sufficiently to confide in him but until then it was all he could do.

"*Humph,*" Hawkesbury said again, breaking into his reflection. "So what are your thoughts?"

"I think," Nick said, "that my cousin could have

been stabbed by a passing criminal who saw a rich man and chanced his luck in the hope of carrying off his purse. Or a hired assassin might have set upon him. Any one of those outraged peers whose sons Rashleigh had cheated could have paid a man to do the job. I think it most unlikely that you will discover the truth now, my lord, and I think very few people care because in so many ways it is poetic justice that he is dead."

Hawkesbury grunted. "Can't argue with that. The man was a scoundrel."

"He was worse than that," Nick said.

"Just so." Hawkesbury sighed. "If we may be sure that there is nothing seditious, nothing treasonable going on that involved Rashleigh and those damned highwaywomen…" Another quill pen broke between his fingers. "But can we be sure?"

"I think that whoever killed Rashleigh used Glory's name to gain more notoriety," Nick said. "I do not think there was any conspiracy. And whilst it is a taunt to law and order to have these women galloping around the countryside and robbing the rich to give to the poor, there are worse crimes."

"It goes against the natural order," Hawkesbury grumbled. "If the poor were meant to be rich, then God would have given them money."

"Which is what he is doing, indirectly," Nick said. "Those are my thoughts, sir, for what they are worth."

"I'll send the militia," Hawkesbury grumbled. "I'll catch them yet!"

"Then I wish you the best of luck, sir," Nick said. He stood up. "If I have fulfilled my commission, then I will ask your permission to resume my furlough."

"You've scarcely fulfilled it satisfactorily," Hawkesbury grumbled again. He flapped his hands irritably. "Oh, very well, go! Go and sort out those papers you inherited from your cousin. Nothing but filth there!"

"Your clerks must have suffered terribly reading through it all," Nick said politely.

He went out into the street. London wilted under a hard blue sky. The dust clung to the trees, turning the leaves a dull green. He found himself thinking of the fresh green fields of Yorkshire.

He wondered what else to do with his furlough. He was meeting Anstruther that night at Whites and he supposed that after that he should go up to Scotland. His great-uncle was hosting a stalking party at his estate in Sutherland. His sisters and their families would be there and he had every intention of seeing them at some point during his leave. What he would be unlikely to do was to spend more time with Charles Cole, who had traveled back with him on the coach and seemed to have taken up residence permanently at his club, drinking his way through bottle after bottle of ruinously expensive port. Charles seemed to be avoiding Nick's company and had offered no excuse for his sudden departure from Yorkshire so close to his cousin's wedding other than some vague comment about urgent business in Town. It was most odd.

Nick walked back to Eaton Square through the stifling heat of the day and stepped into the cool of his great-uncle's hall with some relief.

"There is a gentleman to see you, sir." Danton, the butler, was standing in the doorway. "Or rather, not a gentleman, but a lawyer by the name of Churchward. Apparently the matter pertains to your cousin's estate and he has been hoping to have the chance to speak with you for several weeks past."

Nick raised his brows. He had thought that Hawkesbury had dealt with all aspects of Rashleigh's estate as part of the investigation into his death and that there was nothing else to add.

Danton was hovering. "Shall I show him in, sir?"

"By all means," Nick said.

The fussy-looking little man whom Danton ushered into the study a moment later was clutching a battered leather briefcase in one hand and he extended the other to shake Nick's proffered hand.

"Good day, Major Falconer. Thank you for receiving me."

"Would you care for refreshment, Mr. Churchward?" Nick inquired. "A pot of coffee?"

Danton was dispatched to fetch the refreshments and Nick waved Churchward to a chair before the fire.

"How may I help you, Mr. Churchward?" he asked.

Churchward pushed his glasses back up his nose. "Well, Major, it is more a case of how I may help you."

Nick inclined his head. "I see. This is in connection with my cousin's estate, so I understand? Forgive me, but I thought that all matters had been dealt with by Lord Hawkesbury's office?"

"Indeed." Mr. Churchward shook his head disapprovingly. "Such a thing has never happened in the history of Churchward and Churchward, Major Falconer. A man stabbed to death whilst dressed as a molly and visiting a low tavern in Brick Hill! His papers confiscated by the Home Secretary! Not the sort of client that Churchward and Churchward, lawyers to the discerning, would choose to have at all."

"I can imagine," Nick murmured. "My family uses Wordlip and Charles, but I have heard of your sterling reputation, Mr. Churchward."

Mr. Churchward sniffed at the bad taste of the Falconer family in preferring a different lawyer.

"That cannot be helped, I suppose," he said, "but should you ever require another lawyer, Major, may I suggest that you contact us? We are most discreet and accustomed to dealing with all manner of business."

"Of course," Nick said. "Even—reluctantly—that involving my cousin Rashleigh." He leaned forward. "I understand that my cousin named me as heir to all his unentailed property and his nonexistent fortune?"

"That is correct, Major," Churchward said. "You have inherited the house in Kent and very little else, I fear, and your great-uncle..."

"Reluctantly paid off all Rashleigh's debts in order to preserve the family honor," Nick finished. "So what does that leave, Mr. Churchward?"

"This!" Churchward said, with the air of one producing a rabbit from a hat. He fumbled in the leather briefcase and extracted a thin pigskin folder. Nick held his hand out. Churchward, however, did not immediately hand over the file but held it for a moment, an odd expression on his face.

"This did not form part of the paperwork that I passed to Lord Hawkesbury, Major."

"I see," Nick said. He waited.

"You should know, sir, that this document only came into my possession shortly before Lord Rashleigh was murdered," Churchward continued, "and with it he sent me a note demanding in no uncertain terms that I should destroy it in the event of his death."

Nick's eyes narrowed. "And why did you not, Mr. Churchward, if that was his wish?"

An strange expression crossed Churchward's face. "I read the document, my lord," he confessed. A shade of color touched his thin cheek. "Most unprofessional of me, I admit, but knowing your cousin I wanted to be sure that I was doing the right thing. And when I had read it, I decided that in destroying it, or indeed in handing it over to the authorities, I might be committing a grave injustice."

He put the folder gently into Nick's outstretched hand. "It is your decision, Major Falconer."

The strangest shiver of premonition went down Nick's spine. He was not a superstitious man but as he slid the single sheet of paper out of the folder, he felt some of Rashleigh's venom touch him and turn him cold.

At first glance he did not recognize the document for what it was. The signature was that of his uncle, Robert Rashleigh's father, and the deed was dated December 1798. The wavering writing suggested a man who was already very sick.

Nick had never seen a manumission form before but as he read on, understanding burst on him.

"I, Cecil Anthony John Rashleigh, twelfth Earl of Rashleigh, do grant in perpetuity freedom from serfdom to Marina Stepanova Valstoya and to all her descendants…"

Nick paused. Like an echo in his head he could hear Mari's voice, that night at the Star House.

"I thought it would be you, because you are his heir…"

He put the paper down slowly. The patterns in his

head faded and reformed; his uncle's death seven years before, the rumors circulating in the *Ton* of Rashleigh's Russian mistress whom it was said had stolen from him and run away, his cousin's fury and refusal to discuss the incident, Mari Osborne coming to London to meet with Rashleigh at the Hen and Vulture, the anonymous letters and Mari's vulnerability to blackmail and most of all her absolute terror when Nick had touched her…

Nick ran his hands through his hair. A suspicion was forming in his mind, so loathsome, so unbearable, that he was not sure for a moment that he wanted to face it.…

Mari had been a serf. A slave. Rashleigh's slave.…

"Major Falconer?" Mr. Churchward's voice cut through his thoughts. "I hope that you think I did the right thing in preserving the document and bringing it to you?"

"Oh, yes," Nick said, looking from the manumission form to Churchward's anxious face. He cleared his throat. "You were absolutely right, Churchward. Serfdom is a vile thing and it should weigh heavy on any man's conscience to be instrumental in destroying the evidence of a slave's freedom."

Churchward's expression cleared. "Thank you, sir," he said in heartfelt tones. "You are not like your cousin."

"No," Nick said. "I am not." He shook his head. "This should have been given to her seven years ago."

Seven years, not knowing that she was free, of thinking that she was still Rashleigh's slave.…

Nick tried, and failed, to imagine how that must have felt.

He thought about Rashleigh suppressing the

document for so long and demanding that it be destroyed on his death. Such malevolence could only mean one thing—that he had deliberately withheld from Marina Osborne the proof of her freedom. Perhaps she had never even known the manumission form existed. Rashleigh must have wanted to keep it to have a hold over her.

Churchward was fastening the battered leather briefcase and getting to his feet. "The only matter that still troubles me," he confessed as he shook Nick's hand once again, "is how one might find the lady after all this time?"

"Then do not be troubled," Nick said. He gave the lawyer a rueful smile. "I know precisely where to find her. You can trust me to put the matter right, Mr. Churchward."

After the lawyer had gone out, Nick folded the manumission form and put it carefully in his wallet, and went into the library where Rashleigh's papers were stored. Hawkesbury's clerks had been thorough and meticulous. Everything was filed by year and carefully annotated. But they had not known what they were looking for and Nick did. Sitting down on the window seat he turned to the ledgers for 1798 and 1799. This was the period immediately after Rashleigh had inherited from his father and so there were a great many estate papers. There was a note of all the Russian property and their sale and a note of the number of serfs belonging to each estate. Their names were not given and they were listed in the column under possessions and household items for inclusion in the sale. Nick felt repulsed to see this further evidence of his cousin's inhumanity.

On one page, dated December 1798, he found a note in the estate manager's cramped hand of the purchase of a parcel of land at Svartorsk and a note that Feodor Valstoy, his wife, Maria, and two daughters aged ten and twelve had been granted their freedom from serfdom and established on a farm there.

On another page he found a detailed listing of all the jewelry that Rashleigh had inherited from his father and brought back to England, fabulous jewels of dazzling quality, a staggering fortune. Nick thought it entirely possible that Rashleigh might have sold them and squandered the money like the wastrel he was, but the rumors he had heard at the time, the rumors to which he had paid little attention, had suggested otherwise.

And in a third entry he found payment of passage to the port of London for Robert Rashleigh and Marina Valstoya.

He was beginning to understand now why Mari had struggled so hard to conceal her true identity from him. She was almost certainly a runaway slave and a thief. Or, more precisely, she had thought she was, because his blackguard cousin had never told her she was free.

He wondered again about the ledger entries. Why had Rashleigh, who had never been known for his generosity, given Mari's family their freedom? They had been given land and liberty from serfdom. Mari had come with Rashleigh to London. It looked like a bargain, an exchange....

Nick froze as an icy revulsion trickled through his veins.

An exchange. Their freedom in return for Mari's body... And, judging by her fearful reaction to physical intimacy, it had been an arrangement made under duress.

At last the pattern made hateful, horrible sense. Her fear, her vulnerability, her absolute, desperate determination to keep the truth from him….

He put the ledger under his arm and went out into the hall.

"Danton," he said, "I shall be leaving for Yorkshire in the morning."

The butler looked a little pained. "Already, sir?"

"I am afraid so," Nick said. "There was something that I left unfinished and I have to go back."

Those are matters that cannot be set to rights, Mari Osborne had said, but Nick knew this could not be true. He would not allow it to be. He would give her the freedom that had been denied to her for so long. He would hear her story. He would bring Rashleigh's hateful legacy into the light.

He was going to go back and he was going to put matters right.

CHAPTER THIRTEEN

Ash – With me you are safe

NICK'S FIRST IMPULSE on arriving back in Peacock Oak had been to go directly to Peacock Cottage and demand an interview with Mari. When he arrived there, however, there was no answer to his knock. The house looked as though it had been closed. He had only been gone for ten days, yet it seemed that much had changed.

He was obliged to go across to Cole Court, his impatience simmering inside him and desperate for a way out. The Court was also strangely silent and when the butler answered the door to his knock it was to inform him that the house party had ended and the guests departed.

"No one is at home except for me." Laura Cole came forward to greet him and he saw that she was limping. "The most tiresome thing, Major Falconer—I twisted my ankle when I was out riding only two days ago and so cannot walk, let alone ride. And the hunt is to go out tomorrow and here I am stuck at home like a dowager aunt."

She gestured to him to precede her into her private study. "However, this is most auspicious in one sense as I have been hoping to speak with you if you returned to Peacock Oak and it seems that now I have my chance. Tea, Carrington, if you please."

In the study Laura sat down with a gasp of relief then smiled up at him. "I apologize that I cannot invite you to stay here for your visit, Major Falconer, but with Charles away—" here a flicker of pain crossed her face "—and the house party ended it would not be appropriate."

"Pray do not concern yourself, your grace," Nick said. "I am uncertain how long I shall be staying but I have booked a room and left my bags at Half Moon House."

"Oh, dear!" Laura's eyes were bright with amusement. "Josie will not like that. I am surprised that she did not turn you from the door."

"Perhaps," Nick said, watching her face, "she knows that my presence here is no longer a threat?"

He saw Laura color up delicately and fidget a little with her skirts. Carrington brought the tea in at that moment and Laura stirred the pot with perfect composure, although her color was still a little high.

"I hope," she said with a little constraint, as the door closed behind the butler, "that that is true, Major Falconer, for all our sakes." She tilted her head to look at him. "I understand, you see, that when you were here previously you were anxious to track down and arrest the gang of highwaywomen calling themselves the Glory Girls?"

"Your grace—" Nick began, but Laura raised a hand to stop him in his tracks and Nick could suddenly see that beneath the outer gentleness she had all of a Duchess's authority.

"Major Falconer, if you please…" She waited for him to fall obediently silent and then resumed, "I assure you that this is a matter of utmost importance. So please tell me—is my understanding correct?"

She raised a brow interrogatively and Nick nodded. "It is correct," he said.

"The Glories will not ride again," Laura said. "Nor were they associated in any way with the death of Robert Rashleigh."

"Your grace," Nick said, astounded, "how do you know—" He stopped. He thought of Laura's passion for riding, and then he looked down to see her feet peeping from beneath the hem of her gown. They were very large feet. A moment later she had whisked her skirts back to cover them and he looked into her gentle hazel eyes to see that she was smiling at him.

"They will not ride again," she repeated, adding, "A pity in many ways, but it has to be."

Nick was silent.

"Mari Osborne never rode with the Glory Girls," Laura continued. She passed him a cup. "Tea, Major Falconer? Sugar?"

"Thank you," Nick said, feeling increasingly cast adrift in this unlikely conversation. "No sugar, please."

Laura shot him a look. "I think that you realized that, of course. Poor Mari, she is by far too bad a horse-woman ever to ride out like that!"

"I had observed it," Nick said, taking a gulp of tea and feeling that he needed its restorative qualities.

"Quite. But the idea of the Glory Girls, Major Falconer…" Laura smiled. "That was the scheme of someone who had known immense injustice in their life, someone who wanted to ensure that others did not have to suffer the type of hardships and betrayal and cruelty that they themselves had done. May I press you to a rock bun?"

"Thank you," Nick said automatically, thinking of Mari and all the charitable work that she had done. He had thought before that he had been very slow to see the truth. Now he was starting to realize how close he had been without realizing it. He had known that Mari must have been deeply involved with the Glory Girls, but she had been the cool planning behind the attacks, not the one who rode out to execute them. And she had done it from a sense of justice.

"So Glory was conceived as an avenging angel," he said slowly. "Of course. She was the creation of someone who had very personal reasons for wishing to right some of the wrongs of society."

"And," Laura said, a thread of steel entering her gentle tones, "I am sure that you would not wish to add to the injustices heaped on that person, Major Falconer."

"I am sure that you are correct, your grace," Nick said wryly. He took a bite out of the rock bun. It tasted very good.

"Which brings me rather neatly to Mari herself," Laura said, stirring her tea. "She will not thank me for mentioning this to you, Major Falconer, so pray disabuse yourself of any notion that she has asked me to speak for her."

Nick waited. He doubted that anything else Laura Cole could say to him on this extraordinary day could possibly shock him.

"Mari Osborne has been very badly used in the past," Laura said. "I know that to be true." She gave a little sigh. "How much do you know of Mari's history, Major Falconer?"

"A great deal more than I did when I was last here," Nick said, a little grimly. "I came back in the hope that she would finally be able to tell me the whole."

Laura nodded. "You wish to speak with her. That I understand. But I do hope that you will not hurt her. She has had so much to bear." She hesitated. "I am speaking very much out of line here, you understand, Major Falconer?" When Nick waited politely, she continued with a little difficulty, "I have to confess here to doing something of which I am not proud, Major Falconer. I have to tell you that I know Mari Osborne's entire history at the hands of your cousin, the Earl of Rashleigh. I know it because when Mari first came to Peacock Oak, I asked an inquiry agent to look into her background."

She gestured to the teapot. "Another cup, Major Falconer?"

"Thank you," Nick said. His mind was reeling. So much for thinking that she could not shock him. "I... Uh... You...asked someone to investigate Mrs. Osborne's history?" he repeated.

"I used Tom Bradshaw," Laura confirmed. "You will know of him, I am sure. He is the most discreet and efficient inquiry agent in London."

"I do know him," Nick agreed. He shifted. "Tell me, your grace, what was it that prompted you to suspect that Mrs. Osborne was not all that she seemed—for I assume that that was the reason for your actions?"

Laura nodded. She took her cup and walked away from him toward the fire. "People assume that because

I am female and a Duchess that I must be either stupid or need to be protected from the harsh facts of life," she said, after a moment, "but the truth is that I am well able to take care of myself. I knew as soon as I met Mari Osborne that there was something…not odd about her, exactly, but not precisely *right*. I sensed that she was not the blameless widow of a merchant that she claimed to be." She looked at him. "As you know, a Duchess has many an approach from undesirables, people who want to know me for my money or my influence or some other reason. I developed an instinct for it early. That was why I wondered about Mari Osborne right from the start."

She placed her cup and saucer on the sideboard and rested a hand on its shining surface. "I never told Mari what I had done, of course. When I heard all that she had gone through, I wanted to befriend her. And the irony was that when I tried, I discovered that she wanted nothing from me other than to keep out of my way. She resisted my friendship fiercely." Laura's lips twitched. "Had I not been a Duchess and her next-door neighbor I believe she would have told me to go hang before she accepted my friendship."

Nick was frowning. "Knowing a little of Mrs. Osborne's history, as I do now, I suppose that is no great wonder."

"No," Laura said. "Well, eventually we did become friends. And a great deal later than that, Mari trusted me with something of her story, never knowing that I knew the whole, dreadful tale already." Laura turned to look at him. "I knew your cousin Robert Rashleigh, Major Falconer. We all did, Charles, Henry, John Teague, myself. How could we not, when he was a member of the *Ton* as we all were? But I knew Rashleigh for another reason." She moved away from him with a swish of silk. "When I was young, barely more than a child, in fact, Robert Rashleigh ruined a distant cousin of mine."

Nick shook his head. "I did not know. I had no idea."

"Of course not. The matter was hushed up to preserve the family honor in a manner Rashleigh had so signally failed to do. But I heard my parents speaking of it. I never forgot. So you may imagine that when I heard he was dead, I was not sorry, for so many reasons."

She looked Nick straight in the eye. "I did not kill Robert Rashleigh, Major Falconer, and nor did Mari or Hester Teague. I want you to know that. When I said that the Glory Girls were not involved in his murder, I spoke the truth."

Nick nodded. "I am more than grateful to you for your honesty, your grace," he said.

Laura smiled. "I owed it to both you and Mari to reveal the truth about the Glory Girls," she said. "Mari has kept silent out of loyalty—to protect those she cares about the most. It was time that those of us who care for *her* should put the matter straight."

"You may count upon my discretion in the matter, your grace," Nick said. He laughed. "Though I confess it relieves me to hear the Glories will not ride again."

"Of course," Laura said. "A gentleman in your situation cannot collude at breaking the law, Major Falconer. I appreciate that." She looked at him, biting her lip. "There is, however, one small barrier remaining to your discovering the whole truth, Major Falconer. Mari has gone away."

Nick remembered the shuttered windows of Peacock Cottage. "I wondered if she had," he said slowly.

"Not run away," Laura stressed, "but she required some peace, I think, and some time alone. As soon as Hester and John's marriage had taken place, she left. She has been gone a week." She drummed her fingers thoughtfully on the sideboard. "I suppose she did not forbid me from telling anyone where…"

Urgency grasped at Nick and he sat forward. "Your grace—"

"I need your word, Major Falconer," Laura said. "Your word that you will not hurt Mari in any way."

"You have it," Nick said instantly.

Laura smiled. "Very well. Mari is staying in a convent, Major Falconer, the convent of Our Lady of Mount Grace in Cavenham. It is less than twenty miles from here."

"A convent." Nick saw the problem at once. "So if she does not choose to receive me…"

"Then you have a problem, Major Falconer," Laura said. "If she will not see you, there is no way in which you will be able to speak with her, unless you decide to abduct a lady from a convent." She raised her brows. "Fine behavior for an officer and a gentleman! Do you need time to think about it?"

Nick laughed. "No, your grace. I do not believe I do."

MARI TUCKED HER BOOK under her arm and made her way from the walled convent garden through the archway to the guesthouse. It was late afternoon now and the hot, heavy summer day promised thunder. From the church floated the clear, plaintive notes of plainsong as the nuns sang Compline. It was an extremely soothing sound. In fact, everything to do with Mount

Grace was peaceful and soothing. In the week that she had been there Mari had found more peace of mind than in the past five years.

Nevertheless she was very aware that she was running away. Laura might be kind and say that she had needed to give herself time and space to think, to find some peace, and in some ways that was true. But she had no vocation to be a nun and no intention of staying permanently in her retreat and one day soon she knew she would have to go back. She would have to pick up the threads of her life in Peacock Oak. She would have to dismiss Nick Falconer from her memory, as well as from her life.

She paused in the shadow of the gateway, convinced that someone was standing within the cobbled courtyard and watching her, but when she looked around, there was no one there. With a little shrug, Mari walked down the quiet stone corridor to her room and pushed open the door. There were no locks here. They were not needed.

She placed her book on the table and put a hand up to unfasten her spencer then froze as a movement behind her caught the corner of her eye. Turning, she was just in time to see the heavy door swing shut and Nick Falconer leaning back against it, arms folded. He looked solid, unyielding and dangerously determined. Her pulse jumped.

"What… What on *earth* are you doing here?" Her voice came out as a croak.

He smiled and her stomach dipped. She had scarcely had time to forget that wicked smile. "I wanted to talk to you," he said.

"Most people would call at the gate," Mari said. "It is customary."

"I knew that if I did that, you would refuse to see me."

She could not fault the logic of that. Of course she

would have done. Just seeing him standing there made her nerves trip and the breath catch in her throat. She had thought it would be a long, long time—perhaps never—before she would have to face him again and she was woefully unprepared.

"How did you know I was here?" she asked, and knew the answer before he had replied. "Laura told you, I suppose."

"You did not forbid her to tell anyone."

"No." Mari sighed. "But I trusted her…"

"And she trusted me," Nick said. "I swear, I will not hurt you, Mari. I came only to talk."

The way he said her name, with its caressing undertone, did nothing to help Mari's self-possession.

"If you did not call at the gate, how did you get in?" She could scarcely believe that her haven had turned into a trap.

Nick laughed. "I climbed over the wall."

Mari felt genuinely shocked. "You broke into a nunnery? This is not the Middle Ages, Major Falconer!"

Nick shifted slightly. The way he was standing, with his broad shoulders propped against the panels of the door, suggested that he would not be moving anytime soon. Mari noted his tough, uncompromising stance with misgiving.

"As I said, I wanted to talk to you. If that was what it took…"

"You risk a lot simply to talk to me." Mari turned away. "I thought we had said all that we had to say to one another."

"That is where we differ." Nick straightened, moving toward her with deliberation. "I never thought everything was finished between us."

His confidence shook her. Mari took a step back and almost tripped over the table. He put out a hand and caught her arm. His touch seemed to sear her skin and she pulled her arm away.

"You promised not to press me for the truth until I was ready to speak with you," she said, stiffly. "If you have changed your mind, say your piece now and go."

Nick shook his head. "No. Not here. This is too important. We need to talk properly and to have sufficient time. So you are coming with me."

Outrage flared through her. "I am not!"

He shook with silent laughter. "Mrs. Osborne, you are. Surely you do not think I have gone to all this trouble just to leave you behind?"

He seemed so sure of himself and there was something different about him, she thought. She struggled to work out what it was. Throughout their previous acquaintance he had always had this self-assurance. That had not changed. The difference now, she realized suddenly, was that he seemed in some way more certain, more confident of her. It was almost as though…

"You know," she said, on a whisper.

A shadow touched his face. "I know some things. Other things you are going to tell me. Come on."

She folded her arms. "No. I came here for some peace. Leave me alone."

"You came here because you were running away."

It was brutal but true. She glared at him.

"Mari—" His tone had softened, again with that undertone of intimacy.

"Mrs. Osborne," Mari snapped. "I never made you free of my name no matter how willfully you used it!"

"Mrs. Osborne—" Nick spoke with immaculate

courtesy but his gaze slid over her, reminding her of everything they had shared "—this is not a matter for discussion. Either you come back with me of your own free will or I carry you out of here."

"Back?"

"Back home. To Peacock Oak."

Mari raised her chin and stared at him. "And how do you intend to persuade me? Or is that not a matter for discussion, either? You will simply carry me over the wall with you?"

Nick laughed. "Once I was on the inside I opened a gate. I can easily carry you through that."

He could, too. She knew it. And he would do. She could see it in his eyes.

She could still hear the notes of the music from the church. If she screamed loudly enough, someone would surely hear her. It would cause a huge fuss and a scandal. More importantly, it would be poor recompense to bring so much trouble on Mount Grace when they had given her refuge.

She teetered on the edge of capitulation and saw him watching her deliberations with quizzical amusement.

"I did not have you down as a man who would abduct a woman from a convent, Major Falconer," she said. "It seems I do not know you very well at all."

He laughed again and Mari felt the attraction, ruthless, breathtaking. "You'll know me better hereafter," he said, and it sounded like a promise. "So? Are you coming with me?"

Mari felt a rush of panic. The nerves skittered in her stomach. This was all too sudden. "No—"

He laughed, took her wrist and pulled her to him, then slid an arm around her waist as he opened the door.

"Too bad," he said. "I did warn you."

The corridor was empty but for a convent servant hurrying along at the end of the passage, the slap of her sandals loud in the silence. She did not see them.

"If I screamed—" Mari began.

"Don't." He slanted a look down at her and she remembered someone—Hester?—saying that Nick Falconer had a reputation for ruthlessness. She did not doubt it for one second.

He picked her up. His arms were as strong as steel bands, her cheek was against his shoulder and it was the work of seconds to carry her down the corridor and out into the gardens, bundle her through the door in the wall and inside the carriage that was waiting on the other side. Mari waited for the cries of shock and outrage behind them, but they never came. No one had noticed. She had been carried off in broad daylight, and *no one had noticed.* She felt a little faint.

Nick banged on the roof and the carriage moved off.

"Have you done this before?" she demanded.

He looked pleased with himself. Too damned pleased. She felt annoyed.

"No," he said. "It was a first for me."

He was watching her with the same closed, thoughtful expression that he had worn before. Her stomach curled, melted with a mixture of nervousness and longing.

I know some things. Other things you are going to tell me.

She knew she would. They had gone too far now for lies and deception. Whatever it was that he had discovered in London put further pretence beyond her. He had gone to the trouble of fetching her from the nunnery and she sensed he would now go to any lengths to have the truth from her. So when they arrived back in Peacock Oak, she would tell him everything. Until then she had a little time, a little privacy.

"If you do not wish to speak until we are back in Peacock Oak," she said, with dignity, "I will go to sleep. Excuse me, Major Falconer."

NICK SAT AND WATCHED Mari sleep all the way home. She slept neatly, precisely, curled up like a cat. He recognized this quality in her now. It was a defense in a way, an orderly way of keeping the rest of the world at arm's length. Her head rested against the cushion and her eyelashes fanned across her cheek, dark against the pallor. Her breast rose and fell with the rhythm of her breathing. She looked restrained, collected, all that was buttoned up and tidy. He remembered the wild, passionate goddess swimming in the fountain, he remembered unfastening those buttons and exposing her nakedness and he wanted to tear away the layers and reveal the woman beneath, the woman he knew was there, if only he could find her. He knew now that she was neither the harlot from the tavern, Rashleigh's shameless mistress nor the prim and respectable widow of Peacock Oak, but a woman who was a complex mixture of feelings and emotions. It was that woman he wanted to set free, if he could.

She moved slightly and made a soft noise of contentment in her sleep and his heart squeezed with a tenderness he could not deny. He was no youth; he was a man of two and thirty and he understood his own feelings too well for self-delusion.

He wanted Mari Osborne very much. He desired

her. That was easy to understand. The awareness between them had been explosive from the very first. He wanted to bed her and explore every inch of that pale, voluptuous body until she was sated and he was, too.

But he also cared about what happened to her and that was less easy to explain. When he had left London, he had planned only to deliver the manumission form into her hands and finally hear the true story of her relationship with Rashleigh. Or so he had told himself. Yet the urgency with which he had traveled to Peacock Oak, the utter determination he had felt to take her from the convent and bring her back with him, the tenderness he felt as he looked on her now, argued a deeper and more complicated emotion than he had previously acknowledged. And it had taken root much, much earlier, when he had been in Peacock Oak before and seen Mari's courage and her strength, her generosity and her compassion. It was the same feeling that had prompted him to protect her against Lord Hawkesbury's investigation, to offer her his help.

He loved her.

He thought about Anna then and about the way in which he had loved her in his youth, more as a friend than as a wife. He had loved her but he had not been in love with her. He had taken her for granted, betrayed her, failed her in so many ways. And perhaps his absolute determination to put matters right for Mari was in some sense the result of his failure to give of his best to Anna. He had become a better man through knowing her, but the price had been too high. He hoped fervently that Anna would somehow know of his remorse and could forgive him. One day, perhaps, he could forgive himself.

They were reaching the outskirts of Peacock Oak when Mari stirred. She sat up and rubbed her eyes and looked out of the window as the last of the evening sun gilded the hillside. The road was winding down over the fells with the village in the dip below them and the open fields on either side. And suddenly, out of nowhere, Nick heard the sound of the hunt, and remembered Laura Cole saying that they were meeting and that she could not ride out with them because of her injury. He heard the raucous blare of the horn and the frantic yelping of the hounds as they streaked past in the field beside the road, with the riders pounding along behind them. The hunt in full flight was primitive, a wild thing barely under control. Nick sat still for a moment and watched them pour over the side of the valley and disappear. The baying of the hounds hung on the air, then died away, an echo around the valley until the rising breeze swept in to take its place. The air was hot and heavy still, even though it was evening now.

Then he heard Mari make a sound. It was halfway between a gasp and a sob. Her fingers were clenched so tight on the windowsill of the carriage that he could see the bone-white of her knuckles. She sat frozen still.

Nick put a hand out toward her.

"Mrs. Osborne?" he said. "What is it? Are you unwell?"

He stopped. She had made no sign that she had even heard him. She sat, braced and still, her arms wrapped tight around her now as though defending herself from the world.

Nick moved closer and put a hand on her arm. "Mrs. Osborne? Marina?"

This time she turned to look at him. Her face was

so white it was almost transparent. She was shaking.
Her eyes were blind.

"The hunt…" she whispered.

"They have gone now," Nick said. "It is quite safe.
I know it appears wild, but—"

He stopped. Once again she did not appear to hear
him. Concerned, he moved across to the seat beside her
and put both hands on her upper arms. He could feel
the trembling that racked her body.

"Mari—"

She looked up into his face and the shock hit him in
the stomach like a physical blow. She was terrified. He
remembered suddenly the evening in Laura Cole's
drawing room when Mari had said that the hunt was
barbaric and that he could have no idea what it was to
be hunted. And further back in his memory, like the
echo of a nightmare, he could hear his cousin
Rashleigh's drawling voice one day when he had been
deriding Nick's work.

*Fighting for the forces of justice, Nick? Why bother?
It's such a bore. Summary justice is more my style. If
someone angers me, I set the dogs on them and let them
tear the scoundrels apart!*

He looked down into Mari's face and the final pieces
of the jigsaw slowly came together to form the most
appalling whole.

"Mari," he said, and his voice was suddenly very
rough. "He sent the dogs to hunt you down, didn't he?
Rashleigh *hunted* you. Tell me—" Suddenly it felt so
urgent that he wanted to shake the truth from her, but
he forced himself to be patient. "For God's sake, Mari,
tell me what happened!"

She closed her eyes for a second and he wondered

if she had even heard him. But then she opened them again and looked at him, and her gaze was so clear and dark and soft that he caught his breath.

"It is true," she said quietly. "You are quite correct, Major Falconer. I ran away from your cousin and he set his pack of dogs on me."

THE FIRST FAT DROPS of rain had started to fall as Nick dismissed the carriage and helped Mari into the shuttered hall of Peacock Cottage. Mari moved slowly, as though she was sleepwalking, and when Nick led her into the drawing room and closed the door behind them, she made no demur. She felt very tired, as though she had been traveling for a long time with no rest. She sat down on the blue velvet sofa and watched Nick go across to the table, light the candles and pour her a glass of brandy.

"I have given all the servants leave until I returned from Mount Grace," she said suddenly. "There is no one here, though I think that Frank may be working in the gardens during the day…."

"Don't worry about that for now." Nick came across and sat beside her, handing her the brandy glass, but when she tried to hold it, it almost slipped from her grip. Her fingers felt cold, nerveless, and his hand closed around hers to guide the glass to her lips. Her teeth chattered against the rim and then the sting of the spirit was in her throat and it warmed her and she felt a little stronger.

"How are you?" Nick asked, and she looked at him, and it was as though all the emotions that she had repressed for so long flared into vivid life.

She loved him.

She had been in danger of falling in love with him all along. She had wanted to trust him, wanted to love him. And now that there were to be no more secrets between them, now that she knew him to be the man she had always wanted him to be, she could resist her feelings no longer.

But the thought frightened her. She had never been in love before and it felt dangerous and new, tempting but far, far too risky for her.

Never trust a man, never love a man, never give him that power….

For a moment she trembled on the edge of terror.

"Mari?" Nick was looking at her with concern in his eyes.

"I am sorry," she whispered. She made an effort. "I feel a little better, thank you. I am sorry that I reacted so badly when I saw the hunt. It was so sudden and it reminded me…"

"It would have been strange had you not reacted like that given what you had experienced," Nick said. He stood up and moved a little distance away from her. His voice was hard and there was something in his eyes that scared Mari, it was so primitive and angry. Then she saw him make an effort to smooth the expression away.

"I have something for you," he said. He ran a hand over his hair. "I had intended to give it to you when we got back here. You know that I was Rashleigh's heir?" He made an abrupt gesture as though the idea was anathema to him. "His lawyer brought this to me when I was in London last week." He held out a piece of parchment to her. "I imagine from the things that you have said to me, that you did not know it existed."

Mari took the paper and unfolded it. She read it

once without understanding what it meant and a second time in utter incredulity. Then she read it a third time and started to tremble so much that the paper fell from her hand to the floor.

"No…" she whispered.

"Does it mean what I think?" Nick demanded. "My uncle gave you your freedom before he died—"

"But he never told me." Mari looked up, her eyes stricken. "Why? Why did he not tell me?"

"Perhaps," Nick said, "he did not have the chance."

Mari retrieved the paper and looked at the date beneath the old Earl of Rashleigh's signature. "The day he died," she said. Her head felt strange, light and buzzing with the enormity of what she had discovered.

"Rashleigh found this and kept it, didn't he?" she said. She looked at Nick. Her voice broke. "Why? Why did he never tell me?"

"I do not suppose it suited his purposes for you to know," Nick said. His tone was hard with contempt. "He was a sickening scoundrel. He kept the document against the day he might want to use it as a bargaining tool."

Mari rubbed a hand across her forehead. For seven years she had been physically free yet always afraid, always thinking she was a runaway slave. And now it seemed that she had been granted her freedom years before and Rashleigh had stolen that from her, too. The anger swept through her and made her shake with the force of it. It stung her throat until she thought she would choke, and burned so fiercely that she could hardly bear it. She wanted to scream until her voice was hoarse, to break something and wreak around her the same destruction that Rashleigh had inflicted on her life.

"My freedom," she said. She remembered Laura challenging Charles about buying her from Rashleigh and Charles admitting it. So Rashleigh had cheated him, too, selling her on like a piece of horseflesh when he had no right. The knife of her hatred twisted within her again like poison and she made a conscious effort to let it go. Rashleigh would *not* ruin her future as he had taken her past. She would not allow it.

"All those years, thinking that I was still property, still a man's possession…" She met Nick's eyes. "But I *was* a thief. I stole from Rashleigh when I ran away from him. Did you know about that, Major Falconer? I took all his jewels."

Nick nodded. "I guessed you had. I saw the ledgers with a record of all the jewelry that Rashleigh had brought back from Russia, and I wondered what had happened to it." His gaze was thoughtful. "Why did you take it?"

"I did not realize that the stones were worth so much," Mari said. "I knew that I would not survive alone without any money—without selling my body on the streets—and I thought he owed me that at least." She bit her lip. "When I discovered how much they were worth, I was terrified. I had had no idea. I sold them little by little and when I came here I invested the money." She looked at him a little hopelessly. "I used some to set up the school and the almshouses and my charities, but the rest is safe. It is yours by right as you are his heir. I can pay it back…" She realized that the brandy had gone straight to her head and she was gabbling. "I am sorry," she said. "I am no thief by choice but I was alone and afraid and I could not bear to have to sell myself again."

Once again she saw that look in Nick's eyes, so angry, so primitive, so violent that she shrank back a little. She knew his anger was not for her but it was frightening to see. Then he made an effort and smiled at her, and she felt her tense muscles relax a little.

"You have used the money to do good," he said. "Far more than Rashleigh would ever have done."

Mari sighed. "I should tell you everything, I suppose."

Nick came to sit by her and took her hand. "You need tell me only what you wish," he said.

Mari's hand tightened involuntarily on his. She moistened her lips. "I want to tell you, but—" She shook a little.

"Have some more brandy," Nick instructed, and she picked up the glass again and swallowed some more of the liquid conscientiously, as though it was medicine.

She stared into his dark eyes and saw nothing but concern there. No judgment, no disapproval, no pity.

"I do want to tell you," she said again, and realized it was true.

He nodded. "Begin at the beginning," he said gently.

She did. Once she had started she found it was surprisingly easy, as though she were telling a story that had happened to someone else, long ago. She told him about her childhood and her education and the way that the twelfth Earl had tried to turn her into an English lady. She faltered a little when she came to relating what had happened when Robert Rashleigh had inherited from his father, but Nick's hand was still warm and steady in hers and although she saw the same primitive anger burning in his eyes, she knew his fury was not directed at her. When she related the terms of her agreement with Rashleigh, though, she found that she could not look at him and as she spoke she felt his hands tighten, cruelly hard around hers. She looked up to see that his whole body was rigid with hatred and repulsion, and felt the misery flood her then. What had she expected? No one could hear a tale such as hers and not be disgusted by it. She knew Nick Falconer was a good man and so no doubt he would not blame her for her capitulation to Rashleigh's blackmail, but even so he would never be able to see past it to the woman she really was, and she knew that no amount of longing on her part could make that happen.

"I saw the papers." Nick's voice was so rough she barely recognized it. He got up, strode away from her. The rain was tumbling down from a leaden sky now. High above the fells, the thunder roared. "I saw the record in the ledgers of the farm Rashleigh bought for your parents. I saw the manumission forms for them." He looked at her and Mari knew they were both thinking of the terrible price she had paid for that freedom.

"What happened to them?" Nick asked. "What became of your family?"

Mari laughed without mirth. "That is the irony, Major Falconer. They died. They died in a fever epidemic. Very likely if they had stayed in St. Petersburg they would have survived. So it was all for nothing, their freedom, my sacrifice."

She put her hands up to her face and then let them fall. She wanted to finish this now, have done with it and see him walk away. For surely he would not want to stay when he had heard the whole truth.

"You knew that Rashleigh brought me back with

him to England," she said, "and as soon as he did, I plotted to escape. He kept me locked in my bedroom and had me watched day and night, though, so it was no easy matter. He took away all my clothes. And when we went to the country, he shackled me to his carriage and dragged me along beside it. I still have nightmares about it to this day."

Nick stirred. He was standing by the window, watching the rain run down the pane like tears. "That was why you were so disturbed that night of the Glory Girls attack," he said, "when they tied my hands. I wondered… I knew your reaction could not be feigned."

Mari shook her head. "No, that was no pretence."

There was a silence before she resumed. "One night when we were in Kent, Rashleigh grew careless and I had my chance at last," she said. "He was very drunk. He came to my bedchamber alone and it was easy to overpower him. I went to the study and in the safe there I found the jewels he had inherited from his father. I took them and slipped out into the night and hid in the outbuildings. I thought I had killed Rashleigh but when the alarm was raised and I heard his voice, I realized that I had not hit him hard enough." She looked up and met Nick's eyes. "A pity. I could have saved us all so much trouble later on."

Nick smiled faintly but he did not speak and after a moment she resumed. "I had thought of remaining hidden in the stables or the barns until the hue and cry had passed, but I realized it would be too dangerous," she said. "So I ran away into the fields and concealed myself in a barn that first night…" She shivered, pressing the palms of her hands together. "And then the hunt came." Briefly she closed her eyes. "They lost my trail. But even now I cannot hear the noise of the hounds without remembering."

There was a silence but for the growl of thunder retreating now. Mari turned to Nick and spread her hands wide.

"And there you have the truth, Major Falconer. I stole from your cousin and ran away from him. I am a criminal and an impostor and what I have told you now could see me hang, but—" She swallowed hard. "I wanted you to know the truth at last. I am sorry I did not trust you before, but I did not know then what sort of man you were."

Nick walked across to the mantel and rested his arm along the top. "I understand," he said. "You lied to me to save yourself from the gallows, but you also lied to protect the Glory Girls, did you not?"

Mari's gaze flew to his face. "I—" She bit her lip. She never, ever wanted to lie to him again. She had let go of her own secrets but could she trust him with those that involved the others?

Nick came to sit beside her again, close but not touching. "Laura Cole told me," he said. "I know you never rode with them and I think I understand now why you did it." Then, when she did not speak, "I swear you can trust me, Mari." He shook his head slightly. "It is true that I came to Peacock Oak to find you and to see if you had murdered Rashleigh and to discover the connection between him and the Glory Girls, but now that I know, I promise I shall never speak out."

"Thank you," Mari said. She felt a huge relief sweep through her that the others were safe.

"I suppose that Laura also told you it was Charles

who was the connection between Rashleigh and the Glory Girls," she said, but then she saw Nick's eyes widen with shock and hurried on, realizing she had made a mistake. "She did not tell you that? No, of course she would not. She is far too discreet." She stopped. "He is your friend," she said. "I am sorry."

"Charles?" Nick's tone was incredulous. "Laura said that they had all known Rashleigh, she and Charles and Hester and John Teague—" He broke off. "*Charles* was the one who told Rashleigh about the Glory Girls?"

"Rashleigh was holding the knowledge over my head," Mari said carefully. "He threatened to expose my past and also to expose the identity of the Glory Girls. Charles had told him one night when they were drunk together." She looked down at her hands. "And Rashleigh sold me to Charles. Charles was my black-mailer. He was the one writing the notes, the man I mistook you for."

She saw such fury then in Nick's face that she drew back instinctively, but he made no move toward her. He got up, thrusting his hands into the pockets of his jacket as though to restrain himself from violence.

"Charles…" he said again. "That was how Rash-leigh had the Glory Girls' card. Charles must have given it to him with instructions on where to find you. Rashleigh had it in his hand as he lay dead in the gutter. Poor Laura," he added flatly. "No wonder she threw him out."

"Yes," Mari said. "She has shown me nothing but kindness and generosity."

"He is a weak man," Nick said. "I saw him in Town, drinking himself under the table. I never re-alized why." He shrugged, then moved over to the sideboard, poured himself a glass of brandy and brought another across to her.

"Tell me the rest," he said, a little harshly. "Finish this."

Mari made a slight gesture. "You know almost everything now. After I ran from Rashleigh I created a new identity for myself."

She had, after a time. To start with she had run anywhere that she had thought Rashleigh would never be able to find her; to the slums of Birmingham and the back streets of Manchester, where she had sold the jewels little by little so as not to attract too much attention to herself. Along the way she had found work as a lady's maid then as a governess, each time reinventing her identity and moving a little further away from Marina Valstoya.

"I will tell you about that someday," she said, "but not now." She hesitated. "It was hard sometimes, but I never had to sell myself or my principles again, or lie and steal and beg."

Nick's gaze searched her face and then he nodded. "And Mr. Osborne?" he asked.

"He was an invention, as you guessed previously. When I said that in order to live quietly in the country I needed to appear respectable, I was telling the truth."

"And after five years Charles accidentally blurted out your whereabouts and Rashleigh found you again."

Mari nodded. She took another mouthful of the brandy. It was very reviving and she wondered if she was getting a taste for it. She had never cared for it before. "He did. And that is another irony, you see, Major Falconer. I thought I had killed Rashleigh the night I had run from him and, when he found me again,

I hated him and feared him enough to kill him. I *would* have killed him that night at the Hen and Vulture if I could, but someone else got there first. Someone killed him before I could."

"There were enough people who hated Rashleigh, in all conscience," Nick said. "I did myself." His voice hardened. "I hate him even more now."

Mari looked at him. "I think I was half-mad with fear and the memory of the past that night I met you at the Star House," she said unevenly. "I thought you were going to enforce another unholy agreement, just as your cousin had, and I did not think I could bear it."

She saw Nick close his eyes for a second. The muscles of his jaw clenched but he spoke very softly. "I am not my cousin."

"No," Mari said. "I know that. I knew it then, I think, deep down. But I was afraid that I had misread you. I could not trust you because my very life depended upon it and it broke my heart that I had thought you so much better than it seemed you were proving to be…."

Their eyes met and for a moment it felt as though all the unspoken dreams and desires Mari cherished shimmered between them as fragile as gossamer.

"I thought that about you, too," Nick said quietly, and Mari's heart leaped. "After you ran from me that night I fought my instincts so hard but I knew you could not be the woman you seemed to be."

The heat rose in Mari's face. She tore her gaze from his and fixed it on the amber liquid swirling in her glass.

"So," Nick said, "there are no more secrets between us."

Mari looked up. "Just one. Why were you at the Hen and Vulture that night?"

He laughed. "What I told you that night at the Star House was true. I had gone to meet Rashleigh." His smile faded. "He had been borrowing heavily from impressionable sprigs of the nobility, leading them astray. He owed thousands of pounds."

Mari sat forward. "Then you must have the money back! If Rashleigh had incurred debts, you must allow me to pay them."

Nick shook his head. "Keep the money," he said. "I have more than enough of my own and my uncle settled the debts. And Mari—" he came to sit beside her again "—you must never blame yourself for what happened. It was none of your fault."

It seemed too much. He had given her back her freedom, released her from the secrets of the past and now he was promising his silence forever. Mari's mind tried to grapple with the intimacy that they had somehow achieved—not a physical intimacy but an understanding that seemed far deeper and more profound. She did not understand how it had happened nor did she know how to reverse it and she could feel herself sliding deeper and more hopelessly in love with him all the time. Hopelessly indeed, for his mention of his uncle had reminded her that he was heir to a Marquisate and she was his cousin's former mistress, a thief and a freed serf. Her past was dark and she was scarred by it. How many reasons did she need to realize that there could never be any future for them?

She stood up and her head spun immediately and she realized that perhaps the brandy was not as restorative as she had supposed. "You have given me too much to drink," she said helplessly. "I must lie down."

The rain was lashing down outside and the sky was dark. In her confused state Mari was not even sure if it was day or night. She swayed and caught hold of the back of the sofa to steady herself.

A moment later Nick had scooped her up in his arms and was carrying her toward the door. He held her very securely, her head on his shoulder, and she could hear his heart beating against her ear.

"What on earth are you doing?" she asked, making a grab for the shreds of control.

He glanced down at her. "You said you wished to rest. Which is your bedchamber?"

"I will find it myself."

"I doubt it. You are so drunk you will probably fall down the stairs. I had no notion you had so poor a head for drink. I thought that all Russian women would be able to drink their men under the table."

"That is a ridiculous generalization."

He smiled down at her. "I suppose so." His grip tightened as he started up the stairs. "Now, trust me. I'll keep you safe."

Safe. It was so seductive an idea.

His breath stirred the hair around her face. "Your room?"

She gave in. "The second on the right."

He maneuvered the door open and laid her gently on the bed. "Can you manage to undress yourself?"

"Certainly. You are *not* to do that for me!"

She saw him grin. "Very well. I will leave you to get ready for bed."

Contrarily fear grabbed at her. Perhaps it was the brandy talking but all those nameless terrors that she had suppressed for years were rising to mock at her.

"But you will not leave me alone in the house? Please? I need to know I am safe."

She saw him hesitate for what seemed a long time but then nodded. "I will send word to the village and stay until the servants return. Will that suffice?"

She nodded, feeling only relief. "Thank you."

Her eyelids felt weighted with lead. As soon as she heard the click of the door closing behind him she kicked off her shoes, dragged off her gown and dropped it on the floor and hid under the bedcovers. She did not want to think, did not want to feel. Too much had happened and she was exhausted. It could all wait until the morning. A second later she was asleep.

NICK WALKED SLOWLY back down the stairs and headed for the door. No matter that it was raining. He had to get out of the house. He needed fresh air, to clear his head, to help him think. Besides, the thunderstorm outside was a pretty good match for the violence of the feelings inside him.

He had never felt so angry in his entire life. He had not even known he could feel like this. Whilst he had been talking to Mari he had been able to dampen down on his rage and think only of her. Now, though, he was filled with a furious, impotent hatred of his cousin that could never be quenched. If Rashleigh had still been alive, he thought that he would have hunted him down and killed him with his bare hands. And even that would not be good enough. It would never be good enough.

As it was, he could never make Rashleigh pay for what he had done to Mari and his inability to avenge her filled him with frustrated rage. He balled his hands into fists and thrust them into his pockets for fear of the violence that he might wreak. He had always considered himself a civilized man but now he realized how thin that veneer was. Rashleigh had transgressed every code and had hurt Mari beyond reparation, and he could never make him pay.

He went out of the garden door, onto the terrace and down the steps to the lawn. The rain beat down on his bare head. The sound of the downpour filled his ears, drumming on the stone of the terrace, beating a more muted stroke on the thick grass beneath his feet. He turned his face up to the sky and prayed that there was vengeance in heaven or in the other place to which he hoped Rashleigh had been condemned. The thunder echoed off the fells with distant threat. He was soaked to the skin within minutes, drenched, but the downpour made him feel a little better, as though he could wash away some of the anger from his soul.

He found Frank stolidly closing up the greenhouses and sent him off to Peacock Oak village to find Jane and tell her that Mari had returned, and then he let himself back into the house and stood for a moment in the darkened hallway, the water from his clothes dripping onto the tiled floor. He had no way of knowing how long it would be before the servants returned but he had promised Mari that he would not leave her until he knew she was safe. Unless he was to catch a chill in the process he thought that he had better try to dry himself off. He went into the kitchen and found a towel near the stove, which he used to rub vigorously at his hair. He then removed his shirt, which was so wet that it was sticking to his chest, and draped it over the wooden drying frame in the little laundry room. He was just debating whether or not to light the fire in an attempt to dry off his soaking trousers, when he heard a sound from above. It sounded as though Mari was crying.

He took the stairs two at a time and found her lying tangled in the blankets. Her gown lay crumpled on the floor and she was in her petticoats. Her face was flushed and she was breathing quickly in little gasps. He knew she was having a nightmare.

He touched her gently on the shoulder and she struck his hands away with a violence that was shocking.

"Don't touch me! Leave me alone!"

He had no idea how to soothe her but he caught her flailing hands and drew her into his arms. "Hush." He spoke against her hair. "You are quite safe. I promised to keep you safe and I will."

She opened her eyes. They were dark and soft and then they focused on him and she smiled and he felt as though a fist had squeezed his stomach, turning his feelings inside out. How could Rashleigh have taken this girl and used her and destroyed her innocence? The anger rose in his throat, as thick as bile. Unconsciously his arms tightened about her.

"Nicholas," she said, and he realized it was only the second time that she had used his name. She put a hand against his cheek. Her hair spilled over his bare chest. "Don't leave me," she said.

"I won't," he said, and her eyes closed and she smiled again and he was lost.

CHAPTER FOURTEEN

Clover—Be mine

THROUGH THE THICK, muffling layers of brandy-induced sleep, Mari could hear the sound of screaming. She stirred, resisting the urge to wake. She was warm and comfortable and for the first time in as long as she could remember she felt so safe and so protected that she thought she could sleep forever.

Except that someone was screaming, and it sounded like Jane.

She tried to move and found that someone was holding her close to them. She felt the heat of another body, the slide of warm skin against hers. Something tickled her cheek, a lock of dark hair. And there was a masculine scent that teased her nostrils with it woody, fresh smell.

She rolled over and he made a protesting sleepy noise and moved slightly, trying to draw her back into his arms. She froze rigid. Oh, good God. She was in bed and she was in Nick Falconer's arms. He was holding her close. Her hand was against his bare chest and… She drew a deep breath. He was cuddling her, his cheek slightly rough against hers.

Cuddling. She had heard about that. She had never done it, though.

It felt warm and intimate and entirely delightful and it made her want to burrow even closer to him and drink in the scent of his skin and stay curled up there comfortable and safe forever.

The knowledge of how she felt, the fact that she was not afraid of Nick's physical proximity, stunned Mari for a moment. Then another scream penetrated her brain and she sat up and felt her head spin. When she opened her eyes the floor of her bedroom rose and fell like a ship in a stormy sea. At the bottom of the bed stood Jane. In one hand was an empty brandy bottle and in the other was something that looked suspiciously like a man's shirt. Mari looked from the shirt to Nick, whose bare-chested appearance suggested that he must be the owner. He was starting to stir now.

"Oh, dear," Mari said, inadequately.

Jane had stopped screaming. "Well, upon my word!" she said. "And I thought it was Lady Hester who had the reputation with the gentlemen!"

"This is not what it seems, Jane," Mari began, then put a hand to her forehead as a headache like a nutcracker squeezed her temples. "I beg your pardon, I do not feel quite the thing."

Jane looked at the empty brandy bottle in her hand. "I am sure you do not, madam! Cavorting with gentlemen, drinking and running about in the rain… This is the second time I've found a *shirt* lying around the house." She gave a loud sniff. "I'll heat some water, shall I, and prepare a tisane for your headache? Not that you deserve it, madam. And is the gentleman staying?"

"Yes," Nick said. He sat up and Mari tried to avert her gaze from the hard, defined muscles of his torso.

She knew she was staring like a startled virgin but she had never seen anything so riveting in her life.

"Yes," Nick said again, "I am staying until I have persuaded Mrs. Osborne to accept my proposal of marriage."

Jane sniffed again. "Fine persuasion!" she said. "I shall be in the kitchen if you need me." She looked at him. "Not that *that* seems likely."

"Oh, dear," Mari said again, as the door closed behind the maid with a quietly outraged click. "Major Falconer," she enunciated carefully, "I think that you had better go. I will explain matters to Jane."

"You called me Nicholas when you begged me to stay with you," Nick said helpfully.

Mari blushed. "Begged you? But I…" She cast a look around at the tumbled sheets. "I don't remember," she said helplessly. "I am sure nothing happened between us."

Nick grabbed her hand. "You were having a nightmare," he said. "I promised to stay with you and keep you safe."

"You had no need to take it so literally," Mari said. She dropped her gaze to their clasped hands. "I did feel safe," she admitted in a whisper. "I thought that I would be afraid to be so close to you after what happened that night at the Star House, that it might bring back terrible memories again, but I know that you would never hurt me. I trust you."

His fingers tightened on hers and she looked up to meet the look of brilliant intensity in his eyes. "Then marry me," he said. "This news will be all over the village by now anyway. You are compromised, Mari. Accept me. Be my wife."

"Accept you?" Mari repeated. She felt stunned. "Have you run mad, Major Falconer? Earlier today you abducted me from a convent. Then you plied me with brandy. Now you are proposing to me. This all seems so out of character that I suggest that you need to see a physician."

Nick laughed. He stretched and Mari watched his muscles move beneath the smooth skin and felt a sudden and very hot wave of sensation sweep over her.

"I feel very well," he said. He looked at her and Mari blushed. "In fact, I feel extremely well."

"I still do not think there is any need to propose to me," Mari said. "You must surely understand that the concept of being *compromised*—" she felt faintly amused "—is as foreign to one in my situation as is the idea of marriage, Major Falconer. I fear I must decline your…rather astonishing…offer."

Nick grinned. He looked, she thought with trepidation, like a man who was thoroughly elated rather than one who had just been turned down flat. The change in him was remarkable. It was as though laying the truth bare between them had freed something in him, as well as in her. He seemed to think he could *court* her. It was a shocking idea.

"I could persuade you—" Nick said

"No!" Mari felt a flash of genuine panic. She put a hand on his bare arm and whipped it away equally quickly. He felt warm and smooth and tempting in a way that she did not understand. She wanted to touch him *all the time*. Surely that was not normal. Hastily, she shuffled away from him on the bed as her whole body started to burn.

"Nicholas," she said, saw him smile at her use of his

name and felt a helpless rush of feeling, "I understand what you are trying to do. You are trying to atone for Rashleigh's actions toward me. But you are not your cousin, as you have told me before. It is not your responsibility to make good the evil he has done."

Nick caught her hand in his again. "You mistake me," he said. "That was not why I asked you to marry me." His grip tightened. "It is true that I deplore the way that Rashleigh behaved and I would do anything in my power to put it right—" He felt her instinctive withdrawal from him but held on to her hand and carried on doggedly. "But that was not why I proposed marriage to you. I want you, Mari, and nothing else matters. I love you."

Shock silenced Mari for a moment. "You cannot love me, Nicholas!" she burst out. "You cannot wish to marry me. You do not know me."

She freed herself from his grip, intending to get to her feet and put a little distance between them. Then she realized her state of undress and thought better of it. In nothing but her petticoats she felt hopelessly vulnerable, especially as Nick was sitting and watching her with a look in his eyes that made her tingle with awareness. She swallowed hard, trying to concentrate.

"When you first met me," she said softly, "you thought that I was a criminal and a whore and it was *that* Mari Osborne you wanted. You wanted the woman who kissed you at the tavern and danced naked in the fountain. Then you discovered the truth and thought me a virtuous woman wronged, and it was a different Mari Osborne you wanted then. You wanted to save me." She pushed the tumbled hair back from her face. "But you do not know me, Nicholas! You do not know the real

Marina Osborne. You create these different images yet you know nothing of the real Marina at all."

Nick started to speak but she gestured him to silence. "Please. Let me finish." She looked across to the window where the night was dark now. "Nor do I know you," she said, a little sadly. "Did you never wonder why I did not ask any questions about you, ask about your history, or your interests or your tastes when you were so curious about mine?" She raised her gaze to his. "It was not because I was so self-absorbed that it did not occur to me. It was because I did not want to discover the real Nicholas Falconer. I was drawn to you by instinct but I knew you were here to trap me and I was afraid to see you as a real person; afraid I would *like* you as a real person, like you too much, perhaps. But as a result we neither of us know the other well and that is no basis for marriage, leaving aside the dozen or so other reasons there must be against us."

Nick did not move nor did he touch her but his gaze moved over her face and left her feeling breathless.

"May I speak now?" he asked, with exemplary courtesy, and when she nodded, he said, "You say that we do not know one another and yet I have to challenge you on that. These are the things that I know about you. You are brave and strong and devoted to those people and causes you believe in. I have seen your loyalty to your friends and theirs to you." He did not take his eyes from her face. "You have compassion and gentleness— I will never forget your distress when you untied my wrists after the Glory Girls had attacked us." He smiled. "And you are wild and passionate and sweet and I want you in my arms and in my bed and those are good reasons for marriage." He paused. "Oh, and you are a hopeless horsewoman and I have wanted to teach you to ride properly from the moment I saw you fall off."

He caught her wrist suddenly, tumbling her beneath him on the coverlet and leaned over her, his lips an inch from hers.

"Marry me," he whispered. "You can learn all the things you wish to know about me during our engagement."

"But what if we both discover things about the other that we do not like?"

She saw his lips curve into a smile. "I do not think that likely. Say yes."

"No." Mari tried to remember all the good reasons why she should not agree. It was difficult when he was so close. Her heart was thundering in her ears. "I do not want a husband," she said.

"How do you know? You have never had one." He nuzzled at the tender skin of her neck and she felt the quivers of acute sensation shake her body. "Mr. Osborne does not count," he continued, "since he was imaginary."

He leaned on one elbow beside her. "I know that you are afraid of physical intimacy, Mari." His gentle fingers traced the lines of her face. "I understand that now. I frightened you that night at the Star House and I am sorry for it, but I am sure that, if you trust me, it could be different. You have responded to my kisses before and I can be patient and I believe it *will* be good for you in time."

Mari closed her eyes. She concentrated on his touch, so light, so soothing and yet with an undercurrent of excitement that lit her blood.

"I am not afraid, precisely," she admitted, wanting to be honest with him. "I do respond to you. I *want* to respond to you." She swallowed hard. "When first you kissed me, I confided in Laura that it was amazing and wonderful to me that I could be drawn to a man after all that I had experienced." She saw the flash of masculine triumph in his eyes and laughed. "Nicholas, you are pleased!"

He took her fingers and kissed them. "Of course I am pleased, my love! How could I not be, to know that you want me, too?"

Mari put a hand against his chest, holding him back from kissing her. "Wait! That is true, but after what happened at the Star House…" She stopped. It felt painful even to think of it. "I am afraid," she said honestly. "I am afraid that the same thing will happen again."

Nick sighed. "I understand," he said. His fingers were gentle against her cheek, turning her face to his, "And I would never hurt you, Mari, so we will just go very slowly and see what may happen."

He looked at her and sighed again. "What else is there troubling you?"

Mari looked at him out of the corner of her eye. "Your uncle!" she burst out. "You are the heir to a Marquisate and I am your cousin's former mistress and nothing can change that."

"Hush." Nick's kiss was gentle on her lips. "Neither of those things matter, Mari, if you wish to wed me."

"They *do* matter—"

"They do not matter to me." Nick sounded stern. "And I care nothing for the opinion of others."

Mari was not so sure. "If anyone discovered that I had been Rashleigh's mistress, you would be shunned by society," she said. "Your family would probably cast you out. No one would receive us! For myself, I do not care about such things but it is scarcely fair for you to have to face that future when all you wish to do is put matters right for me."

Nick's face was dark and he did not answer immediately, proof, she knew, that what she had said was true. For all her life she would live with her history and if she married Nick, he would, too.

He gave a sigh and sat up. "I cannot deny that may happen. I would hope that, in time, my family would come to love you as I do. I am sure that they will. But the *Ton* is riven by scandal and slander, and if your secret were to come out…" He kissed her again. "As I say, it matters nothing to me because I love you, but are you strong enough to live with the threat of that, Mari? Could you do that with me by your side?"

"I do not know," Mari said. She rubbed her fingers thoughtfully over the curve of his bare shoulder. "I do not know if I can. I don't want to bring that upon you."

"I make my own choices," Nick said, a little harshly, "and my choice is you."

Mari dropped her gaze to the bedcovers and fidgeted with the material.

"You have given me much to think about, Nicholas," she said, "and it is too soon. All this is too new."

Nick smiled ruefully. "Well, that is honest."

"I am sorry," Mari said. "My head hurts and I have had too much brandy to think properly—"

He kissed her, a little less gently this time. It was tender but beneath the sweetness ran something heated, something more demanding. Mari raised a hand to his cheek and felt his stubble rough against her palm. She felt dazed and confused, trying to see past this assault on her senses to the truth beneath.

"I feel strange," she said, "and that is not entirely due to the brandy."

Nick laughed. "I will go," he said. "But I will be back tomorrow, and I will not have changed my mind." He paused. "One word from you, though," he said, "will silence me on this subject forever and I will leave you in peace."

Mari looked at him. Now was the moment to speak, to tell him that she could give him no hope, that the odds were stacked against them, that she was too afraid to take the risk of loving him. She looked at him and saw the steadfastness in his dark eyes and felt her stomach melt with a mixture of longing and fear.

"I will think about it," she whispered, and saw the light leap in his eyes.

"Thank you," he said. He kissed her again, a hard kiss of masculine satisfaction and demand and desire that had her head spinning once again. She was glad that she was lying down.

There was a knock at the door, it opened a crack and there was a muffled squeak from the other side.

"Lord 'a mercy!" Jane said, as they broke apart. "Have you not persuaded her yet, sir?"

"No," Nick said, standing up and reaching for his shirt, "but I will do, Jane." He smiled at Mari and her heart turned over.

"I will see you tomorrow," he said, and once again it felt like a promise.

"I HEAR," Josie said, slapping a huge plate of bacon and eggs down in front of Nick in the parlor of Half Moon House, "that you have proposed to Mrs. Osborne."

Nick looked up, somewhat startled. The landlady

was standing next to the table, blocking out the light. Her hands were resting menacingly on her hips and behind her he could see Lenny standing by the bar polishing a glass with the violent intention of a man who was about to smash it and use it as a weapon. Nick cleared his throat. Suddenly his appetite for breakfast had fled and he regretted the impulse that had led him to choose Half Moon House for his accommodation over The King's Head.

"Yes," he said, meeting Josie's furious glare. "Yes, I have."

The landlady's frown deepened. "You should watch yourself," she said. "What would you want to do a thing like that for, now?"

Nick looked at her. He had guessed by now that Josie and Lenny, along with Laura Cole and Hester Teague and a great many other people, were extremely protective of Mari and he realized that nothing but the absolute truth would do now unless he wanted to leave Half Moon House on his ear.

"Well," he said, pushing the plate away, "I love her. I love her and I want to be with her and protect her and care for her."

He heard the clink as Lenny put the glass down and started to move toward him and braced himself. Then Josie's face split into a huge smile that was possibly more frightening than her glare had been, and she slapped him on the back, driving all the breath from his body.

"Damn me, but he means it, Lenny," she crowed. "Major Falconer has fallen in love with little Mrs. O."

"Better see he looks after her properly then," Lenny said. He was not smiling, but Nick thought that perhaps that was too much to ask.

"I will," he said, "if she will give me the chance."

Josie gave a massive sigh. "Know what you mean. Proper stubborn, is Mrs. O."

"Strong-willed, independent, slow to trust," Lenny said lugubriously.

"And who can blame her," Josie said. "Most men are bastards, begging your pardon, Major Falconer, and no offense, Lenny."

"Tell you what you need to do," Lenny offered, sliding onto the seat opposite Nick and resting his elbows on the table. "You need to woo her. Bring her flowers and the like." He frowned. "Well, not flowers, maybe—she's got plenty of those. But gifts and trinkets—show you care. Court her."

"Lenny, you old romantic!" Josie said admiringly. She dropped a heavy hand on Nick's shoulder and he sank a little in his seat. "More bacon, Major Falconer? You'll need your strength now."

"Thank you," Nick said, recognizing this for the sign of approval it surely was. "Thank you very much."

"YOU KNOW WHAT Major Falconer is doing, of course," Hester said. She was brown and glowing with newly wed happiness. She and Mari were sitting on the terrace at Peacock Cottage, drinking homemade lemonade as they watched the sun sink below the line of the fells. August had given way to September now and there was the faintest nip of autumn in the air.

"He is courting you, Mari." Hester smiled. "I think Lenny has been giving him hints! Can you imagine Lenny doing that? It's priceless that he and Major Falconer are now such good friends..." She paused, took a sip of lemonade. "Anyway, he brings you presents—I saw that beautiful little watercolor that he purchased for you in Skipton—and he is even trying to teach you to ride. That shows true devotion." She laughed, reaching for a biscuit from the tray. "Is he a better teacher than me?"

"He is certainly more patient," Mari said, with a smile.

"I never was any good at the theory," Hester admitted. "Just like with love." She stretched. "Now the practice is another matter—"

"Don't tell me!" Mari besought. "Although I am glad that you are happy."

"Very, very happy," Hester said. She yawned. "So when are you going to agree to marry him?"

Mari felt a slight chill and drew her shawl closer around her shoulders. "I do not know," she said. "There are difficulties…."

"Pish," Hester said, her eyes bright. "He loves you. You spend all your time together. What difficulties can there be that cannot be overcome?"

Mari bit her lip. "Perhaps you are right. And it is true that we spend a great deal of time together." She sighed. "But there are plenty of things that we do not discuss, Hes. Nicholas never talks about his wife. And though I love him, I have grave doubts about marrying him. I have only just found my freedom again. Am I to give it all away in marriage?"

Hester laughed. "Marriage is not slavery!"

"Surely that depends upon the husband," Mari said. She smiled reluctantly. "I do not know, Hes. The money is his by rights, of course. It is not that which concerns me. But my liberty is another matter."

Hester nodded slowly. "I cannot pretend to understand, Mari, but I do know that you must do what feels right."

A frown furrowed Mari's brow. "Nick's furlough is due to end soon," she said. "I fear I cannot expect him to wait for my decision forever. Each day I almost expect him to tell me that he is leaving. He has promised to visit his family in Scotland before he goes back, and—"

"Mari," Hester said, putting out a hand to quell the tumbling flow of words. "Major Falconer is probably not a patient man by nature but he is showing the most tremendous patience with you. He will not rush your decision. I dare swear," she added, "that he has not even kissed you."

Mari blushed. "What has that to do with anything?" she demanded. She felt annoyed that Hester had guessed so accurately. "And anyway, how do you know?" Each day she had waited, filled with anticipation and a strange kind of hunger that had grown sharper all the time. Nick had kissed her on the night that he had proposed, but since then he had barely touched her. Each day, as he had ridden away, her disappointment, frustration and puzzlement had grown. She felt that they were growing close now, matching the physical awareness that flared between the two of them with an emotional intimacy that was entirely new to her and was very, very appealing. So why did he hold back? The riding lessons made matters worse, for whenever he would throw her up into the saddle or lift her down, whenever he leaned over to show her how to hold the reins or to demonstrate the way to shift her balance in the saddle, his body would brush hers, or his thigh would press against her briefly or he would touch her hand impersonally before he moved away and resumed an entirely proper distance. It was driving her mad.

"It has everything to do with everything," Hester said calmly, helping herself to another biscuit. "It shows remarkable respect for you, Mari, and even more remarkable restraint." She looked at Mari with amused exasperation. "Mari, this is a man who is all that is honorable, who knows what you have experienced in the past. He is hardly going to pounce on you like a callow youth or try to sway your decision with physical intimacy. All the same," she added thoughtfully, taking a bite of the biscuit, "I'll wager he has already bought a special license. He wants you, Mari, body and soul, and I don't think he intends to let you go."

Mari shivered, as though a shadow had crossed the sun.

"What is it?" Hester asked. "What have I said?"

"It's nothing," Mari said. She was remembering the night in the Star House when Nick had told her that he wanted to possess all of her, claim her body and soul. She had seen his passion then and it had burned her, shaken her to the core. Since then, apart from on the night he had proposed, he had kept his desire hidden from her, banked down, waiting. But she knew that if she loved him and gave herself up to his loving, she could keep nothing back. She would be giving a part of herself away. Could she do that when she had only just found her true liberty? She did not know.

"It's nothing," she said again, turning away from Hester's concern. "Nothing at all."

THE SEPTEMBER days crept past and autumn began to close in. In the garden the green of the leaves was tinged with bronze and gold, and the purple heads of the Michaelmas daisies flaunted amongst the late flowering roses. By now Mari's riding skills had improved so dramatically that she and Nick had taken to riding out together each day and on a dry sunlit day in mid-September they took a picnic to the ruins of Bolton Abbey.

Nick smiled inwardly as he watched Mari in the saddle. She would probably never be a natural horsewoman but she did seem to take pleasure from the ride and at least she no longer looked as though she was going to topple off backward from the sidesaddle. He had been as slow and persevering in tutoring her as he had been patient in awaiting her answer to his proposal, and at times he had thought that both would be the death of him.

There had been many occasions when she had been close to him over the past few weeks and her proximity had put a severe strain on his self-control. There had been the times when her face had been tilted up to his and her full lips, so unconsciously sensuous, had curved in a smile that had brought a tiny dimple to her cheek. There had been the times when her body had grazed his as he had helped her up into the saddle or lifted her down. Her scent had wrapped itself around his senses, the cool, slightly husky sound of her voice had stirred him, her laughter had warmed him. He wondered if it were possible to love her more than he already did and thought probably not. He wanted to spend his life with her. He wanted to *claim* her publicly, formally, officially as his wife. And he wanted to claim her privately, passionately, perfectly as his own. His body ached with the frustration of denial. He was in an almost permanent state of near arousal when he was close to her and today the cool, clear water of the river beckoned temptingly to him as a way to soothe away that frustration, if only for a little while.

Today, however, there was also something very important that he had to say to Mari before any of those physical discomforts could be addressed and Nick was disturbingly aware that if he got this wrong, there would probably be no future satisfaction for him anyway, of any sort. There was something he had not told Mari and his guilt gave him no peace. He had to tell her about Anna.

They had chosen a spot beneath a spreading oak tree at the side of the river and he had laid out a blanket on the ground for them. Mari sat down, neat in her blue gown, and started to unpack the picnic.

"We have gammon," she said, peering into the basket, "and fresh bread and cheese and game pie and apples and lemonade." She looked up, smiling at him. "I do believe that Jane must like you a little these days, Nicholas, to give us such a fine meal—"

"I'd like to tell you about Anna," Nick said abruptly. He picked up a stick; snapped it between his hands. He was already aware that this was not quite how he had intended to broach the subject but he seemed powerless to do this with his usual confidence.

Mari's hands stilled in her lap. "Of course," she said.

Nick looked at her. Her eyes were scared and he suddenly realized that she was afraid of what he was going to say.

"Mari," he said, wrenched by tenderness.

She shook her head, confused, and put out a hand

to ward him off when he would have reached for her. "Tell me," she said.

Nick threw the broken stick in the river and watched it bob away downstream.

"I loved Anna," he said, after a moment. "I loved her but I was not very good at caring for her." He looked up and saw that Mari was watching him intently. He tried to explain.

"We were betrothed almost from the cradle and we married when I was one and twenty. I think—" he had thought about it a great deal "—that because Anna had always been there I did not really see her properly. I…I took her presence for granted and although I loved her with a deep affection I was not in love with her." He was talking quickly now, uncovering things that he had never told anyone before, things he had never thought to speak of. "For most of our marriage we were apart. I was away in the army and Anna stayed at home."

Mari's beautiful dark eyes opened wider in surprise. "Anna did not travel with you?"

"No." Nick shook his head. "She was…delicate." He took a breath, deliberately exposed the harsh truth. "I did not want her with me. Not because I did not care for her but because I knew she would crumple beneath the strain. It seemed better for her to stay with her parents." Little had really changed for him on his marriage, he thought. It was almost as though he and Anna had not really been married at all.

"She wrote to me each week," he said. "And I was glad when I saw her. I did love her." Almost he felt as though he had to prove it. "But I loved her tenderly, with none of the passion I felt the moment I saw you."

Mari's gaze fell but a second later she raised her eyes and met his very straight. "You were faithful to her?"

Nick's heart stuttered, missed a beat. She had gone straight to the point. And how could he lie to her? He had to be honest. But if he told the truth, he would crush the delicate trust they were building between them. To have any trust from Mari at all seemed a miracle after all she had gone through and now he was going to destroy it willfully by telling her the truth.

He closed his eyes. Opened them again. She was still waiting. "No," he said at last. "No, I was not. I did try. It only happened the once. Anna had been ill for two years and we had not been together…" He stopped. "And I am making excuses where there can be none."

There was a silence. The breeze rippled along the surface of the river. He looked at Mari and saw that her eyes were dull with shock. He wanted desperately for her to say something, anything at all, to prove that she was still prepared to speak to him.

"Many people behave as you did," Mari said. She cleared her throat. "I know it is the way of *Ton* society. But I did not expect that you…" Her voice trailed away.

"I did not *want* it to be the way that I behaved," Nick said. "I was angry with myself, so remorseful…" He stopped. He was not going to tell Mari all the details— how Anna had been bedridden for over two years and he a young man who had tried so hard to suppress his natural urges, how it had happened just the once when he had been drunk and had allowed himself to be seduced by the wife of a senior officer. Even now, thinking about it, it seemed tawdry and shoddy and shameful

UNMASKED

that he had not been able to withstand the temptation. It had been the guilt and remorse that had kept him from doing the same thing ever again. He had betrayed Anna and betrayed his own principles. But he would not tell Mari all that because it sounded as though he was trying to excuse the inexcusable.

He snapped another stick viciously in half and hurled it into the river. He knew he had to finish this now and tell her everything.

"I neglected Anna," he said, with difficulty. "My infidelity was a part of that neglect. My cruelty was not deliberate but I hurt her, nevertheless. I think she was lonely and I was seldom there. And then, suddenly, she was taken from me. I had not been there to protect her and my guilt was so huge, so monstrous, that I could scarcely live with it."

"Nicholas…" Mari had moved to sit close to him. A strand of her hair brushed his cheek and he put a hand up to twine it absentmindedly around his fingers. "I failed," he said baldly. "I was so complacent. I feel sick to think of it now, and Anna lying there alone at the end…"

Mari said nothing trite to try to comfort him. Perhaps, he thought, she knew from her own experience how impossible it was to bind deep hurts with commonplace words. But she put her arms around him, spontaneously, for the very first time, and pulled him to her and held him tightly and it felt good. Her body was so warm and soft that he felt a huge urge to hold her and kiss her and lose himself in her. He held back, though, knowing that he might never have that right now, and freed her.

"What are you thinking?" he asked, wondering if he really wanted to know the answer to that question.

She looked up at him and her eyes were the clear, candid dark that he loved. "I am thinking that when you proposed to me all those weeks ago, I told you that you did not know the real Mari Osborne, and that because I had been wronged, you had put me on a pedestal," she said. "And now I see that I did the same thing with you. I loved your integrity and your strength and thought you too good for me, little realizing that you, too, had made mistakes."

"You made no mistakes," Nick said gruffly. "You have done nothing wrong."

Mari ticked them off on her fingers. "Theft, lying, highway robbery…"

Despite the dread and misery inside him, Nick's lips twitched involuntarily into a smile. "You had a good reason," he said.

"Nicholas, stop it." She sounded very stern. "I may have excuses but I am not perfect. Don't try to make me so."

He looked at her. "And what do you think of me now, now that you know I am very far from perfect, too?"

She held his gaze. "I think that you should forgive yourself."

He felt the rush of emotion flood his body. "I love you," he said. "I failed when I tried to love before, so I probably have no right to tell you that or ask you to marry me. But if you will let me, I will look after you and care for you and be faithful to you and love you in the way that I never could love before. I will not fail you. I swear it."

If you will let me…

He saw the uncertainty in her eyes and knew he asked too much.

"You can't do it." He spoke flatly. "You can't trust me." He scrambled to his feet. "It is no wonder. I can understand that."

He turned away and walked across to where the horses were grazing. Of course she could not trust him. How could she, when he had revealed so many painful reasons as to why she should not? He knew that what he had told her was true. He would not fail her, he would always love her, be faithful to her, cherish and protect her. But he could not make her believe it, not Mari, who already had so few reasons to trust.

"Nicholas." She put a hand on his shoulder and he turned.

"I will think about what you have told me," she said. "And I will give you my answer soon. I promise."

"Of course," he said, masking his disappointment. "Thank you."

They rode back in silence and when he helped her down from the saddle, he was careful not to touch her for a second more than was necessary in case he gave in to the impulse to hold her and take her and never let her go.

But he rode back to Half Moon House thinking of Anna.

I think that you should forgive yourself.

How wise Mari had been. He had to forgive himself before he asked anything more of her.

When he got back to Half Moon House, he went upstairs to his room and took out the locket with the tiny miniature of Anna inside. He held it in his hand as he walked down to the bridge over the river, feeling the warm, familiar shape of it against his palm. He stood for a moment on the bridge, looking down at the smiling, painted face of his first wife, and remembering everything that had been good for them, without the shadow of guilt to cloud it. Then he closed the locket softly and let it drop into the water below. The sun caught the shining silver arc as it fell and for a moment the light dazzled his eyes before it hit the water and disappeared from his sight.

He turned back to the inn and as he walked his heart felt lighter. He knew he did not need the locket now. Anna lived on in his memory, would always have a place there and one that was finally without bitterness or guilt, or regret. All that remained now was hope that his past would not be the ruin of his future. And all he could do was wait.

CHAPTER FIFTEEN

Tulip-Enchantment

NICK WAS LYING on his bed at Half Moon House staring up at the ceiling. None of Josie's blandishments had succeeded in persuading him to eat. She had tried to tempt him with mutton stew that smelled delicious, and with Yorkshire pudding and onion gravy, and now she was here again, tapping on the door. He knew it was Josie because her tap was like someone else's hammering.

"Mrs. O is here to see you," she said, sticking her head around the door. She looked at him closely. "You look like a proper wet weekend, Major. Done something to upset her, have you?"

"Yes," Nick said. He knew that this was probably an unwise disclosure given Josie's strength and propensity toward violence but he did not care.

"Can't let her up to your room, wouldn't be proper," Josie said. "You'd better come down to the parlor. Lenny and me will give you some privacy."

"Thank you," Nick said. He stood up and reached for his jacket. His stock was undone and his shirt unfastened and he knew he looked unkempt, but since he was probably going to be given his marching orders, it did not seem to matter. He followed Josie down the stairs.

The parlor was dark. The sunlight that had accompanied their trip to Bolton Abbey earlier in the day had gone now and rain clouds were massing above the fells. At least, he thought, Mari had not made him wait too long.

Mari turned as he came in. In the gathering dusk her gown looked a deep lavender-blue. He thought that she looked nervous. He sketched a bow.

"Mrs. Osborne."

She smiled and he felt hot all over. She could do that to him with just one smile. He could not believe how nervous he felt. He started to fumble for his neck cloth in order to loosen it and then realized that it was not there. Josie went out and left the two of them alone.

"Major Falconer," Mari said. "I have a few questions for you."

His throat was dry. "Ask them."

"You say that you love me."

He nodded. "I do."

"Hmm." Mari was looking at him very intently. "You promised to cherish and protect me and be faithful only to me."

"I will. I promise."

"I see."

She spun on her heel; walked a little way away from him.

"Do you have a special license?" she inquired.

He did, but he hesitated to admit it. It seemed rather presumptuous now, given all that had been said between them.

"Major Falconer?" Mari sounded ever so slightly impatient.

"Yes, I have one," Nick said.

She nodded. She came right up to him and stopped when she was within touching distance. "You said that you love me, but are you *in love* with me?" Her eyes were fixed on his face, her lips slightly parted. "Specifically, Major Falconer, do you desire me and wish to make love to me? Do, please, be honest, as you have not touched me since the day that you proposed so I cannot be sure."

Nick found that he was staring. Was she mad? Could she not see how much he wanted her? Just thinking about it made his body harden into almost unbearable arousal.

"I do."

Had she flicked a glance down at his breeches? He could not be sure. He was feeling as hot and hard as he had done that night when he had seen her in the fountain. If she did not end this purgatory soon...

"Then I will marry you," she said decisively. "I have been thinking about what you said." She drew so close to him that their bodies were touching. "I think you were very honest with me and that you deserve a second chance, just as I have been given one. For a while I was afraid that, if I allowed myself to love you, I would never be truly free. I thought that in loving you I would give away something of myself." She tilted her face up to his. "But I see now that in loving you I will gain something, not lose. There is no freedom without you."

He grabbed her and she was real in his arms.

"You love me?"

She laughed. "Have I not just said so?"

He kissed her deeply. "Enough," he said. "Enough of this teasing. You know—surely you *must* know—that you drive me insane with wanting."

The parlor door crashed open, making it all too obvious that both Josie and Lenny had been eavesdropping shamelessly. "Better get to the church then," Josie said threateningly. "Mr. Butler is waiting to make the arrangements."

"IT WAS A LOVELY WEDDING," Hester said, kissing Mari on both cheeks and standing on tiptoe to do the same to Nick, "but now I am sure that you are wishing us all anywhere but here, so—" she slipped her hand through John Teague's arm "—we are gone!"

Teague slapped Nick on the shoulder. He had stood as groomsman. "Congratulations, old fellow."

"Good luck, Mari. I wish you every happiness." Laura Cole gave her a brief, hard hug and though she smiled Mari could feel how she hurt. How could it not, seeing someone else's happiness but with Charles so singularly absent and her own marriage so empty? Mari's heart ached for her. But Laura, so quiet, so self-contained, was already drawing away.

Mari stood on the terrace of Peacock Cottage and watched them all walk away through the garden gate and start across the deer park toward Cole Court. Hester was holding John's hand and had taken off her bonnet and was twirling it by the ribbons. Laura walked a little apart. Mari sensed Nick come up behind her and a moment later he had slid an arm around her waist, drawing her back against his body.

"It was a lovely day," she said, a little wistfully, leaning back against him. "And so thoughtful of Jane to choose to visit her brother in the village after the wedding breakfast."

Nick laughed and nuzzled at her hair. "I expect she

has had enough of our shocking behavior. Come inside. It is going to rain. I have never known such a season for storms."

He was right. The day had been bright, airless and very hot, but now that night was falling the storm clouds were boiling up over the fells and even as he spoke the first big drops of rain fell on the parched ground.

"I love that smell," Mari said, not moving. "The earth so hot and dry and greedily gasping for water—" She broke off with a gasp herself as the heavens opened and the rain fell, straight and hard. Nick was pulling on her hand but she freed herself. "My greenhouses! Oh, no! All the windows are open! My plants will be destroyed!"

Grabbing her skirts in one hand she ran down the gardens toward the glasshouses. The grass was slick and wet beneath her feet, soaking her silk slippers. The rain ran into her eyes and she dashed it away. Her pearl headdress flew off and her hair fell down around her shoulders. Her bodice was drenched. Nick was running beside her and she looked at him and laughed, and when they reached the bottom of the garden he dashed into one hothouse and she into the other. The rain thrummed on the roof in a torrent. Puddles splashed on the floor and the plants quivered and bent under the onslaught. Mari rushed from one end to the other, the window catches slipping in her wet fingers. Finally she reached up for the last one and turned, panting, half laughing, a stitch in her side, as Nick came in and closed the door behind him.

"Thank you!" she said, collapsing into his arms. "I could not have married a man who cared nothing for my plants."

He was as sodden as she, the shirt sticking to his back, the rain wet on his face and spiking his eyelashes. She raised a hand to his cheek and he turned his lips against it and then suddenly he was kissing her, as hard and greedy and quenching as the rain falling on the grass outside.

It was hot inside the greenhouse now, scented with the heady fragrance of the flowers, damp and dark. Mari tore her mouth away from his and took a step back. He was breathing hard, his chest rising and falling fast. He looked dangerous. She felt the heat spread through her veins, melting her, scalding her.

"Your gown is soaking," he said.

"Then take it off me." She felt drunk with the storm, drunk with power. She remembered his words to her in the Star House. "Undress me," she said. "Take my clothes off."

Heat flared in his eyes at the same time as the first shaft of lightning ripped the sky. He turned her around and started to unbutton the gown. One button. A second, a third. She lost patience, tearing it from her body, stepping out of it, letting it fall to the ground. The thin cotton of her chemise and petticoats stuck to her, transparent. He made a sound halfway between a groan and a sigh, wrapped his hand around the back of her neck, his fingers tangling in her hair, and kissed her again, devouring her. She grabbed his shirt, pulled it away from him and ran her hands over his chest and shoulders, relishing the cool, damp feel of his body.

The thunder crashed outside and echoed in her ears. She did not want to stop, did not want to think. She had been fearful about her wedding night, wondering inevitably how she might feel and what might happen.

She had been afraid that Nick would be anxious, too, anxious not to frighten her or hurt her. But now, with a huge feeling of liberation she let go of that fear and pressed closer to him, seeking and finding the passion she had always known he had for her.

When he picked her up and sat her on the edge of her workbench, she drew him close, replacing the touch of her hands on him with her lips and tongue, tasting him, learning the flavor of his skin, the salt and the sweet, the smooth and the rough. Suddenly there seemed so much to learn and so much she wanted to know. He stood braced, his head back and eyes closed as she explored him, but when her questing fingers reached the band of his breeches he caught her hand.

"Not yet. My turn."

He pushed the damp shreds of the chemise down from her shoulders to her waist, and held her naked breast in his hand, and the rub of his palm against her nipple made her want to cry aloud but she could not, for he was kissing her again, deep, possessive kisses that demanded everything that she could give. The heat built within her, pooling low in her belly, clamoring for release. He put his hand to her shoulder and gave her a little push and she fell back, scattering the remnants of her pots around her. The bench was hard beneath her back and his hands moved over her bare stomach, stroking upward to the underside of her breasts, teasing, raising sensations she had not even dreamed existed. She opened her eyes and looked up at him helplessly. His expression was concentrated, hard. It excited her.

"I want…" she whispered.

"Trust me." The smile he gave her made her shiver.

She closed her eyes as he leaned over her, his mouth brushing her nipples so lightly, tormenting her. She arched.

"Ah! Nicholas, please—"

The damp, moist air touched the inside of her thighs as he slid her petticoats up. She let her legs fall apart with a kind of dizzy relief mixed with aching longing. The drumming of the rain was like a beat in her blood now. She tried not to think. Soon…

His fingers touched the core of her, stroking, caressing and she shook, the muscles in her thighs and stomach clenching. Then, suddenly, his hands held her hips down and his tongue plundered her, seeking and finding. The shock exploded in her mind. She struggled to sit up and his grip on her hips tightened and he held her ruthlessly still and open to his ravishment. The knowledge of it fused with the wanting in her and she screamed, sliding over the edge of pure pleasure, her body rocked by hard, tight spasms, her mind splintering.

Yet even in her bliss, unimagined, unknown bliss, she knew something was missing. She reached for him and he pulled her to the very edge of the bench and entered her in one hard thrust.

She cried out again, her hands braced against the surface of the table, her legs spread wide. He had a palm resting on either side of her body and he bent his head to her breasts and started to move inside her with slow, deliberate strokes. She arched to the demand of his mouth in willing submission and felt each thrust of him like a blow of pleasure through her entire body. When he finally ceased tormenting her breasts and raised his mouth to hers, she wrapped her legs around his waist and felt him move deeper still within her. Again the spiral of desire tightened around her. She tried to stave it off, tried to wait for him, but she could not. Bright white light flooded her mind, and her whole body clenched and tightened around him and she heard him shout and lift her up so that they were breast to breast, entwined, their skin sliding slickly one against the other in an exquisite friction that made her gasp and score his shoulders with her nails. She felt his seed spurt into her and pulled him in closer still to her body and felt him shake with the force of his release. His mouth was buried in the curve of her shoulder, his hand in her hair, his arms around her, and gradually their breathing slowed and calmed and eventually she found that she could speak again.

"I didn't know it could be like that. That…that's never happened to me before." Mari was incredulous. "How did you… How did I…"

His fingers moved, stroking the bare flesh of her inner thighs and her heart raced uncontrollably. Her still damp body shook and an echo of the same raw passion stabbed hard through her, making her gasp.

"Shall I help you do it again—more slowly?" She could hear the smile in Nick's voice. He drew back from her a little, caressing her gently.

"Not yet. Please." Her body still tingled, still shook. She was almost begging him. "I can't…"

"You can."

His mouth claimed hers again and she forgot all about thinking and forgot about doing it slowly, as well. The knowing, expert slide of his hand against her was relentless, intimate and unbearably good. She felt the sensations shimmer through her, the swift, slick strokes taking her to the brink again. He stopped and she groaned with frustration against his mouth, unable to stifle the sound.

"I want you to come again," he whispered, and drew a finger over the swollen bud of her femininity, caressing the tiny hard tip. He bent his head and his mouth touched her breast. Mari whimpered as pleasure, hot, slow and sweet as honey this time flooded her veins. She dug her fingers into the muscles of Nick's shoulders and rested her bowed head against his chest as her body throbbed.

"You shouldn't—"

"I should." He pressed a kiss against her hair. "I like doing that for you, Mari. I intend to do that and much, much more." She felt his chest move as he laughed. "Even so, it wasn't meant to be like that."

Mari raised her head, frowning a little. "What do you mean?"

Nick sounded rueful. "I mean, my love, that I had intended to wait until we were in bed and it could be gentle and decorous."

Mari gave a little splutter of laughter. "Decorous?"

"I didn't want to hurt you or shock you."

Mari sat up a little. "You have done neither." She looked at him. "Though I am a little surprised to see that you still have your breeches on."

"I was in too much of a hurry to take them off." He sounded very pleased with himself all of a sudden, she thought. He straightened, adjusted his clothes and then before she could protest, he picked her up off the bench, racing up the garden with her clasped in his arms. The rain was still pouring steadily down now but the thunder had passed. He carried her up the stairs, kicked open the door of her bedroom and placed her gently down on the bed.

"Bed," he said. "Gentle and decorous."

Mari sat curled up on the covers and looked at her reflection in the mirror. Her chemise and petticoats were crumpled and still damp, her face was flushed pink, her eyes bright, her hair tousled. She stared. She had never seen herself this way before, never looked like this before, never *felt* like this. It was not the shameful, sickening horror that had possessed her after Rashleigh had taken her. That had gone. For the first time, she could remember it with regret but no pain. It was in the past, and now she could see that she had become a different person, freed, transformed.

"Oh!" She stared at herself. "I look…" She hesitated but it was the right word. "Beautiful."

"You are," Nick said. He came to sit behind her and put his hands on her shoulders. She could feel his heat and the press of his body against hers. He bent his head and touched his lips to her neck and she leaned back to allow him to kiss her. His mouth was like a brand on her skin and he slid his hands down from her shoulders to her waist, holding her tightly against him. He was nipping at the soft skin of her neck now with tiny sharp bites that raised the goose bumps on her arms and sent the quivers of sensation right down to her toes. His hair brushed her bare shoulder, a soft caress.

Mari turned her head and he kissed her, a sensual kiss of demand and possession that had her melting fast. She had not suspected it, had not imagined she could want him again so soon. Her body's responses were mysterious, unknown to her before now but as his tongue swept across hers she felt the sweet low ache in her belly again and pressed back against him in a mute plea. His hands came up to palm her breasts, his fingers caressing her nipples through the shreds of her chemise. Wicked, delicious sensation made her shiver. She turned back and opened her eyes to watch in the mirror as he drew the bodice of her chemise down from her shoulders and bared her breasts to his hands. His fingers were tanned dark against the whiteness of her skin. His thumb flicked over her nipple and she had to bite down on a scream of pleasure.

He turned her in his arms so that they were kneeling opposite one another, tangled his hands in her silky hair and held her face up for his kiss. But there were things that she wanted to know now, things she wanted to do. She put a hand against his chest and pushed him backward, taking him by surprise. Before he could protest she had scrambled up his body, straddled him, the tips of her nipples brushing his chest as she leaned forward to kiss him. She heard him groan and felt his erection swelling against her thigh and felt feminine and powerful.

Her hands went to the fastening of his breeches and he groaned again but he did not stop her this time, and taking courage, she freed his shaft and removed all his clothes and allowed herself to explore his body with her fingers and her tongue. She took her time, running her palms over his shoulders and down his chest, trailing her mouth across his abdomen and feeling a secret and very female satisfaction when his erection strained toward her and he fisted his hands in the bedsheets in sheer desperation. She was excited, fascinated, by the contrast of the hardness and the velvety smoothness of his shaft. She took it in her mouth, wanting to torture him with the same agonizing pleasure he had given her and spin it out into ecstasy but he caught her shoulders and drew her against his naked body, turning her over and coming down on top of her in one fluid, possessive movement.

"Next time," he ground out.

He entered the tip of his shaft into her and had her squirming beneath him. Her hands fluttered at his back and his buttocks, frantic to pull him closer. He slid inside her one slow inch at a time, deeper and deeper until he was buried to the hilt, then he raised her bottom in his hands and thrust hard. She felt stretched and full and beneath the fullness was exquisite pleasure.

He smoothed the hair back from her face with the same gentleness he had shown her once before.

"Mari?" he whispered.

"Yes." This time she allowed herself to think and to feel. Slowly, carefully, she opened her heart and her mind and waited for the feelings to come, happiness where once there had been misery, healing sunlight banishing the dark.

"I love you," Nick said. "I will love you always."

He started to move, taking her with him, their bodies entwined on the bed, their images in the mirror locked in a tangle of sweet, erotic pleasure. Mari opened her eyes and gasped to see the reflection; the slide of his hand over her thigh, the hard thrust of his body into hers, the whiteness of her skin as she lay in pleasured abandonment on the covers. The sight of it was her undoing. She watched as Nick's eyes closed and his muscles tautened and his face tensed with pleasure as he quickened the pace, carrying her with him until the sensual delight seized them both, flinging them together over the edge and they lay gasping in sweet oblivion.

After a long moment Nick drew back the bedclothes and pulled her beneath them, still curled in his arms. It was a long, long time before either of them spoke but they did not need words.

At last Nick stirred. "Decorous," he said thoughtfully. "Perhaps we will have to work a little harder to achieve that."

Mari pressed a kiss against his jaw.

"Nicholas…"

"Mmm?" His voice was already very sleepy.

"Frank will find both my gown and your shirt in the greenhouses," Mari said. "What will Jane say this time?"

Nick put out an arm and drew her close in to the warmth of his body. "She will say it is a very good thing that we are married at last," he said, "and so it is."

CHAPTER SIXTEEN

Rose—Everlasting love

"I HAVE BEEN INTENDING to ask you, Nicholas," Mari said a few days later, "when you plan to go to Scotland. I know that you wished to visit your family before the end of your furlough."

They were walking through Laura's rose garden and Nick was enjoying the simple pleasure of watching Mari and knowing she was his wife.

His wife.

It seemed little short of miraculous.

Then he saw her snap the head off one of Laura's roses, an action so unexpected that he recognized she was nervous and her nervousness was making her clumsy. He realized then that during the brief, heady days of their honeymoon he had given her no reassurance about the future or indeed where she fitted into his plans. They had been too wrapped up in the present to look ahead but now he knew Mari was anxious.

Catching her fingers in his before she shredded too many more flower heads, he brought them to his lips.

"I thought perhaps next week," he said. "As a wedding trip? Hester and John plan to travel to the Lake

District for their honeymoon and we might go part of the way with them and continue on to Sutherland after."

Mari's face lit up at the idea and he felt a rush of pleasure to have made her happy. He was learning to read her reactions these days and he could see that there was still one matter that troubled her. His furlough. Of course. She would be wondering what would happen when that came to an end.

"As for the army," he said carefully, "I had thought perhaps to sell out and come to live with you here at Peacock Oak? In time we will have Kinloss, as well, of course, but I do not wish you to worry about living there for I am almost certain that the garden will be in need of remodeling by the time I inherit and so you will have a great deal to do…" He stopped as Mari wrapped her arms around his neck and gave him a spontaneous hug. "Oh, yes!" she said. "That would be entirely delightful." She released him. "But in the meantime what are you to do? You are not a man accustomed to sitting around with nothing to occupy himself."

"I thought," Nick said, "to buy some land and learn to be a farmer. Not the type like Sampson who encloses the common land and steals people's animals," he added hastily, seeing her frown, "but the sort like John Teague who is a good landlord. What do you think?"

Mari slipped her hand through his arm. "I think you will be good at it."

"Charles is selling," Nick said. He cast a sideways look at her. "Did Laura tell you?"

"Selling Cole Court?" Mari stopped and stared at him. "But surely he cannot. Is it not entailed?"

"The house and some of the land is," Nick said,

"but not much of the farmland hereabouts. I have of-fered to buy."

Mari was biting her lip. "That means he does not intend to come back," she said. "He is severing all the ties he can with Peacock Oak. Poor Laura. What will she do?"

"Live apart from him, I imagine," Nick said. "You did not truly believe that after all that has happened they would be reconciled?"

Mari shook her head slowly. She still looked trou-bled. "I suppose not," she said, "although I did wonder if they might set aside their differences in order to preserve the appearance of a happy marriage."

"I do not think Laura would settle for that," Nick said. "You know her better than I, of course, but she does not strike me as someone who would compromise over anything that truly mattered."

"And she loved Charles so much once," Mari said. "If only he had had the will to see it and not to waste what he had."

They had reached the lawns where Laura had had the tea table set up beneath the plane trees. Hester, John and Laura herself were already seated around the table and they waved to Mari and Nick to join them.

"We have some of your apple cake here, Mari," Laura was saying, as they sat down, "served with cream from our own dairies—" She broke off, lowering the teapot with a slight thud. "Good gracious, is that Jane over there? I have never seen her *run* before, and so quickly…"

Nick turned. Jane was running across the deer park, positively sprinting, in fact, which was most unlikely in one of her years. By the time she had skidded to a halt beside the tea table she had her hand pressed to her side and was panting so much she could barely speak. John Teague stood up to set a chair for her, but she waved it away. She looked at Mari and the tears started to flood down her cheeks though she barely had the breath to sob.

"The constable's men are coming, ma'am! Mr. Anstruther is with them. They have a warrant for your arrest for the murder of Lord Rashleigh! I came across the park but they are already on the drive, ma'am! You have only a minute—"

Nick felt a cold, cold fear settle in his stomach. Mari grabbed his hand. Her face was ashen. Laura was looking stunned, Hester stricken.

It seemed impossible. They had barely begun to talk about their hopes and their plans, had been married all of three days, and now the past had intruded in the most abrupt and unbearable way.

"I don't understand," Mari said. She looked at him. "I thought they knew I was innocent. I thought…"

Nick had thought so, too. He could only assume that Hawkesbury had disregarded his views and decided to press charges on the basis that Mari was the most likely perpetrator. He saw the terror in her eyes. She was breathless, the panic rising in her chest, silencing her. He drew her to him and held her tightly.

"It will be all right," he said. "I will protect you. I swear it."

He could see the terrible blankness in her eyes, the pain he had hoped was banished forever, and he could tell she could not hear his words. He felt an unbearable wave of protectiveness swamp him, and an equally powerful surge of anger. He knew he had to keep his promise to her. All the fragile happiness, the liberty, the security was fading away now, leaving Mari exposed and alone. Nick knew she was thinking that the past had finally come for her, that they would lock her up, discover the truth of her history so that even if they could not prove her a murderess they would hang her for theft and take away her freedom and her life and her love forever…

He could never let that happen.

He got to his feet. "Mari," he said, "trust me. I will *not* let them take you."

There was the scrape of a chair as John Teague stood up.

"I am the one they should have come for," he said. He looked desperately tired. "If they are here to arrest a murderer then they should take me. I killed Robert Rashleigh."

THERE WAS A TERRIBLE, frozen silence. Stirring from her stupor, Mari saw that Hester's face had gone very white. She leaped to her feet, clutching John's arm, her eyes wild.

"John, no!"

"Hester, darling—" Teague released himself gently as though he was already starting to take the painful step of distancing himself from her. "I am afraid that it is true." He looked at Mari and Nick, and gave them a tired smile. "They will not take you when I have told them the truth, Mari."

Hester was standing there, unbelieving, anguished, and even through her own shock Mari wanted to go to her and put her arms about her to try to comfort her, but she knew she could not. Hester could not even see her—

all her thoughts, all her attention was focused on John alone.

"I don't understand," Hester said. "*You* killed Rashleigh, John?" She looked across at Mari. "But why? Was it for Mari's sake? Did you do this for her?"

Teague's eyes never left Hester's face. He was as pale as she was now. "No," he said, and his voice sounded rusty. "I did it for you, Hester. When you told me that Rashleigh was blackmailing Mari by threatening to expose her past and her connection to the Glory Girls, all I could think of was how to protect you from his malice."

Hester gave a little, dry sob. "It was my fault then," she said. Her voice broke. "I should never have told you about Mari and about Rashleigh. We were friends and I always confided in you. But—" she shook her head slowly "—I never thought, never imagined, that you would take his life…."

Teague took her hand. Mari saw her flinch at his touch as though she could not bear it when she knew it might be the last time they ever touched one another.

"I had been in love with you for a long time, Hester," Teague said. "I thought that you would never be mine and I think I was a little mad with wanting you. When Rashleigh threatened Mari and through her you, I could think of nothing but how to remove the danger. I knew your plans, knew that Mari was to meet him. So I went to the Hen and Vulture, too, and watched and waited. And when I had my chance, I killed him." He gave her hand a little shake. "Please tell me you understand. Tell me you love me."

"I love you," Hester said, without hesitation. She

was in his arms, her head buried against his chest, her arms holding him so tight. The expression on her face was naked, a compound of love and unbearable loss. Mari felt her eyes fill with tears to see it. She looked at Laura and saw the same anguish in her eyes as they watched Hester's life being torn apart.

"It was my fault," Hester said again. "If only I had realized what I had done to you! I pushed you too far. If only I had thought about anything other than myself!"

The constable's men were approaching across the grass now and at the head of the procession Mari could see Dexter Anstruther, his face drawn, a bleak light in his blue eyes. Mari saw Nick straighten and look at Teague and Teague give the very slightest of nods and put Hester away from him with the gentlest of gestures.

"Mr. Anstruther," he said, before the younger man could speak, "I understand that you have a warrant for the arrest of Mrs. Falconer for the murder of Robert Rashleigh?"

Anstruther was looking perplexed and wary. He looked from Mari to Nick to Teague. "Yes, my lord, but I am sorry, I fail to see what you—"

"I am the murderer of Robert Rashleigh," Teague said deliberately. "Mrs. Falconer is entirely innocent of the deed. I can provide witnesses who will testify that I was in London on the date of Rashleigh's death and should there be any other doubts about my veracity I can describe what he was wearing that night and other details that must surely satisfy a court of law."

Anstruther looked stunned. "If you can prove it, my lord…"

"Oh, I can," Teague said tiredly. He was still looking

at Hester, had not taken his eyes from her. "Of course I can. I give you my word of honor."

The constable cleared his throat and Teague looked up as though he was wakening from a dream.

"I have to go now," he said. "Forgive me, Hester. I have to go."

And without another word he turned and walked away across the grass, leaving Anstruther and the stupefied constable to follow in his wake.

"I HAVE PUT HESTER to bed," Laura said. It was late and she and Mari were sitting alone in the drawing room. John Teague had asked Nick to accompany him to Leyburn jail with Anstruther and the constable, and Nick had sent a note that Teague was to be taken to Skipton castle in the morning. From there he would be taken to London for trial.

"I gave her laudanum," Laura said. "It was the only way I could get her to sleep. She is half-mad with grief and despair." She looked at Mari. "John will never tell the truth, Mari," she said. "He will never mention the Glory Girls. When they ask him why he wanted to kill Rashleigh he will make up some reason about a debt or a quarrel of some sort. He will go to the hangman still protecting Hester, and through her us, too."

"I know," Mari said. She got up and walked across to the window. "What can we do, Laura? We cannot just let this happen! How can we help them?"

"There is only one way we can help them," Laura said. She looked up, met Mari's gaze directly and Mari felt a shiver go down her neck as she anticipated Laura's next words.

"The Glory Girls," Laura said. "Tomorrow, when they take John to Skipton, the Glory Girls must ride to save him."

Mari felt cold. She rested one hand against the window and looked out into the dark. Carrington had not been in to draw the curtains; the whole house was at sixes and sevens, utterly stunned into shock and silence by what had happened.

"You know that Nick will probably be with them?" she said. "Given that Lord Hawkesbury commissioned him to find Rashleigh's murderer in the first place… And he knows everything, Laura. He knows about the Glory Girls. He could give us all away in an instant."

Laura looked thoughtful. "Do you think he would?"

Mari rubbed her forehead to try to dispel the pain behind her eyes. She did not know what Nick would do; she could only guess, hope, pray… But she did not want to ask it of him. She never wanted to ask him to compromise his principles for her sake. They were what made him the man he was, the man she loved. He was good and true and honorable and if she expected him to watch the Glory Girls ride again, and keep his silence, then she would be trading on his feelings for her and taking advantage of a love that should never be treated in that way.

But then there was Hester, who had also loved her as the best of friends, stood by her through thick and thin. Hester, who needed her help.

Laura was watching her struggles with sympathetic eyes. "I do not think that you should ride with us, Mari," she said. "It is not fair to ask it of either you or Nicholas—"

"I'll do it," Mari said abruptly. "You need me. There

is only you and Josie and Lenny, for Hester is in pieces. She is my friend and I have to do it for her."

Laura frowned. "You cannot ride well enough," she said.

"Yes, I can," Mari said. She smiled faintly. "Nicholas has taught me. And I can shoot straight. Don't forget that I am the woman who almost shot Glory!"

Laura laughed. "So you did. And what will you do if Nicholas denounces us? And how will you explain this to him even if he does not?"

Mari wrapped her arms around her cold body, seeking comfort. "I can only tell him the truth and hope that I can make him understand," she said. "I am certain that he will not denounce us but whether he will be able to forgive me is another matter." She shivered. "I don't know, Laura. I can only hope."

MOLLY from the Hen and Vulture stood in the middle of the road from Leyburn to Skipton, wringing her hands in a very pretty fashion as she surveyed the wreck of her carriage, which was half in the ditch and half blocking the road. To her right was a copse of trees between the road and the river, and to her left the steep side of the Yorkshire fells climbed toward the sky. Today Molly was wearing a red wig rather than a blond one, courtesy of a chest of theatrical costumes belonging to the Duchess of Cole, a cloak with a hood, and a blue velvet mask. Her lips were painted a deep cherry-red and her cloak was unfastened to reveal a scarlet dress that was very low cut indeed. The Captain of Dragoons who had stopped to offer Molly assistance was barely able to take his eyes from her extremely tempting décolletage.

"Oh, Captain," Molly said, casting her eyes modestly down, "I cannot think what happened! My groom says that a fox ran across the road and the horses shied and—" She gestured helplessly toward the ditch where the carriage was canted at a sharp angle and a very thin groom and a very large coachman had unharnessed the horses and were struggling ineffectually to right it, all the time swearing beneath their breath.

"Lord Tremblett will be so disappointed if I am late," Molly said, letting her fingers drift across her décolletage and noting that the Captain's avid gaze followed the movement. "He and I have a very special arrangement. Captain—" she put a soft white hand on his arm "—you are a man of the world and understand such matters. Could your men—" she glanced hopefully at the five soldiers who were drawn up and evidently guarding the closed carriage that had come to a standstill in the middle of the blocked road "—would you mind terribly… Would you be able to help? Please, Captain. It means so much to me…."

The Captain cleared his throat. On the one hand he had a particularly important prisoner to deliver to the jail in Skipton Castle. On the other there was Molly, with her deep red lips and her equally deep cleavage. And her carriage was blocking the way, after all. It would take only a moment to shift. He smiled at Molly.

"Come on, lads," he called. "You heard the lady. Set to!"

The soldiers put down their weapons and came forward eagerly enough to help the groom and the coachman, and there was much good-natured banter as they pushed and pulled at the obstinately wedged coach. The Captain had no intention of dirtying his uniform and stayed beside Molly to engage in a little heavy-handed gallantry.

"I should be most obliged to know the name of the lady I rescued," he said, stroking his moustache and smiling down at her.

Molly cast him a look from under her lashes. "I am Molly Lane, sir."

The Captain took her hand and raised it to his lips. "Well, Miss Lane, I wonder if you might make an old soldier happy and remove your mask? I long to look on your prettiness."

Molly simpered. "Oh, Captain, I would love to make you happy but my Lord Tremblett insists on secrecy! Indeed I do think that he feels that for a woman to be masked adds a special little thrill to our trysts—"

Something like a groan escaped the Captain's lips. "Please, ma'am…" He was very nearly begging.

"Oh, Captain, I don't think so." Molly was coy. She tilted her face up to him so that her pretty, painted red lips were very close to his own. "My Lord Tremblett is most possessive," she whispered. The Captain leaned closer. "Indeed if he could see me now, Captain," Molly continued, "I do believe that he would most likely put a bullet through you, but it would be worth it for just one kiss—"

And as the Captain leaned in to kiss her, something very hard and heavy came down on the back of his head and he crumpled silently to the ground.

"Thank God," Mari said. "I did not think I could sustain that much longer."

"He will be having sweet dreams," Laura said. She swung her horse around, the bay mare with the white blazon on its head, and faced the soldiers. Lenny and

Josie, the groom and coachman, had whipped pistols out from beneath their cloaks and were holding the bemused redcoats at gunpoint. Laura rode up to them and brought the horse in close, so close that her black cloak brushed against their bodies and their eyes were level with the barrel of her pistol.

"We are the Glory Girls!" Her voice was steady. "We ride for justice and to free your prisoner." She nodded at Lenny and Josie. "Tie them up."

"Stone the crows," one of the soldiers said. He scratched his head. "Never thought to see the day I'd see Glory ride."

"Quiet!" Laura snapped. "On the ground."

The soldiers were no martyrs. They had already been tricked into laying down their weapons and now they put up no resistance whilst Lenny and Josie bound them and tumbled them unceremoniously into the hedge. Mari bent down beside the Captain's prone body, retrieved the keys to the closed carriage and tossed them up to Hester.

"He won't be alone in there," she warned as Hester turned the black stallion toward the coach. "Be careful."

There were two men in the carriage beside John Teague. One was Dexter Anstruther. The other was Nick.

Mari's heart turned over to see him.

"Put down your weapons," Hester called. "We are armed and we have the soldiers hostage."

Nick's eyes met Mari's and for a long, long moment they looked at one another and then he threw his pistol out of the carriage and jumped down onto the road. He lowered the steps and John Teague came stumbling down, blinking in the bright sunlight, Dexter Anstruther behind him.

Hester gave a muffled squeak and leaped down from the black stallion, running across the track to hurl herself on John Teague. His arms were shackled and he stood still beneath Hester's embrace as though he could not quite believe she was there, but when she unlocked his chains, he caught her up and spun her around as though he would never let her go ever again.

"Come on," Mari said, giving them a gentle shove away from the coach as Laura and Josie came over to cover Nick and Anstruther. "John, your horses are in the trees. We've packed your saddlebags. There's food and money. Make for Liverpool." She broke off, a lump in her throat, as Hester turned to her and grabbed her in a bear hug.

"Write to me," Mari whispered. "As soon as you can."

Over Hester's shoulder she could see Nick watching her. He had not taken his gaze from her once and she could not read his expression.

Hester's eyes were bright with unshed tears. "Look after Starbotton for me," she said, and Mari knew that it broke her heart to leave. "Maybe one day I will come home, but if I have John, then I have my world, and I think that America will be the very place for me." She raised her chin bravely. "I hear it is *marvelous*. Glory—" she turned and blew Laura a kiss "—thank you!"

"Go," Laura said. "Good luck!"

Hand in hand they ran for the trees whilst Laura and Josie kept their pistols trained on Nick and Anstruther, then Laura rode forward slowly, grabbed Dexter

Anstruther by the neck cloth, leaned down from the saddle and kissed him long and hard on the mouth.

"Lord save us," Josie said as Laura released Anstruther and tossed him one of Glory's calling cards with the flaunting peacock on it. "Glory's never done that before!"

"Time to go," Laura said. Josie and Lenny had gone to take the carriage horses. Laura was holding the reins of Hester's black stallion, and looking at Mari with a very quizzical expression.

Mari squared her shoulders. It had been part of the plan for her to swap horses with Hester to throw any pursuers off the scent, but now the moment was upon her she was not at all sure she could do it. The horse looked absolutely enormous from where she was standing and not very friendly, either.

Then she saw Nick's face. He was looking at her and at last there was a smile in his eyes, a look of challenge; the sort of look that said he might have taught her to ride properly but *of course* she would not be able to handle a horse like that. He looked as though he fully expected her to beg Laura to take her up instead and a fine ignominious end that would be to the exploits of the Glory Girls.

Mari's heart lifted to see the smile but the challenge was all the incentive that she needed. She put her foot in the stirrup and swung herself up to sit astride, triumphant in her scarlet dress. She looked down at Nick and gave him the biggest, most jubilant smile that she could. She saw his eyes widen in disbelief and an expression of extreme apprehension come into his face. She turned the horse expertly and passed so close to him that her ruffled petticoats brushed against his body like a promise. She heard Laura laugh and then they were away, Josie and Lenny thundering behind them, as they galloped across the fields to the river, splashed through the ford and up into the beech woods and the track for home. The blood was singing in her veins, the breeze cool on her face, and she felt elated and free.

"At last," she said to Laura, slowing to a canter and leaning forward to pat the stallion's neck. "At last I understand why you enjoy riding!"

Josie and Lenny left them where the track to Half Moon House cut southward. They took the black stallion and the bay mare with them to stable, leaving Mari and Laura to walk back down the path to Peacock Oak.

"I must go home," Mari said, "if I am to have time to change before Nicholas returns." She kissed Laura's cheek. "You were splendid," she said.

"You, too," Laura said, returning the squeeze of her hand and neither of them said anything about what Nick might say or do when he returned, but both of them thought it.

Mari walked across the deer park and through the gate in the wall. It was a very quiet autumn day, with the leaves drifting gently down from the trees in the great park and the sheep wandering peacefully amongst the grass. Mari hurried up the garden, shedding her blue velvet mask as she went and slipping off the red wig, which had made her head itch. She ran her fingers through her hair as it fell around her bare shoulders.

She mounted the steps on to the terrace. And stopped.

Nick was standing by the garden door. Mari's first thought was to wonder how on earth he had got back so quickly. Her second was that even though he had smiled at her earlier and she had dared to hope that everything might be all right, he was now looking stern, unyielding and very, very angry.

Mari's heart did a strange little flip and sank so low she felt faint all of a sudden and had to put a hand on the balustrade to steady herself. She had taken a risk and now she faced the reckoning. She had done it for Hester because Hester was her friend and had stood by her and she owed Hester so much. But suddenly she feared more than anything else in the world that this was the moment in which she lost everything that had come to be important to her, her love, her life, her freedom, if she lost the one man that she loved more than anything else.

For what seemed like forever they stood and looked at each other, and then Nick straightened up.

"I guessed what you would plan to do so I sent word ahead," he said. "To Liverpool docks. I thought they would seek passage to America. I trust I guessed correctly."

Mari closed her eyes. All the hope in her was blotted out in a huge burst of grief. He had sent word ahead to the authorities to capture Hester and John. She could not bear it. She knew she had asked a lot of him, but she had dared to think that he might understand.

"I thought they would need a fast ship," Nick said. He was watching her face. "I wanted to make sure that it was waiting for them and ready to sail. I sent word last night."

Mari's gaze came up to his slowly, as his words sank in.

"You helped them…" Her voice came out as a whisper. "You understand?"

Nick did not answer at once and so she hurried on. "I had to do it," she said. "I am sorry, Nicholas. I love you so deeply and I did not want to put you in that position because it was not fair to you, but I owed it to Hester. You do understand?"

Nick's face was still expressionless. "I do," he said. "Hester is your friend. She and Laura cared for you when there was no one else. Of course I understand." He drove his hands into his pockets, moved away from her a little. "And I understand for another reason, too," he said. He rested against the balustrade, staring out across the garden. "I understand because I would have done the same as John Teague did." He turned his head to look at her.

"That day when you told me what Rashleigh had done to you," he said, a little harshly, "had he still been alive then, I would have found him and challenged him and killed him, and no power on earth would have stopped me because I love you so much."

He covered the distance to her side in two steps and pulled her to him so tightly that she gasped for breath.

"It might not be good," he said against her hair, "it might not be admirable, but I could not be enough of a hypocrite to see a man condemned to death for what I would have done myself."

For a long time they stood there, locked in each other's arms, and then Nick loosed her a little and stood looking down into her flushed face.

"All the same," he said musingly, "I should be angry with you. I think. I *am* angry. You could have been killed."

"I know," Mari said. She was trembling a little from emotion. "I am sorry."

He turned her face up to his and kissed her fiercely.

"When I saw you on that horse," he said, releasing her as they both gasped for breath, "I was terrified. Did you fall off?"

Mari frowned. "Certainly not! How could you think that when you taught me yourself?"

He kissed her again, more gently this time. "Then I am proud of you. But even so, there will be no more Glory Girls."

"No," Mari said. "No more. That really was the last time."

"Molly, though," Nick said, his gaze roving over the scarlet dress and the scattering of freckles on her shoulders, "is a different matter. I would be very happy to renew my acquaintance with her. I have wanted her since that very first night in the Hen and Vulture."

Mari put her hand on his nape and brought his lips back down to hers. "She is yours," she said softly. Their kiss was sweet and deep and passionate, an ending and a promise and a new beginning.

"I told you once that had I known who you were that night at the Hen and Vulture, I would not have chosen you," Mari said. "But it was not true, Nicholas. It was you I was drawn to. It was you I wanted."

Nick smiled and drew her closer into his arms. "So you *were* looking for someone in particular that night," he said.

Mari nodded. She stood within the circle of his arms and felt her heart swell with the pleasure and the passion and the pure freedom of being alive and being loved. "I was looking for someone special that night," she said. "I was looking for you."

AUTHOR NOTE

IN 2007 THE UK CELEBRATED the bicentenary of parliament's abolition of the slave trade in the British Isles. The trade was outlawed under the Slave Trade Act of 1807 with penalties of £100 per slave levied on British captains found importing slaves. However, this did not stop the British slave trade. If slave ships were in danger of being captured by the British navy, captains often reduced the fines they had to pay by ordering the slaves to be thrown into the sea. It also did not mean that existing slaves were automatically freed. Further reform was needed and the trade was finally legally abolished in the British Empire under the Slavery Abolition Act of 1833.

This struggle for freedom was one of the ideas that inspired me in the writing of this book. I wanted to explore the concept of liberty and the influence that an experience of slavery might have on an individual.

My heroine, Marina, was born a Russian serf. In that sense she was a slave, part of a tradition of slavery that covers many different forms of human exploitation across many cultures and throughout human history. A definition of slavery might be the systematic exploitation of labor for work and services, without consent. It also covers the possession of other persons as property.

The origins of serfdom in Russia date back to the eleventh century. Russian landowners eventually gained almost unlimited ownership over Russian serfs. The landowner could sell the serf to another person while keeping ownership of the serf's personal property and family. Mari was therefore the property of her owner and could be sold at whim.

Slaves could be freed through a process of manumission, by which the owner would grant liberty to their serfs, but the system of serfdom in Russia was not abolished until 1861.

REQUEST YOUR
FREE BOOKS!

2 FREE NOVELS
FROM THE ROMANCE/SUSPENSE
COLLECTION PLUS 2 FREE GIFTS!

YES! Please send me 2 FREE novels from the Romance/Suspense Collection and my 2 FREE gifts (gifts are worth about $10). After receiving them, if I don't wish to receive any more books, I can return the shipping statement marked "cancel." If I don't cancel, I will receive 4 brand-new novels every month and be billed just $5.49 per book in the U.S. or $5.99 per book in Canada, plus 25¢ shipping and handling per book plus applicable taxes, if any*. That's a savings of at least 20% off the cover price! I understand that accepting the 2 free books and gifts places me under no obligation to buy anything. I can always return a shipment and cancel at any time. Even if I never buy another book from the Reader Service, the two free books and gifts are mine to keep forever.

185 MDN EF5Y 385 MDN EF6C

Name _____ (PLEASE PRINT) _____

Address _____ Apt. # _____

City _____ State/Prov. _____ Zip/Postal Code _____

Signature (if under 18, a parent or guardian must sign) _____

Mail to **The Reader Service:**
IN U.S.A.: P.O. Box 1867, Buffalo, NY 14240-1867
IN CANADA: P.O. Box 609, Fort Erie, Ontario L2A 5X3

Not valid to current subscribers to the Romance Collection,
the Suspense Collection or the Romance/Suspense Collection.

Want to try two free books from another line?
Call 1-800-873-8635 or visit www.morefreebooks.com.

* Terms and prices subject to change without notice. N.Y. residents add applicable sales tax. Canadian residents will be charged applicable provincial taxes and GST. Offer not valid in Quebec. This offer is limited to one order per household. All orders subject to approval. Credit or debit balances in a customer's account(s) may be offset by any other outstanding balance owed by or to the customer. Please allow 4 to 6 weeks for delivery. Offer available while quantities last.

Your Privacy: Harlequin is committed to protecting your privacy. Our Privacy Policy is available online at www.eHarlequin.com or upon request from the Reader Service. From time to time we make our lists of customers available to reputable third parties who may have a product or service of interest to you. If you would prefer we not share your name and address, please check here. ☐

BOB08R

Nicola Cornick

77211 LORD OF SCANDAL   ___ $6.99 U.S. ___ $8.50 CAN.

(limited quantities available)

TOTAL AMOUNT $ _____
POSTAGE & HANDLING $ _____
($1.00 FOR 1 BOOK, 50¢ for each additional)
APPLICABLE TAXES* $ _____
TOTAL PAYABLE $ _____

(check or money order—please do not send cash)

To order, complete this form and send it, along with a check or money order for the total above, payable to HQN Books, to: **In the U.S.:** 3010 Walden Avenue, P.O. Box 9077, Buffalo, NY 14269-9077; **In Canada:** P.O. Box 636, Fort Erie, Ontario, L2A 5X3.

Name: _____
Address: _____ City: _____
State/Prov.: _____ Zip/Postal Code: _____
Account Number (if applicable): _____

075 CSAS

*New York residents remit applicable sales taxes.
*Canadian residents remit applicable GST and provincial taxes.

HQN™

We *are* romance™

www.HQNBooks.com   PHNC0708BL